CONTINUING
THE
PASSION

CONTINUING THE PASSION

Continuing the Passion follows the story of Connor Edmond Blake, a best-selling Fantasy and Science Fiction novelist who, after suffering the tragic and unexpected loss of his father decides that the best way to honor the memory of his father is by carrying on the legacy that his father left behind.

Connor's father, William Edward Blake, a Hall of Fame High School Baseball Coach had led his team to numerous state championships. Most of Connor's memories and moments he shared with his father have something to do with and revolve around the sport of baseball. As a former coach himself, of a men's softball team, Connor decides to at least make the attempt to coach a High School team in attempt to honor his father.

In the midst of his efforts, Connor is deeply entrenched in family concerns and doing his best to help his mother and siblings in this trying time. Rather than letting the death of his father crush him, Connor rises to the challenge, ready or not, and becomes the central figure in the family that is there for everyone else.

Through a new government program sponsored by the Governor, Connor is presented with the opportunity to become not just an assistant coach, but a head coach of a new school and baseball team. The school itself is a statewide school of choice in an attempt to reduce the stress and attendance of primarily inner city and other over-populated schools. In it's inaugural year, there was little hope for an athletic program until a heartfelt recommendation from the Principal of the school Connor's father previously coached attracted the attention of the Governor, Superintendent, and Principal.

With assistant coaches from his softball days, years of drills, notes, and progress reports from his father, and a deeply ingrained knowledge and passion for the game, Connor begins his new career as a head baseball coach, hoping to live up to the name that his father had created. His task is not an easy one, with players who had never played before, establishing an entire athletic program, acquiring uniforms, funding, and even approving a schedule with the state league.

Through personality conflicts with members of the team, working to help a dyslexic player remain academically eligible, managing injuries, overcoming diversity and public scrutiny, and fighting to overcome additional tragedies that will impact every player on the team, Connor Blake will claim his father's passion and struggle to persevere. He continues his father's legacy, his passion, and slowly helps his family, and himself, move beyond the loss of the late William Edward Blake.

Continuing the Passion is seen through the eyes of Connor Blake as he experiences the tragedy of the loss of his father, and his pursuit to help his family find a way to overcome the loss. In the end, after fulfilling his tribute to his father, Connor feels as if he did honor his father's memory, and that if it were possible, his father was watching with love and pride.

CONTINUING THE PASSION

Clifford B. Bowyer

HOLLISTON, MASSACHUSETTS

First printing, May 2009
10 9 8 7 6 5 4 3 2 1

ISBN # 097877826X
ISBN-13 # 978-0-9787782-6-2
LCCN # 2008908510

Silver Leaf Books, LLC
P.O. Box 6460
Holliston, MA 01746
+1-888-823-6450

Visit our web site at www.SilverLeafBooks.com

In loving memory of a man who took pride in what he did, who loved unquestioningly and unreservedly, who selflessly sacrificed time and again for those that he loved, who befriended everyone he met and treated them all like cherished family, who always knew the right thing to do and the right thing to say, who taught and guided me, helping to turn me into the man I am today, my father, Warren Edward Bowyer. I love you and miss you dearly.

FOREWORD

For those readers who are fans of my writing, you'll find that this book is quite different from the normal fantasy world of the Imperium Saga and the militaristic and espionage Science Fiction story of Gen-Ops. When I originally began writing, I had had an idea for something that could be classified more like a movie romantic comedy, but decided to "practice" by writing a fantasy novel where I could sort of make up the rules on my own and refine my style. Several months later, everything I was developing and creating grew exponentially, and not only a single fantasy novel was created, but an entire world with a trilogy, a young adult spin-off series, a few other things that I have plotted and developed along the way, and now even an RPG game that has been developed based upon my world.

In the time since I began "practicing," my love and excitement for the genre has grown. Almost daily, I wake up with ideas for my characters and adventures that they can go on. Little thoughts, concepts, and tales that I weave into current or future books. The same is true for the Science Fiction novel, Gen-Ops, which I had written as something I really wanted to do before beginning another Imperium Saga trilogy, the prequel.

However, through all of this, where my daily routine has become either a Fantasy or Science Fiction one, I had always thought that perhaps one day I would still try my hand at that original novel, or something in a genre completely different. I do not mind being considered a Fantasy and Science Fiction author, because the journey as one has been full of great memories, tremendous fans, and enjoyable stories. But, deep down, I did always think that I would write something else.

On October 22nd, 2006, while at an RPG Development Team meeting, I received a phone call with the news that my father had died. The experience was unexpected and profound. A few weeks later, I had the urge to write, to just create something, but I could not bring myself to continue working on the game, or a sequel, or a prequel. The desire was there, but not for the things that I usually dive into and immerse myself with. Instead, all I wanted to do was write something in honor of, as a tribute to, my father.

Hence, *Continuing the Passion* was conceived. When I began, I knew that this would be a book far different from my normal Fantasy and Science Fiction novels, and that my publisher did not normally publish books of this genre. However, it was a story, even if it were never published, that I just had to tell. I needed to tell it. I am very grateful that Silver Leaf Books has seen how important this book is to me and decided to go beyond their normal expertise and publish this book.

When I began, I typed twenty pages in the first day, tears flowing down my cheeks as I did so. I knew what the "fiction" would be, but also included some parallels to what was experienced by my family at the time of the loss of my father. This has been a highly emotional project, but one I just needed to write. Not to capitalize on such tragic events, but to honor a man who I respected, loved, and lost far too soon.

- Clifford B. Bowyer

CONTINUING THE PASSION

Baseball is a game to some, but a passion to others. The passion, whether it is from a fan, a player, or a coach, is what keeps the game pure and inspirational. It is not about free agency, corporate sponsors, and business; it is about dreams and the pursuit to fulfill them. It is about teamwork, striving with your peers for a common goal, and for nine innings at a time, putting it all on the line in hopes of achieving those goals.

For eight-year-old Connor Blake, baseball was more than just a game: it was a way of life. Not because he was captivated with his favorite Major League Baseball team—because truth be told, sitting through nine innings of a game in the living room could become rather dull for an eight-year-old—but because he enjoyed playing it, listening about it, and learning about it from his father.

Connor's father was not just a passionate fan who liked to talk about trades, free agent acquisitions, and how a season was going. He was, instead, a baseball coach. Not in the major leagues where everyone would know his name, but in the town of Corinth, Massachusetts with a population of a little over 20,000.

In Corinth the name William Edward Blake, a high school history teacher and varsity baseball coach, was well known. He was the man who led his team to over a dozen division championships, and even had two teams compete on the national level, one of which brought home the trophy. He was not Mr. Blake, William, or Bill, but "Coach," and whenever that simple word was spoken, everyone in Corinth—student, parent, faculty, staff, or administration—knew exactly who was being referred to.

Being a high school teacher and coach is never about the money or the fame, but about the desire to help others, to guide and teach the next generation, and the pride in seeing those whose lives you impacted becoming successful. Coach had more than a few players make it to the major leagues, and whether they were on his beloved Red Sox or not, he would follow their progress and statistics throughout their baseball careers. With every win, he felt a sense of pride and accomplishment; with every loss, he felt confident that his "boys" would get them the next time.

The demands of his time on teaching and coaching never took away from his family life. His beautiful wife Melony, who he called his "Angel," and his son Connor, were his heart and soul. Whether he had a good day or not, the moment he stepped foot in the door, he had a smile on his face and warmly welcomed his family.

During the summer break, the three would travel. There were always times when they went to military bases since Coach was also a member of the Army Reserves since serving in the Navy during World War II. If not, then they would drive south—always driving because Coach hated flying more than anything—every summer, making it an adventure. As a history teacher, Coach would stop off at Civil War battle sites and talk about what happened there. It may sound dry to some who groan at the thought of history, but Connor always had his hands on the windows, watching the fields, listening to the stories, and visualizing what his father was telling him.

They also stopped at outlet malls, sometimes spending three to four hours shopping just for the sake of seeing what was there. Coach would joke that they only managed to make two hundred miles that day, but nobody was complaining. Every stop along the way, they made new friends—the hostess at a Marriott, the waiter at a diner, the cashier in a supermarket. The ironic part, year after year, these newfound friends would remember the Blake's, and even if just sitting for a meal, it was like spending time with long-lost relatives that you needed to become reacquainted with.

The odyssey ended in Florida, where after several trips to other locations around the country, all three agreed that Disney World was the place that they all wanted to be. There were always new things to see, new shows, new attractions, and even year after year, none of them ever grew bored with their destination. Disney was like a second home.

On that year, however, when Connor was eight, Coach was invited to spend some time at Disney's Wide World of Sports Complex. Each year, there was an intense baseball clinic for high school athletes from around the country, and, in some instances, from around the world. The coaches asked to come to the clinic changed annually, allowing the athletes who attended to receive a wide array of training styles from different regions. That year, after five straight divisional titles, Coach was asked to host a batting clinic.

Melony opted to stay by the pool, working on her tan, but Connor was overjoyed to see his father coaching others. He sat on the bench, watching his father working with each athlete who came to the clinic. They began at dawn, took a break for lunch—Connor and his father each had a couple of hotdogs—and then continued on until early evening when the session ended.

Connor never grew tired of watching his father. Coach gave the same attention to every player, whether they were the most prolific batters Connor had ever seen, or if they spent fifteen minutes swinging a bat without even touching a ball. Coach always spoke calmly, encouragingly, and found ways to help the athletes improve their swing. Whenever the batters who could not hit finally began hitting, Connor felt like clapping his hands and cheering: his father had the gift, and not a single athlete walked out of the batters box feeling as if they did not learn something insightful from Coach.

When the day was done, Coach held the bat out for Connor, smiling and waving him over. "Ready to give it a whirl?"

"Really?" Connor asked, eyes widening in anticipation of the opportunity to play.

Coach smiled wider, handing the bat to his son. Some people might want nothing more than to go home and relax after a long day at work, but Coach never once had that thought, desiring only to have his son have some fun too.

Coach walked up to the mound, reached into the bucket for a ball, and looked at Connor. "Are you ready?"

Connor nodded, watching his father and waiting for the pitch. He was batting right-handed, his stance similar to the one Dwight Evans used to use with his left foot slightly raised on his toes. Connor knew that his parents both loved Dwight Evans, and he had seen more than a few Corinth batters in a similar stance. When Connor first began using it, Coach spent hours throwing him balls and giving his son tips on balance, grip, motion, and always keeping his eye on the ball.

Coach motioned into his windup and threw a perfect batting-practice pitch to his son. Connor swung away, watching the ball the entire time, and hit it down the third-base line. After a dozen pitches, Coach said, "They shifted to the left on you, what are you going to do?"

Connor nodded. He may only be eight, but he knew what to do if there was a shift put on him already. He remained in the same stance, but as the ball came in, instead of stepping into it, he stepped slightly to the right, angling his body toward first base. The ball connected with the bat and hit a line-drive between second and first.

"Great," Coach said. "You're hiding that much better now."

Connor couldn't keep the look of pride from spreading on his face. He had been at a Little League game where he wanted to hit it down the right-field line because the right fielder was actually sitting down and pulling grass from the ground. The only way he could at the time, though, was over-compensating by shifting his entire stance. He hit the ball where he wanted to, and nobody on the other team seemed to notice what he was doing, but Coach worked with him over the next couple of weeks to mask where he was aiming so that future opponents couldn't shift themselves to make the play easier.

"You ready to bat lefty?" Coach asked.

Connor stepped to the other side of the plate, and got back into his stance. Once he nodded that he was ready, his father threw him a pitch, right down the middle. Connor swung and missed.

"That's okay, just keep your eye on the ball and choke up a little on the bat."

Connor tightened his grip and slid his hands a little up the barrel of the bat as his father instructed. Another pitch went by and Connor barely tipped it foul.

"Better," Coach said, encouragingly. "You were just a second off. You'll get this one."

The third pitch, Connor connected with such ferocity and determination that he looked like a Major League Baseball power hitter. The ball did not soar out of the complex, but it went high and far, trailing most of the way to the wall.

Coach walked in to the batters box, excited, and hugged his son. "Did you see that? That shot would have been out of every field you play in back home."

Looking at it that way, Connor didn't mind so much that he didn't quite reach the fence. His father was right: in every Little League park that had a fence, it would be a home run. In the parks that didn't have a fence, with his speed, it would probably still be a home run.

"How about a few more pitches?" Coach asked.

"I'm ready," Connor said, keeping his hands choked up on the bat.

Coach threw until the bucket of balls was empty. In the end, Connor had just about the same number of pitches from both sides of the plate. There was definitely a pattern that could be seen from his hitting. As the two walked around the field shagging balls together, Coach imparted a few tips about batting.

"How did you feel?"

"I was more comfortable batting righty, but I hit better lefty," Connor said.

"You hit with far more power lefty, but you were more consistent righty," Coach said.

"Which is better?" Connor asked.

"You tell me," Coach said. "Would you rather bat over .300, get on base a lot, score a lot of runs, or bat closer to .200, hit home runs, and maybe drive in more runs than you score?"

"Everyone likes home runs," Connor said, frowning, knowing what his father was thinking.

"You're right," Coach replied. "A home run is exciting. Everyone cheers and that one big hit can mean the difference in a game."

"So I should bat lefty?" Connor asked.

"You said you were more comfortable righty," Coach reminded.

"I am," Connor admitted. "My stance feels right."

"I would go with how I was most comfortable," Coach said.

"But I don't hit for power righty," Connor said, his shoulders sagging.

"Be a line-drive and gap hitter," Coach suggested. "Or, we'll work every day on batting lefty and try to get you to be more consistent. In time, you'll probably feel comfortable batting both ways."

"Can I be a switch hitter?"

"Of course," Coach said. "Some people bat lefty against right-handed pitchers, and righty against left-handed pitchers. You could certainly do that. Or, just bat for consistency most of the time, and if that big hit is needed, show them what you can do."

"Okay," Connor said. "But we can work on it some more?"

"We definitely can," Coach said. Tapping Connor on the hat, he pointed to the scoreboard for the time. "We should get back to the room. I'm sure your mother will want to do something tonight."

Connor nodded. Knowing his mother, she probably already had something planned for the evening. Coach drove them back to their motel, Disney's Caribbean Beach Resort, and the two chatted about baseball the entire time. When they got home, clothes were already set out for them: they had reservations for a dinner show at the Polynesian Luau.

With baseball now in the back of their minds, the pair took showers and got ready for the night. The three took the Disney shuttle to the Magic Kingdom, and from there the monorail to the Polynesian. The night was full of laughs, stories, memories, and awe. Disney never failed to deliver, and the Blakes' would cherish the memories of their times there.

CHAPTER 1

By the time Connor was thirty-one, he had loved, lost, loved again, and risked everything to follow a dream. His dream was not baseball—though he did coach a softball team in a men's league for nine years—but instead for writing. With a Bachelor of Science in Business Administration and an MBA in Business, Connor was a very successful employee in Corporate America, working for SJC—Stanley Jalbert & Company—a financial investment firm. His field specifically was Business Continuity, which was known by numerous buzz names, including Business Contingency and Disaster Recovery.

The goal of his focus was the ability to continue normal business operations in the event of an emergency. It could be as simple as a power failure, or as devastating as a terrorist attack. Regardless of the scenario, it was his job to make absolutely certain that if something unexpected happened, there was a way to resolve the problem effectively and efficiently.

He inherited the plan from his division and decided very quickly to scrap the entire thing to make a new one of his own design. Forging a team of experts from around the division, Connor questioned everything, and designed a new plan that truly did take into account every contingency for every scenario. Even something like a tsunami—which was considered virtually impossible as a natural disaster in Massachusetts—was taken into account.

Connor was known throughout the company for his ability to question the normal guidelines and to find more-effective ways to achieve his goals. The reputation was well deserved, and reached well beyond the walls of SJC. It was in large part because of this that Connor was handpicked for a project management team that was tasked with revolutionizing the way the company did business. Though excited by the opportunity, Connor felt out of place in the new unit, and also found the company beginning to go through numerous layoffs, feeling that his future with SJC was no longer as certain as it had once been.

The entire time Connor had been working and finishing his Masters program, he had also been writing a fantasy-adventure novel. He had an idea for some kind of romantic comedy swirling around his actual experiences with softball, but wanting to refine his writing style, decided to go with fantasy since, as he often explained, he could make up the rules as he goes along.

When the company decided to offer a voluntary separation package, Connor took it, deciding to finish his novel and see what would happen. He understood the dynamics of being an author. After all, his research showed that a first-time novelist, on average, sold only 3000 books a year. Even if he made a dollar or two per book in royalties, that would be a substantial pay cut from the six figures he was currently enjoying. Regardless, Connor was unhappy with the project team, and he decided to take the plunge to follow his passion.

His first book and series was published six months after he "retired" from SJC under his full name, Connor Edmond Blake. As he expected, the books sold, but not anywhere near the extent that he would need them to in order to live off of them as a profession. He did find, though, that the fans of his work became quite passionate, the reviews were overwhelmingly positive, and his family and friends were more proud of him than they ever had been when he was making more money, working crazy hours, and being an executive.

A few years later, the fantasy series was continuing to grow in popularity, including more than a few inquiries optioning the rights to create a film series based on the books. Connor, long-forgetting his original book idea of a romantic comedy, wrote numerous books, including a prequel, a young adult spin-off series, and even began working with a development team on transforming his world into a role-playing game.

It was not, however, until he decided to write something different—an espionage suspense novel with a slight touch of science fiction—that Connor became a best-selling author. Finally making money again, Connor asked his girlfriend of three years, Marina Norton, to become his wife, and the two wed on the beach on the Cape.

Throughout all of this, Connor kept a single tradition going with his family: Saturday would always be the family movie day. Marina worked Saturdays, so Connor would go to his parents', taking them out to the movies and either lunch or dinner. His mother loved nothing more than going to the movies, whether it was one, two, or even three a day. His father, retired from both teaching and coaching, enjoyed the stimulating discussions of trends in the game of baseball, roster moves, player development, and how things were progressing with their favorite team, the Boston Red Sox.

Just like their annual trips to Disney, Saturday became their weekly day together. There were times when someone may have been too busy to go, or something important came up, but more often than not, the movie theater was where the family would be. There was one time when the three saw two movies, went to dinner, and then came back and saw two more! It was not entirely intentional, as they were just going to see the sneak preview of For Love of the Game with Kevin Costner, but the showing allowed them to stay for another movie afterward, and they did.

In the new Costner movie, during a scene when Costner was tiring and thought his perfect game would be ruined, when the catcher told him that the team was there for him, Melony looked over at her husband and saw tears in his eyes. Leaning over to tell Connor that his father was crying, she was shocked to see that he, too, had streaks flowing down his face.

It was not that the movie was sad, or that the two men were upset, but the Blake men always believed strongly in looking after your own, and pulling together to help each other out. It really did not matter where that theme was found, whether a sports movie, a military movie, or anything of the sort, the sentiment always made both men cry.

With their tradition in place, it was not unusual on October 21ˢᵗ, 2006, for Connor to make the trip to his parents' house to go to the movies. Marina was working and then had plans with an old college friend. The two would be staying in Mystic Connecticut for the night. Connor knew that his father would like him to spend the night, but he had a meeting in the morning with the RPG development team and still had a good six to eight hours worth of work to prepare for it. The plan was for a pair of movies, dinner, and then he would head home.

The first movie was going to be at a relatively new theater built, the "Premium Theater," where you have to buy seats like going to the theatre and seeing a play. Each seat was large, leather, and had a table in front to eat. Viewers could order food before the movie, and then have their food brought directly to them before the show started. The Blake's loved the Premium Theater, and whenever there was a good movie playing, they preferred to go there first.

This particular weekend, Flags of Our Fathers was the featured movie. Connor had spoken with his mother earlier that morning: they were going to go to the 12:00 movie, have lunch at the theater, then go to see another movie, and have dinner after that. It had been several weeks since they had seen their Saturday movies for one reason or another, and Connor was looking forward to it.

While driving, the phone rang. "Connor Blake," he said, his customary way of answering the phone since his very first day working at SJC.

"Connor, my tire just blew up!"

Connor recognized the panic in his mother's voice. His father had always been the one who drove places, handled all car repairs, and fixed whatever needed fixing. But a year before, his foot slipped from the brake to the gas and he hit three cars in a parking lot before he could stop the car. He was showing signs of the early stages of Parkinson's disease, and it was then that Coach had realized that he had to stop driving unless some kind of cure could be found. It broke his heart, but he did not want to be the cause of an accident where someone could get hurt.

Since then, his mother had the responsibility of driving and doing things thrust upon her. She already worked a sales job that caused her to feel stressed and anxious twice a month. Now, with being the one having to drive to doctor's visits, to every store, to restaurants, to visit family, to movies, and more, the sense of anxiety only grew.

"Are you okay?" Connor asked, trying to stay calm and relay that to his mother.

"I'm fine," Melony said. "But my car!"

"What happened?"

"I just had to make one last delivery," Melony said, her voice cracking and Connor knew she was on the verge of tears. "I figured I had a little more time before you got here, and wanted to try and get something done."

"Where are you now?" asked Connor, glancing down at the clock and seeing that he was still half an hour away.

"I'm home," Melony said. "I drove it home."

"With a blown tire?" Connor asked, cringing.

"I didn't know what to do," Melony said. "Your father always handled these things! What do I do?"

"First off, I want you to sit down," Connor said. "We'll take care of this and then it will be nothing more than a bad memory."

"How though? We're going to miss the movie."

"We can go see a later show," Connor said. "We can go and have the tire replaced. Maybe I'll change the tire, then I'll follow you to BJ's or something."

"They'll change tires on a Saturday?"

"Of course," Connor said. "We can drop it off, go see our movie, and then pick it up."

"Okay," Melony replied, sounding calmer.

"I'll be there in half an hour, and I'll take care of everything then. Just relax until then."

"Okay, I'll try," Melony said. "I was so looking forward to lunch at the Premium Theater. I haven't eaten anything yet."

"Well, after I get there, we'll see about getting some lunch. Then we'll go to a later movie."

"Okay," Melony said. "Thank you."

"Anytime," Connor said. "I'll see you soon."

"I love you," Melony said.

"I love you, too," Connor replied, hanging up the phone. Glancing at the clock, he checked the time and then pulled out the list of movie times, glancing up and down at the road while driving and the list to see their options. They could see the 3:00 movie in the same theater, so perhaps something small for lunch like a sandwich would be good.

The rest of the trip to his parents' house met very little traffic, and Connor pulled up next to his mother's car. A few months earlier, because his father was having trouble getting in and out of her car, she had purchased a Buick Rendezvous. Getting out, Connor saw that the front right tire looked almost shredded, but there appeared to me no damage to the body of the vehicle. Of course, there could be damage to the rim, especially since she drove it home like that, but the first step was changing the tire.

Melony walked out of the house and headed to the car. "I don't know what happened. I dropped something, but was at a stop sign; so I bent down to pick it up. When I was up, the person across from me waved me to go, and without thinking I went. But there was a curb there, and rushing for the other man, I hit it. It sounded like an explosion, or at least like thunder."

"And you're okay?"

"I'm fine," Melony said. "Shaken up a little, but fine."

"When I bought my truck, I had a roadside assistance plan where they would send people out to me. Did you get something like that with this?" Connor asked.

"You know what, I think I do," Melony replied, nodding hopefully.

"Why don't we give them a call? At least they'll be able to come and switch tires for you. Then we can get a replacement."

"Okay, I'll do that," Melony said.

The two walked into the house where Connor was met by both the Chihuahuas, Chip and Dale, and the cats, Boots and Mittens. After spending a couple of minutes petting them, he went into the den where his father was looking at a couple of videos.

"Hi, Sir," Connor said, grinning as he saw that his father was wearing the hat from his old softball team, WildCard. "I like the hat."

"It's my son's," he replied, looking up, smiling affectionately, and winking. "Your mother is a bit nervous."

"I think she's okay," Connor said.

"Don't change the tire yourself," he warned. "Call triple-A and have them do it."

"We've got it covered," Connor replied. "Mom is making a call now."

His father nodded. "Remember, if you ever do change a tire, make sure you don't put your arms or legs under the car, in case it falls."

"I'll remember," Connor said. "So what have you got there?"

"Just some old tapes," he replied. "Vacations when you were younger. I'm trying to organize them."

Connor smiled, remembering the trips to Disney. The last vacation they all took together had been on the Disney Cruise Line. It had been wonderful. "I'm going to go help Mom."

"Thank you," his father said, taking Connor's hand and squeezing it.

Connor walked over to his mother, who was pulling out the materials she received when buying her car. "Here it is," she said. "Can you help me find the right one?"

Connor picked it up and glanced through the pages until he found the right form. He put the page down with the number for his mother, and then scanned the page. "We need your VIN number," he said. "I'll get it." Taking a piece of paper, Connor went back to the car and wrote the number down. He came back inside, handing the page to his mother, and waiting as she made the call.

"Thank you," she said as she put the receiver down. "Up to two hours."

"So why don't I go pick us up some lunch," Connor suggested.

"What are you in the mood for?" Melony asked.

"Whatever you and Dad want," Connor said. "Subs maybe?"

"Eddie, do you want a sub?" Melony asked.

"Sure," he replied.

"Okay, let's do that," Melony said. "I'll go with you. I get a senior discount."

Connor looked at his watch. "Sure, we'll have the time."

As they got into Connor's truck—a Cadillac Escalade EXT—a tow truck pulled up in front of the house. Jack, the owner of Central Garage himself got out. "I got the call and came right away."

"Oh Jack, thank you so much," Melony said.

"What happened?" Jack asked.

Melony told the story again, and then Jack got to work on switching the tires. He told her that she needed to make sure she got the exact tire because of the warranty. Rather than looking around and driving on the temporary tire, Connor suggested just having Jack do it. He said it wouldn't be a problem, and took the tire with him. He said that he'd call on Tuesday and we could just drive up and he would switch the tire right there.

As Jack drove off, Melony looked at her watch. "Think we can still make it?"

"Probably," Connor said.

"Okay, I'll tell your father."

Walking back into the house, Connor's father got up and met them in the kitchen. "That was quick."

"Jack already changed the tire. We're going to still try and make the movie."

"No subs?" he asked.

"Oh, honey, I'm sorry," Melony asked. "Do you have something here?"

"Don't worry, I'm sure I'll find something," Eddie said.

"You're not coming?" Connor asked.

"Not today," he replied. "I feel like just staying home and watching the videos."

"Okay, Sir—have fun," Connor said.

"You too," Eddie replied.

❖ ❖ ❖ ❖ ❖

As it turns out, they did miss the movie, but bought tickets for the next show. Buying a quick sandwich from Burger King so as not to completely lose their appetites for the Premium Theater, Melony and Connor both felt bad that they hadn't actually gotten the subs. Coach would never say anything to get in their way, but they could both see how disappointed he had been. Subs and donuts were two things that Coach had always loved. Connor remembered numerous times going out of the way to little places that his father had found where they made nice, thick sandwiches or extra-tasty donuts.

With time to spare, mother and son did a little shopping, and then went to the theater early. Melony ordered a turkey club, and Connor got teriyaki glazed chicken wings. They talked until the movie began, laughing and joking, and then enjoyed the film.

By the time they drove back home, it was already late. Coach walked out to greet them again, smiling. "Hi, how was the movie?"

"It was good," Melony said. "I didn't remember everything from back then though. I only remember Ira."

Coach, flipping on both his history teacher and World War II hats, began telling his wife and son all about what happened, recapping the entire movie he had not seen as if he had also been there. When he finished, he said, "So, where are we going for dinner?"

"Oh, Eddie, we ate at the theater," Melony said. "I'm sorry."

"I can go pick something up for you, sir," Connor suggested.

"No, I'll just have some soup," Eddie decided. "Can you make it for me, Angel?"

"I've got it," Connor said. "What kind would you like?"

"Just the ramen noodles is fine," he said.

"Ramen noodle soup, coming right up," Connor said.

Eddie walked back to his chair and sat down, looking at two tapes that were out of their boxes. "I just need to figure out which one is which," he said.

Connor walked in with the soup, and looked at the boxes. "I don't think it really matters, Sir, neither box is marked."

"Okay," Eddie replied, dropping the tape on the table.

"What would you like to drink, Sir?"

"Soda would be fine."

While Connor helped his father, his mother listened to messages and returned a few phone calls. When she was done, she came in and sat down with them both. "You know, I wish you came today," she said.

"I was fine," Eddie said. "And you had a good time, too."

"We did," Melony replied.

"A great time," Connor added.

"Good, good," Eddie said. He then looked straight at Connor. "Marina isn't home tonight, right?"

"No, she's in Mystic," Connor replied.

"Then you should stay."

"I really should get going," Connor said. "I'm still working on the descriptions for the 'Items and Equipment' for tomorrow morning's meeting. I probably have a good six to eight hours of work to do."

"Where's the meeting?"

"In Milford," Connor said.

"So you'll be coming back to this area in the morning," Eddie pointed out. "You should definitely stay."

"If I had brought all of my materials for the meeting I would have," Connor said, "but I don't have anything, even if I decided not to finish the descriptions tonight."

His father's eyes dropped to his bowl of soup, but he didn't push the point any further.

"Well, I should get going," Connor said. "Thank you again for a lovely day."

"Oh, my pleasure," Melony said.

"I love you, Sir," Connor said, leaning over and hugging his father.

"I love you, too."

Connor then said a quick farewell to the four pets and then made his way home. Along the way, his mother called because her glasses were missing. Connor had taken the phone number to the Premium Theater just that afternoon to make future reservations and gave her the number. He said that if they had it, he would pick her up after his meeting in the morning and take her to get them. If they were somewhere in the house, and the dogs took them, then he would come and help her look after the meeting as well. With that, he hung up, finished his ride home, and then went straight to work until well after 2:00 in the morning working on the game.

CHAPTER 2

A sure sign of being a workaholic is sleeping fewer than four hours. When the alarm sounded at 6:00 AM, Connor turned it off and leapt from the bed. It was not so much as being energized in the morning—he had always been a night owl—but a sense of responsibility to his meeting and being there for his team that had him instantly awake.

Connor went through his morning routine in the bathroom, and then stopped at his computer both to see if there were any emails from his development team members, and to spend a few spare minutes checking out the baseball rumors and news. Like his father, the offseason was always Connor's favorite part of the baseball year: it was the time when strategy came into play in forging the team that you go to war with. Even coaching softball for nine years, Connor always saw the season as seeing just how good his preparation and strategy had been in the offseason. Some decisions work, some do not. There are tweaks as the season goes along, but the major moves always happen when there are no games.

Getting dressed, Connor picked up a box of materials that he had for the meeting. The last thing he had done before going to sleep was putting everything together—all of the development materials, printouts, updates, notes, agenda items, and books. One thing nobody would ever accuse Connor Blake of was being unprepared.

The meeting usually was scheduled for 9:00 to 11:00 on the third Sunday of every month. Originally, the team met in Connor's living room and sat on his sectional couch discussing the game. With work schedules and other conflicts from the team members, they shifted their meetings to the Milford Dunkin' Donuts, where they could all have breakfast and talk for two hours without interruption.

This month, however, one of the team members had early afternoon plans and asked if the meeting could be pushed up from 9:00 to 8:00. Since nobody else on the team had any objections, Connor made the schedule change. As the member who lived furthest away, he was the one who had to wake up the earliest to make the meeting.

When Connor arrived, he was two minutes early, but everyone was already there—eating and discussing the game. It was currently in testing, something that Connor felt was a bit premature, but the team wanted to try and push the game out in time for the 2007 holiday rush. It meant many long nights and hours of writing for the game instead of on his fiction, but Connor accepted whatever the team desired for timing and just kept working at it. One thing his parents always quoted: "If you want something done, give it to the busy man." Connor had always been the busy man, and he had always found a way to juggle however many projects wound up on his desk.

At the last meeting, there had been some problems circulating around the team. Two members felt that a third wasn't doing enough work, but Connor knew that the third member was going to be doing far more once the number crunching was done. Still, as the team leader, he had to manage the situation, bring it all out, try to get both sides to see the perspective of the other, and go from there. Whether the fire was completely out or not remained to be seen, but for now, everyone was working productively again.

This month's problem was the size of the book. Connor's materials for writing were so detailed, that when information was pulled from that to put into the game, the book just kept growing and growing. One of the members was anxious to begin cutting things out, and to even skip developing certain sections because there was already so much, but Connor was adamant about leaving everything in there. The argument went back and forth for most of the meeting, until Connor finally just overruled the team.

"We have to cut it out! It's too long! Nobody will buy it!"

"It all stays," Connor said, trying his best to keep his own aggravation and frustration from creeping into his voice. "Listen, I don't care if the book is 2000 pages when we're done. Everything will be useful and complete. We can cut things down from there. In the end, the final book will be between 300 and 400 pages, but we're not going to start skimping now and taking short cuts."

"That's extra work for nothing."

"Not for nothing," Connor tried to clarify. "You keep mentioning that you want future supplemental books. If we have the game fully developed, and decide not to use certain portions, it's those portions that can then be used for the supplements. A few additions here or there, but the overall theme will remain consistent and uniform. We will not cut anything out now."

"Fine."

Satisfied that the matter was resolved for the day, Connor checked it off on the agenda. He then glanced at his watch and was shocked to see that only an hour had passed. Usually, they struggled to fit everything on the agenda into their two-hour sessions, and here he was actually done early for a change.

"Well, that's all I have for today," Connor said. "If any of you have something you want to bring up, feel free."

The discussion then began casually about the testing and how things were going. There were a few things—like player races or classes—that had to be adjusted because they were not properly balanced as they should be. Overall though, testing was going fairly well.

Connor's phone rang. He pulled it out and saw the readout say, "Mom and Dad." Pushing the button to silence the ringer, he put it back into his pocket.

"You're not going to get that?"

"She knows I have this meeting," Connor said. "She's probably just reminding me to stop by the house to help her find her glasses. I'll call back after the meeting."

Under a minute later, the cell phone began playing a little tune, different from the ring.

"She's persistent."

"That's just voicemail," Connor said, pushing the button to silence his phone again. "Don't worry about it. Where were we?"

Just as the group began discussing the next testing session, the phone rang again. Connor pulled the phone out, cursing under his breath at the constant interruptions during a business meeting, and decided to answer it rather than have it keep ringing every few minutes.

"What?" Connor practically shouted into the phone, not trying to hide his annoyance at the interruption at all. Patience was one of his father's strengths, but Connor always seemed to struggle to try and maintain it.

His mother said something, something fast and clearly hysterical. He couldn't hear her, but began thinking that one of the pets got outside and was hit by a car or something. All four of them darted for the door trying to get out whenever someone wasn't careful. One time, Chip made it outside, ran down the driveway, and just began running down the street. Melony had been hysterical calling and running after him, terrified that he would be hurt. Something had to have happened to one of the pets.

"Hold on, I can't hear you," Connor said, standing up. "Let me get outside." Stepping out the side door of Dunkin' Donuts, leaving his team without so much as a word of explanation, Connor covered his other ear so that he could hear better outside. "Now, what did you say?"

"Connor, Dad's dead! Connor, he's dead! Dad's dead! Connor!"

Standing there, with one hand to his ear and the other on his cell phone, Connor could not believe what he was hearing. How could his father be dead? He was having trouble walking lately, but all he needed was a wheelchair or one of those electronic chairs. He wasn't dead. He couldn't possibly be dead.

"Calm down," Connor said, trying to rationalize what he was hearing. His mother was hysterical, but she had to have made a mistake. He just saw his father last night. He had been strong, better than Connor had seen him in a long time. His most recent medicine was doing great. "What did you say?"

"He's dead! Connor, Dad's dead! I need you!"

"I'm on my way," Connor said, hanging up the phone, still trying to come to grips with the news he just heard. Deep down, he knew it was a mistake; his father was fine. He had to be fine. Taking a breath to collect himself, Connor walked back into Dunkin' Donuts, took his notes and put them into his box. Without looking at any of his development team members, he said, "I have to go. My...my father just died."

With that, Connor pulled the box and made his way for the door. Behind him, he heard his team say the right things: "If there is anything we can do, let us know," and "I'm so sorry." Connor had no idea who said it. He heard the words, but they barely even registered. Nothing registered at the moment. All he knew: he had to get home to see his father.

For years, Connor had always been the rock in the family. His older sister, Lauren, one of two daughters from his mother's first marriage, had been diagnosed with cancer when she was in college. Connor remembered many days of being in hospitals and waiting to see how his sister was doing. To this day, he still despised hospitals and hated to go anywhere near one unless he absolutely had to.

Whenever a family member or friend had died, Connor was the one who stood vigilant guard over his sister, watching her carefully and trying to keep the sentiment of death away from her. Funerals were tough, but for those who have diseases like cancer, it becomes even more difficult. It is not just a matter of grieving and paying respects, but of wondering how much time you had left before you were the one up there. Connor watched for this, never leaving his sister's side.

But how could he be strong now? This wasn't just a cousin, an in-law, or a friend. Those were all tragic losses, and Connor would never diminish the emotions and feelings of them, but he was always the strong one—the one there to take care of everyone else. He remembered vividly the pain in his grandmother's eyes after the funeral when she walked up to him, looked at him, and asked, "Aren't you sad that Grandpa died?" The question broke his heart, but not once did he cry that day. He had been there for everyone else, and remained strong. It wasn't until months later, late one night when he began weeping and thinking back of the grandfather he had loved. The man who played soccer with him in Florida. The man who always challenged him to races and ran exaggeratedly slow so that Connor could get to the finish line and back. The man who loved hamburgers and said that there was nothing else like them in the world.

But this was different—this was his father. The man who was always there for him. The man who never lost faith in anything that Connor did, and always took pride in his son. How could Connor be strong now? But he needed to be. If his father was really gone, he had to be the strong one. Not just for his sister, but especially for his mother. She needed him now more than ever. He had to be strong for her. He just had to be.

The Milford Dunkin' Donuts was about fifteen minutes from the house. A quick trip down Rte 16 into Holliston, and before he knew it, he would be at his parents'. That is, if the cars in front of him did not insist on driving ten to fifteen miles per hour under the speed limit.

Finally cracking down and unable to contain it any longer, Connor shrieked on the top of his lungs: "Get out of my way!" His windows were up, his eyes were tearing, and he knew nobody would hear him, but he shouted it again and again, giving in to the emotion, punching his steering wheel along with the screams. He just wanted to be home. To be there with his father and for his mother. To see for himself that this couldn't possibly be real.

Knowing that he was in denial, and that when he got home he would find that his father was truly dead, Connor broke down entirely, barely able to keep his eyes on the road with the intensity of the tears clouding his eyes and flowing freely down his cheek.

"I'm not ready," he cried, knowing the sincerity of the words. He had seen the shift coming, with the family responsibility passing from one generation to the next. His parents, or his uncle, Aaron, had always been the ones who looked after the family and helped them through the tough times. That had gradually been shifting to Connor, the business-minded child, and though he accepted that he would one day be seen as the leader and strength of the family, he could hardly accept that that time was now.

Connor picked up his phone and dialed voicemail. He knew what his mother was about to say in the message, but he just had to hear it.

The voicemail in its mechanical voice told him that he had one new message, from October 22nd at 9:04 AM. His mother's voice came on next: "Connor, Dad's dead! Connor, Dad's dead! Connor! Why won't you answer? Dad's dead!"

Connor pushed the save button, feeling his hands and body beginning to tremble. "God damn it, no! No, god damn it!" he shouted, then began screaming at the cars in front of him again.

Knowing deep down that he could not handle this alone, Connor opened his phone again, fighting back the tears and the choking sensation in his throat. Pushing the speed-dial button for Marina, he prayed that she would answer the phone.

Very groggily, she said, "Hello?"

Connor knew she'd had a late night—not like he had, working long into the night, but out with her college friend. The two got together about once a month, went to dinner, and then sought out different clubs or bars to dance in. They loved dancing. She often told him that things didn't even really get started until after 11:00, so she could have been out well into the night.

"My father's dead," Connor said, trying desperately to speak clearly so that he sounded strong for her. He made the attempt, but the emotion seeped through the phone and broke Marina's heart.

"Oh my god," she said, suddenly completely awake. "What happened?"

"I...I don't know," Connor admitted. "I'm going there now."

"I'm on my way, too," Marina said.

"You don't have to," Connor said, not sure what was going to happen once he got to his parents' house.

"I'm leaving now," Marina said.

"H-how long will it take you?"

"Two hours, at most," Marina said.

"Okay," Connor said, feeling somewhat relieved, but unable to contain his emotions any longer.

"Connor, I'm so sorry," Marina said. "I'll be there soon."

"Okay," was the only word Connor could get out of his mouth. After hanging up, Connor punched the steering wheel several times again, knowing that the truck had done nothing to him, but also needing to release his emotions somehow.

The phone rang again, and Connor looked at the display. Half expecting either his mother or Marina to be calling back, he was shocked to see the name of his niece, Chrissie, on the display.

"No," gasped Connor. I don't know anything yet, he thought. How can I be strong for my niece when I don't know anything myself? Flipping the phone open, taking a deep breath to try and steady himself so that he would sound strong enough, he said, "Hello?"

There was no answer. Connor spoke several times again, and then hung up. Either it was a bad connection or Chrissie had hung up. Taking another breath, Connor pushed the speed dial number for Lauren, Chrissie's mother. The phone rang five times, but nobody answered. He could have called Chrissie back, but he wanted to talk to his sister before his fifteen-year-old niece. He had no idea what to tell her. Do you protect a fifteen-year-old, or tell them the truth? Right now, Connor had no idea.

The phone rang again, and he saw that it was Chrissie again. As cheerfully as he could act, he said, "Hey there," as he answered the phone.

"Connor?"

It wasn't Chrissie, but Lauren. "I thought you were Chrissie."

"My batteries died," Lauren said. "Mom said you're heading home?"

"I'll be there in a few minutes."

"You will be?" Lauren asked. "Where are you?"

"Pulling into Holliston now," Connor replied.

"That was quick," Lauren said.

"I had a business meeting in Milford," Connor explained. "Do you know anything?"

"Nothing more than what Mom told me," Lauren said. "How are you holding up?"

"I'll be okay," Connor said, wondering how many times he would lie and say that to people in the days to come. That, and the infamous, "Thank you."

"Since you're going to be there soon, I'm not going to come right now," Lauren said.

"I have Chrissie and Jimmy with me, and I don't want them to see Dad like that," Lauren explained.

"Okay," Connor said, hearing the words but not really registering what she was saying. The whole conversation was beginning to blur.

"We will be over later though. Let me know when they take Dad away."

"Okay," Connor said, feeling the tears welling up again at the thought of some coroner or funeral home taking his father away.

He was sure Lauren said something else, perhaps "Goodbye," or "I'll see you later," but Connor only knew that he hung the phone up. For a second, he hoped he had not been rude and hung up on her, but only for a second. Right now, even if he did, she would understand.

Pulling into Queens, a residential part of Holliston, Connor saw an ambulance driving away. "No!" he shouted, defying the medical staff for even thinking of removing his father before he had a chance to see him. Praying desperately, the words, "Please don't let them have taken my father away," kept repeating both through sobs of tears and in his mind until he reached his parents' house.

In front, a police car was parked on the street. Connor parked his truck next to his mother's car and jumped from the seat, rushing toward the house. A police officer met him by the door.

"Are you here for the Blakes'?"

"My father," Connor managed to say coherently.

"Connor?" Melony shouted when she heard her son's voice. She ran over, grabbing him in a hug, holding him tight. "He's dead, Dad's dead."

Connor held his mother tight, not able to hold his emotions back at all. Both were weeping as they held each other. "Where is he?" Connor asked.

"He's in the den," the officer said.

Connor brought his mother into the kitchen and helped her into a seat. He then walked into the den and saw his father beneath a white blanket. Only the socks on his feet could be seen from his angle.

"Mr. Blake, I know this is a difficult time for you, but there are some things that you must consider," the officer said.

Connor wanted nothing more than to drop to the ground and hold his father in his arms, but he pulled himself away, walking into the other room with the officer, grabbing a pad of paper from the kitchen counter as he went by so he could take notes. He sat on the steps leading upstairs, looking up at the officer, ready to take notes on whatever was needed.

"The paramedics have already been here and have officially pronounced your father dead. There is no sign of foul play, so we just have to wait for the Medical Examiner to release the body. Once he does, we'll contact a funeral home for someone to pick your father up. I'd recommend Cheston, because it's close, but you can use any funeral home that you want."

Connor listened and nodded, writing everything that the officer was saying. "You said that all arrangements have been made?"

"All we need is to know the funeral home and I'll take care of everything," the officer said. "Do you want me to call Cheston? It's really a good home and they'll take good care of your father."

"He's going to Bourne, to the national cemetery," Connor said. "Would Cheston bring him there?"

"Yes, they could," the officer said. "They'll take care of all of that unless you want a different funeral home."

"No, Cheston is fine," Connor said.

Melony walked in, looking back and forth between the two. "What?"

"The funeral home," Connor said. "We want the one here in town, not another one, right?"

"Oh, yes, I would assume so," Melony said.

"That would be fine," Connor said. "Thank you."

"I'll see to it," the officer said. When Melony returned to the kitchen, the officer added, "The best thing you could do right now is take care of your mother, and also start thinking of who you need to contact to let know about your father."

"Okay," Connor said, standing up and walking into the kitchen. Dropping to his knees, he hugged his mother again, who was sitting.

"Why?" Melony cried. "Why did he leave us? Why? Do you think it was because he thought that he was becoming a burden to me?"

"No, don't think like that," Connor said, his heart breaking all the more for what his mother was thinking and going through. After several minutes of trying to comfort his mother, Connor could not stay away any longer. Getting up, he walked into the den, and sat down next to his father. His father's hand was against the cathouse, stern. Connor held his father's hand, feeling how cold it was, and felt the tears flowing from his eyes again uncontrollably.

"I'm so sorry," Connor cried. "I shouldn't have left last night. I should have stayed like you wanted me to. I am so sorry."

Melony came in and saw the two on the floor. "Do you think we can turn him?"

"We can try," Connor said, afraid that by trying to move his father he might in some way hurt him.

Melony pulled the blanket off of her husband, and began screaming when she saw him lying like he was. "Oh my god, Eddie! Why? Eddie!"

Connor looked at his father. His head was by the sliding door in the den, perched awkwardly on another of the cat's little houses, which was tilted beneath him. His walker, which he only used sparingly, was half beneath him and half on top. The way his right arm was against the cathouse, Connor thought that it looked like his father had been trying to push himself up, but his other arm was pinned by the walker and the way he was laying.

"Could he have broken his neck by the fall?" Connor asked, horrified by the thought of his father being in pain.

"They told me that it was instantaneous," Melony said through pained sobs. "A heart attack or a stroke."

Connor stared at his father's arm pushing at the cathouse, like he was trying to get some kind of leverage. Then, at his father's neck, almost like he might not have been able to breathe because of the way he was laying. The paramedics could have said something about a heart attack or stroke and that it was quick to spare the family, but Connor wasn't convinced. It only added to his own guilt. If his father had fallen, and lived as he struggled to get back up, then if he had spent the night, he certainly would have been here to help his father back up.

Just like the last time they had gone golfing, when his father hit the ball into the woods and went to go look for it. Every time they played golf, his father seemed happier waving others on and searching for balls in the woods than actually playing. It was nothing new, but that day, on a New Hampshire country club course, his father had fallen on some stones and couldn't get up. Connor had to lift his father up, and then help him to the cart. The rest of the day, he just drove around and told Connor to keep playing, and that he just wanted to watch and keep him company.

If this had been like that, then staying overnight would have made all the difference in the world. The weight of that decision, of forcing himself to leave his parents when he had an empty home to go to and little more than a computer to keep him company as he worked until all hours of the night, was making him mad. Was it really so important to get another few pages of "Items and Equipment" developed for a meeting? Was it really so vital that he had his notes for the meeting when, being who he was, he had everything memorized anyway?

"I'm so sorry," Connor said again, caressing his father's hand. At the tip of his father's head, fallen to the ground, was the WildCard hat. Connor saw it, viewing it as a symbol of his father's love and pride in the things that he did, and broke down again. Time became surreal. He did not know how long he had sat there with his father, but the officer came back in and said that the people from the funeral home were there.

Two men came in—one who had gone to high school with Connor—and said that Connor and his mother should probably leave the room. The officer escorted Connor's mother, but Connor had to stay with his father. He did not want his father to feel abandoned, to think that they were just going to leave him with strangers to take him away.

Connor watched, horrified as the two tried to turn his father over, fighting the rigor mortis in his body. They put him in a black bag and zippered it up, then lifted the bag onto a stretcher, which they used to wheel him out.

In the kitchen, Melony asked if she could see him, and they opened the bag. She hugged him, holding his head, and crying as she kept telling him again and again that she loved him so much. Then, the officer told her that she had to let him go, and Melony backed away, promising that she would see him soon, that he was not alone.

After bringing Connor's father to the funeral home van, one of the men, Kyle Cheston, returned to the house. He gave the normal condolences, and then said that they should come down to the funeral home around noon to take care of the arrangements.

"Marina may not be here until then," Connor said. "And we still have to call everyone else."

"Can we do it later?" Melony asked.

"Anytime you want," Kyle said. "How about 4:00?"

"4:00?" Melony repeated. She then looked at Connor. "That sounds good, doesn't it?"

"We'll see you at 4:00," Connor said. "Is there anything we need to bring?"

"If you have it, his birth certificate, his military discharge papers, and if you have something personal you would like put in the newspaper announcement, that as well."

"Okay," Connor said, making notes of each item on the same pad he used with the officer. Following Kyle to the door, and making sure his mother did not hear, Connor added, "May I ask you a question?"

"Of course," Kyle said.

"Do you have any estimate as to my father's time of death?"

"Based on the rigor mortis, I would say about six or seven hours," Kyle said. "It takes a good twelve hours to really set in, and he was about halfway there."

Connor quickly did the math and calculated that his father died somewhere between 3:30 and 4:30 in the morning. "Thank you."

"Call me if anything changes or you need anything," Kyle said.

"Thank you again," Connor said.

Once the funeral home people and the police left, Connor sat his mother down. "What happened?"

"Last night, it was a little after midnight, and your father called up to me, all excited. He thought that he had found my eyeglass case under the couch. Can you believe it?" she said, beginning to break down and cry again. "How much trouble he has getting up and down and he was crawling around the floor looking for my stupid glasses?"

Connor could imagine it. It was exactly what his father would do. Both of them, the Blake men, would always go out of their way for the women in their lives. It was something he admired about his father, and something he cherished as having adopted as a part of himself. No matter the consequences, Blake men always made the sacrifices to try to make the women in their lives happy.

"He was so excited," Melony continued. "But they weren't my glasses. I told him to forget about the stupid glasses and come to bed. The last thing he said to me was 'Okay honey, I'll be right up'."

"He didn't come up?"

"I didn't know," Melony gasped for air, the tears beginning to flow again. "The doctor has me on some new prescription to help me sleep through the night. I went to lie down, and the next thing I know it was morning. I rolled over and he wasn't in bed with me. When I came down and saw him, I just thought he had fallen. I never imagined he was dead. I kept saying, 'Oh my god, Eddie, you fell! Are you okay?' But he didn't answer.

"He was probably locking up, and either had a heart attack or fell. It's that damned disease he has. He lost his ability to drive, he lost his strength and I have to even take out the trash, we even hired people to mow the lawn, shovel snow, and clean the pool. How could I take away his feeling of protecting us too? I used to let him check all the doors and windows and turn on the alarm before he went to bed."

Connor thought of where his father was laying. It was quite possible he fell while he was checking the sliding door to make sure it was secure.

"Oh Connor, what are we going to do? What are we going to do?"

For perhaps the first time in his life, no matter what problems or decisions he had always been faced with, Connor found that he did not have an answer.

CHAPTER 3

The phrase "calm down" has little meaning when such a profound incident like the unexpected death of a husband or father occurs. Neither Melony nor Connor really calmed down, but they did ultimately manage to contain—at least for a short while—their emotions so that they could form the list of who needed to be notified.

Connor wrote all the names as they thought of them, beginning with the obvious close family, and then moving out to cousins and other relatives. Then there were friends, business associates, former students, and people that Coach served in the military with.

Making the calls would be difficult. Nobody knew that more than Melony and Connor. Relaying the cold message that Coach was dead, and then being inundated with sympathy, apologies, and regrets was not something either was looking forward to.

Connor took the close family, as all of their numbers were programmed into his cell phone. He made his way up a flight of stairs into the living room so that both he and his mother could talk on the phone at the same time without interrupting each other.

Looking at the list, Connor dialed his oldest sister, Cindy, first. It was Sunday, and she would be going to work at her weekend job as a waitress at an Italian restaurant soon, so Connor wanted to make sure he reached her first.

The phone rang three times, and then a masculine voice answered. "Hello?"

Ever since Dan and Robert reached high school, Connor could no longer tell them apart from their father. The same was true for Kimberly, Robert's twin sister, and her mother. "Matt?" Connor said, taking a guess that it was his brother-in-law and not one of his nephews.

"Yes," Matt replied.

"Hey Matt, it's Connor," he said.

"Hi Connor," Matt said. "What can I do for you?"

"Is Cindy home?"

"No, she went out on a few errands," Matt said.

"Do you know her cell phone number?" Connor tried, knowing that the number he had for his sister's cell phone was given to Dan when he went to college.

"I'm sorry, I don't have it handy," Matt said. "What's up?"

"I...I just called to let you know that my...my father passed away."

"Oh my god," Matt said. "Connor, I'm so sorry."

"Thanks," Connor said. "Will you have Cindy call me when she gets in?"

"Of course, of course," Matt said. "Oh man, oh god. How did it happen?"

"They think maybe a heart attack or stroke," Connor said, sure that this was also going to become a common question. He sincerely did not believe that his father died from a heart attack or stroke, especially with the way his arm was braced to try and get leverage, but it was the answer he would tell people. Somehow, it was easier for people to think that a heart attack or stroke was a blessing and a good way to go. How any way to go before your time was a blessing, Connor would never understand.

"Oh man," Matt repeated. "Should I have Cindy call you on this number?"

"Yes, please," Connor said. "I'm trying to talk to as many people as I can personally so that Mom doesn't have to."

"Okay, no problem," Matt said. "Oh man, I'm so sorry."

"Thanks," Connor said again. "Bye."

Hanging up the phone, Connor took a deep breath. He looked at the list and then called his Uncle Aaron, his mother's brother. Uncle Aaron wasn't home, so Connor left a message to call him back. He wasn't sure if he should leave the news on voicemail or not, but decided that at least his uncle would know what the call was about.

Connor called one of his cousins next, knowing that she would then begin spreading the word to the rest of the cousins. His mother had suggested Maeve as the one to call first, and if he did not get through to her, gave a couple of other names. About a dozen years ago, one cousin created a "Cousins' Club," where everyone met a couple of times a year, stayed connected, and received news and information about other family members. The call to Maeve would filter its way through the entire Cousins' Club network.

When he was done with his calls, including a returned call from both Cindy and Uncle Aaron, Connor called his other sister, Lauren, to let her know that his father had already been taken away.

"We're just cleaning up from Jimmy's football practice, and then we're on our way," Lauren said.

"Okay," Connor replied. "Take your time; we have until 4:00."

"What's at 4:00?"

"We have to go to the funeral home to make the arrangements," Connor said.

"I don't want the kids to be there for that," Lauren said. "We'll come, help Mom for an hour or so, then I'll take the kids home, and come back after that for the meeting."

"Okay," Connor said. "See you soon."

Connor heard a car outside and looked out the window, seeing Marina pull up. Walking back down the stairs, Connor listened for a moment to hear his mother talking to someone on the phone, and then walked outside to meet his wife.

Marina walked right up to him without saying a word, and embraced him in a hug. Connor clung on tight, the tears he had been fighting beginning to flow freely again. She held him as long as he needed, and then said, "Let's go see how I can help your mother."

The two walked in, and Marina went right to work. With the first round of notification calls done, the phone began what would undoubtedly be a weeklong, non-stop ringing. People calling back to see if anyone needed anything, to see how things were going, to get details on the funeral and any services. Marina answered every call, answering any and all questions and only handing the phone over if it was someone new for Melony to talk to.

She also made sure that the pets were fed, that Melony had taken whatever medicine she needed to take, and took over the note-taking that Connor had been doing to make sure that everything that was supposed to be done actually was.

Lauren and the kids—Chrissie and Jimmy—arrived next. Chrissie gave Connor another long hug, and once again, he completely broke down. He wanted to be strong for Lauren and the kids more than anybody, but just could not keep everything bottled inside of him.

This breakdown, however, began by a comment of his father being "better off." Connor knew it was one of the sentiments people say when they really did not know what to say, but the comment alone infuriated him. How was his father better off? Everything had been great just yesterday. He may have trouble walking, but so do many senior citizens. They don't die from that, they get a wheelchair and live for another decade or so. Chrissie could see the frustration in Connor, and hugged him for comfort. It had been then that the emotions overwhelmed him again.

By the time Uncle Aaron arrived, who coincidentally was coming from Mystic same as Marina had, Lauren decided to take the kids home and give everyone else some time to try and eat before the meeting. Connor offered to go with Uncle Aaron, but he only took directions and orders and went on his own.

He returned with subs, not happy at all with the barren supplies at the restaurant, and the four had lunch together. They ate in the den, Melony sitting in her husband's chair, and Connor staring at the spot where his father had been laying more than anything. Marina kept holding his hand, knowing that he was upset and just needed her to be close.

It was good to eat, but neither Melony nor Connor ate much. They both had about half of their sandwiches, which was something, though nowhere near the amount of food that they usually had at a sitting. As it had since Marina first arrived, the phone continued to ring, and she kept excusing herself to answer it, not once interrupting anyone else in the den.

While Marina was cleaning up and putting the leftovers away, Connor saw that his father's WildCard hat was not where he had put it. He had picked it up from the floor and put it atop of the cathouse. He knew it was silly. It was just a hat. But, seeing it suddenly and unexpectedly gone, Connor grew frantic. A panic attack, desperate to find the hat that his father always wore and loved.

"Where is it?" Connor whispered, then spoke more loudly as he searched around the cathouse. "Where is it?"

Melony, who had gone into the kitchen to make sure Marina was okay, rushed back into the den. "What is it? What's wrong?"

"The hat, where's the hat?" Connor asked. "It's gone!"

"Oh honey, I'm so sorry, I put it away in the closet," Melony said.

Connor rushed through the kitchen, into the front hall, and opened the closet. There, the hat rested atop of the shelf with the rest of his father's hats. Sighing in relief, Connor tried to contain himself.

Marina and Uncle Aaron were watching him, looking to see if he was all right. Melony rushed into the room, crying, and hugged him. "I'm so sorry, I thought it would be helping you. That you wouldn't want to see the hat and be reminded of this morning. I'm so sorry."

"It's okay," Connor said, fighting tears. "It's silly, I know. But, that hat was just something he took pride in. Of me. Of my team and accomplishments. I just couldn't deal with losing that too."

❖ ❖ ❖ ❖ ❖

At 4:00, everyone met at Cheston Funeral Home. Marina drove Connor, Uncle Aaron drove Melony, and Cindy and Lauren both met them there. They all walked in together, and Connor found Kyle working in a side room on his computer. As he was earlier in the day, he was very pleasant and understanding, and came right out to talk to the family.

A small table was set up with chairs for everyone. Marina had the notepad to continue taking notes of anything that they may need. Connor had a page that he and his mother had written after lunch that they wanted for the newspaper listing. Melony also had all of the military papers, birth certificate, and materials that Kyle said he needed.

Kyle did his best to make things as easy as possible on everyone. He had a short form that needed to be filled out and asked the questions to whoever in the room could answer them. When he was done, he took the military discharge papers and the birth certificate and made copies for the paperwork on the death certificate and for the cemetery at Bourne.

"Now, did you want to do some kind of service?" Kyle asked.

"Absolutely not," Melony replied. "My Eddie always used to say that wakes were barbaric, and that he never wanted people to walk in and just look down at him."

"I completely understand," Kyle said. "If you would like, I could arrange for just you and the close family to see him."

Melony glanced at Connor. "That would be good, right?"

"Yes," Connor said.

"I do want to see him," Melony said. "I just don't want other people to be all over him."

"Not a problem at all," Kyle said. "Now, at Bourne, you usually need at least two days notice. The way it works, when I let them know that we are bringing Mr. Blake there, we will get the next available time slot for the day. Every ceremony is fifteen minutes, and the graves are in order of ceremony. What time did you want me to try for?"

"Oh, I don't know," Melony said. "How does 11:00 sound?"

"I will definitely try for 11:00 or close to 11:00, but that may change if there are a lot of funerals on Tuesday. Unless, I try for Wednesday, and then we can probably get any time that we want."

"What do you think?" Melony asked, looking at Connor again.

"I remember when Grandpa died that Dad walked up to the funeral director and asked him if he was sure that Grandpa was really dead. That he had read articles of people who had been buried alive, and that it was a great fear for him. Maybe the extra day would be good."

"That settles it then," Melony said. "If my Eddie was afraid of being buried alive, then definitely, let's wait the extra day."

"Since it's Sunday, Bourne isn't open until tomorrow morning, but I'll have everything sent over first thing in the morning with a request for 11:00," Kyle said.

"Thank you," Melony replied.

"Now, did you already have a casket, or would you like to see some?"

"We don't have one," Melony said.

"That's okay," Kyle said. "I have a good variety here, and even if there isn't something that you like, we can order one for you, too."

"Okay, thanks," Melony said.

Kyle stood up and led everyone into another room. There were about eight metal caskets and a dozen wooden ones in the room. Melony made it clear that she did not want wooden, and then took opinions on which one to go with. Connor, Cindy, and Marina all liked a black one, but Melony thought that it was too fancy for what her Eddie would have liked. She ultimately decided on one that was mostly brown and looked to her the most like a military casket.

After a few more details and arrangements were made, Kyle apologized again for everyone's loss, and walked them out to their cars. Cindy and Lauren went their separate ways from there. Uncle Aaron drove Melony home again, and Marina drove Connor.

Once they reached the house, Uncle Aaron suggested that even if they weren't hungry, they should try and get something for dinner. The four agreed on the Ninety-Nine Restaurant and Pub, and Aaron and Connor went to order and pick up the food. Both Connor and Melony ate much better at dinnertime than they had at lunch, though still not as much as they normally would have eaten.

As Marina went to clean up, Aaron whispered to Connor, "Are you staying here tonight?"

"I am," Connor said.

"That's probably for the best," Aaron said. He then got up, and said to Melony, "Well, I've got a long ride ahead of me, and I'm going to head out."

"Oh, thank you so much for coming," Melony said. The two embraced, and then Aaron headed home.

About an hour later, after everything was cleaned up, all of the notes were organized, and all of the phone messages were answered, Marina also headed out to go home and take care of Fribble, their lop-eared bunny.

With everyone gone, Connor and Melony were alone. Melony watched some television, the movie Speechless with Michael Keaton and Geena Davis, as Connor read a book. As fatigue finally caught up to him, and he could hardly keep his eyes open any longer, Connor stretched and asked his mother, "You about ready for bed?"

"No, you go ahead honey; I'm going to watch a little bit more."

"Okay, call me if you need anything," Connor said. He leaned over, gave her a hug and kiss, and headed for the stairs. He reached them and had an image of coming down in the morning and finding his mother in the same spot as his father had been. Was this not what happened last night? She went to bed and he said he'd be right up? Now, Connor was going to bed and leaving his mother downstairs alone. That was something he could not do.

Heading back into the den, Connor said, "You need your sleep. You can finish watching in bed."

With tears in her eyes, Melony looked up. "Okay, I guess you're right."

The two went upstairs and Connor waited until his mother was in bed, had her movie on, and the lights off. "If you need anything, just call."

"I will," Melony said.

Connor then went into the bedroom he grew up in, changed into his father's boxers to sleep in since he had no extra clothes of his own, read a couple of more pages in his book, and then went to sleep.

CHAPTER 4

The next few days were like a blur to Connor. Marina's schedule had her working Tuesday through Sunday, with classes for her Master's degree on Tuesday, Wednesday, and Thursday evening. Since she had Monday off, she contacted her professors to let them know that she was not going to make school this week, cancelled all of her appointments for Tuesday and Wednesday, and did some assignments for school so that she wouldn't be completely behind.

During a break, Connor spoke with her on the phone and she sent an email to everyone in his personal directory letting them all know that his father had passed away. She put in a note that Connor was not looking for phone calls at the moment, but did want people to at least be aware of the news.

Two minutes after the message was sent, while Connor was driving his mother to the bank to transfer the money for the funeral expenses, the phone rang. It was an old friend, Dominic Petrioli, who played third base for Connor during eight of the nine seasons he coached.

"Hey man, I just heard... are you okay?" Dom asked.

"I guess you can say I'm doing as well as expected," Connor replied.

"This sucks man, I'm so sorry."

"Yeah," was all Connor could say.

As Melony went into the bank, the two spoke for several minutes, with Connor telling Dom the story of what had happened. They talked about how good his father had been the day before, and Connor's guilt at not staying overnight. They also talked about softball, and how Connor's father always gave his support and encouragement to them, and that he would be missed.

By the time Melony returned, Connor got another call, this time from his long-time friend and roommate before he had moved in with Marina. In college, he had been reading a Calvin and Hobbes book, and somehow the name Hobbes had stuck. Connor talked to Hobbes for a while, relaying the story again, and then gave the phone to his mother, who considered Hobbes to be like another son.

Over the next few hours, the phone became a constant, especially once people began seeing the announcement in the newspapers. Conversations with the funeral director about arrangements, talking to family and friends confirming arrangements, and more calls continuing to come in throughout the day. The deliveries also began starting, with plants, flowers, and food baskets. Somewhere in the midst of it all, Marina came back and took over again, logging in everything that arrived and taking over the phone duties.

At one point during the day, they got the call from the garage and went back down to have the spare tire replaced by the good one. Jack said that he heard about Connor's father through the newspaper and expressed his deepest sympathies. Connor thanked him.

That night, Connor decided to go home. He considered it the best time. Sunday was when his father had died. Tuesday was when he and his mother would see his father again for the first time. Then Wednesday was the funeral. He'd spend Monday night at home, pack for the rest of the week, and then return early on Tuesday.

Marina was going to spend Tuesday night as well, so they left Connor's truck in Holliston and Marina drove. Connor sat staring out the window at the clouds as they drove on the highway. One cloud formation looked identical to the helicopters used by the United States Army. Connor stared at it, not taking his eyes from it even once, wondering if this was some kind of sign from his father.

"Are you okay?" Marina asked.

"What?" asked Connor, taking his eyes from the clouds and looking at her.

"Was this song making you sad?"

Connor paused to listen. He hadn't even registered that the radio had been on. "No, I'm fine."

Thinking of songs, Connor remembered one that he had at home. It was by Luther Vandross, titled "Dance with My Father." At the moment, all Connor wanted was to go home, find the CD, and listen to that song. When they made it home, that was exactly what he did, sobbing loudly as Vandross sang about choosing a song that never ended for his parents to dance to. Marina, on her knees, lay her head down on Connor's lap, wrapped her arms around him, and just sat with him listening to the song.

The next day was an even bigger blur, with people visiting in the morning, the phone continuing to ring off of the hook, and then the moment that Connor was both looking forward to and dreading at the same time: it was time to go see his father.

Marina drove this time, bringing Connor and Melony to the funeral home. Uncle Aaron met them there, as did Cindy, and Lauren's husband Jon. Everyone had a short amount of time to say what they wanted, and then backed off, sitting and talking amongst themselves. Connor remained with his father, holding his hand and caressing it gently.

When they met with Kyle on Sunday, Connor had been adamant about his father having his tie tied "the Blake way." His father had taught Connor how to tie a tie, as his father had done with him. It looked normal enough when worn, but under the collar, the knot was never quite a perfect triangle. It may seem like a small point, but Connor wanted his father dressed the way he did in life, and that meant using "the Blake way" with the tie.

Fortunately, they had all been to a cousin's wedding just a month earlier, and when Connor's father took his tie off, he just loosened it a bit and took it off rather than completely untying it. Connor and Melony actually gave Kyle that entire outfit, including the tie that just needed to be tightened, for his father. Melony also liked the idea of seeing pictures of the wedding and being able to visualize her husband, knowing that he was eternally like that.

When Melony came to the casket for her final goodbyes, Connor reluctantly let go of his father's hand and backed away, giving his parents some room and time together. He went and found Kyle and confirmed all arrangements one last time for the following morning. Kyle recommended leaving no later than 9:00 in case there was traffic getting to the Cape.

And then, just like that, it was over. The family left the funeral home, never to see the man who had been William Edward Blake again. To Connor, it seemed to go so quickly. He was not sure what he wanted. His father was gone, after all. But he just did not feel as if he had had enough time with the man he looked up to, respected, and loved so much. Does anyone ever truly have enough time?

That night, cousins were planning on coming. Melony, Connor, and Marina were all exhausted, both emotionally and physically. None of them truly wanted company, but they knew that their cousins meant well. When they arrived, all doubts and dread were lost, as the cousins began making everyone laugh, shared pictures of the recent wedding, and put on a display of the newlyweds taking little humorous shots at each other. When they did leave, everyone felt better.

After the three were alone with only the pets, Connor played the Luther Vandross song for his mother, which made her cry too, and said that she loved it because it was so perfect. Connor then worked on his eulogy for his father, reading it to his mother and wife, both teary eyed and saying that it was beautiful. Connor wasn't sure he wanted to give the eulogy, crying in front of everyone who came, but everyone who was there that day felt that he should say a few words and make the service more personal.

Marina went to bed first, leaving Connor and Melony up for awhile longer. Just like Sunday night, Melony watched television as Connor did some reading. Then, the two went upstairs together, setting alarm clocks for the funeral in the morning.

❖ ❖ ❖ ❖ ❖

Marina had offered to drive, but Lauren suggested driving herself. She had a van that could fit seven, meaning that Melony, Connor, Marina, Lauren, Jon, Chrissie, and Jimmy could all ride together in one car. Melony wanted to get there early to look around the cemetery and try to see when her husband would be buried. They did get there early, but only received information about where to go to get ready for the funeral.

The official ceremony for an officer with full military services included soldiers from the Army and the flag folding ceremony. The gun salute and playing of taps was no longer customary. Since Connor had played taps in high school both on Veteran's Day at the various cemeteries, and at the police station in honor of an officer who had fallen in the line of duty, he wanted it for his father. He tinkered with the idea of doing it himself, or having Jimmy, who also played the trumpet, do it. That, however, would have been quite inappropriate. Kyle looked into it and found a gentleman who would come to play taps since it was important to the family.

When it was 11:00, the hearse led the cars lined up to an alcove where the ceremony would be performed. Two U.S. Army soldiers were there, waiting, saluting as the coffin was taken out and rolled between them. The American flag was already draped over the coffin.

Connor took his mother by the arm and led her to where the ceremony would be performed. They were outdoors, in what looked like a small gazebo with flowers around the structure. One soldier was behind them, holding a bugle. The two soldiers who had welcomed and saluted when they first arrived stood at attention on either side of the coffin, and three chairs were arranged. Connor helped his mother into one, and then went to stand behind her. Lauren and Chrissie took the two other chairs, one on either side of Melony, and held her hands tightly.

The turnout was rather good, though Connor honestly expected to see more people. Family was all there, but no friends, former colleagues, or ballplayers. It was, however, a relatively far drive for those who may have wanted to come, and it was on a business day.

A minister welcomed everyone and began saying some words. Connor hardly knew what was being said, his eyes moving back and forth between the soldiers, the coffin, and his mother. Far more quickly than Connor would have thought, the minister was asking him to step forward and say some words.

Connor took a deep breath, walked forward and stood before his father's coffin. As he was taking out his notes, he began by saying, "I would like to begin by thanking each of you for coming today, the minister for his kind words, the soldiers who are here representing my father, and Kyle Cheston for helping to take such good care of my father these past few days."

With his notes in hand, and the formalities behind him, Connor began speaking the words he prepared. "What can I say about my father? A man who I love, a man who I respect, and a man who helped shape not only my life, but the lives of so many people who he touched. For a while, I went to school with my father and substitute taught. While I was there, I saw that my father was not only a teacher and coach, but like a member of the family. Everyone who saw him greeted him warmly. Everyone who heard that I was Coach's son got really excited and told me how great my father was.

"It was not only the people from school though. Every year we would travel south on vacation. There were people we met along the way—waiters, waitresses, people at hotels—they would always remember us when we walked in, and treat us like family. My father always greeted them with a smile, a little joke, and welcomed them like long-absent friends or family."

Connor heard his mother sobbing, remembering the times he was talking about and crying at the loss. He too was emotional, but he could not look at her, afraid that if he did, he would never make it through. Instead, like a good orator, Connor made eye contact with others there, moving slowly from one to another and holding their attention, avoiding the chairs before him.

"But his outgoing personality, his friendliness, his warmth, compassion, and love are things that we will remember, but my father has always been so much more. Not the grand memories of vacations and adventures we took—like the gas tank being on empty when avoiding a detour, driving through fields of cows and corn with no sign of highways or gas stations, and him calmly and comfortingly telling us that we'll be there in just a little longer...and we were!—but the little things that are what we shall cherish.

"I remember being at an ice show at Cypress Gardens when I was younger, with my father putting his arms around me, caressing my arm, and just showing how much he loved me. I remember the times I did something foolish, and he would very calmly give me a look that let me know I did something wrong, but never lost his temper or got angry. We'd talk about it later, but it was always positive and encouraging, guiding me to learn from my mistakes. I remember playing sports and my father giving me encouragement and advice: even when I was coaching, he always had some positive words to help me and the team improve.

"Even as recently as this past Saturday, his guidance was there as we were working to fix a flat tire. The gentle reminder not to let my hands or feet get under the car in case the jack slipped and the car fell. It was little comments, little reminders, little looks, little touches: these are what I'll remember most and cherish about my father."

Connor took a deep breath. He had read this twice the night before, and it had always been the next part where he lost control of his emotions and began to cry. Without looking at his mother, he continued.

"Above all of this, my father has also been generous, giving, and loving. Just last Christmas, my father no longer was driving, and asked me if I would take him shopping to buy presents for my mother. After I picked him up, I wasn't sure where we would go or what we would get, but he knew exactly what he wanted. First, he wanted a hand-held television. He said that he wanted to get it so that my mother could watch her stories while taking him to his doctor's appointments, or when she was at the pool. And did he get just any TV? No. We looked at a few, got a recommendation from the salesman, and then my father picked the best and said that no price was too high for his honey.

"Then, instead of heading home, he said he had another stop he wanted to make: he wanted to get her a necklace. We went right to the jewelry counter, and as I was browsing and checking prices, he pointed to one he liked, told the woman he would take it because my mother would love it. He never looked at the price, just smiled and said that 'his Angel' would love it.

"I love my father. I am so proud and lucky to have had him in my life, and I shall miss him more than words can say."

As Connor finished, he finally looked at his mother, and saw the tears flowing from her face. He knew that if he looked at her while speaking, he would not have made it through. It broke his heart seeing her like this. Everything about the past few days broke his heart.

One of the soldiers shouted something, and then the officer with the bugle began playing taps. Connor stared at the coffin, holding Marina's hand with his left hand, and his right on his mother's shoulder. Near the end of taps, a pair of F16's flew overhead. Whether it was part of the ceremony, or just part of a normal patrol from nearby Otis Air Force Base, nobody knew for sure, but it was a lovely addition to the ceremony.

The two soldiers by the coffin then lifted the flag, and in full ceremony, folded it, stepped over to Melony, leaned over and presented it to her, saying, "As a representative of the United States Army, it is my high privilege to present to you this flag. Let it be a symbol of the grateful appreciation our nation feels for the distinguished service rendered to our country and our flag by your loved one."

With the ceremony complete, Melony, Uncle Aaron, the three children, spouses, and grandchildren all took a single red rose, walked up to the coffin, and set it on top. Some said a final farewell; a few just put it down and walked away. After Connor put his down, he made it a point to seek out each of the soldiers and thank them for coming and being there for his father.

Kyle directed everyone to sign the book so that the family would know who had been at the funeral. After people signed, some spoke in groups, expressing condolences and well wishes. Kyle then told everyone that they needed to get going, that everyone could go to the main building to talk, but that the next funeral would be coming in soon.

Marina had done some research and made reservations at a nearby restaurant. Listening to Kyle, everyone got into their cars and followed Lauren's van, who was getting directions from Marina. Lunch was pleasant, and then some family returned to the house. People came off and on throughout the day and night, spending time and offering condolences.

Throughout it all, Connor watched his mother closely, feeling protective, but also wondering what he would do next. Writing, developing some kind of RPG game—those thoughts were buried deep in his mind, and he did not think that he could possibly even think of doing either.

At least, not yet. But if not that, then what? It was a question that would be going through his mind the next few days as he stayed with his mother and helped her through everything, but one with an answer that eluded him.

CHAPTER 5

In several weeks, as was expected, the phones stopped ringing, and for most, life returned to normal. Normal, that is, for everyone but Melony and Connor. Connor had tried to get himself back into a routine by writing and working on the development of the game, but he just found that he could not concentrate enough to bring himself to doing it. Instead, he thought of doing a little plot development for down the road, but everything he came up with was dark, dismal, and largely depressed.

Rather than tainting his work, he decided to push it aside and be more proactive by working out and doing physical training exercises. By doing the treadmill, an exercise bike, and working on his weight bench, Connor managed to lose fifteen pounds since the death of his father.

His mother, on the other hand, was trying her best to resume her normal routine. She seemed to be doing so, but she still called Connor frequently and was either crying, or broke down crying in the midst of the conversation. She kept apologizing, saying that she had to stop doing that, but Connor kept telling her to do so as long as she needed to, regardless of what anyone else said or felt.

In the midst of this, there was a convention in Springfield where Connor was hosting a booth and doing a book signing. He was dreading it, but he and his mother both decided to go host the booth, and for at least eight hours each of the days of the convention, they were focused on something productive and good. It actually turned out to be a phenomenal event in terms of sales, and Connor felt that he made many new acquaintances amongst other authors, artists, and even some celebrities who also attended.

Through everything though, Connor just felt even more determined to find something to do to honor the memory of his father. Marina joked, asking him if he was going to join the military and go to Iraq for a year, but that was not what Connor was thinking about at all. Instead, the more he thought about it, the more he wanted to continue his father's passion and try coaching high school baseball.

Of course, being late November, the opportunity to find an opening as a coach was one that Connor did not feel overly optimistic about. First, he may have coached softball, but never baseball. Second, most schools probably already had a coach, or even a coaching staff, firmly in place by now. That rationalization, however, did not sway Connor. He put in a call to Principal Bill Murphy of the Corinth High School where his father had taught. From his name alone, he would at least be granted an audience. Anything could happen from there.

Tying his tie "the Blake way," Marina, sitting on the bed and keeping him company, said, "Are you sure about this?"

"I'm not sure about anything," Connor admitted. "I just feel like I have to do this."

"Do you think you'll get the job?"

Connor shrugged as he finished with his tie. "It's probably too late. I still have to try though."

"What happens when your editor calls and wants to see some progress on the next book?"

"Writer's block is something that has never hit me," Connor said. "I have five books already written that have never been submitted. That's more than enough to spend a year or so honoring my father."

Marina stood up, walked over to Connor, and hugged him. "Good luck. I hope you get it."

"I don't want you to worry," Connor said.

"Worry? About what?"

"The money," Connor added. "I know coaches don't make much money, but even without writing at the moment, we'll be fine."

"I'm not worried about the money," Marina said.

Connor looked into her eyes and saw her concern. He knew what she was thinking. She wasn't worried about the money, she was worried about him. What if, on some elaborate quest to honor his father, possibly an obsession, he lost himself?

"I have to get going," Connor said. "Bill's expecting me within the hour."

"I'll be right here waiting for your call," Marina said.

Connor kissed her on the forehead. Money probably should be a concern, even if Marina said it wasn't. Her company had recently shifted the services to clients, and though she had more kids now, she was actually working fewer hours. Instead of working Tuesday through Saturday, she actually had Wednesday, Thursday, and Sunday off now. The royalty checks would keep coming, making up the difference, but if his readers' thought that he was no longer writing, that could harm sales of his series as well.

"Wish me luck," Connor said.

"Good luck," Marina replied, walking him to the door and kissing him before he left.

Connor stepped outside, closed his eyes for a moment, breathed deeply, and got on his way. He knew that what he was trying to do would probably never work, but he also knew that it was something he had to do to find a way to connect more with his father before moving on. Hopefully, Principal Murphy would be able to see that.

❖ ❖ ❖ ❖ ❖

"Connor, come on in," Bill Murphy said, opening the door to the office and welcoming him in. "I'm so sorry to have heard about your father."

"Thank you," Connor said. "And thank you for the floral arrangement as well. It was beautiful."

"It was the least we could do," Bill said as he gestured for Connor to take a seat. "How is your mother?"

"Taking it day-by-day," Connor said. "The news about Social Security and military retirement benefits was a bit upsetting, but we're working through it."

"Good, good," Bill said. "If there is anything that we can do to help make this easier for your mother, please don't hesitate to ask."

Connor's eyes shifted over Bill's shoulder to a display case with trophies. All baseball trophies all won when his father was coaching. Pictures of the players, the coaching staff, and his father were on plaques and hanging above the trophies.

"So Connor, what brings you here?" Bill asked, getting right to the point.

"I wanted to talk to you about baseball," Connor said.

"Baseball?" Bill asked, confused.

"Yes," Connor said. "I would like, in some way, to honor my father by doing the thing he loved most: coaching."

"Connor, he loved you and your mother most," Bill said. "Not coaching."

"It was his passion," Connor said. "I wish to share that with him. I need to share that with him."

Bill held Connor's gaze for a moment, seeing the intensity and determination in his eyes. Then he broke contact, turned around and looked at the display of trophies. "Connor, there was nobody who I respected more than your father, but he retired thirteen years ago. We have a new coach."

"I don't need to be the head coach, I just need to be involved," Connor said. "Besides, I don't see any new trophies. Maybe another Blake is just what this school needs."

Bill turned around again, his lips clenched. "We actually have what looks to be a really good team this year."

"Bill, that's wonderful," Connor said.

"Yes," Bill said, "we can use another championship around here."

"Let me be a part of it," Connor said. "Please."

"Connor, if there was anything that I could do, I would. Please, believe me on that. But we had to lay three teachers off this year. Our sports budget has been cut again, and the players are using old uniforms. The coaching staff has been in place, and even if there were an opening for another assistant, the budget probably wouldn't give me the flexibility to bring someone on board. Especially someone who is not already a teacher in this school system."

This time, Connor's eyes lowered. It was what he expected, but he had hoped somehow for something more. "I understand."

"I wish I could help," Bill said, looking genuinely sad at not being able to offer a position.

"You would if you could," Connor said. "I know that."

Bill stood up, nodding. "I still need your next book for my collection."

Connor grinned at the comment, but his heart was not into it. His father had been the one to tell Bill about the books and got him to buy them. Bill did have an autographed copy of every book he wrote, but at the moment, it was just another reminder of his loss.

CHAPTER 6

Rather than just heading home after the meeting with Principal Murphy, Connor called Marina first and then his mother. They all agreed to meet for a movie and to then go out to dinner afterwards. Marina loved penguins, so a movie about penguins seemed to be the perfect choice for a relatively light evening.

When the movie was over, Connor pulled his cell phone out of his pocket and saw that he had a missed call and voicemail. "I'm going to head outside and check this," Connor said, knowing that his mother enjoyed watching the credits in case the movie came on again.

"We'll see you out there," Marina said, squeezing his hand affectionately.

Connor walked outside, turned up the ring volume from silence all, and then dialed voicemail. It was from Bill Murphy. "Connor, I really hated not being able to help you today, so I made some calls. If you are serious about coaching, I have a possible opportunity for you." The message then went on to say that he was heading out for the day, and he gave Connor his home phone number. Connor quickly pulled out a pen and wrote the number on the back of his ticket stub. He pushed the button to replay the message and confirmed that the number was right.

Once he hung up, Connor dialed the number and waited.

"Hello?"

"Hi, Bill? This is Connor."

"Connor, hello, hello," Bill said. "You got my message? Good."

"I did, thanks for the extra effort," Connor said. "So what is the opportunity?"

"What do you know about the Governor's new Education program?"

Connor winced. "I'm afraid that I don't pay attention to the news very much." That was an understatement: he read about baseball rumors and transactions, but paid little attention to any other kind of news. Sometimes in conversations, people marveled at how little he actually knew about what was going on in the world around him. Connor always justified it by saying that as a writer, he had to be interested in what was going on in his world, the one he created, not the real one.

"Oh, well, Governor Shilalie's biggest campaign push was to reduce overpopulation at schools, especially inner city schools where dropout rates and teenage crimes were quite high, and present an alternative by having one statewide school of choice."

"Statewide?" Connor asked dubiously.

Bill chuckled briefly. "Ultimately it would be a set of regional schools, but the first one—built in Farmington—was open to those from the state who were interested, though admittedly, it is expected to have more of a regional appeal due to the potential commute."

"Okay," Connor said, listening intently.

"Well, every effort was made for the school to be a viable alternative to what these students were used to, in a hope to attract students into what would become a better lifestyle and future for them. Everything is new: the building, the books, and the buses. The teachers were recruited from around the state to have an experienced and creative curriculum.

"The only thing that was not focused on were the extracurricular activities. School plays, sporting programs, the band: the facility was designed to accommodate these programs, but they have not yet been developed and integrated."

"If there is no program, how do I come into play?" Connor asked.

"They may not have a program, but they do want one," Bill said. "Very badly. It is believed that if these students had extracurricular activities to become involved in, they would feel more attached to the school rather than think of themselves as outsiders attending there. When I mentioned that you were interested in coaching baseball, there was tremendous interest in you doing so at Farmington."

"Even though I've never coached baseball before?" asked Connor, hoping that this opportunity was not too good to be true.

"Don't get me wrong," Bill said. "The fact that you are a best-selling author who will potentially bring publicity to the Governor's program is quite alluring as well. But, this is what you were hoping for, and it is a win-win for everyone."

Connor nodded, agreeing with Bill. "I have to agree with you. What division is it?"

"Well, without a sports program in place, there is no schedule or division officially, but the size of the school, if the schedule can be arranged, would be Division 1 ball."

"Division 1," Connor repeated, smiling. "So what's next?"

"If you can make it, they want to meet with you tomorrow morning at 10:00."

"Just go to the office?" asked Connor.

"That's it," Bill said. "Just be prepared to show them that you are the coach that they need. The one who will get this program started, get the students to feel a sense of ownership and pride in their school, and the one to carry on his father's passion competently and completely."

"Bill, I don't know what to say," Connor said. "Thank you. Thank you so much."

"I'm glad this may work out for you," Bill said. "Besides, if our program is as good as we think it is, and you prove to have even half of the skill your father did coaching, maybe we'll see each other in the play-offs."

"I would like that," Connor said. "Thanks again."

Marina and Connor's mother were just behind him, waiting for him to get off of the phone. "Who was that?" Marina asked.

"Principal Murphy," Connor said. "He got me an interview for a head coaching job."

"Really?" Marina asked. "Where?"

"Some school-of-choice that the Governor created in Farmington."

"Oh Connor, no," his mother said.

"Why not? What's wrong?" Connor asked.

"Those kids are all trouble makers. When the Governor first proposed it, there was a near-panic about the location of the school. Farmington took it, and a rash of robberies in the area happened shortly after. I don't want you to put yourself in danger like that."

"These sound like kids trying to escape trouble and build lives for themselves," Connor said. "That's something I can respect. But don't worry about me. I'll be fine."

"Oh Connor," Melony said again, visualizing her son in a hospital after being attacked by someone with a knife.

"Mom, if nobody gives these kids a chance, then it creates a vicious cycle that they can never escape. I want to honor dad, and if I can help these kids along the way, then that's even better."

"Just be careful," Melony pleaded.

"I will, I promise."

❖   ❖   ❖   ❖   ❖

At precisely 10:00 the following morning, Connor walked into the front doors of the new Farmington school system. The building was pristine, almost more like a college than a High school. Principal Murphy had been right: no expense was spared with building this school.

Connor also thought that his mother would be somewhat relieved as he looked around. He could not find a single item of litter, vandalism, or graffiti anywhere near the school. The grounds were also well tended, looking more like the work of a professional sports groundskeeper than anyone a high school would hire to mow the lawn.

To the left of the front door was a sign for the main office, and Connor stepped inside. There were two students talking to the woman behind the counter, but everything else looked much like any school as far as he could tell. On the right hand side at the end of the counter were faculty mail slots. A large clock was on the wall for everyone to easily see, and several benches and chairs were lined up for students to wait if they had to.

Once the two students finished their discussion, they walked out of the office with a pass. Connor walked over to the woman behind the counter. "Good morning. I'm—"

"Connor Blake?" she said, cutting him off. "There has been a buzz about you coming all morning."

"Why, thank you," Connor said, not sure what the proper response should be.

"Let me take you back to the Principal's office," she said. "Everyone is waiting for you."

"Everyone?" Connor asked, not sure all of a sudden whom he was meeting with.

The woman opened a door that was opposite the mail slots. She held it open and beckoned Connor inside. "This way."

They walked by several small offices, and Connor saw people working intently inside. He assumed that it was the Assistant Principal, perhaps some kind of disciplinarian, and maybe even a Guidance Councilor, though normally they had an office of their own.

The woman knocked on a door, which was promptly opened. "Here you go," she said.

Connor stepped inside and saw three people in the room. He may not pay attention to the news all that often, but he immediately recognized Governor Mitchell Shilalie standing in the room. There was another man with the Governor, and a woman sitting at the desk. All three were wearing suits and looked like power-brokers in an Investment firm.

"Mr. Blake, welcome," the woman said, standing up and extending a hand for him to shake. "I am Principal Daniels, Rhonda Daniels."

Connor shook her hand, returning with, "It's a pleasure. Connor Blake."

"This is Superintendent McGovern," she continued.

"Paul," Superintendent McGovern said, shaking Connor's hand as well.

"And of course, Governor Shilalie."

"An honor to meet such a brilliant and talented artist from the Commonwealth," the Governor said.

"The honor is all mine," Connor replied.

"Mr. Blake, would you like a drink or something to eat?" Principal Daniels asked.

"I'm all set, thanks," Connor said. "And Connor is fine."

"Connor then," she said. "Have a seat."

Connor sat down, and glanced at each person in turn. "I have to admit, I didn't expect such a welcome."

"This is an important day for Farmington," Principal Daniels said.

"Principal Daniels is right," Governor Shilalie said. "It is the culmination of our dream to run not just a successful educational alternative, but an actual school system where all of the needs of our students can be met. When I learned of your interest in heading the Athletic Department here at Farmington, I was overjoyed."

Connor noted the comment about the Athletic Department, and not just head coach of the baseball team. "What do you foresee for the baseball program?"

"I am inclined to allow you some flexibility there," Principal Daniels said. "As long as the school policies are maintained, athletics shall be your purview."

"I see," Connor said. "Well, do you have any questions for me? Game plans? Strategies? Goals? Why I am doing this?"

"If I may be frank," Governor Shilalie said. Seeing Connor gesture for him to do so, he continued. "Your interest in this school system alone brings a certain credibility to it. You are a well-known best-selling author. Does that mean you can coach baseball? Who knows? But, my office has received no fewer than fifteen phone calls already just this morning asking to confirm whether you were in consideration for this position or not. That, in itself, is exposure that would be invaluable for this school and program."

"I see," Connor said.

"I trust you have also picked up a few tips from your father along the way," Paul said.

"A few," Connor agreed.

"I knew your father," Paul said. "By reputation, not personally. I could not think of someone better to bring sports to this school system than the son of the true Coach."

"Thank you," Connor said, thinking to himself about how easy this process was going. The entire interview was more of a welcome-to-the-team meeting than a job interview.

"Do you have any questions for us?" Principal Daniels asked.

"Of course," Connor said. "What kind of budget does the athletic department have for baseball?"

"Well, I'm going to use a little of my discretionary fund here," Governor Shilalie said. "But even then, you will have to be a bit innovative with your expenses."

"Meaning?" Connor asked.

Principal Daniels folded her hands. "The money that Governor Shilalie is providing will cover most transportation costs, field maintenance, some equipment, and a small stipend for yourself."

"I'm not in it for the money," Connor said, bypassing the issue of his pay. "What about Assistant Coaches?"

"I don't think that would be in the budget," Paul said.

"Junior Varsity coach?"

"Mr. Sullivan, one of the Physical Education Teachers has agreed to do it on his own time," Principal Daniels said.

"Okay, that's something," Connor admitted. "Uniforms?"

"Not the best quality, but the Governor's contribution will help," Paul said.

"What about equipment?"

"Bats can become expensive," Paul winced. "Find out what the kids have and what you need, and we'll go from there."

"I see," Connor said, deciding that the picture being presented was not a very good one. "How about buses to and from games?"

"That will be covered," Principal Daniels confirmed.

"What about the rules of having the same sport offerings for both boys and girls? Will there be softball, or are girls going to be trying out for the team?"

"It is our intention to offer all sports next season," Paul said. "Governor Shilalie has worked a gradual infusion into the Farmington budget over a three year span, and sports will be the next priority."

"It is important for our students to feel a sense of pride, accomplishment, and belonging," Principal Daniels said. "Sports help foster that environment."

"Of course, we do have to follow the rules," Paul added, "So we will also be looking to have a softball team this year. Probably a volunteer coach this season, with a more definitive program going forward after the budget increase next year."

"Sounds reasonable," Connor nodded. "How is the field?"

"I'll take you for a walk when we're done here," Governor Shilalie said. "I'll show you myself."

"Fair enough," Connor said.

"So, what do you think?" Paul asked.

"I think that if this program is going to work, I will need assistants. Assistants that I pick and choose on my own. We'll also need equipment and uniforms without worrying about finding the lowest cost provider."

"We don't have the kind of budget for that," Principal Daniels said.

"If you tell me right here, right now, that the job is mine, and that I can run the Baseball department as I see fit, then I'll take the financing headache away from you. I'll take whatever you have in the budget, and then find a way to raise the funds to augment it myself."

"For baseball only?" Governor Shilalie asked. "We would like you to consider running the entire Athletic Department."

"I want to honor my father by coaching baseball," Connor said. "I will put my heart and soul into coaching baseball, but, for now, that is all. Maybe after this school year, I'll look at things differently. But, right now, you need some form of athletics, and I need a baseball team to coach. So how about it?"

Principal Daniels stood up and extended her hand, "I think I speak for everyone here when I say, welcome Coach."

"Coach Blake," Connor said. "There was only one true Coach."

"Coach Blake, then," she corrected.

"When do I get started?" Connor asked.

"Right away," Principal Daniels said, handing him a three ring binder and a book. The binder was information about the Farmington School of Choice program, the school itself, faculty, and academic policies and guidelines. Inside the binder Connor also found an application for employment in the Farmington School system, as well as a few tax, background check, and legal forms. The book was the MIAA—Massachusetts Interscholastic Athletic Association—Handbook. "You should review both and come to me with any questions."

"When can I begin putting together the roster?" Connor asked.

"Usually practices begin in March, but since this is a new school with no established program, we'll let you at least contact the students for interest after the winter break," Paul explained. "We'll plan an auditorium speaking session to discuss the program and invite participation."

"Practice begins in March?" Connor asked. "Can I see the players before that?"

"All the rules are in the Handbook," the Governor said, winking.

"Follow the handbook," Connor said. "Got it."

"Now, how about that tour?" the Governor asked.

"Let's go," Connor said. As he stood up, both Principal Daniels and the Superintendent thanked him for coming in, congratulated him, and said that they would be in touch.

Connor and the Governor then made their way through the school and out to the fields. The entire time, the Governor spoke about his hopes and dreams for this program, and how the success that the school has already demonstrated has been more than he ever could have expected. Connor got the distinct impression that the Governor had high hopes that a best-seller's publicity, honoring a fallen coaching legend, and leading a new school to a Divisional Title was something that would become a reality to launch future schools in the program.

The two walked out to the fields. It was not bad, but Connor had seen better fields. There were four baseball fields in all, which would be quite helpful for practice fields. Instead of dirt, there were crushed red stones for the infield. That would make sliding difficult, but also could help them get onto the field and start practicing a little earlier even after the winter since there was no dirt that had to dry out. There were no fences for home runs or stands for fans, but it was a brand new sporting field. As Connor looked, he saw this not as just any field, but his field. This was where he would do battle with other coaches and schools, and where he would honor the memory of his father.

CHAPTER 7

That night, Connor, Marina, and Connor's mother went out to celebrate. Melony still wasn't eating all that well, but she always seemed to be doing better when she was with Connor. The food of choice for the evening was Italian, with Connor ordering chicken parmesan, Marina getting a mini-pizza for one, and Melony deciding to go with steak and shrimp.

The conversation began fairly light, with discussions about movies and television programs that each watched. Melony also had information after hearing back from the Veterans' Representative about what to expect in terms of continued financial payments now that her husband was gone. As he often did, Connor promised his mother that he would help her out, and offered also to come over with his laptop and create an entire financial analysis and budget for her to see exactly what she had and what she owed, including even topics ranging from utilities all the way down to the smallest of groceries and luxury goods.

Melony was open to the idea, and quite thankful, but until everything was settled between the military, Social Security, and school payments, she knew that she could not accurately project anything.

About halfway through dinner, Connor decided it was time to mention the Coaching offer. "I have some news."

"Oh?" Melony asked. "Good news I hope."

"Well, I know you had reservations about me interviewing in Farmington, but I had my meeting today."

"Oh," Melony said, putting her fork down and looking expectantly at her son.

"I met the Governor today, as well as the principal and superintendent."

"The Governor, really?" Melony asked.

"In person," Connor said. "They wanted me to take over the entire athletic department for the school."

"I hope you said no," Marina said, wincing. "That's not what you want."

"You're right," Connor said. "I only want baseball."

"Did they agree to that?" Marina asked.

"Reluctantly," Connor shrugged. "So, I'm going to be coaching baseball this year. Division One baseball."

"Congratulations," Marina said, reaching over, taking his hand and squeezing it lovingly. "This is what you wanted."

"It's what I need to do," Connor said. He then looked at his mother. "Are you going to be okay with this?"

"I wish that your interview went poorly," Melony said. "I don't want you to risk your life."

"Mom, the school is immaculate. There isn't any graffiti or vandalism at all. These are kids who are looking to escape the stereotypes and futures they see themselves locked into, and have better lives. We both have something that we're trying desperately to achieve: for them, it's a better future; for me, it's honoring the past. I think this is going to be good."

"What about your writing?" Melony asked. "Your father was always so proud of your writing."

"I'm sure I'll get back to writing," Connor said. "That's in my heart and mind. I dream sometimes about plot ideas and things to do with my characters. I drive down the street and my mind is swirling with possibilities. Sooner or later, that's going to begin pouring out of me into another book. Right now though, I just need to do this."

"You know I've always supported you in everything that you've done?"

"I know," Connor said. "Both you and Dad."

"This is no different," Melony said. "Any reservations I'm making are only because I'm concerned about you. But I am proud, and I do support you."

"I know," Connor said, putting his hand out to clasp his mother's across the table.

After dinner and a delectable desert, Connor drove his mother home, took the dogs out, and made sure the house was locked and secure before leaving. He and Marina then drove home, Connor lost in thought about the things he wanted to do.

"Penny for your thoughts?"

"What?' Connor asked, realizing that he did not actually hear Marina but registering the fact that she had said something.

"What are you thinking about?"

"My staff," Connor said. "There's no budget for it, but there's people I want to bring with me."

"You always bring people with you," Marina snickered.

"Not true," Connor said.

"Oh no?" Marina said, amused by his rebuke. "So is it just a coincidence that wherever you go, your friends and colleagues wind up going shortly after?"

"I may have helped a few people get jobs along the way," Connor shrugged.

"And when you left to work on your own thing, you brought people along to work on the Development Team of the game, or on the testing teams, or something that you've got your fingers dabbling in."

"Fine," Connor said, acceding to the point. "I bring people with me."

"So who did you want now?"

"A few names pop into mind," Connor said.

"Such as?"

"Dom for one," Connor said. "When I coached softball, he was the one guy I spoke to daily, emails back and forth about scouting reports, lineups, strategy, and anything and everything that might impact the game." Connor laughed to himself for a moment.

"What? What's so funny?"

"Our emails tended to get quite long. I always put subjects like 'Update,' or 'Status Report' so that if we were ever monitored, at least the letters may appear somewhat legitimate. He used to use headers like, 'Man, I'm so friggin'...' and then went right into his letter."

"Why did that make you laugh?"

"He got in trouble for it, and said that he couldn't write during office hours anymore," Connor explained. "Then, one day, I got an email with an attachment. The attachment was a Word document that had a three page letter, explaining all about how using Word looked like he was working and not sending emails, so he could still provide replies in depth that way."

"It didn't work, did it?" Marina asked, shaking her head at the thought.

"Not quite," Connor laughed again. "He came back from lunch, found the Word document printed and on his keyboard with a note from his boss saying 'See Me'."

"Lovely," Marina said. "Did he get fired?"

"His company had a strong union. He got in trouble, but not fired," Connor said. "Still, he didn't care. Softball came first. It always did. Of everyone I know, other than my father, of course, he is the one with the most passion for the game. There is no one better qualified than him to come with me. Nobody I would trust more."

"Will he do it?"

"Probably," Connor said. "He's always wanted to get back into the game. That's one of the reasons he opened Pure Hitters—helping kids, and adults, with batting instructions and a place to go for batting cages."

"Who else?"

"Do you think a bunch of high school boys would listen to a female coach?" Connor asked.

"You're thinking Corey?"

"Coach Corey," Connor said. "Best pitching coach we ever had."

"You only had her for one season," Marina pointed out.

"She was in high school herself at the time," Connor shrugged. "People do tend to go to college and things change."

"I don't know if she'd be interested," Marina said. "Do you even know where she is?"

"I'll find her," Connor confidently replied. "I was also thinking of Joe and Rick."

"Why them?"

"Joe was the Physical Trainer for the team, and really helped to get us where we needed to be athletically. I'd like him to take a similar role here. As for Rick, he may be a little flashy and unusual at times, but he definitely knows what he is doing."

"Anyone else?"

"That about covers it," Connor said. "There's others I'd like to have involved. My loyal players, but these four are the ones who I think would be best for the team and teaching. After all, our goal is to teach and guide in high school, and this group would be able to do that."

"When are you going to start trying to reach people?"

"Tomorrow," Connor said. "I want to read over all of the materials tonight to make sure I'm not thinking of doing something I shouldn't. Then I'll organize the coaches and go from there."

Connor pulled into the driveway and turned his truck off. As he reached for the materials he was given at school, Marina added, "If there is anything I can help with, just ask."

"I will," Connor said. "Thanks."

❖　❖　❖　❖　❖

Connor read every word of the Farmington project, school information, and then began reading the MIAA Handbook. He had a notebook by his side and jotted down notes of anything that he felt was especially pertinent: things like requiring permission forms from parents, academic eligibility requirements, attendance policy, authorized team meetings and practice schedules, and season logistics.

There were some things that bothered him: with softball, he put the roster together beginning on January 1ˢᵗ, had people in the batting cages in February and early March, and had rigorous physical training for most of March, with field practice beginning as soon as the fields were dry enough to play on. By the end of April, they had daily scrimmages, and the season began in May. With high school baseball though, practice could not begin before the third Monday in March. There could be Captain's practices, but a team that never had a prior roster or Captains seemed to be at a distinct disadvantage with such a clause.

Connor put down a few more notes and ideas on ways to try and have his people practice and do something before the season. It could not be organized and exclusive to the baseball team only, but if he set up an after-school program open to the entire student body, it could be a way to at least do the physical training before the first day of practice could begin. He also wrote the word "Captains" and underlined it three times. Even if there were temporary Captains, the fact that they could begin practicing earlier was something he had to find a way to take advantage of. A new team needed all of the practice it could get. Certain aspects of the game, like chemistry, coordinating defenses, and the game plan were something acquired through repetition and knowledge of those around you. These kids would all be learning from scratch.

Connor flipped back to the beginning and read again. "Does this seem right to you? 'Grade Point Averages of students improve during seasons in which they are participating in athletics'."

Marina, who was reading one of Connor's manuscripts that had not been published yet, paused to answer. "The kids probably try harder."

"Yeah, but grades going up? There is more activity, more demands on the student's time, more pressure and stress. Doesn't it just make sense that grades may dip a bit?"

"The students have a larger incentive to do well while playing sports. They don't want to be disqualified. Besides, think back to high school yourself: sure, there were times when there was a lot of home work, but did you ever feel completely overwhelmed, or were you able to do other things?"

"I played sports and worked," Connor admitted.

"See?" Marina said. "So with the student's desire to play, they focus on maintaining their grades, and actually do better."

"I guess," Connor conceded. The academic requirements seemed, to him, to be fairly lenient. To be eligible to play, students had to be passing four traditional year long classes. As someone who always emphasized learning, school work, and continuing education, Connor wanted a somewhat more stringent policy for his team. Four passing grades meant that a student could fail one class. That wasn't going to work. Connor wrote down the letter 'B' and circled it. His players would need to maintain at least a B-average without failing anything, or they would be ineligible to play.

Marina put the pages down and took her glasses off. "You almost done?"

"I think so," Connor said. "I'm just going to go send an email to Dom, Rick, Joe, and Corey, see if I can get some quick feedback."

"Okay," Marina said. "Goodnight."

"'Night," Connor said, kissing her on the forehead as he got up, shut the light, and closed the door behind him. Walking into his home office, he sat down, opened email, and typed in the names for the four assistant coaches he wanted. For the subject, he typed 'Opportunity.'

Connor then stared at the screen for a moment, wondering what to write. Taking a deep breath, he decided to just begin.

Hey Guys,

I know I haven't been in touch very much since I found out about my father, but I wanted to take this moment to thank each of you for the support you have shown since then. We all appreciate it.

I myself have done quite a bit of soul searching in these past few weeks, and have decided to do something meaningful in honor of my father. It may be a small gesture, but it is something that I feel that I need to do. As of this afternoon, I am officially the head coach of this year's varsity baseball team at the new Farmington school system that the Governor formed this year. Division One ball, too.

It's not going to be easy. There currently is no athletic department, equipment, uniforms, or even opponents to play against, but between now and the season, I'll work all of that out. As I do take this step though, there are certain things that I know that I will need in the months to come, and the largest part of that, is all of you.

I understand that each of you have your own lives, families, and careers. That makes what I'm proposing somewhat difficult. However, over the nine years I coached and played softball, we have fought together, bled together, triumphed together, and cried together. We have been together for the playoff years, and the seasons where we were lucky to scrape by with a single win. I would like us to be together for this, too.

If you can't, don't worry about it. I'm certainly not trying to force or guilt any of you into this. However, if you would be willing, I would truly be grateful to have you all on this journey with me. Think about it. Give me a call if you have any questions.

I hope that all is well with all of you.

Connor

Connor reread the letter and then clicked the send button. It said what he wanted it to say, and if his people decided to join him on this, then he would be glad to have them. If not, he would make do on his own.

The phone rang, and Connor picked it up quickly so it wouldn't disturb Marina as she tried to fall asleep. "Hello?"

"Hey, Connor!"

"Dom?" Connor replied. "How's it going?"

"I just read your letter, man," Dom said. "You're really doing this?"

"I haven't signed the contract yet, but yes," Connor said.

"And you need help?"

"Always," Connor said.

"Then count me in man, you know that."

"Thanks Dom, thanks a lot."

"So what's my role going to be? General-Ass-Kicker-and-Roughneck? The guy who makes sure everyone listens to you or else?"

"Yeah, sure," Connor said, remembering the Roughneck Squad from the softball team. "As long as you don't stick with the philosophy of, 'If you can't beat them, then beat 'em'."

"Oh man, I forgot all about that," Dom laughed.

"High school kids," Connor said slowly and clearly. "No roughneck business."

"No problem, man," Dom said. "Seriously though, what do you want me to do?"

"How about being my Batting Coach and doubling as my Bench Coach?"

"I'm game if you are," Dom said. "Do these kids know how to hit?"

"No clue," Connor admitted. "We'll find out though."

"Yeah, we'll teach them how to hit," Dom said. "No problem. No problem at all."

"Well, Dom—welcome to the team."

"Oh yeah, coaches unite, the WildCard is back together again!"

CHAPTER 8

With Dom Petrioli officially on the coaching staff, Connor waited patiently to hear from the rest of the people he wanted. Joseph Lane, the former EH—the Extra Hitter in softball, a position similar to the Designated Hitter, but since pitchers bat, it was an extra batter off of the bench—and occasional outfielder, was the next coach he heard from.

Joe was one of the fastest people Connor ever knew. They knew each other briefly in high school, where Joe had set or broken almost every sprinting and cross-country record in the Middlesex County. His four years of high school were champion years, and trophies with his name on it were still on display in the lobby.

He had not played baseball since he had been in Little League, but came one day to a practice with Hobbes, who he stayed in touch with since high school, and tried out. He had a great arm and bat, a winning attitude, but his speed was used against him in the field—if he broke too soon, he overran a ball and then had to chase after it. If he tried to wait, he would find that it would drop in. Even chasing a ball, with his speed, batters rarely could take extra bases off of him, but while he was practicing in the field, he was EHing in the games.

Joe had been on the team for one season before Connor made him the Physical Trainer. They had begun jogging in November—rain, snow, or shine—and were doing sprints for a month before the team got onto the practice field. Connor and Joe used to tell the team as they ran laps that if they could do it, then the team could do it. Of course, neither ever told the team that they had been doing it for four months already.

Joe had also run the Boston Marathon every year for five years, coming in second twice, just behind a Kenyan who won. He was an example of what hard work and discipline could do for physical stamina, and a man who was pure speed.

Joe had a good job, a wife, and two children. They had just bought a new house as well, and though he was interested, he made it clear that his family and ability to keep the roof over their heads was his first priority. The job, however, had fantastic hours for coaching, working 6:00 AM to 2:00 PM, giving Joe enough time to get to Farmington before any game or practice should be scheduled.

With the understanding that Joe may have to miss a few things for work and family, he accepted the position of Physical Trainer and became the second assistant coach for Connor. The third, was Rick—Rickey—Urban, Connor's former center fielder and leadoff batter.

Rickey never liked to do things easily, and always tried to put some flare into his game, like a swan dive leaping through the air with his glove stretched to the left and catching the ball. Ninety-nine out of one hundred times, he would make the play when doing that; of course, that one time the ball dropped, Rickey received tremendous criticism from the players, and Connor had often been besieged with requests to cut him from the team. They didn't need a show-off; they needed a player who would just do his job. Every time a request came in, Connor watched Rickey making a diving catch, or scale the chain fence and rob the batter of a home run. He had his quirks, but he was one tremendous player.

In the final season that Connor coached, he had made Rickey his Fielding Coach, under much scrutiny from the team. One thing Connor knew immediately: Rickey may like to have a style of his own while playing, but he had a solid grasp of fundamentals and could convey that to other players with ease. It was that skill and ability that Connor was looking for now, and Rickey was interested.

Rickey had gone to college for radio broadcasting, but found himself moving from job to job in a suit and trying to forge a career in Corporate America. He lived in a tiny one-room apartment and rode his bike wherever he had to go. Keeping his needs modest, he felt that he could make changes in his life if the opportunity for sports broadcasting ever presented itself.

When Connor sent the email, Rickey had been bored in his current job, and turned in his two-week notice. Without a guaranteed job, coaching sounded as good as any other. Connor had not been offered much as a Head Coach, but he made the same offer to Rickey, as well as an offer to try and get him a ride back and forth to the school each day. Even if Connor had to finance it himself, he was willing. Without reservation, Rickey agreed.

That left only Corey Forester. Connor originally met Corey through an ex-girlfriend, who coincidentally, also had been the reason he met Marina. It was a rather awkward scene, as the two saw Connor at a soft-ball game, after tracking him down from a few internet conversations. They went out for nearly nine months, and then broke up. It was years later that Connor and Marina bumped into each other again, but after their third date, when she got food poisoning and Connor nursed her back to health, they had been together ever since.

Back then though, the former girlfriend had a best friend who was an All-State pitcher. She, Corey, had long discussions with Connor about softball, and had plenty of ideas about how he could turn the team around, which, at the time, had only played one full season and another in a frostbite league. Feeling that her insight and commentary was good, Connor invited Corey to become the Pitching Coach and work with the pitchers directly.

Her first session, Corey had brought a resume of sorts, and pre-pared an entire presentation to give to the pitchers to show them that she was qualified to teach and guide them. There were five pitchers at the time, and of them, one was removed for refusing to listen to a girl, and the other four all made tremendous strides and had years far better statistically than before she worked with them.

Her style was a bit unique, as she used to have pitcher and coach conferences by sometimes dancing with her pitcher on the mound, but every one of the pitchers who worked with her respected her, and numbers never lie: they all got better.

The email Connor sent had been bounced back as undeliverable. That pretty much ended his pursuit of Coach Corey, as everyone had called her. Marina then got involved, making a few calls, and finally reaching Corey. She was hesitant at first, not sure if she wanted to coach a high school boys' baseball team, especially since the pitching style between baseball and softball were so different, but ultimately she agreed. The fundamental of pitching she knew, and just because she pitched underhand did not mean she did not understand how to pitch or teach people how to pitch for baseball.

With his coaching staff complete, Connor was ready for the next step. It was time to announce the program and his taking on the role of coach. There had been rumors that leaked about it, and Connor had been receiving quite a bit of fan mail and inquiries. Principal Daniels also called and told him that the school's phones were ringing non-stop, and all asking to verify whether best-selling author Connor Edmond Blake was leaving the literary world for academia. It was time to tell the world exactly what was happening.

Connor spoke briefly with Superintendent Paul McGovern, and agreed to a press conference, which Connor decided would be best to have on the baseball diamond. It was scheduled for Wednesday, the day before Thanksgiving. The timing could have been better, but Connor was ready. It was time to let the world know that he was honoring his father by continuing the legacy of coaching.

❖   ❖   ❖   ❖   ❖

At 10:00 AM on November 22nd, Connor Blake stood on the pitching mound of what would be the field he would be calling his own in the months to come. Chairs had been brought out from the cafeteria for people to sit, and were arranged for those involved to be near the mound, and the media along the infield. Each of Connor's assistant coaches made it to the press conference, as well as the Governor, Superintendent, and Principal of Farmington High School.

The Superintendent walked over to join Connor on the mound, and raised his arms to quiet everyone down. As he was doing so, Connor stepped back and took a seat. "Good morning," Paul said a couple of times until everyone's attention was on him. "Thank you all for coming this morning. We have some exciting news and announcements for you this morning, and then we'll open up to any questions that you may have.

"To start off, it is with great pleasure that I am here to announce that the Farmington School of Choice High School is going to be able to offer an Athletic Program a year early. We originally believed that athletics would not fit into this year's budget, but in light of a few opportunities that have presented themselves, we are quite fortunate to be able to have a Spring season.

"Since this entire school system and project was founded by the inspiration and hard work of Governor Shilalie, I am going to step down for him to say a few words," Paul concluded. "Mitch?"

"Thank you, Paul," Governor Shilalie said as he stood up and walked over to the mound. "As someone who spent my youth in the inner city, I have always striven to find a way to help those who find themselves in situations that are less than desirable: streets ruled by drug lords, gangs, and violence. Since becoming Governor, I have sworn to increase public safety, reduce gang- and drug-related violence, and to provide an environment that would foster learning and education for our youth.

"When the Farmington School of Choice High School opened its doors for the first time this Fall, it was the culmination of my dreams, my passions, and my goals. But just because I achieved that which I set out to do does not mean I am done. I have never been one to be complacent. Instead, I want more. I want a better education for our youth. I want better programs, better opportunities. Not only for the students here, but for all students.

"But, as Superintendent McGovern indicated, this school system had a tiered approach: Tier One was to build the school, attract top faculty, and secure innovative technology and textbooks for the students. Tier Two was to then encourage parents and students to choose to come to Farmington, leaving a school system that they know and are familiar with to journey into an unknown opportunity. The response to Tier Two has been overwhelming, with overpopulated and under-achieving school systems around the state having students interested in this opportunity. But, our early studies show that not only is the Farmington School system prospering, but with smaller class sizes and more manageable teacher-to-student ratios, the other schools within the state are showing improvement as well. The future for our youth has never looked brighter.

"As any good politician would tell you, though, change must be made gradually, and not all at once. This is not only for acceptance, but, unfortunately, for budgetary constraints. If we did everything we wished with our school systems, taxes would be increased so high that it would put a hardship on all of the people of the Commonwealth. So, we decided to focus on education, and not athleticism, for the first year of implementation.

"Tier Three, which we were looking at for the next school year, would begin having a more developed extracurricular schedule, including sports, theatre, music programs, and other activities that the students desire. Well, Tier Three is here. Not a full rollout of the program, which will still take place next year, but a beginning.

"The success of this school system gives me great pleasure, and knowing that this spring, a full season early, there will be students wearing Farmington High School uniforms and competing in organized sports, is more than I could have hoped. But with the hard work and determination of myself, the dedicated staff in my office, Superintendent McGovern, Principal Rhonda Daniels, and all of the students and parents here at Farmington, there will be sports this Spring.

"The schedules and details are still being finalized in conjunction with the Board of Directors of the Massachusetts Interscholastic Athletic Association, but the first sports available here at Farmington shall be Baseball and Softball.

"Now, to run this program, and lead Farmington from a collection of students from around the state into a community of individuals who feel a sense of acceptance, belonging, and pride takes a very special individual. I am here to tell you that we have found just such an individual.

"Who he is will not be a surprise, for people recognize him and know exactly who he is. The choice of this man though, may be a bit of a surprise because of just who he is. Who is our new Athletic Director and Baseball Coach? He is a best-selling novelist who is known wherever he goes. He has had three movies made of his books already, with a fourth in the works. He is a Massachusetts native, and has always had pride in his home.

"All of this is terrific, but you probably wonder, how does that make him qualified to run an athletic department or coach a baseball team? Well, this man has also been raised by a former coach who is in the Massachusetts State High School Coaches Hall of Fame. Baseball has fueled his life for as long as he can remember. Not just playing the game, but the mechanics, the strategies, and the principles behind the game. He has also been a coach himself: not baseball, but softball, where he has had success building a team, forging a bond and chemistry between players, and leading them.

"This is a man who really needs no introduction, so without further ado, I give you, Connor Edmond Blake."

Governor Shilalie stepped back off of the mound, nodded to Connor, and sat down in his chair. Connor stood up and walked back over to the mound. "Well, for not giving me an introduction, your words were very kind."

Governor Shilalie grinned and nodded.

"I want to begin by thanking you all for coming out here today, especially to such an awkward meeting location for this press conference.

I'm sure the auditorium would have been a better venue, and you certainly could all hear me better at a podium, but as this field is where we shall be living our dreams, I felt that our beginning should be right here with it."

Connor paused, looking at each of the reporters and the mini-recorders pointed in his direction. "As you just heard, I am going to be coaching the Farmington Baseball team. This is a challenge that I am looking to embrace, and one I feel that I am ready for. I have always enjoyed building things from the ground up, whether it is business, my old softball team, or the worlds I write in, so I feel quite at home and comfortable with beginning a program rather than taking one over.

"For giving me the opportunity to build this program, I would like to thank Governor Shilalie, Superintendent McGovern, Principal Daniels, all of the voters and supporters of the Farmington School project, and Corinth High School's principal, Bill Murphy who originally referred me for this position. I am especially grateful because I am not only here to build this team and program, but to honor the memory of a great man, my father, William Edward Blake.

"To carry on the legacy of coaching excellence, and to feel the passion he had, and we shared, for this game, is something that I feel that I need to do. To be provided with the opportunity to do this, like the Governor said, is more than I could have dreamed of. I will do this job, I will build something great, and I will honor a man whom I love.

"To assist me along this journey, I have brought a few very talented individuals with me. Sitting to my right is my Pitching Coach, Corey Forester; my Batting Coach, Dominic Petrioli; my Fielding Coach, Rickey Urban; and my Physical Trainer, Joseph Lane. Each of us would be more than happy to answer any questions at the end of today's planned events.

"To conclude, I could not do this without the love and support of my family, especially my wife, Marina, and my mother. I also appreciate the understanding and support of my readers and fans. Thank you," Connor concluded. Pausing for a moment, and then added, "If there are any questions, we'd be glad to answer them."

Connor walked back to his seat, and for nearly an hour, fielded questions about his writing career, whether he was giving it up, what type of players he was looking for, what kind of team did he expect to have, and more. The questions were not all geared toward him, as his coaches, the Governor, Superintendent, and Principal all had questions posed to them as well. When all questions had been asked, Connor and Governor Shilalie thanked everyone for coming, and with the press conference behind them, they each faced the pre-holiday traffic as they went home to their families.

CHAPTER 9

Ever since the first year they had been dating, Connor and Marina did their best to split their time and spend the holidays with both families. It was often suggested that they should pick a holiday, such as Thanksgiving with one family and Christmas with the other, but the two always wanted to spend time with each, even if it meant only for a short time.

Connor's oldest sister, Cindy was hosting Thanksgiving for the third year in a row. They used to alternate houses, but Cindy had been doing it most recently, first because Dan and Robert had football, and more recently out of convenience. Matthew was also famous for his cinnamon bread, which he baked whenever they hosted a holiday, so it worked out well for everyone.

Dinner was originally scheduled for 2:00, but to get to the Cape and the second dinner, Connor and Marina would have to leave around 2:30, so Cindy said she would try to move everything back to 1:00. Of course, there was still morning high school football, all three of the Griffin children were at the games, and the entire Kerrigan family also went to support their home team. As a result, most people did not expect to arrive until 1:00.

Connor did not mind leaving at 2:30, but the thing he enjoyed most about the holidays was spending time with the kids. This was never more apparent than the first time he missed part of Christmas to be with an old girlfriend and arrived too late to see the children open their presents. It was an experience he vowed never to repeat. So, knowing he had to leave early, Connor had asked if it would be all right to come early and spend some extra time at the beginning. Cindy suggested noon.

As the first holiday—other than Halloween of course, but that hardly counted as a family event—Melony and Connor were both dreading the day with the obvious absence in the family. Melony also was afraid to drive on her own, unable to drive at night, and was actually considering skipping the entire holiday. Connor offered to pick her up as long as someone else could drive her home afterwards since he would be leaving early. His sister Lauren agreed to drive her home.

Even then, Melony had reservations. She thought that it was ridiculous for Connor to drive an hour to pick her up, and then another hour to Cindy's house. Connor would hear nothing of it, assuring her that it would not be a problem at all. Besides, he explained over and over again that he wanted to go early to spend time with the family, and if she either did not go, or waited until Lauren was able to pick her up, then that would be less time with everyone. Ultimately, with much reluctance, Melony conceded and let Connor and Marina pick her up.

While driving, engrossed in conversation, Connor glanced around and realized that for the first time ever, he had gotten lost going to his sister's house. He reached the highway and knew that he had definitely done something wrong, though he thought he probably drove by the house without realizing it because he was preoccupied. Turning around, he watched every house that he drove by, shocked not to see his sisters.

They returned to a small square in town, and Connor recognized the gas station and World War II veterans' statue, and knew where he was again. He had merely missed a left turn by the third gas station—he had taken the right at the first one, the left at the second one, and then missed a left at the third one. As he looked at it, in all honesty, he never remembered having to take two lefts, but as he took the turn, he knew he was on the proper road this time.

The little adventure of getting lost did not last long, but it did make them fifteen minutes late to arrive at Cindy's. Connor pulled into the gravel driveway, drove down and backed into the first clearing so that it would be easy for them to leave first.

It was not the best Thanksgiving Day ever: it was raining in various degrees, sometimes in torrents, and others a light drizzle. The wind was also quite ferocious, driving the rain even harder at times. Connor looked out the truck to gauge how bad the rain was. "Do you want an umbrella?"

"No, I'm fine," Melony said.

Marina got out first, heading to the house to let Cindy know that they were there and to open the door. Connor walked over to his mother's door, opened it for her, helped her with the things she had brought—crackers and cheese for an appetizer, and sweet potatoes for dinner—and also made sure she got out of the truck without any problems, especially since he had parked so close to the grass.

"Oh Connor, please go ahead, you're getting soaked."

"I'm fine," Connor said, holding his hand out for his mother.

Melony took his hand and had him guide her from the truck. Once she was on the driveway, Connor closed the door, then held his arm out for her to take it. The two then walked up the sidewalk and to the house, where Marina was waiting along with Cindy.

"Hi there," Cindy said.

"Do you want me to take anything?" asked Marina.

"I'm all set," Connor replied.

As they stepped inside, Cindy and Melony went right into the kitchen with the things Melony brought.

"What should we do with our jackets?" Marina whispered.

"Usually Cindy puts them on her bed," Connor said.

"But they're wet."

Cindy walked back over to the foyer. "Come on in. Can I get you anything?"

"What should we do with our jackets?" Connor asked.

"I'll take them," Cindy said, holding her hand out. "I'll put them on the bed."

"Marina was concerned because they are wet," Connor added.

"Oh, well, I'll think of something," Cindy shrugged as she took the jackets upstairs.

Connor and Marina then walked into the kitchen and joined their mother. Melony was putting the crackers and cheese out for people to eat. As Connor looked around, it was the cleanest and most organized kitchen he ever remembered seeing around the holidays. Usually there was food everywhere, in various stages of preparation, some ingredients that were on the counters, drinks, and more. Now, it looked as if it was any normal day with everything clean and in it's proper place.

"So how is everyone?" Cindy asked as she rejoined them.

"Good, good," Connor said. "Everything looks so clean."

"Well, everything is done," Cindy shrugged. "The kids are still at the game. They'll be home soon."

Connor heard a footstep behind him and turned around just enough to see Matt coming in and trying to scare him.

"Boo!" Matt said, his arms out to poke Connor as well. "Did I scare you?"

"Did you see me flinch?" asked Connor.

"Guess not," Matt shrugged. "So, are you keeping the kitchen afloat, or are you going to go sit down?"

"That depends," Connor said. "If you're going to join us, we'll go sit down. If not, we'll stay where we are."

"Let's go then," Matt said.

They went into an adjoining room with a couch, a sofa chair, and a television. The football game was on: the Miami Dolphins against the Detroit Lions. Other than Cindy, everyone came in to sit and chat. Since Melony and Marina were not football fans, Matt changed the channel and found some kind of beauty contest for bred dogs. Everyone watched, the conversation centering around the dogs, types of dogs, and dogs that they used to have.

Dan and Robert came home together. They had left the game early, with their town annihilating their rivals. Robert headed up to take a shower and get dressed as Dan stayed downstairs to spend time with the family. Since he was a freshman in his first semester at college, every question was geared toward how things were going, what his classes were like, his dorm, how he liked everything, and the normal banter surrounding new college students.

Dan thought that college was quite easy, and that he was the smartest one in his school. Like his father, Connor could never tell when Dan was being serious or joking. They both had the ability to say complete falsehoods with straight faces and no hints of deception. There was one time when Melony had called to talk to Cindy that Matt acted frantic. He said that Kimberly had swallowed one of her toys, it lodged in her throat, and the paramedics were there now. Months later, after numerous conversations where Matt reiterated how horrible of an experience it was, Cindy said quite clearly, "Kimberly never got a toy stuck in her throat!" For all Connor knew, Dan could have been miserable in college, but with a straight face said everything was perfect.

When Robert was done with his shower, Dan went upstairs to take his. Several minutes later, Kimberly got home with the news that Uxbridge did indeed win the Thanksgiving game. Then she headed up to get ready herself. Not even a minute after she walked in the door, the rest of the family arrived at the same time in two different cars. The Kerrigan's pulled in first—Chrissie, with her newly-printed driver's permit driving—and then Uncle Aaron directly behind them.

After the pleasantries, Happy Holiday wishes, and hellos, Chrissie came in and joined Connor, Marina, and Melony on the couch watching the dog show. They remained there, talking, until Cindy called and said that it was time for dinner.

Connor got up and went to go to the bathroom, but somebody was in there. Waiting, he watched Jimmy walk over and hug him. "Hey buddy," Connor said.

"Can I talk to you for a minute?"

"Sure," Connor said, stepping back into the room where they had been watching television. "What's up?"

"I heard about you coaching at Farmington," Jimmy said.

"It's official," Connor said. He saw Robert in the other room lean against the doorway, listening to the conversation.

"You're doing it for Grandpa?"

"I am," Connor said.

"I want to do it for Grandpa, too," Jimmy said.

"Do what?" asked Connor.

"Play for you."

"You already have a school in Hopkinton," Connor said.

"I don't play baseball," Jimmy pointed out. "I do football, wrestling, and lacrosse. All three are to help me be a better football player."

"So why do you want to transfer out of that and become a baseball player?"

"I want to do it for Grandpa," Jimmy said, with conviction in his voice and eyes.

"I don't know," Connor said. "I admire that you want to do something for your grandfather, but you're on the fast track for a football career. You bypassed the Freshman team and became a starter on Junior Varsity your first year in the system. You have a good coach, a good school, and a potentially lucrative career ahead of you. I'd hate to think you might jeopardize that for any reason."

"You're jeopardizing your writing career," Jimmy pointed out.

"That's different," Connor said. "I have books stockpiled. I'm not going to miss deadlines or become a worse writer for doing this. You, however, need to play football if you want to be scouted and drafted."

"Maybe it's baseball I really want," Jimmy argued.

"Jimmy, be honest. You liked baseball, but always thought it was too slow."

"I am being honest. I want to do this. Like you, I need to do this. Besides, wouldn't it be nice to know you have at least one pitcher who can pitch on your team."

"How do you know I won't have good pitchers already?"

"Come on, Uncle," Jimmy scoffed. "You taught me how to pitch when I was a kid. I remember pitching for hours outside of your apartment. I can do this, and you know I can."

Connor saw Robert slide off of the doorway and head to the dinner table. "What do your parents think?"

"They don't know," Jimmy said. "This isn't their decision, it's mine."

"That's not entirely true," Connor said. "My first recommendation is to stay where you are. You're happy now. You're established in your school and community. You've got your whole future ahead of you. I would not even consider transferring if I were you. But, if it is something you have to do, and my objections don't sway you at all, then talk to your parents. It's a family decision, not yours alone."

"You'd take me if I did transfer?"

"You'd have to try out just like everyone else," Connor said. "No favoritism. Besides, you're a freshman, so you'd have to be pretty impressive to land a roster spot on varsity. The odds are against you. Do yourself a favor and stay where you are."

Cindy leaned into the room, "You boys coming?"

"We're coming," Connor said. Standing up, he checked and saw that the bathroom was free. He washed his hands quickly and then went to the dining room. Since there were so many of them, they for years had two separate tables: one for the adults and one for the kids. Jimmy joined Chrissie and his cousins, Robert and Kimberly, at the kids' table. Dan, for the first time, had a seat at the adult's table.

Connor took his place next to Marina and looked at the chair at the head of the table, the one his father usually occupied. His mind drifting back, seeing that moment yet again when he had walked into the house and saw his father lying on the ground, Connor pushed the memory aside.

Cindy was placing the platters of food on the table. There was the turkey, stuffing, potatoes, sweet potatoes, corn, Matt's cinnamon bread, olives, and assorted pickles. When everything was out, Cindy stood behind the chair at the head of the table, and after a lengthy pause, sat down.

"Everyone help yourselves," she said.

Holiday dinner with the family was always festive. People at each end of the table were engaged in conversations, some about sports, some about the food, some about family in general. Connor looked back and forth, picking up pieces of each conversation, relishing the time with the family.

When dinner was winding down, Connor saw that his mother was looking rather sad. "Are you okay?"

"I was just thinking," Melony said. "I've been with your father since I was twenty-nine years old."

That single comment, soft, heartfelt, and full of sorrow, was enough to quiet the entire table. After a lengthy pause, Lauren spoke first, with a simple, "Well."

Cindy followed suit, "Well."

"What a deep topic," Uncle Aaron said.

Melony glanced up, tears welling in her eyes. Of course the death of her husband was a deep topic.

"Wells," he added.

Jon was the first to laugh. "That was a good one, Uncle Aaron."

Connor watched as even his mother smiled.

"Wells," she said, shaking her head and laughing a little herself. "That's cute."

As the women began cleaning up, Connor stayed at the table and talked to Uncle Aaron, Jon, and Matt. Between the baseball offseason and rumor mill about potential trades and free agents, as well as an upcoming football game and the Patriots in the playoff hunt again, there was quite a bit to discuss.

Connor saw Marina signal him that it was time to get going, and he glanced at his watch. There was never enough time with the family, especially after what had happened to his father.

"Mind if I steal a little stuffing?" Connor asked. He had already discussed it earlier in the week with Cindy, and knew that it wasn't a problem, but it was always nice to ask. The stuffing was a recipe passed down from generation-to-generation—from his great-grandmother to grandmother to mother to sisters. It was delicious and he loved it. Last year, at Marina's parents, he had tried the stuffing there, and it was a sausage stuffing. He made do, but Connor found the stuffing to be the best part of the meal, and if he were having two Thanksgiving dinners, he wanted to have stuffing both times.

"Not at all," Matt said. "Take what you want. Do you want some bread, too?"

"Seriously?" asked Connor.

"I wouldn't have asked if I wasn't serious."

"Great," Connor said. "I'd love some. Your bread is always delicious."

"Go ask you sister for a bag."

Connor walked into the kitchen and asked Cindy for a bag. She pulled out a sandwich bag at first, but when she heard what Matt was giving him, she put it away and gave him a larger storage bag with a zipper on it. Connor brought it back to Matt who had cut almost two-thirds of the bread to give to him.

"You really want to give me that much?"

"Are you going to eat it?" Matt asked.

"I am," Connor said.

"Then take it," he said. With the knife, he put a few grooves into the top. "Here, so you'll know where to slice it."

"Thanks again," Connor said.

Lauren also brought cookies and brownies that she had baked for Connor. She and Melony put together a little take-out bag of deserts for him as well. Connor loved cookies and brownies. Far more than the pies and cakes that were also baked, though if they were staying, he definitely would have had some of the pie that Marina baked for the family. The crust was a giant chocolate chip cookie with bananas, pudding, Cool Whip, and chocolate shavings.

After collecting the food that they were taking with them, Connor and Marina made their way through the family, wishing everyone a

Happy Holiday and saying their farewells. Just as they arrived fifteen minutes late, they left fifteen minutes late too. Matt had given Connor directions that would shave some time off of driving to the Cape, so he wasn't too worried. Back in the storm, the truck blowing at times from the ferocity of the wind, Connor made his way to the Cape as Marina slept soundly. The first part of the holiday was done, and in under two hours, they would be having another Thanksgiving feast.

❖   ❖   ❖   ❖   ❖

The holiday with both families had been wonderful. The food was great, and Connor felt stuffed. As Marina and her sisters were in the living room and talking, Connor and Marina's father were discussing baseball and the Red Sox offseason in the kitchen. Marina came in, interrupting them, saying that she wasn't feeling well and wanted to head home.

With desert packed up instead of eaten, they got into the truck and began heading home for the night. When they were coming, they drove around the rotary where you would take the turn to go to Bourne where his father was. Connor knew that the National Cemetery would be closed, but he had the burning desire to wish his father a Happy Thanksgiving. Even if he just drove by the area and saw the sign for the cemetery, it would be close enough.

Going home though, even though he thought he took the same roads, Connor was shocked to find that he was going over a bridge and off of the Cape without ever reaching the rotary.

Noticing that Connor was visibly becoming agitated, Marina asked, "What's wrong?"

"Where's the rotary? Where's my father?" Connor asked, not quite frantic but feeling as if he was getting there.

"This is a different bridge," Marina said. "Why? Do you want to go?"

"I just want to wish him a Happy Holiday and tell him I love him,"

Connor said.

"I can get you to the other bridge," Marina said. "Do you want to go back?"

Every fiber of his being was screaming for him to say "yes," but Connor knew that if he ever went over a bridge two more times on a stormy night when he did not have to, his father would have been outraged. "No," Connor whispered.

"Are you sure?" asked Marina.

"Yeah, I'm sure," Connor said. Touching the driver's side window with his hand, Connor whispered as he was driving over the bridge, "Happy Thanksgiving, Sir—I love you."

After they were over the bridge, Connor collected himself and was fine. The moment had passed.

"Do you want to listen to some music?" Marina asked.

"Sure," Connor said.

She turned the radio on and found Christmas music. Connor approved. Christmas was always one of his favorite times of year: the lights, the music, the festivities, and sometimes even the first snow. It was a time of year his father loved too.

After a couple of songs, Connor's phone rang. He had asked his mother to call when she got home so that he knew she made it home safely.

"Hello," Connor said.

"I'm home," his mother replied. "Lauren and Chrissie brought me after they dropped Jon and Jimmy off."

"Is everything all right?" Connor asked.

"Yup," she replied. "Chrissie took the dogs out for me, and now everything is locked up."

"Okay, good," Connor said. Pausing for a moment, he added, "I wished Dad a happy Thanksgiving."

"You did?" Melony asked, and Connor could hear her voice crack and could visualize the tears welling in her eyes.

"I couldn't go, it was the wrong bridge, but as we crossed over the

Cape, I said it." Connor then told her that Marina offered to go back, and she said the same thing Connor felt: his father would have been outraged to know that he did extra driving on a stormy night for nothing—especially on a bridge.

With the topic of his father already being discussed, Melony said, "Cindy was a wreck after you left."

"She was?" Connor asked. "Why?"

"She had to sit in Dad's chair," Melony explained. "She didn't want to."

"I'm so sorry," Connor said. "If I knew that, I would have sat there. I thought that she should as hostess. Her and Matt at each end."

"Yeah, well it really bothered her," Melony said.

No matter how hard people tried to act like everything was normal, no matter how much people seemed to have moved on, a loss such as this was always deeply heartfelt. Connor's heart broke for his sister. Everyone was trying to act strong for each other, and each of them was breaking down inside.

CHAPTER 10

Over the next few weeks after Thanksgiving, Connor spent numerous days with his mother. Most times they went through drawers and cabinets, slowly examining each and every memory, article of clothing, award won, and items used. The process was slow-going and very painful, but it was something they had to do.

They were told more than once that they should just throw everything away, but neither could bring themselves to do that. Connor's father meant far too much to both of them to just take all of his belongings and drop them in a dumpster. The man deserved to have his belongings, his memories, the things he cared about and cherished handled with respect and care, no matter how difficult it may be.

While going through things, Melony had found little coaching journals from the Baseball Coaches Association Annual Hall of Fame Dinner. Connor had thought that he already had all of his father's notes and materials on coaching, but the journals were far more than drills, assignments, scouting reports, and strategies. The journals had his father's actual thoughts: tips of the day, little things like positioning of feet and the balance of the stance to discuss with his players. Some notes were commonsense, others made Connor think of things differently than he had before.

Connor spent much of December going through the journals, coaching notes, and reports. He even found what could amount to a hand-written Coaching Handbook, including all aspects of the game and fundamentals that his father used to review, update each season, and teach to his players at the beginning of each year. The preparation and thoroughness of his father had been incredible.

As he went through the materials, Connor computerized most of it, forming his own version of his father's handbook and even updating it further with other notes he found or his own thoughts and ideas. By the time he was done, the handbook was almost two hundred single-spaced pages. Everything he needed for strategy, fundamentals, instruction, and tutorials were in the document. Just like his father before him, Connor expected the document to be a work in progress as he added coaching experience, but for now, it was a pretty all-inclusive guideline.

With the information fresh in his mind, Connor began putting together materials for his first meeting with the students. There were the required documents that he would need, such as the parental permission forms and a passed physical, but as someone organized and analytical, Connor also wanted to have information from each of his prospective players. Something more thorough than a name, age, and grade point average. Who were his prospective players? Why did they want to play baseball? Do they have experience, or was his team going to be filled with novices?

With those thoughts swirling in his mind, Connor opened another document and began typing out questions. He typed in the obvious identifying questions first, for the student to fill out their name, grade, age, address, phone number, and email address. Once this was done, he began with the questions.

> Have you played high school baseball before?
> If yes, where and at what level?
> What baseball experience, including Little League,
> do you have?

Connor finished typing the first three questions, and then paused. Perhaps a student was an athlete in another sport, but had never played baseball before. Joe Lane had been a track star, and when he joined Connor in softball, he was one of the fastest players on the team. The speed alone was enough to get him onto the roster, with the fundamentals being taught from then on.

> What other sports have you played?
> Where, what level, and what positions?

Satisfied that that was enough to cover the non-baseball athletes who may be interested, Connor began with the specific baseball questions.

> What hand do you throw with?
> What side of the plate do you bat from?
> What is your preferred position?
> What other positions have you played?
> How comfortable do you feel in each position?
> What are your athletic strengths?
> What are your athletic weaknesses?

Connor looked back at the questions. He wanted to know what the prospects thought of themselves, and not necessarily begin plugging people into a lineup. One student may think that they were God's gift to shortstop, but if he thought they belonged in the outfield, they would play in the outfield. The questions were just a way to dig into the thoughts and desires of the students, and try to gauge how they felt they would do and what they could contribute.

His thoughts lingering on how students actually thought they had a grasp on things, Connor added one more talent question.

> On a scale of 1 to 10, 1 being not at all, and 10 being
> an expert, please rank your proficiency in each of the
> following:
> Fielding:
> Throwing Power:
> Throwing Accuracy:

Pitching:

Batting for Average:

Batting for Power:

Placement Batting:

Bunting:

Speed:

Base Running:

Stealing Bases:

Awareness of Fundamentals:

Awareness of Game Situations:

Some students may have trouble differentiating between fundamentals and game situations, Connor thought, but they were different enough to list. The fundamentals were the grasp of the entire game of baseball. Did an outfielder know when to hit the cut-off man, and did the cut-off man know what to do with the ball next? Did a base runner know how big of a lead to take when trying to steal a base? Did an infielder know how to properly field a ground ball? All of this and more were the fundamentals of the game. These are the things that he and his staff would be coaching to perfect.

On the other hand, the game situations were something based more on the player's ability to be aware of what was happening around them. He can drill it into their heads to turn two if there is a runner at first, but if the shortstop gets the ball and throws to first because they think there is two outs, no amount of coaching will fix that. It's a matter of awareness and ability to know what needs to be done. The fundamentals may say to hold a runner at third and then throw to first to get the out, but it is up to the player to be aware that there is a runner at third with less than two outs.

Placement batting may also bring up a few questions. Connor did not know how many people would understand that either. Anyone can get into a batters box and try to hit. If they are successful, that's great. But, not everyone can get into the same batters box, see that the third baseman is playing a bit far off of the third-base line, and then hit a ball right down the line. Or, see the right fielder shifting toward center, and then hitting a shot into right field. Connor would be pleasantly surprised if he had even a handful of players who could manage this.

With the skills section complete, Connor began thinking about equipment, what players have, and what either they or he needed to acquire. Most schools provide the equipment, at least uniforms, bats, and catcher's gear, but he was beginning everything from scratch and wanted to see exactly what people had and what they needed. Of course, most towns were also charging roster and participation fees now, but Connor also needed to determine if his team would have that option, or whether he needed to find some alternative way to fund the season, such as a sponsor.

> Do you own a glove?
> Do you own cleats?
> Do you own an athletic cup?
> If you answered no to any of the above, will you be able to supply one for yourself in time for the first scheduled practice?
> Do you have any other equipment that you intend to use?
> If yes, what is it?
> If there was a roster fee to cover the expense of uniforms and equipment, do you feel that you could afford this expense?

Connor did not like the way the last question was worded. It was vague. Too vague. How could students answer unless they had some idea as to what the roster fee may be? Opening the Excel document that had all of his contact information, Connor went through to find the contact name for the store that had made all of his uniforms during softball. Finding the information for Kenneth Carlson of Custom

Sports, he picked up the phone and called.

"Custom Sports."

"Hi, is Ken Carlson there?" Connor asked.

"May I ask who is calling, please?"

"I'm an old customer, Connor Blake."

"Connor Blake?" the man asked. "Really?"

"That would be me," Connor said. "Is Ken available?"

"Oh, yes, of course, I'll get him right away."

Connor waited, grinning at the thought of how far he had come since he had first begun writing. The day he got a call on his cell phone while at a Red Sox game and was told that he was on television and the commentators were talking about him was the day he knew he had really made it to the big time. A celebrity in the midst. He always saw Stephen King and actors or actresses making it onto television, but the fact that they had found him was awe inspiring.

"Connor? Ken Carlson here. Long time."

"Hi Ken," Connor said. "It has been awhile."

"So what can I do for you? Is the team starting up again?"

"Not quite," Connor said. "I've taken the head coach position at Farmington High School, and we have absolutely no equipment at all. I was hoping to get some kind of projection for what to expect."

"How many uniforms?"

"We'll probably have eighteen varsity, another eighteen for JV."

"Different uniforms or the same?"

"Probably different colored shirts, but the same pants and hats," Connor decided.

"The same logo, design, and markings though?"

"Sure," Connor said.

"The color of the shirt isn't a problem, that'll save you some money putting it through as an order of thirty-six shirts," Ken explained. "What kind of fabric?"

"How about you go identical to what we had for now," Connor said.

"Let me see, that was 100% polyester, button-down shirts, team name and number on front, player name and number on back, and team logo on left sleeve, right?"

"That works," Connor said.

"Will the logo be fancy or generic?"

"Assume fancy for the moment. I'd rather have an over-quote than quote not enough."

"Of course," Ken said. "If you recall, the logo design will be an extra $25 for the first time, and then is included in all future shirts, hats, jackets, or whatever you need."

Connor wrote down the $25.00 logo fee on a separate piece of paper. "What are the shirts looking like?"

"We can do it for $35 a shirt," Ken said. "If you need to reorder though, anything less than twelve shirts would be $55, and between that and twenty would be $45."

"Not bad," Connor said, grateful that the cost of shirts had not gone up significantly since he had coached. "How about the pants?"

"Full color, one stripe, pinstripe?" Ken asked.

"Give me the most expensive and we'll figure it out when the actual design is done."

"No more than $26 then."

Connor added the pants to the list. "How about the belt and socks?"

"$5 for the belt, and $3.50 for the socks."

"Hats?"

"Fitted or regular?"

"Give me both," Connor said.

"We can do it for $9 regular and $11 fitted," Ken said.

"Thanks Ken, if I have any other questions, I'll be in touch."

"No problem," Ken said. "Just try to get me the order about four to six weeks in advance."

"Will do," Connor said, hanging up the phone and wondering how he could actually meet that time frame when the league rules had him working with his players for only three weeks. Perhaps he had to skip player names, or try for multiple shirts and pants of different sizes. Regardless, he'd work it out.

Uniform numbers, he thought. Then scrolled back up in the document for the questionnaire and added a question about desired uniform number before the expense question. Then going back to where he was, he quickly calculated the uniform expense, using the high numbers for everything, and came up with $80.50, without counting the one-time logo fee. Adding in a $50 roster fee, which would be used to purchase catcher's equipment, bats, balls, and any personal equipment players may lack, Connor decided to go with $120 as his estimate for player contribution requirements. He inserted that into the form in parenthesis as "No more than $120.00 per player."

Moving on to a different section, Connor wanted to see if the prospects had any scheduling conflicts. Since students came from around the state, staying for practice or games could create hardships for transportation and availability.

Do you have any after-school commitments that would impact your ability to make a practice or game?

Do you have any transportation concerns that we should know about?

Please list your estimated availability:
  Monday:
  Tuesday:
  Wednesday:
  Thursday:
  Friday:
  Saturday:
  Sunday:

All of this would be beneficial to know, but Connor also wanted to see if his prospects could begin doing activities that would make the pre-season more effective. In softball, he had players in batting cages until the weather was good enough to have his players begin physical training and drills. If possible, he would like to run a similar program, even if he was not allowed to physically be present for it. Knowing what he wanted, he added:

Would you be willing and able to go to batting cages prior to the start of the season?
Would you be willing and able to take advantage of an after-school physical training program in the gym?

The physical training program, Connor knew, he needed to get approval for from Principal Daniels. The batting cages though, he could have people visit Pure Hitters. Dom would probably let the students in for free, too, so that wouldn't be a problem.

Glancing at his notes on league rules for eligibility requirements, Connor began typing questions to see if the prospects were even eligible to play.

What is your current course schedule?
What grades have you received thus far?
What grades do you anticipate receiving at the end of the year?
Do you have any academic concerns about playing baseball?
Do you have any health concerns about playing baseball?
Do you smoke, drink alcohol, or use illegal drugs?
If yes, what?
Would you be willing to take a drug test if requested?

Connor grinned at the last three questions. Even if a student did all three, drink, smoke, and do drugs, he doubted he would have anyone admit to doing it. However, if they said that they did not, and then indicated that they would not take a drug test, then either they were morally opposed to taking it, or they were lying.

MIAA rules indicated that "During the season of practice or play, a student shall not, regardless of the quantity, use, consume, possess, buy, sell, or give away any beverage containing alcohol; any tobacco product; marijuana; steroids; or any controlled substance." The rules however did not specify how this was monitored or tested, and in fact, Connor saw that there was very little testing done, if any.

The rules did also indicate "This rule represents only a minimum standard upon which schools may develop more stringent requirements." Connor's idea of a more stringent requirement was a zero-tolerance policy. There would be no drugs, smoking, or drinking by any of his players—at least not during the season. The testing question would lead into that, and demonstrate his conviction with this matter, even if there was not even a single test administered. No matter how good his intentions, he doubted that drug tests for all of the prospective players was something the school would accept.

Deciding that the questionnaire was pretty much done, Connor finished with two final questions:

> Who, in your eyes, would be the top five students in
> this school who should be considered for this team?
> Is there anything else you feel that the coaching staff
> should be made aware of: the program, the team,
> and about yourself?

Asking for the five students might put players on the spot, but the students would know each other at this stage far more than he would. That way, he could see if the people peers thought should make the team actually tried out and showed interest in the team. If someone was on the list who had not, it may be worth looking into and investigating to see if there is talent that has reservations that he could work through.

Satisfied with the questionnaire, Connor wrote a quick email to his coaches and asked them to look it over and see if there was anything that they wished to add. He then attached the form and sent it to them. With the form done, Connor looked at the clock. It was late. Marina had been asleep for a few hours already. Deciding that that wasn't such a bad idea, he shut the lights, checked all of the locks, and went to bed himself.

CHAPTER 11

The holiday season was a near blur. It was the greatest time of the year, and Connor grew up loving the holidays. He remembered nights when he and his parents took a little ride just to drive through residential neighborhoods and look at all of the colorful lights and decorations that were shining. More than once, as Connor was driving on December nights, he saw the lights and smiled nostalgically, only to become quiet with the thought that his father was not there to enjoy it with him this year.

That month, he and Marina saw Chrissie in the winter production of *The Pajama Game* at her school, and the very next night picked out their Christmas tree. Connor never had a real Christmas tree growing up. The Blake family had a sparkling silver tree that they assembled each year, and Connor used to love decorating it with the numerous ornaments from places they have been or that his mother had bought from AVON. They had a color-wheel light, which they set near the tree, making the tree look green, then red, then blue, and then yellow as the wheel rotated. It was quite pretty, and majestic for Connor.

Marina though, had always had real trees. She loved the sight and smell of them, and the day when you went out to find the perfect tree for the holidays. The two had gone on Sunday, after Marina spent most of the day doing her end-of-the-month reports on her kids, and Connor had a chance to watch the Patriots play in a game that they won, despite double-digit penalties. To be kind: it was not the best game the team had ever played, but, as Connor thought, at least they won.

The first place they went to allowed people to cut down their own trees. Connor and Marina pulled in, but they did not see anybody there, and decided that it must have been closed because it was getting late on a Sunday. They then drove to another spot that Marina thought of, one that was across the street from a school where a couple of her clients were. The place was open, and hundreds of trees were on display, separated by size and type.

The couple walked through the trees, searching for that perfect one for the holidays. Some looked like it was not entirely full, some were a bit lopsided, and some were a bit thin. There was one, however, that they kept going back to. It was just shy of nine feet, full, and was perfect.

They brought it home and began decorating, only to find that the tree was larger than their previous ones, and they had to buy a new tree stand and even more lights, which was mind boggling since Marina had boxes of them for both the holidays and her own hobby—making lamps out of fancy bottles that she found.

With a few trips to the stores, and a couple of days, the decorations were up, the tree was full of lights and ornaments, and the wrapped presents were under the tree. Each night, Connor would sit on the couch or his chair, reading, going over coaching notes, or watching a movie, but regardless of what he was doing, he would pause frequently, look at the lights and decorations, and just smile to himself. Like his father, he loved this time of year.

A week before Christmas, Connor and his mother bought a wreath that was decorated and a small graveside tripod stand, and brought it to Bourne for the gravesite. The cemetery allowed holiday decorations from December 4th until January 3rd, and both wanted to have something so that in some way they were all sharing the holiday together.

The trip brought on tears, but Connor was glad to see his mother doing something for the holidays. She had decided not to take out any of the decorations this year and make the house festive at all. Without her husband, her Eddie, she just could not see having a festive house. The same was true for Christmas cards, which she sent out religiously. This year, she paused, not wanting to have to write something other than "The Blake Family" at the end of the card. Writing only "Melony" tore her apart.

She still did her shopping for the family and for her customers, but anything that would have been something she would do with her husband she skipped this year. That included Christmas day itself.

Not even half a dozen years ago, the Blakes went on a Disney Cruise. It was during December, and everything about the cruise was magnificent. The ship had a giant Christmas tree in the main lobby, and as a family who loved both the holidays and Disney, the combination of the two was magnificent.

Connor's father, however, hated flying above anything else. Every year they drove, and Connor became accustomed to driving to Florida himself. This particular year though, because of work schedules and vacation time, Connor did actually have to fly. His parents met them at the airport, both picking them up and dropping them off again when the vacation was over. Connor managed to be home for Christmas day, but his parents were still on the road.

That day, there was a sense of being incomplete and somehow wrong. Melony called from the road, and everyone spoke to her one at a time, but it was not the same. More than once, in almost a guilt-trip way, it was mentioned that they couldn't believe that the family wasn't completely together because of a vacation. Well, this year, the Kerrigan's were going on vacation and Christmas was cancelled altogether.

Almost. Lauren was hosting a Christmas celebration the Friday night before the holidays. Everyone was coming for that, but then on the actual day, the Griffins would stay by themselves, Uncle Aaron would remain in Mystic rather than driving up twice, Connor would be spending the holidays with Marina's family, and Melony was left all alone, without her husband, and without the family on Christmas day.

It was a thought that broke Connor's heart. Marina invited her to join them and come to the Cape with her family, but Melony politely refused. She later told Connor that she had three reasons: the first was traveling, they lived closer to the Cape, and if Connor had to drive an hour to get her, an hour back, and do it again at night, it was four extra hours of driving. The second was the fact that she did not want to become a burden to Connor and Marina, making them feel pressured or responsible to always have to include her in the things that they do. The third was that she did not want to interfere with Marina's family, and interrupt their normal traditions and activities. She tried to make it clear that she would not be alone, that she would be with her four pets.

Connor wasn't so sure. He hated the thought of her being alone. Every year, even after he had moved out, he used to go back home for Christmas morning. The three of them would sit in the living room, his father on the right-hand side of the couch, his mother in the middle of the couch, and he on the floor leaning against one of the chairs nearest the tree. He would search the presents and sort them, handing them out to his parents and putting his aside. Then, together, as a family, they opened their gifts, one at a time.

This would not only be the first year that they were without Connor's father, and it would not be the first year where the family would not be together for the day, but it was also the first year that Connor was breaking the tradition and not coming over in the morning. Depending on when Marina's family was getting together, Connor hoped to still be able to go over in the morning. Since they were celebrating Christmas early, there would be no presents, and—this year—no tree, but he could at least go and make Melony a Christmas breakfast, share that with her, watch the Christmas parade, and then go from there—and since two of the four hours of extra driving would already be done, maybe, just maybe, she would change her mind and join them with Marina's family.

Connor hoped that she did. The last thing he wanted was for his mother to be alone for the holiday. Besides, if she did, maybe, in some small way, just as he did when driving near the cemetery on Thanksgiving Day, she would feel closer to her husband, as if she were not truly alone. It was not something that could be planned; but he did hope, and in a few days, would see.

CHAPTER 12

The closer it got to the actual holidays, the more things began to change. It was as if the family's plans were in a constant swirl of motion. First, Melony finally decided to join Connor in going to Marina's family's for the actual Christmas day. A friend of hers, a fellow AVON sales representative, had pointed out that perhaps it was Connor who needed to be with his mother for the holidays, like always, and that he was not only doing it for her. Melony then decided to go, and bought a gift for Marina's parents to bring with her.

Since Marina traditionally goes on Christmas Eve and sleeps over, Connor decided to do the same with his mother, spend the morning like they always had opening their gifts, watching the parade, having breakfast, and then going from there. With this idea in mind, they decided not to exchange any gifts for each other on the Friday night at the Kerrigan's, preferring to wait until Christmas morning.

But, things would change again: the Griffins were not all able to make it to the Friday night celebration—Cindy was working at the restaurant and Robert was delivering pizzas; Matthew had gone for knee-replacement surgery only a week before and wasn't up to going out either; Dan was back from college and went along with his sister, Kimberly, but the rest of the family could not be there.

Rather than them missing out on the family holidays as well, Cindy offered to have a family Christmas on Christmas day for everyone. She said that they did their morning presents and traditions, but would be glad for Melony, Connor and Marina, and Uncle Aaron to come over whenever they wanted for a celebration.

Melony was not certain, because now that she committed to going to Marina's family's, she did not want to offend or insult anybody. Also, in case her friend was right about Connor's motivations, she did not want to upset him, either. As she thought about it, she found herself lost without any clear direction on how to reach a decision.

Her other problem, if she went to Cindy's, was driving. She had trouble driving at night, and did not want to have to drive home alone. Cindy offered to drive her home, taking a car of her own and having one of the kids drive Melony's car so that she would make it home safely, and then the driver would have a ride.

Still not certain what to do, Melony spoke with Connor, who immediately told her to go to Cindy's. It was quite generous of Marina's parents and family to make the invitation for the holidays, but if Melony could be with family, then Connor thought that she should be. He merely had not wanted her to be alone, and if she was with the Griffins, she would not be.

Melony agreed, but still was hesitant about driving. Even with the generous offer of driving her home, she said that she had never driven to Cindy's on her own, and the last time that Connor drove for Thanksgiving, they had actually gotten lost. Connor then offered to drive her, saying that he would stay on Christmas Eve as planned, spend Christmas morning with her, drive her to Cindy's, and then head to the Cape from there.

The discussions continued all the way until the Friday night at the Kerrigan's for the holidays, but the final plan sounded like the one that was going to be implemented. For this night, however, traveling arrangements were also a little up in the air. Marina was working, and said that by the time she got home, got together with Connor, and then headed to the Kerrigans', they would probably not arrive until 7:30, when Lauren said that people should start coming for 5:30.

Marina suggested that since her last client was closer to route 495, and she could get to Hopkinton faster than if she went home first, was for Connor to go earlier. Connor had originally considered picking his mother up, but Melony said that Uncle Aaron was going to do it, if he could then drop her off at the end of the night.

Once again, plans changed: Uncle Aaron would go straight to the Kerrigans', and Connor would pick up his mother, with Marina meeting them at the house. Connor got out a bit later than he would have liked, spending most of the morning doing a little writing for something he wanted to finish up before the New Year's, and then headed out. Melony was not happy that he was late, indicating that she should just have gone with Uncle Aaron.

The comment was not meant to be hurtful, but Connor got upset. He had planned on leaving at 4:15, and he left only ten minutes late. Fighting traffic, checking his mail, and picking his mother up, timing was not all that bad. Marina called while he was driving, letting him know that she got out of work early. By the time Connor was pulling into the Kerrigans' driveway, Marina had also just arrived, and Connor took a little pleasure in seeing that he had beaten Uncle Aaron there, and that even with his mother's comment of making a mistake by having him drive, she got there earlier by going with him.

Jon met them at the door, coming out and helping Melony inside first, and then coming back to help Connor and Marina bring the presents in. It had begun to rain a bit, not heavy, but enough to make everyone want to hurry inside before the presents got too wet.

Chrissie, Kimberly, and Dan were upstairs in the living room, waiting for everyone else to arrive. Lauren was out picking up Jimmy, who was at wrestling practice. As a freshman, he made the varsity team in the 160 pound weight class, even though he weighed in only at 153 pounds. He was losing most of his matches, but even other freshman weighing more than him could not stand a chance against him, so varsity was the best place for him. By the time he was a senior, the coach thought—and Lauren had agreed—that Jimmy would be unbeatable.

For about an hour, they sat around talking, as the others gradually arrived at the house. Conversations about Dan at college and his finals, artists that Kimberly knew who might be good for Connor's RPG game, the holidays in general, and normal catching up discussions reigned one room. In the other room, Melony and Uncle Aaron went over some financial documents that he usually helped her with. They had her investment portfolio and options, and when she had shown them to Connor, there had been a few questions about a really low interest rate and possibly switching into a different investment vehicle. Uncle Aaron agreed and took the materials to look into further.

While they had been talking, they called Connor into the room since he was the one who would help Melony finish everything up in the end. He listened intently to everything that Uncle Aaron had to say, and even suggested that they fill out one of the forms—a form requesting the physical certificate of title that Uncle Aaron thought Melony should have so that she would not one day be forced to sell it through the same bank—right then and there.

The last thing they had to go over was Melony's will. It had arrived from the lawyer earlier that week, and Melony was quite concerned by the verbiage within it, thinking that it was wrong. Connor was named as Executor, but—the way Melony read it—he had the right to determine what everyone got.

Connor thought that highly unlikely. The whole purpose of a will and testament was for the desires of the individual to be fulfilled, with assets and belongings going where *she* wanted. She had already made it clear that Connor was getting the house, and Cindy and Lauren would be getting everything else—with certain things going to the five grandchildren as well.

Jon, who was putting Christmas music on, said that Connor was very trustworthy, and that Melony should not worry. They were in good hands. Melony said that she was more afraid of problems arising between Cindy and Lauren over certain things, and she did not want that. Jon assured her that there would be no problems between them.

To try and put her mind at ease, Connor suggested creating a separate document, one for the family and not a legal form, which would serve as a guideline of her wishes. Before his grandmother died, there was a bird sculpture that she kept telling Connor would one day be his since he collected birds and thought they were beautiful. That was not in any legal will, but after she passed away, nobody but Connor knew that she had said that. If they prepared a document for Melony that indicated certain things that she really wanted to go to certain people—such as the fancy china, her jewelry, or her collections of figurines—then there would be no mistakes to her wishes.

When the business was done, Lauren set out the plan for the evening, with dinner first, then opening presents, and desert after that. Dinner was a combination of pasta—stuffed shells that Jon made himself—hand-sandwiches, and deli wraps. The adults sat and ate at the dining room table, with the kids in the kitchen table. After everyone finished eating, they moved into the living room for presents.

Melony started first, handing out her presents to everyone, one family at a time. All the girls—Lauren, Chrissie, and Marina—got plush bathrobes. Kimberly was asked to go into the other room for a minute since she was getting one too, but not until Christmas day so that she would still have presents to open on the actual holiday. Jimmy got a leather wallet that looked almost Native American, and he absolutely loved it. He also got a CD player for his room. Chrissie also got slippers to go with her robe. Both received a check as well with their gifts.

Melony then gave family presents to the Kerrigans and to Connor and Marina. They had their new annual Christmas ornament with the date on it, and a few other smaller gifts like a snowman soap dispenser and a small wall clock. Connor and Marina also got a new shower curtain that had pockets to put things like shampoo bottles into it.

Chrissie walked a present from Melony over to her father, handing it to him.

"Who is it from?" Jon asked.

"Grandma and Grandpa," Chrissie said, then, with a complete look of panic on her face, glanced at Connor worriedly, and corrected herself, "Grandma."

"That's okay," Connor said, trying to let her know that there was nothing wrong with what she said.

Jon opened it up and found an automatic grill cleaner. It was a handheld tool with changeable bristles so that it could do the work instead of scrubbing it after each barbeque. He was quite pleased.

All of the gifts for Dan and Kimberly would wait until Christmas day, so she did not have anything for them with her. Melony finished off by giving a gift to Uncle Aaron from his cat, Midnight, indicating that Midnight told her what to get. It was a small grooming kit with a comb, nail clippers, and file. She then gave him a gift from her, which was a bottle of Seagram's VO.

When Melony was done, Connor completely lost track of gifts that people were receiving. Every year, since Connor was a child, his parents used to alternate a present at a time so that everyone could see what everyone else was getting. It seemed like lately, over the past few years, presents were just sorted out, and then it was a mad desperate dash for people to see what they got.

Connor didn't really like it that way. He enjoyed seeing the reactions on people's faces as they opened their presents, whether it was good or bad. With that being the case, he always kept his presents aside to hand out after everyone was done. It sort of forced them to open it without anything else so he could see their reactions.

Kimberly had been next to hand out presents. She walked around the room giving all of the Griffin presents to everyone. Connor saw a couple of movies, and some Patriots sweatshirts, which he thought had been from the Griffins to Chrissie and Jimmy, but he wasn't entirely certain. He and Marina had a pair of gifts. The first was a gift certificate to the restaurant TGI Fridays. The second matched Cindy's home warming gift, a jar that looked like a woven basket with apples on the top—Connor and Marina had received a set of three when they had a home warming party, and this one was the biggest of the group, for cookies.

Lauren handed out her gifts next. Connor saw some Patriots shirts that were for Dan and another bag that would be given to Robert. Melony received a pair of dog stuffed animals holding movie theater gift certificates—Lauren said that the stuffed animals were supposed to be Chip and Dale, with the right coloration even though they were not Chihuahuas.

Connor and Marina had two gift bags. One had silver tinsel wrap, the other red tissue paper. Marina handed Connor the one with the tissue paper, saying that she wanted the sparkly one. Each had a gift certificate in it: one was to the Ninety-Nine, the other to Olive Garden.

With everyone apparently done, Connor handed out envelopes with his gift to Chrissie and Jimmy. He told Dan and Kimberly that he would give them theirs on Christmas day since Robert wasn't here to get his gift with them. Chrissie and Jimmy knew exactly what they were getting, and even joked about it being such a big surprise—it was the same gift he had given for the past five years: a Day Out With Uncle. It included lunch, a movie, and money toward a shopping spree. Every year Connor wondered whether they would still want to do it, since they were getting older, but every year they were really excited and had a great time.

When Jimmy opened his, he looked at the typed out gift certificate, and said, "This is the same background as last year."

"Actually, last year was a blue water-drop background," Connor corrected. "That's the background from two years ago."

"I knew I recognized it," Jimmy said.

Connor decided to go home that night and create a brand new one for next year, with an added line in small print: "*This is a new background, happy?*"

The family broke off into different groups for a while: Chrissie and Kimberly went up to Chrissie's room; Jimmy went to play some video games; Melony, Marina, and Jon stayed in the living room talking, as Connor and Dan were also there but having a discussion about video games; and Uncle Aaron and Lauren were in the kitchen having a conversation of their own.

After about another thirty minutes, everyone pulled back together for desert. Once desert was done, Marina, tired, decided to head home. It was getting late and she was working Saturday morning. Connor walked her out and saw her off, then came back inside. Downstairs, Kimberly had joined Jimmy and was playing some kind of skateboarding game.

Connor went back upstairs, ultimately winding-up in the living room with Jimmy and Dan after Jimmy was done with his game. Kimberly and Chrissie soon joined them. In the living room they put in one of the movies Jimmy had gotten, *Christmas Vacation* with Chevy Chase. Shortly after it began, Cindy arrived, coming straight from work. About a half-hour later, Robert showed up.

The entire family remained together for a little longer, and then Connor and his mother decided to call it a night. Connor loaded the car and then came back in to say his farewells to everyone. In addition to "Happy Holidays," he wished the Kerrigans all a good trip. Kimberly said that she would see him in a few days on Christmas.

Connor brought his mother home, took the dogs out, made sure the house was locked and secure, and then headed home for the night.

CHAPTER 13

Christmas Eve morning became Christmas Day for Connor and Marina. Since they were both planning on spending Christmas Eve with their parents, they could either wait for Christmas night to open their presents and have their own celebration, or do it on the morning of Christmas Eve, so they opted for the latter.

There was a bit of a discussion about breakfast. Connor suggested pancakes or an omelet, but Marina seemed hesitant. When he asked if she wanted to go out for breakfast, she said that sounded good. Then the question was whether to go to breakfast first, or to do presents first.

They decided to do presents first, but then Marina realized that she left her camera in the car, and wanted to be able to take pictures. Connor suggested getting ready and going to breakfast, and then bringing the camera up when they were done. However, after taking their showers, Marina saw that is was getting late, and thought that perhaps they should skip eating all together because she had to leave to get to her parents on the Cape.

Marina went downstairs to get her camera as Connor put in a tape to record the Patriots game to watch later on. When she came back up, it was time for Christmas.

Connor closed the doors and set up the barriers as Marina let Fribble out of his cage. The bunny was excited to be free, though opening presents did not seem to be of much interst. Fribble's presents, a leash and a harness so that he could be taken outside for walks, were in a holiday bag under the tree. Marina took a bunny-snack and put it into the bag so that maybe Fribble would show *some* interest in his present.

Since her camera had been in the car, Marina began recharging the battery, not wanting to do it for long, but making sure there was enough of a charge to at least take some pictures of them opening their presents. Fribble, who had shown no interest in the presents at all, hopped over to his, stuck his head inside his bag, and disappeared into it searching for the snack.

"No, no, no!" Marina shouted as she lunged for the battery and began fiddling with it. "Pull it away from him."

"If I do that, he'll never go back to it," Connor countered.

Marina slid the battery in and turned the camera on just as Fribble got his snack and went off beneath the tree, nibbling happily. "I missed it."

"We can try another one," Connor said, getting up for another snack. It turned out that the third snack was the charm. Fribble got the second one quickly, and got away again before Marina could get a good picture. By the time Fribble went sniffing around for his third one, Marina switched from pictures to video, and recorded Fribble getting his snack from the present.

"You have your first present in the bedroom," Marina said.

Connor turned and looked at the door, surprised. He had been the one to close the doors when they let Fribble out, and hadn't been aware that she put anything in there. Getting up, he went inside and found his stocking lying on the bed. An instant smile appeared on his face as he anxiously went to the bed to see what it was.

Several times this holiday season, Connor said that they needed to get Marina a stocking. She, however, said that they never did stockings growing up, and didn't really want one. Just the other night, Connor had been talking about stockings, and how he used to try and buy candy that his mother liked to put into it for her since she was the one who did the stockings for both Connor and his father. He had teased that it was almost like a reverse-order, with the children trying to stay up later than the parents and sneak the presents in.

From the top of the stocking, Connor saw a white teddy bear. He was cute and cuddly, but Marina frowned, saying that she thought it had been wearing a Santa's hat. There was also a candy bar with holiday decorations of snowmen, a can of goofy string—which matched one that she had given him last Easter, and Connor began visualizing them laughing as they ran around spraying each other with the two cans—and something really special, a custom designed ornament of two snow-men snuggling together holding a heart, and their names and the year on it.

Marina took a picture of Connor holding the ornament, teasing him by saying, "By your reaction, that's probably going to be the gift you like the most."

"I love it," Connor said. It was always the little things, especially this time of year—the things that created memories that you could look back at years later that were the most important thing.

Marina followed Connor to the tree and recorded him as he put the ornament onto it. With the stocking done, there were three packages for each of them. Connor handed Marina her first package.

The box was decent-sized—actually, it was a shipping box, full of tissue paper and a second much smaller wrapped present. Connor had done that all of his life, wrapping presents in the wrong-sized boxes so that it would throw people off and not let them guess at what they were getting in advance. Marina opened the smaller package, and found sapphire earrings that matched a sapphire and diamond bracelet that he had bought for her last Christmas.

She put them on right away, modeling them for Connor. "How do they look?"

"On you—beautiful."

Connor had the next present, opening a mug that Marina had specially made for him. Last Christmas, she had given him flight lessons—for years Connor had said that he would love to learn how to fly. The day that he had gone, she took pictures of him by the plane, and a video of him actually flying in the air. The mug itself was black, but when something hot was in it, like Connor's daily hot chocolate, pictures of him by the plane appeared in perfect clarity.

Marina's second present was a wrapped envelope. Inside the envelope was a certificate that Connor designed to let her know what her gift was: they had talked for quite some time about learning ballroom dancing, and he had gotten them both three introductory lessons at a local dance academy.

With Connor's next present, Marina teased, saying that it was probably the one he was going to like the most. Like the mystery-wrapping for the earrings, this box looked like it was a shirt or some kind of outfit. Inside, however, was *Kingdom Hearts 2*, a video game that was created by both Disney and Square Soft, a company that made RPG-style video games. Connor had loved the first *Kingdom Hearts* game, and was looking forward to playing this one. Disney gifts were always a good bet for Connor.

Marina's last present was an off-white jacket vest. One night when they had been shopping, Marina saw it, loved it, tried it on, and then put it back saying that she really shouldn't be buying anything for herself. Connor went back later and picked it up for her.

Connor's last present was huge. For two weeks, he had been clueless as to what it could be. Marina had also complained at the time she bought it that it had been sold-out the first place she went, and his mind was swirling with things that were popular and could sell out during the holiday season. It was far too big though to be some kind of new game system, and all of his other thoughts he found hard to believe that they would sell out.

Marina even wrapped it in special Disney Christmas gift-wrapping paper. The package was so large that it took the entire roll. The time finally there to see what it is, Connor paused briefly, looking and admiring the paper, and then tore into it like a child.

It was an executive office chair, with plenty of cushions and padding. When Connor first got an apartment with Hobbes, he had bought himself a chair that he loved. It was comfortable, and he could spend hours at his computer writing, working, or even playing video games. When it broke, becoming lopsided, he had very quickly gone out to search for a replacement chair. It was shortly after he left SJC, and

Connor did not want to spend his money foolishly, so he bought one that was a little shy of $50. From the very first day he sat on it, he regretted it. He could feel the screws while he sat, as well as the metal swivel plate. After writing for a day, his back was always aching.

A few months after buying the chair, Connor's parents had both suggested that he go and get a better chair. It was not like he was just sitting in it to check email or browse the sports section online—he spent more time in his office chair than he did on any other piece of furniture—to write, work, correspond, and any other use of his computer. Still, Connor did not want to spend a lot of money on a chair, and, he had a hard time seeing himself replacing a chair that was not broken, no matter how miserable he was with it.

Marina knew the entire story, and she could see how much trouble he had with the chair when he stood up and clutched his lower back. It was actually an old sports injury—when he had pinched a nerve from playing in a softball frostbite league—but sitting in that chair always made it tweak. This chair was an extra-cushiony executive model. It was designed for people to be in it all day, and to provide the utmost comfort. It was far better than either of the chairs that Connor previously had.

The two opened it up and put the chair together. Once assembled, Connor sat down and let out a little moan of pleasure. "This is really comfortable."

"Are you sure? We can get you a different one?"

"Nope, this one is perfect," Connor said.

After spending some quiet private time together, enjoying the day, the two got ready to go. Connor suggested they at least grab a sandwich, but after Marina called and spoke with her mother, she said that going out to IHOP for breakfast was still okay, since she knew that even at 3:00 in the afternoon Connor still really wanted breakfast.

They went to the restaurant, ordering their breakfast. Connor actually got both the pancakes and omelet he had suggested at breakfast. Marina had an egg and ham sandwich. When they were done, they hugged each other goodbye, and went their separate ways—Marina to her parents' house, and Connor back to the apartment to watch the football game.

He watched the first half, playing video-game baseball at the same time. He was two seasons behind in the game, but was finally into mid-September, and only had Red Sox games instead of the three minor league team games left to play. Near the end of the half, Connor was beginning to doze off, so he decided to get ready to go, take another shower to help wake him up, and head off to Holliston to spend the night with his mother.

They had spoken several times throughout the day, so she knew he had intended to watch the game before coming. She said that she did not want to do dinner, but perhaps an ice cream and a movie. Well, he was running late, so a movie was not going to work unless they went to the 10:00 show that night, but he knew she wouldn't be interested in that. Instead, he brought movies with him to watch with her.

While driving, Connor saw that most things were closed, including restaurants. Rather than going to Holliston, picking her up, and then going back out to try and find someplace open for ice cream, Connor decided to do takeout. He was quite relieved to see that the lights of Friendly's was still on, with cars were in the parking lot, and people inside. Of course, as fate would have it, as he walked up to the door, it was locked.

With the prospect of ice cream out, Connor began thinking of actual food. The one thing that was definitely open was a Chinese restaurant. He passed several on his way to Holliston, and the parking lots were mobbed. Instead of picking food up and bringing it with him, he figured that he would place an order after getting to his mother's house just in case she had changed her mind.

It turned out to be a good decision so he ordered an appetizer platter that had chicken wings, beef teriyaki, chicken fingers, and spare ribs. He also ordered a separate order of chicken wings, which was his personal favorite and also all that his mother said that she wanted.

Taking the dogs for the ride, they went and picked up the food, and then returned home again to eat while watching a movie for the second night in a row. On Saturday night, when Marina had gone out with her friend for a birthday celebration, Connor had gone to Holliston and he and his mother watched the movie *Fever Pitch* with Drew Barrymore and Jimmy Fallon. On this night though, Christmas Eve, there was only one choice as far as Connor could see it: *Die Hard.*

Technically, it was a Christmas movie, though certainly not a warm and fuzzy holiday movie that one would expect to watch every year. But, since first getting the video the year after the movie had come out, Connor had religiously watched it every Christmas Eve. That continued use was evident by the lines on the screen every few seconds that come from excessively watching a tape. One day Connor would have to switch over to DVD for the movie, but he had an extensive video and DVD collection, and refused to spend money on the same movie twice—if he had it on VHS, he watched it on VHS.

They watched the movie, ate all of the Chinese food, and then made their own sundaes with fixings that Connor's mother had available. There was chocolate ice cream, hot fudge that she once bought special in case they wanted sundaes at the house, and chocolate jimmies. Connor's mother asked if he wanted marshmallow sauce, too, since he would have from the restaurant, but Connor decided against it for tonight. The all-chocolate experience would more than suffice.

When the movie was over, Connor's mother headed up to bed, and Connor put on the second half of the Patriots game. He had also brought his laptop, and played a pair of Sox and Yankee games while watching football. After a win for the home team, both on television and in the game, Connor packed up his things, made sure everything was locked up, and headed up to bed himself.

Since he had to be at the Cape by 2:00, Connor and his mother decided to try and get up early to do their holiday rituals in the morning, and then get to Cindy's house with enough time for Connor to stay for at least an hour before having to leave. Setting his alarm clock feature on his phone, Connor read a couple of chapters in the book he was in the middle of, and then went to sleep.

❖   ❖   ❖   ❖   ❖

The alarm clock was not what woke Connor, but an acidic feeling in his stomach. He had rolled over and felt a little pain, and when he burped, he could taste chicken wings. It was a reaction he sometimes had from certain foods, especially Chinese food, so he was not concerned. When he woke up, there was a pill to take, and then he would be fine.

But two other things kept him awake and got him up before his alarm went off. The first was scratching and banging at the door. Connor knew from past times sleeping here that it was Boots, one of the cats. Boots always acted like an alarm clock, jumping onto the beds and waking everyone up. Connor learned from this and put his bag securely against the door to make sure Boots could not force it open—normally the doorknob would be enough, but it had been broken and would not seal properly since Connor had been in high school.

Boots's attempt to get in Connor could ignore. But, the second thing is what got him up and out of bed: the sound of his mother crying. If she needed him, there was no way that he was staying in bed and being selfish.

Putting on his old softball game shirt and his Santa hat, Connor opened the door and went to see how his mother was doing. When she saw him, she wiped the tears away and pretended like everything was okay—festive on this Christmas morning. She had told Connor numerous times that she cried every morning while looking at his father's picture, but obviously she did not want to acknowledge that today.

She asked him if he wanted breakfast, but since his stomach had been bothering him, he decided against it for the moment. Instead, they fed the pets and went into the living room, taking the seats they always took every Christmas morning, and began with the presents.

The pets got their presents first. Unlike with Fribble, the dogs and cats needed no extra incentive to begin tearing into the packages. Chip took each gift and ran behind the couch, hiding it and growling at anyone that came near him. Dale was just happy to have the gifts and chewed his bones right in the middle of the floor. The cats were in a state of heaven themselves, batting around little balls with bells in them, and some toys that had catnip.

Connor had his mother do her presents first. She had gifts from a couple of friends and AVON customers, the woman who cleaned her house, and the one Connor had for her. She got a lovely handmade decoration of Santa to hang on the wall, scratch tickets, an ornament with both a dog and cat on it, and a handmade doily.

In between her gifts, Connor opened his as well. They alternated, one for his mother, and one for Connor. Connor had a stocking that had some candy, lip balm, and hand cream in it. He also received a lovely ornament of Minnie Mouse skiing in a Christmas outfit with a snow baby carrying a bag of toys on its back holding on. His second present was a gift box with black suede cologne, aftershave, and deodorant, the brand both he and his father used. He also got a night-light that fastened onto a book so that he could read in bed after Marina was asleep without disturbing her as much as he did with his current light. There was also an outfit that his mother and cousin had seen and fallen in love with, and a check so that Connor could pick out a few things like games or movies that he wanted as well.

Once both were done with most of the presents, Connor gave his mother her last gift. Unlike with Marina, he did not try to hide the fact that this was only an envelope. Marina opened it up and her eyes widened. Inside was a printed announcement that the certificate entitled her to a night of seeing *Dancing with the Stars* live. It was a show that she and her husband had watched every week, without failure, and she got so excited she could actually go and see the show and share it with Connor.

The idea had been Marina's. She saw something about it shortly after his father had died and suggested it, and Connor jumped at the opportunity, signing up for tickets the day that they were released. He had been considering jewelry, trying to find something similar to what his father had bought the year before, but this was perfect, and from his mother's reaction, he could tell that it was a gift that she would treasure.

When the presents were done, Connor and his mother scratched off the tickets, winning $2.00 on the first, but nothing more on the next nine. The first one at least had been exciting. They then went to begin getting ready, but Connor's phone rang, and he spent a few minutes talking to Marina and sharing their Christmas moments.

After Connor's shower, Lauren called as well, from the airport, to wish them both a Merry Christmas. She had sent an email to Connor about how good he looked in the outfit he wore to their Friday-night Christmas—it had been black pants, a black shirt, and a suede vest with a silk back—and to say that her whole intentions for their Friday night celebration was to let Mom have a good time, and it seemed like she did indeed enjoy herself.

While his mother was talking to Lauren, Connor loaded the truck with gifts for the Griffin family, his overnight bag, his laptop, and his gifts. When she was ready, they were off, though it was later in the morning than they had expected, and the odds of Connor being able to stay at the Griffins for more than thirty minutes were probably not good.

Unlike on Thanksgiving, Connor took all of the right turns and got to the house without any problems. Kimberly was the first out of the house, coming down to see if they needed any help. Dan ran down too, jumping over the fence and landing right before his uncle, wishing Connor a Merry Christmas.

"You on the track team now?" Connor asked.

"Me? No," Dan said. "Not anymore."

"Even with jumping over fences?"

"I'm not good enough for the college team," Dan said.

"Even if they saw that?"

"Well, if they saw that, then of course they would recruit me," Dan replied, stepping aside as his grandmother made her way up the stairs to the house.

Inside, Connor and his mother hugged everybody and wished them all a happy holidays. In the kitchen, Matt was reading one of Dan's history books, and put it down to welcome the two in. He immediately began playing host, offering cookies, candy, and drinks.

After a few minutes, the kids headed into the other room where they were watching the end of *My Cousin Vinny*. Cindy was finishing up a salad that she was making, and then began heating the oven. Dinner for the holiday was going to be a lasagna and chicken cacciatore.

She pulled a pan out of the cabinet and placed it on the stove, dumping the chicken cacciatore into it. Matt put the top on the pan, and then looked at Connor and Melony. "You know, this came with a book."

"Oh?" Melony said.

"Yup," Matt replied. "It was directions on 101 ways to Wok your dog."

Connor chuckled, immediately getting the joke. His mother seemed oblivious to it though.

"Walking dogs? Really?" she said.

"Oh, come on," Matt said. "This is some of my best stuff."

"What?" Melony asked.

"I got it," Connor said.

"There's a tear forming in my eye," Matt said, sighing.

"You know, I almost bought you a dog for Christmas," Melony said, moving on from the joke. The day before her husband died, the Griffins dog had also died. "I didn't know if it was too soon though, or if you would want to pick one out yourself."

"We're getting another dog," Matt said, nodding.

Robert walked into the kitchen and nodded as well. "We're definitely getting another dog."

"What kind?" Melony asked.

"Maybe a hybrid," Matt said.

Robert and Cindy both suggested some hybrid pairings that they thought would be cute. Matt then said, "What I really want is a cross between a Shitzu and a Bulldog."

Cindy began laughing: "A bullshit dog?"

Matt winked.

Connor glanced at his watch and saw that it was already past time when he should have headed out for the Cape. He promised Marina that he would be there two-ish, though he pushed the "ish" part and he knew she wanted him there for 2:00.

"May I use your bathroom?" Connor asked as he stood up.

"No," Cindy said.

Connor sat right back down again. "Okay."

"I'm just kidding," Cindy laughed. "Go right ahead."

Connor went to the bathroom, washed up, and then headed into the living room to find his presents for the kids. For the past three years, he was told that all that they wanted were gift certificates to Best Buy. This year, he saw something that he wanted to give even more. Not because the Best Buy gift certificates were getting old, but because when he was standing in line at the bookstore, he saw that the gift certificates had a holographic dragon on it. Since there were dragons in the fantasy books that he wrote, he thought that it was perfect. So, instead of Best Buy, they all had gift certificates to Barnes and Noble.

At the Friday night party, Connor had told Kimberly that she was not getting a Best Buy gift certificate this year. She quickly retorted with, "What are they, Circuit City?" Connor hoped that the bookstore card would be a bit of a surprise, and also something that they would enjoy. As a writer, he definitely did not mind promoting reading to others, especially family.

Dan opened his first, getting really excited. Melony pointed out that they had some music and movies there too if he wanted, but Dan replied that books were great, and that he loved books. Robert and Kimberly thanked him as well.

Connor then picked up his jacket, saying, "I hate to give gifts and run, but I need to get going."

Everyone shared a final parting hug, another round of Happy Holiday wishes, and then Connor was in his truck and driving toward the Cape for the rest of the holiday with Marina's family. He and his mother spoke again while he was driving home, sharing the details of what was done at each house. He then wished her a good night, officially ending the first Christmas without his father. It had not been easy, and there were certain things that he had found very difficult, but for the most part, everyone did seem to enjoy themselves, and the holidays were now behind them.

CHAPTER 14

To Connor, the best thing about baseball was building a team. You find the players who are interested, perhaps encourage some talent who has reservations, determine where everyone fits and how the team meshes together, and then the actual season is a matter of testing your strategy. As Connor stood at the podium, an hour before the assembly where he would be talking to the students for the first time, his excitement was obvious. It was the first day of determining just what his team would be.

Would they have speed or power? Would they be a strong offensive team or a dominant defensive unit? Would they have great pitching or pray that their bats could overshadow their lack of arms? The best strategy was balance: not all power hitters, not all speed and defense guys, but some of each. Unlike college and the pros, where coaches can actually do recruiting, in high school, Connor had to work with the talent he had available. In the months to come, everything would begin coming together.

Of his coaches, only Dom and Rickey were able to make it with him for the assembly. Dom picked Rickey up on his way over so that both could be there. This assembly though, was addressing the entire student body, and not just the baseball hopefuls. Corey and Joe promised to take some time off for the first meeting with the actual team.

Connor had everything prepared. He had been giving speeches for what seemed like all of his life. Whenever he did, he wrote the speech out, made some highlights of the key issues, jotted down some notes in the margins, put the speech on the podium, and then walked away from it. A good speech meant that he never went back to the podium and looked. He knew the speech, could interact with his audience, and was energetic. A bad speech had him looking for his psychological crutch and checking his notes mid-speech. He did not recall a bad speech since undergrad in college, when once, he did need to look at his notes after losing track of what he was saying. He did not anticipate needing to look today, even though he probably needed to stay by the podium so that people could hear him better over the audio system.

Next to the podium were four chairs, one for Connor and each of his coaches, and one for Principal Daniels. On the other side of the stage, there was a table with forms on them, including the questionnaire he designed, the parental permission forms, and the physical sign-off sheets. Anyone who was interested would need to take and return each to the office over the next two weeks.

Dom walked over and joined Connor. "You ready?"

"Are you kidding?" Connor laughed. "This is me we're talking about."

"Yeah, of course you're ready," Dom said. "How do you think it will go?"

"Quickly," Connor said. "I don't want to hold up the entire school. I'm going to let them know about the program, announce a couple of things, and then have them come up if they are interested."

"Sounds simple enough," Dom said.

"Things will begin to take shape from there," Connor said.

The three went over a few things, then began discussing the softball days. Right before the bell rang, there was an announcement for every student to report to the auditorium. Principal Daniels made her entrance moments later, and the four of them sat and waited as the students began filing in.

Connor was watching every face as they walked in. Every student was a potential player. Every person in the auditorium was someone who could become a star and help the team. In his mind, he tried to select the individuals who he expected to be interested. There were the normal high school cliques, and there were definitely kids he thought would be signing up.

When the bell rang again, Principal Daniels stood up and walked to the podium. "If I could have your attention please," she said, raising her hands and gesturing for the students to quiet down. "If I could have your attention please!"

Once the sea of voices began to subside, Principal Daniels added, "Thank you. By now, most of you have probably heard that we will be able to offer a limited athletics program this school year. We shall be beginning with baseball and softball, with plans to expand to all other sports next year. For those of you who are seniors and missed your sport this year, I wish to express my sincerest sympathies, and thank you for your understanding and patience as this program is being introduced.

"Sitting on stage with me are three individuals who shall be working with those of you who are interested in the baseball program. Each has volunteered to give up their time to dedicate themselves to making this program a success, and regardless of the outcome, I believe they deserve a round of applause."

Principal Daniels began clapping, and was soon joined by the students. Connor smiled, feeling a cross between honor and a little embarrassment at the sight. After a couple of minutes, Principal Daniels raised her hands to quiet the students down again. "Now, let me introduce you to the first baseball coach of Farmington High School, Coach Blake."

Connor stood up, heard a few more claps and cheers—wondering briefly whether it was sincere or just students humoring or making fun of him—and headed to the podium. Principal Daniels shook his hand and then left him alone and took a seat.

"Thank you, Principal Daniels," Connor said. "It gives me more pleasure than you know to be up here before all of you today. The same is true of my assistant coaches, Coach Petrioli and Coach Urban." As he said each name, Dom waived and Rickey nodded.

"I have a tendency to go on in speeches, but I promise you that I'll be brief," Connor continued.

"Be long!" someone shouted. Several students cheered, others snickered.

"More time out of class, eh?" Connor said, laughing along. "Well, we'll see what we can do. Anyway, as Principal Daniels mentioned, we will be having a baseball and softball team this year. Based on the size and population of this school, we will be Division 1, though who exactly we are playing will be determined over the next month or so.

"Officially, other than putting together a list of people interested in playing, we will be unable to begin practicing until the third Monday in March. Between now and then, we'll be looking at those of you who are interested in playing, and also implementing an after-school program that will be available to every student of Farmington.

"That program will be a physical training program. One of my assistant coaches who is not here today, Coach Lane, has agreed to come down three days a week after school to keep the gym open and allow any student who is interested to run laps, use the weight room, or participate in a variety of strength-training and endurance exercises. I think anyone who is interested in physical fitness should take advantage of this program, and those of you interested in either baseball or softball this spring should make it routine to come to each session available."

Connor paused and looked at the kids in the auditorium. "For those of you who are interested in spring sports, this year is going to be quite a challenge. Most schools have a system in place—a routine if you will—returning players, and a few new students who shine and make it onto the roster. We have none of that. There is no chemistry. There is no team history or pre-established pride. There is no routine. Everything we do starting right here today will be new.

"We will be working twice, if not three times as hard as any other team looking to compete. We will be going to schools we have never played before, or face teams that some of you used to be a part of, and be considered the underdogs wherever we are or go. This entire program will depend on hard work, intense effort, constant preparation and readiness, and a willingness to go above and beyond anything we have done to this point. That goes for the players, the coaches, and the fans who will support us all season long.

"This will not be easy, but if any of you think that life should be easy, or that your opportunities should just be handed to you, then this team is not for you. I want players who are going to be willing to give it all for their dreams. Players who know they have to fight for what they want. Players who want to prove that they have what it takes to succeed, not only in baseball, but in life.

"If that is the kind of individual you are, that is the challenge that you are looking for, then my coaching staff and I are here to support you, guide you—even make you despise us at times—but overall be there for you as we embark on this monumental journey. I cannot guarantee that we will win and be successful, but I do know that those of you who try, will feel proud of the accomplishment we shall make this year, and of the foundation of what we are building."

Connor stepped away from the podium and walked to the front of the stage. "That's my speech. That's my spiel. My door will always be open for anyone who wants to talk. I'd be happy to answer each and every question you may have. But to begin, you need to think of yourself, evaluate your own motivations and desires, and decide whether you wish to play ball or not. If you are interested, there are forms on the table at the front of the stage. Come up and one of my coaches will give you what you need.

"There is a questionnaire. Take it yourself and do not share your answers. Be honest, and be thorough. If you're playing softball, pretend the questions about baseball say softball. All questionnaires and permissions slips must be completed and turned into the office by next Friday. Those of you who do shall be in contention for the rosters of both the varsity and junior varsity teams of each sport.

"Good luck to you all," Connor concluded.

Stepping back, he watched as students made their way to the front of the auditorium to pick up the materials. Dom and Rickey spoke with each student individually as they handed things out. As Connor watched, he thought that at least the interest level was high. By next Friday, he would be able to begin reviewing questionnaires and seeing just who exactly was interested in baseball, and what skill level, if any, they had. Biting his lip, Connor realized that it was going to be a long two weeks while he waited.

CHAPTER 15

Over the next couple of weeks, Connor spent much of his time getting organized and ready for the season to come. He was given his office, which was attached to the boy's locker room behind the gym, and gradually made it his own. He did not want to risk his father's materials, leaving them at home, but had all of his electronic updates and variations of them on his computer. He also had numerous baseball lineups, statistical analysis programs, and documents ready to go once the potential players began filtering in to plug them into the system.

The office itself was full of baseball and softball memorabilia. Connor had his bat, the one he used to win three batting titles and three MVP awards in softball. Dented, battered, and even split at one spot now, it was unusable in a game, but Connor paced when he thought, he had his bat in his hand the entire time. He also had several baseballs and softballs throughout the room, which, like his bat, he sometimes picked up and tossed up and down as he was thinking.

There was also a display with a baseball on his desk. The baseball had a clock in it and had Red Sox markings all over it. On the walls there were pictures of his softball teams and of his father in uniform. On top of the filing cabinet, all of Connor's trophies were displayed, including the batting titles and MVP awards, as well as two Home Run Derby Championships, an Infield Gold Glove, and a Most-Improved Player award that he received the season after fracturing his skull by taking a line drive to his left eye. There were also a few Little League Championship trophies, one State Championship trophy, three Softball League Championship trophies, and a baseball stein that he had gotten for Christmas one year.

The setup was far different from his home office, which after writing fantasy novels for a while was full of swords, collectibles, and memorabilia from various movies that he enjoyed. There were also books in several cases ranging from research references in mythology, and medieval weapons, to role-playing game materials and other fantasy novels. His own novels were prominently displayed and available for him to pick up and flip through at any given moment. On his wall he also had the map of his world, and his computer's screen saver rotated through the various cover art images for his books.

The league had been in touch with Connor several times a day working out the schedule of games that they would be playing. Connor picked up a map at the local convenience store to see just where the schools he would be having his team play against were. Their schedule was filling in nicely, but they were playing games in towns all over Massachusetts. One game was on the Cape, the next was in western-Massachusetts, then the third was just outside of Boston. Each game would probably have them on a bus for at least an hour, which would be trying, but at least they had games to play.

Connor jotted down a few notes on a scrap paper about the schedule, and then put it in the top drawer of his desk. They still needed at least three more schools willing to play them to complete the schedule. The way things had been going though, he should have the final schedule available by the time he was meeting with his players for the first time.

Thinking of the players, Connor got up and decided to go check his mailbox. He was a little surprised that he had not even received a single questionnaire response since the session in the auditorium, but having the permission form signed and the physical taken could account for the delay. It was Wednesday, three days before the deadline he had announced. Students seemed interested, but hopefully that would translate into submissions over the next few days.

Connor stepped into the office and smiled pleasantly to Edna Barrows, one of the secretaries and, as Connor quickly discovered, the true force driving the organization and efficiency of the office. "Morning

Edna."

"Coach Blake, good morning to you," Edna replied.

"Any mail for me today?" Connor asked.

Edna's eyes widened excitedly as she bit her lower lip. "There was some for you today," she said.

"Really?" Connor asked, trying to contain his own excitement.

"Here you go," Edna said, getting the mail from his slot personally and handing it to him.

Connor flipped through and counted five envelopes. Five prospects were better than none, that was for sure. Each envelope had a name on it, and Connor froze when he saw a couple of familiar names: Robert Griffin and Jimmy Kerrigan.

"Edna, these two students, have they been here all year?" Connor asked, hoping that it was just a coincidence and his nephews did not really transfer to Farmington.

Edna took the envelopes and looked at the names over her glasses. "Oh no, Coach Blake, both boys transferred here right after the holidays."

"Wonderful," Connor bemoaned. "Could you page them both and have them come down to my office?"

"Of course," Edna said. "I'll see right to it."

Connor took the envelopes back and returned to his office, dropping in his chair and rubbing his eyes. Robert and Jimmy transferred. He could just imagine what his sisters were thinking and feeling right now.

Over the intercom, Connor heard their names and the instructions for them to report to the main office. Knowing that they would then be escorted here, Connor opened up their envelopes and began going through their submissions. Both had permission forms signed by their parents. Matt signed Robert's, and, surprisingly, Lauren had signed Jimmy's.

Connor was not surprised to see that both boys took and passed their physicals. All of that was in order. He then scanned their forms and saw no surprises there either. Jimmy wanted to pitch and was willing to do so in any capacity the team needed. Robert wanted to play shortstop, but was willing to be flexible as well.

The door knocked and Connor glanced up to see his nephews in the doorway.

"They said you wanted to see us?" Robert asked.

"Come in," Connor said, quickly adding, "Close the door behind you."

Jimmy closed the door and took the seat next to Robert.

"So you both transferred?" he said.

Robert and Jimmy exchanged a glance. "Yes," Robert said.

"How did your parents feel about this?"

"Um, okay," Jimmy said, though Connor had known his nephew long enough to see this reply the same as every Christmas when he said his mother wouldn't have a problem if they came home from shopping with a puppy, a cat, a ferret, a bird, a snake, or whatever else caught his attention that particular year.

"I see," Connor said. "How did they really feel?"

"Mom was upset," Robert said. "She thought I was being foolish. Dad just told me to be a man and make up my own mind. When I said I wanted to come, he took care of everything from there."

"And is your mother okay with that, or did this just cause World War Three at home?"

"She doesn't like me driving so far for school, or the fact that Kimberly and I will graduate from different schools, but she's okay with it otherwise. She understands."

"I see," Connor said, taking a deep breath and slowly exhaling. Robert was a Junior and had his own car already. If he wanted to drive forty-five minutes to and from school every morning, they must figure that that is his choice.

"What about you?" Connor said, looking expectantly at Jimmy, knowing his sister would have had quite a few reservations and opinions about this.

Jimmy shrugged. "What can I say?"

"What happens the next time I call your mother to go out for breakfast?" Connor clarified. "Does she come in peace or do I have to worry about her coming to kill me?"

"Um, I think she'll be fine," Jimmy said. "She was upset. *Really* upset. But when I told her this was what I wanted, she gave in."

"She gave in?" Connor repeated, thinking about just how little that sounded like his sister. "How did you manage that?"

"I brought it up every time I saw her from Thanksgiving night until she finally agreed to let me try," Jimmy said.

"What's the price of your transfer?" Connor asked, sure there was something.

"She drives me to and from school without exception," Jimmy said. "I have to maintain a straight 'A' average or she has me transfer back, and I have basically become a maid."

"Excuse me?" Connor asked.

"She's created a list of chores, and things I'm now responsible for: changing the cat-litter, cleaning the cars, vacuuming, mowing the lawn, raking leaves—there's different things for different seasons."

"I see," Connor said, suppressing the urge to rub his eyes again. "Why did you both do it?"

"I told you at Thanksgiving," Jimmy said. "I want to do this for Grandpa, just like you."

Connor shifted his gaze to Robert. "And you?"

"I liked his argument," Robert said. "I think this is something worthwhile. What was I doing before? Delivering pizzas after school. Now, I have something meaningful to do."

"You both gave up baseball after Little League," Connor reminded them. "Are you sure you want to change your entire lives to come back and play again?"

He watched both and saw the conviction in their eyes. They had thought this out, and they were his first recruits. Accepting that, Connor knew he would have to keep an eye on them or face the wrath of the family.

"No special privileges," Connor said. "You have to try out like everyone else."

"We know," Robert said.

"Okay then," Connor said. "Welcome to Farmington."

CHAPTER 16

The last couple of days until the deadline had been busy ones. Overall, ninety-six students submitted their forms for consideration for the team. Connor went through each and every one thoroughly, taking notes and placing students into various groups. He had asked everyone where they wanted to play, but only was using that as a quick reference of insight into the player's image of their abilities. In spring training, every player would play every position, and then he would determine who got to play where.

The level of knowledge varied tremendously though. There seemed to be more people with football, basketball, and even track backgrounds than baseball. Those who did have baseball backgrounds were varied as well. Some played Little League, some had a little high school experience, and quite a few only played at their local field or on the street in a completely unorganized fashion.

These ninety-six students though, these were the basis for his team. Somehow, these ninety-six names would be cut down to eighteen for varsity, and another eighteen for junior varsity. With the names ready, and his plans set, Connor scheduled an after-school meeting for Tuesday. He would have the opportunity to meet with the students who were trying out, and set them up with their schedule and pre-season activities.

Connor knew he could not have official practices, but he could do things like open the gym for the entire student body to participate in a physical training regimen. Connor would emphasize the importance of that school-wide program to his players. He also wanted to begin some form of baseball activity, even if it was not organized. Fortunately, Dom presented him with the perfect opportunity: students could come to Pure Hitters, free of charge with a Farmington school ID.

The last thing, and one Connor wanted to also get his team involved in, was Captain's practices. For the time being, he would name Robert and Jimmy as interim co-captains. He trusted their abilities and judgment, and they could keep him appraised on what was happening with the team.

The schedule had been finalized, and largely because they were a new team and doing their best to accommodate the openings of other schools, they had more away games than home games. The schools that they were playing twice—Andon, Blackfield, Millwood, Newbridge, Rockton, Stonington, Tynesfield, and Weirfield—split a game each home and away. However, the schools where Farmington only was playing once—Corinth, Dennis-Yarmouth, Mondale, and Quallin Regional—were all scheduled as away games.

Going over his materials and preparing a few final things, Connor was ready for his meeting, and not a minute too soon. Rather than meet in the auditorium again, Connor had everyone go to the gym and take a seat in the bleachers. As long as they could hear him, that was all that he needed. All four of his assistant coaches were also present, directing the students to the bleachers and having them sit down.

Connor watched, waiting until Dom gave him the thumbs up that everyone was there, and then walked over to talk to his prospective players. As he looked at the faces of the students, he thought that everyone looked so young. It hadn't been that long ago since he had been in high school himself, but never did he remember looking so young. That, he assumed, with the cost of age. He sincerely doubted that the current generation just happened to look younger than his own.

The students were small, too. He recalled his father's comments and strategies when working with power hitters. There was no ego greater than that of a power hitter, but his father had found a way of using his power hitters to his advantage. Pitchers, especially in high school, often took a little something off when facing the bottom of the order. It wasn't much, but their best efforts were to the top five or six batters, figuring that those were the best players facing them. The seventh through ninth batters were when the pitchers tried to slow down, get a few quick outs, and prepare themselves for the top of the order. Knowing this, Connor's father always used to tell him how he batted his best power hitter eighth, taking added advantage of the reduced effort and driving in some runs. As Connor looked though, he would be surprised to find very many power hitters in this group—which, considering the fact that there were numerous information packets claiming football backgrounds, Connor was relatively shocked by.

"Good afternoon," Connor said. "I am Coach Blake, and we are here to put together a baseball team. Those of you here have expressed interest in said team, and over the next four months, we're going to find out which of you have what it takes to become members of the varsity team.

"To make this determination, to guide you, to at times drill and grill you, shall be the coaching staff you see before you. The Batting Coach is Coach Petrioli."

Dom did not move, just glared at the students as if trying to intimidate them. His only response to announcing his name was a snort, never taking his eyes off of the students in the bleachers.

"The Pitching Coach shall be Coach Forester."

"Pleased to meet you," Corey said.

Connor heard a few students mumbling in the bleachers. A couple of laughs followed as well.

"Pipe down!" Joe shouted. "You want to talk out of turn, you want to laugh like a little girl and show disrespect for your coaches, then you're going to run!"

The comment was enough to silence the crowd. Everyone's attention was on Joe. Connor continued: "Coach Lane here will be your Physical Trainer."

Joe just shook his head back and forth. "You guys keep that up, and I'll be in heaven with all the shoes we'll be wearing out this season."

"Lastly, we have our Fielding Coach, Coach Urban."

"All right, all right," Rickey said, clapping a couple of times. "We're going to work hard, but we're going to have a good year."

"Coach Lane and Coach Urban shall also double as your base running coaches," Connor added. "All of us, at any time, have an open door policy. If something is bothering you, if you have a question, come to us and let us know. Does anybody have any questions so far?"

Connor waited, looked around at the students on the bleachers, and then continued. "Okay. Our official pre-season begins on Monday, March 19th at 3:00 PM. Mark your calendars, because on our first day, I expect you all to be here not at 3:00, but at 2:55. We'll have a little pre-practice chat, and then from 3:00 to 6:00, you'll be working harder than you probably ever have in your life. If you're late, you'll find yourselves working even harder."

"Coach Blake," one student raised his hand as he spoke.

"Name, sir?" Connor asked, looking at the boy whose skin was dark, but his hair was dyed a fluorescent-orange and trailed well past his neckline. As Connor looked at him, he wondered if this student was a fan of anime, where fluorescent-orange and other radical shades of hair were commonplace.

"Troy Kane," the student said. "I don't mean to speak out of turn, but I've played varsity baseball for two years, with a year of JV before that. Practices are only supposed to run for two and a half hours, not three."

"Very good," Connor said. "Thank you for bringing that to my attention. Mr. Kane is absolutely correct: practices throughout the league are only two and a half hours. Now, can anyone tell me why we're going to be practicing for three hours?"

Connor waited, looked around at the students again. "Anyone? Someone here has to know why we're practicing more than other schools."

A hand in the back row went up.

"Name, sir?" Connor asked.

"Nauth, sir, Roger Nauth," he replied. He had blonde hair, trimmed almost in a military-style cut, and a sternness about him that

Connor recognized from the soldiers he saw at his father's funeral.

"Go ahead, Mr. Nauth, why are we going to have longer practices?"

"Because we neither have an established team nor an established program, sir."

"Very good," Connor said. "Mr. Nauth is exactly correct. Our weekday practices will be three hours, and we'll have two three hour practices every Saturday." He caught a few groans about the double-sessions on Saturdays. "Now's your chance. If anyone has changed their mind, you can walk out that door right now and nobody will think any less of you."

When nobody got up, Connor heard Dom whisper, "Your funeral," and smirk deviously.

"Good," Connor said. "Mr. Nauth's observation is also why we find ourselves the underdogs this year. I have our schedule, and not one team on it finished under .500 last season. We're also going up against last season's State Champions—Rockton, twice, and Corinth, who is expected to win States this year as well.

"How come nobody expects us to compete for States?" Connor asked.

A student in the front row, who was best described as thin and wiry, raised his hand, and when Connor looked at him, he quickly said, "Dane, D-Dane Olney."

"Why are we not expected to compete for States Mr. Olney?"

"Because everyone against us is so...so good," he said, his voice trailing off at the end as if he was losing confidence in his own idea.

"They are good," Connor agreed. "But that doesn't mean they can't be toppled. Why else?"

"Because nobody knows us!" someone shouted.

"Who said that?" Connor asked.

"There," Rickey pointed.

"Name, sir?" Connor said.

"Ryan Wolf, senior, starter, power hitter," Ryan said, his tone full of cockiness.

He was short, but Connor could see that he was built. He had a fu-man-chu mustache that Connor thought had gone out of style years ago. His eyes looked bored, as if he could not care less about what was going on.

"Nobody knows us," Connor repeated. "So, nobody knows what to expect? And since our opponents are so formidable, we're expected to fail. I see. You're right. That makes a lot of sense.

"But that is also exactly why we will be practicing longer and harder than anyone else. We may be seen as the underdogs, but we have every right to be champions as everyone else. And that pursuit of greatness, that pursuit of perfection, that pursuit of proving to everyone that hard work and determination pays off, *that* is what will be driving us. I expect nothing less than your best from each and every one of you.

"That is also why I expect more than just pre-season beginning on the 19th," Connor continued. "We began the after-school conditioning program, and though it is open to the entire school, I would highly encourage each and every one of you to be here for each session."

"That means be here, or don't bother showing up in March," Joe added, challengingly.

"We also have an added advantage: Coach Petrioli owns his own batting cage. I don't care if you go with your teammates, with your friends, with your fathers or siblings. Go. Between now and March 19th, I want every student in this gym to have logged at least four one-hour sessions in the cages."

Dom reached into his pocket and pulled out a stack of postcards. "Call me at Pure Hitters to schedule your sessions. Take one of these before you leave. It has the location, contact number, and directions."

"Any questions so far?" Connor asked. Glancing around, he nodded when nobody said anything else. "The last thing I expect from each of you before the 19th is to make an honest effort in conducting any activities that your captains request of you. It's called Captain's Practice, it is completely legitimate with the league, and it allows you to actually throw and catch a ball. Do it."

"Who are the Captains?" Ryan Wolf asked, not raising his hand.

"For the moment, Mr. Wolf, we do not know who the final captains shall be," Connor said. "The coaching staff shall select captains based upon efforts, skill, and leadership in March. For the time being though, I have designed interim co-captains of Robert Griffin and Jimmy Kerrigan. Stand up, boys."

Robert and Jimmy stood up, both looking a bit shocked.

"Get to know these two, because between now and March 19th, what they say and tell you to do is as good as me or one of the coaches telling you to do something."

"No way, man—he's a locker-stuffer," Ryan barked.

"A 'locker-stuffer'?" Connor asked, seeking clarification.

"He means, a freshman, sir," Roger Nauth clarified. "As in someone to stuff in a locker."

"Thank you, Mr. Nauth," Connor said. "Let me make one thing perfectly clear. What grade you are in does not mean a thing to me. If the eighteen best players in this auditorium are freshmen, then we're going to have an all-freshman team. Mr. Kerrigan may be a freshman, but he is also one of the students I selected as an interim captain. You will listen to what he says, and do what he asks, or do not bother coming on March 19th."

Ryan folded his arms, scowling, but he did not say another word.

"Moving on. I have a few simple rules that I expect to have followed throughout the pre-season and season," Connor said. "The first is communication. I cannot coach effectively unless I know what is going on with each of you. While I expect each and every one of you to be here for every practice and every game, I understand that there are external factors in your lives that could, at times, prevent you from doing so. If that is the case, I want to know as soon as you do. Not five minutes before the game, but the moment you know there is a conflict.

"I don't care if we're talking about a family commitment, an injury, or anything else that may impact your performance. I want to know," Connor continued. "By knowing, I have options. I can make adjust-

ments and keep the team running smoothly. By not knowing, I am re-
acting to unexpected events. I will not tolerate that. Your first no call no
show, to a practice or game, will result in an automatic and unappeal-
able two game suspension. I don't care if you're the star of the team or
a utility fielder. A second offense and you're gone, no excuses.

"This goes along with that open-door policy I was talking about earlier. It does not take much to pick up a phone. If you can't do it because both of your arms are in casts, have a parent call me. I don't care
if it's 4:00 in the morning—I want to know what impacts this team."

"I can vouch for that," Dom said, grinning devilishly.

He would be able to, Connor admitted. While coaching softball,
Dom called at random hours—more than a few times. One night, before Connor had moved out on his own, his reaction one of Dom's
calls had woken the entire Blake household. The phone rang, and instantly alert, Connor had answered the phone thinking that something
was wrong. He asked Dom again and again: *Are you all right? Do you
need help? Do you need a ride?* To each, Dom just shook it off, saying
that he was "happy" and wanted to say "hello."

When Connor focused on the clock and saw that his ecstasy-
induced friend was calling at 4:00 AM, he shrieked on the top of his
lungs at Dom for calling that early just to say hello and that he was
happy. After slamming the phone down, Connor rolled over and went
back to bed. Hours later, when he went downstairs, his mother
smirked, and then repeated, word for word—expletive and all—exactly
what Connor had shouted.

"The second thing is respect. There will be respect on this team.
Mutual respect amongst yourselves, and with your coaches," Connor
said, his eyes glancing over at Ryan Wolf. "There will be no heckling,
insulting, or demeaning each other. You may think that is fun, a real
hoot, but it only takes away from the integrity of yourself, your teammates, your team, your coaching staff, this school, and even the Governor for placing his faith in you and us. If you have something negative
to say, say it to me behind closed doors. Otherwise, keep your mouths

shut.

"If there are hostilities or animosity amongst the players and team, the coaching staff will take whatever steps we deem appropriate. I assure you, your best bet is to follow the rules, and not test the penalties," Connor advised.

Joe's smile widened from ear to ear, helping the students to visualize just what the penalties may be.

"Third, I mentioned it before, but it's important to reiterate: tardiness, especially without communication, will not be tolerated. We begin every practice with laps. You won't need to be told to begin, when the clock hits 3:00, you are running. If you are not running so much as one second after 3:00, you are tardy, and your laps are doubled. For every minute you are late from that point on, your laps are doubled again."

A student several rows from the front raised his hand. He was big, very big. Taller than Ryan Wolf and just as muscular. "Name, sir?" Connor said.

"John Turner, sir," he said. "What if we can't finish the laps?"

"You will finish the laps," Connor said. "Whether it is one or one hundred, you will complete your laps or you will not be eligible for this roster."

"But, what if we can't?"

"Do you expect to fail, Mr. Turner?" Connor asked.

"No sir," John replied.

"Then why do you sound like you do?"

"I'm just not good with running, is all," John said. "I'm strong, I can barrel through people in football, but I've never been good at speed or distance running."

"You will complete your laps," Connor said with finality. "You may not be the fastest one running them, and you may be here late with only the coaching staff remaining, but you will finish your laps. It's a matter of effort, persistence, and determination."

"Yes, sir," John said, still skeptical.

"This leads me to my fourth rule: every single one of you will always try your hardest. I don't care if you fail, as long as you try. In life, everyone fails. Each and every one of you either has failed or will fail. But you will try, you will not give up, and you will give this team, and yourself, your best effort.

"I remember one time coaching an intramural softball team in college. I had a player who lasted all of one at-bat for me. He hit the ball to shortstop, decided halfway to first that he was going to be out, turned and began making his way back to the dugout. In doing so, he actually fell and landed on his ass, which is funny, but the point is he gave up. I will not have a player who gives up and does not try playing ball for me. That batter did not go back in the game. If any of you do the same, you will not either.

"I expect each and every one of you to run out each hit whether it is a ground ball, a line drive gap shot, or a home run. You will hustle every instant you are on the field. If a ball is hit anywhere near you, you will converge on it. You will not make any assumptions about what will happen: you will play as if every play needs *your* personal assistance. In this game, you never know what will happen. Only by being alert and playing hard will you master this game and make this team.

"Why would a center fielder run in toward second base?" Connor asked. When he saw that nobody was offering an answer, Connor said, "Coach Urban?"

"To back-up the throw-down to second."

"Correct," Connor said. "It may be infrequent, but it happens. The ball is thrown, and the fielder covering the ball misses it. Surprise, surprise, the other middle infielder who is backing up the play also misses it. Well, if the center fielder is playing deep, then the batter makes it to third—possibly even scores—with ease. But if the center fielder was running in as an extra back-up, then the runner will stay where they are, or the center fielder can make a play at third.

"Effort, awareness, preparation, hustle," Connor said. "These are words you will all learn and know quite well. My fifth rule is academic excellence. The eligibility requirements of the league is that you pass four year-long traditional courses. That means each of you could be failing a major class and whatever electives you are taking. This policy is too weak for this school.

"Those of you here chose to be here to seek better lives. To leave overcrowded schools or areas that were less than desirable. You wish to play sports, and that is great, but for you to go forth and really make changes in your lives, your education should and will be paramount. Those four classes you have to pass to be eligible? Those will be a 'B' average. The rest of your classes, the one's you normally could fail? Anything lower than a 'C' and you're done."

"That's crazy," Ryan Wolf groaned. When Connor looked at him expectantly, he added, with sarcasm dripping off of his tongue, "Sir."

"What would be crazy is requiring you to have a straight 'B' average, which is what I would like to do. I understand that some of your grades may not be in this range at this moment. I have contacted the teachers of those of you who signed up, and will be receiving your report cards and progress reports on a monthly basis until the season begins, and then bi-weekly from there.

"You may be below the eligibility requirements now, but you have until opening day, April 4th, to have your grades raised and reach eligibility status. I would hate to have to cut players that I want because you are not maintaining your academic credentials, but I shall not hesitate to let ineligible players go.

Finally, my sixth policy is a zero tolerance policy on drugs of any kind. I do not care if you drink, smoke, do drugs, or anything of the kind: you will not be doing it during the season. Coach Petrioli here has considerable experience with this topic, and would be able to recognize whether there has been a violation to the policy or not."

"Coach Blake," John Turner said as he raised his hand. "I can't even smoke? I'm old enough to legally be able to buy cigarettes."

"That's fine, and what you do in the offseason is your own business," Connor said. "During the pre-season and season though, you will be giving up the cigarettes. Maybe then you'll be able to get those laps in you are so worried about."

Connor could see that John wasn't happy with the response. He could see that many of the players were not happy. He wondered how many of them smoked cigarettes. He wondered how many more smoked pot, shot themselves up, or did any number of other activities with narcotics. If they did, they were gone. There was no room on this team for players who do things like that.

"Any other questions?" Connor asked.

A Hispanic student in the front row raised his hand. He was short, thin, and at first glance, looked like he had the potential to be quick. "Julio Diaz," he said to introduce himself. "What about uniforms and equipment?"

"We'll have uniforms once we know who is on the team," Connor said. "We'll also have a supply of balls, bats, helmets, and catching equipment. All other gear you will be expected to produce on your own."

There was not enough money in the sports budget for all of that, but Connor had been considering an announcement that he would be donating his royalties to the Farmington School System's athletic department. At least then they would have some form of seed-money to get good equipment for the players.

"If there's nothing else, make sure you pick up a copy of the pre-season schedule, information and hours for when the gym will be available to you over the next three months, about the batting cages, and contact information for your captains. If any of you have to talk to me, my office is in the locker room, and my door is always open. If not, I'll see you all on the field on the 19th."

CHAPTER 17

Over the next month, Connor reviewed the player's questionnaires again and again, nearly memorizing all ninety-six players' responses. He also reviewed all report cards and progress reports, and kept a chart of the players who were already eligible, who were borderline, and who were struggling academically.

Each week he also received a report from both Dom and Joe about what was happening with the players who they saw either in the batting cages or at the gym after school. Connor broke down the reports and kept an active file of each student and the progress they were making.

From the early outlook that he was seeing, the players trying out for the team were quick. Joe had been impressed with the speed of many of the guys, and thought that they would have a fairly speedy team. Connor definitely did not have any problems about going with a team that focused on speed and defense. In the field, a quick team was energetic and solid. On the base-path, they would always be on the go, a constant threat. A running team definitely had promise.

That is, of course, if they could field, and could hit. Though it was too early for Captain's practices to give him a heads up about whether or not people could field, the reports he was receiving from Dom were somewhat less than desirable about batting. Dom was downright pessimistic, thinking that only a handful of prospects had a chance to do anything with the bat.

His view was so low, that Connor asked him to come to the school personally. Checking his Red Sox ball-clock, Connor saw that Dom should arrive any minute. With a knock on his door, Connor looked up and saw his long-time friend and former ballplayer.

"Dom, come in," Connor said, beckoning him.

Dom stepped into the office and closed the door. He then sat down, slouching and groaning. "We have no hitters."

"None?" Connor asked.

"Well, there's some guys who can hit," Dom conceded. "Grounders and line drives. I haven't found anyone who inspired me as a cleanup batter though."

"Speed and defense, Dom, speed and defense."

"A power hitter or two would be nice," Dom argued.

"I saw a few kids who had potential to be power hitters," Connor said.

"Who are you talking about?" asked Dom.

"How about John Turner?" Connor asked, thinking of the big student whose profile said he was a varsity defensive end in football before choosing to come to Farmington.

"Connor, let me be honest: if you or I had his body, we would be belting homers for the home team. The parking garage attendants across the street from the Green Monster would have a better chance of catching our hits than any fielder ever could. But this kid—he's awkward, clumsy, and doesn't have a clue how to even get into a stance."

"He doesn't have a stance?" Connor asked, wondering how someone trying out for baseball could not possibly know how to stand even somewhat properly in the batters box.

"He has this whole legs-spread-thing, no step into the pitch, and just swings with his arms. It's ugly is what it is."

"We can work on that," Connor said.

"I *have* been working on that," Dom said, gritting his teeth. "I told him to take a step into the pitch, and how it's all timing and mechanics."

"What happened?"

"He steps one giant step like he's Godzilla trying to smash people under his foot, stops, and then swings with his arms like he used to. He'll be lucky if he ever hits the ball out of the infield."

"A work-in-progress," Connor said. "What about Wolf?"

"Dangerous," Dom said. "Very dangerous."

"What do you mean?"

"I see the potential in that boy, but he is all attitude. He thinks he's the best, and feels like he should be treated like he's the best. He doesn't listen, he's argumentative, and he just raises his hand and brushes off suggestions saying that 'he's good.' Like I said, dangerous."

"You think he's a cancer?"

"Definitely," Dom said. "He has more talent than anyone else there, but he could also destroy the chemistry of any team. We need to tread carefully."

"How about his hitting?"

"Pure power to left," Dom said. "Won't even consider trying to hit anywhere else."

"Okay," Connor said. "We'll work on him too. See how things go."

"Yeah, well, I'm not all that optimistic," Dom said.

"Are you ever?" asked Connor. "You always see the down-side. The perfect Devil's Advocate."

"That way I never get my hopes too high," Dom admitted. "But I do have high hopes for one player."

"Who is it?"

"The name's Aronson. Lamont Aronson."

Connor leaned back in his chair. The name didn't sound familiar at all. He thought he had learned everyone's name already. "Which one is he?"

"None of our boys," Dom said. "Nobody's boy, actually."

"What do you mean?"

"He's in the system at the moment," Dom said.

"What system?" asked Connor.

"Department of Youth Services," Dom clarified. "He's in juvie."

Connor folded his arms. He did not like the sound of bringing a criminal onto the team for any reason.

"Oh, don't do that," Dom said. "I know this kid. He's a good boy.

He was in the wrong place at the wrong time."

"Isn't that what everyone who has been arrested says?" Connor skeptically asked.

"Yeah, but this kid is telling the truth."

"How do you know him?"

"Back in my youth, when, you know, I wasn't as ethical as I am today," Dom began.

"Oh boy," Connor said. "With an intro like that, this has got to be good."

"Yeah, well, my boy Antwone and I were tight. Real tight. But he got himself into trouble, you see? But instead of ratting me out—which he could have done—he didn't. He went to jail instead. They tried him as an adult."

"Drugs?" Connor asked, suspecting that was it, knowing Dom.

"Yeah, drugs," Dom said. "Well, anyway, Antwone didn't know, but after he was arrested, his girl found out she was pregnant. She had a son, Lamont. As he was growing up, he needed a father figure at times, and I tried to help out, since I was free and Antwone was in jail, and we both had been involved.

"Anyway, Lamont was raised right. He knew his father was gone because he was in jail for dealing drugs. He was straight as can be. All A's in school, and he played sports year-round. His Mom and I were talking about trying to get him recruited for college under some kind of scholarship or something. Then, six months ago, completely out of the blue, he was arrested."

"What happened?" Connor asked.

"He was the black man with the knife wound," Dom said. "If it was us, or one of our kids, white, we would have been rushed to the hospital and treated. Lamont though? Oh no, they see this big black boy, check his name and see that his father is in prison, and they assume that he was involved in what went down."

"What did go down?"

"It was some stupid gang thing. There was a fight and Lamont went to try and break it up. The gang members pulled knives, and in the fray, Lamont got hit bad from his right ear down his neck to his shoulder. When the police arrived, one gang member was dead, and there was Lamont bleeding on the street. They just assumed he was the other gang member, and everything happened quickly."

Connor took a deep breath and slowly let it out. "How could he help?"

"Lamont is pure power. Just like his father, who was jacked; Lamont is bigger than John Turner, and has a better bat than Ryan Wolf. He could come onto this team and make us a legitimate power threat. But, he's also quick, good agility, and knows exactly what is going on and what needs to be done. If you give him a chance, he won't let you down."

"You make a compelling argument," Connor said. "But you said he's locked up."

"He's out the first of March," Dom said.

"There's still the matter of recruitment," Connor pointed out. "We can't ask him to come here and recruit him."

"The boy's got the right to complete his education," Dom said. "This *is* a school of choice. He could choose to come here. Trust me: give him a chance."

"Fine," Connor said. "I'll give him a chance. I'll meet with him. Then we'll see what I think from there."

"I'm a step ahead of you," Dom grinned. "We've got a meeting with him in an hour."

"What if I said no?"

"Then I would have gone and visited him myself," Dom said. "But I knew you'd say yes."

"We'll see," Connor said.

"Yeah we will," Dom said excitedly. "I'll drive."

❖　❖　❖　❖　❖

Connor had always considered himself to be a straight shooter. He did not drink, he did not smoke, and he did not do drugs. When he was younger, his older brother had died from a drug overdose, and Connor decided that very day that no matter what, he would not even experiment. In college, he hosted parties, and his only condition was that people did not try to force him to drink or do drugs, and that they had to do things that non-drinkers could also do.

He never held it against anyone who wanted to drink or do drugs, and if he did, he and Dom never could have been friends. He could hardly remember a phone conversation with Dom in their softball years where Dom wasn't smoking a joint while on the phone or doing something else. The choice was his, as long as it did not somehow impact Connor.

But with a high school team, he would not tolerate it. Players abilities could be diminished, and there were times when a player would be relied upon, and then let the team down. In high school sports, letting a team down could often be at a time when others could get hurt. If his kids wanted to drink and do drugs, then they had to give up baseball to do so.

Besides, none of his kids were old enough to drink, and drugs were illegal, so he wasn't stressing a policy that denied them their legal rights. Smoking may be pushing the borders a bit, but Connor decided to lump all three together.

As he and Dom sat in a room with what looked almost like cafeteria tables waiting for Lamont Aronson, he wondered how many kids were in here because of drugs and drug related crimes. Probably far more than he wanted to imagine. He remembered one year talking to his coaches about instituting a no-drug policy on the softball team, and being told point blank that that would leave him with only a handful of his twenty-five-man roster. Connor knew about Dom and a few others, but the mere thought that nearly everyone was doing something was staggering.

A door opened and Connor watched as a guard walked in with a boy—black, bald, with a long scar where Dom said he had been stabbed, and as Dom said, bigger and stronger than anyone on the team. He looked more like a professional body-builder than a high school student.

"Lamont," Dom said, standing up and hugging him.

"Hey Dom," Lamont said.

"This is Coach Blake," Dom said, walking back to the table with Lamont. The guard stepped back and stood by the door, watching, but acting like he wasn't eavesdropping.

"Hello Coach Blake," Lamont said, reaching his hand out and shaking Connor's with a very firm grip.

"Dom tells me you might be interested in playing ball at Farmington this year," Connor said.

"I would like that," Lamont said.

"Why don't you want to go back to your old school?" Connor asked.

"It's the principle of the matter," Lamont said.

"What do you mean?"

"I was President of the National Honor Society," Lamont began. "When I got stabbed, they revoked my status. They even had my mother return my certificate saying I was part of the NHS. I can't go back there. To them, I'm nothing more than a common criminal."

"And what are you?" Connor asked directly.

"Not a criminal," Lamont said.

Connor held his gaze. If Lamont had been lying, he could not tell.

"If you come to Farmington, we have strict academic policies," Connor said.

"Well, I'm a junior," Lamont said. "Dom and my mom did some checking for me, and I can finish out the school year and then take summer classes to cover what I missed. It looks like I'll still be able to graduate on time at the end of next year."

"Dom told me you're a good student," Connor said.

"President of the National Honor Society," Lamont reiterated.

"Good. I expected B's in four classes and no less than a C in the rest from my players. If you come in—since most of your schooling at Farmington will be after the season is started—I'm giving you a higher standard. Nothing lower than a B, and at least a B+ in those four classes."

"I'll have all A's," Lamont said confidently. "That's not a problem."

"One last question," Connor said, "do you, or have you ever taken any drugs?"

"Not once," Lamont said. "And I would be happy to take whatever drug tests or polygraph tests you may need of me."

Connor glanced at Dom. "Did you coach him on that one?"

"He's sincere," Dom said.

"Fair enough," Connor said. "You get out March 1st?"

"Yes sir," Lamont said.

"I'll see about getting you your course work to begin your schooling now. But, if Farmington is what you want, and baseball is your desire, then I'll be glad to welcome you."

"Thank you, thank you so much," Lamont said. "I won't let you down."

"I know you won't," Connor said, standing up and feeling certain that he was right. "Welcome to the team."

CHAPTER 18

With a full week before practice would officially begin, Connor was taking the lull in baseball activities to work on his RPG book so that the development team would not be held up. It had been far too long since he touched the game, and he knew there were things that his people were waiting for. Nothing like a week of eighteen-hour days to make sure you get caught up with what people needed for creative development.

The baseball-side of things was as covered as they were going to be at the moment. He was still receiving regular reports from Dom and Joe about their activities, but also now daily emails from Robert and Jimmy about what was going on with their Captain s' practices. He also had his first two weeks worth of activities for practice scheduled and plotted out. Baseball was a waiting game now, so writing was back in high gear.

Connor heard the phone ring, but he let Marina answer it. The phone had been ringing all week, but unless it had to do with baseball or his mother, Connor was ignoring the calls until the RPG materials were complete.

Marina knocked and poked her head in the room. "Corey's on the phone."

"I'll take it," Connor said.

Marina handed him the cordless phone and then made her way back to what she had been doing.

"Hi Corey, what can I do for you?" greeted Connor.

"You know your nephews' report on pitching?"

"I do," Connor said, recalling that their estimate on the quantity of people interested in pitching was pretty high, but the *quality* of pitchers was not nearly so vast.

"I have a solution," Corey said.

"I'm listening."

"You used to work at SJC, right?"

"I did," Connor said, not sure where this was going.

"Have you been paying attention to the news?"

"Unless it has to do with baseball, there's very little news I pay attention to," Connor admitted. "Why?"

"SJC has just been acquired by Ishikawa, from Japan. Billionaire Satoshi Ishikawa has come to Boston to oversee the transition personally. Reports indicate that Boston will be his new base of operations."

"Okay," Connor said, not sure how this impacted him since he left SJC quite some time ago.

"You really don't know anything, do you?" Corey asked, amused with herself.

"I'm listening."

"Ishikawa has nine children. Eight daughters, and one son," Corey said. "The son is a pitcher."

"Okay," Connor said.

"Come on Connor, this isn't just business, this is baseball. Osamu Ishikawa is known as the best high school Japanese pitcher in Japan. It's reported that he actually has five pitches, including a fastball in the 90's."

"A fastball in the 90's? For a high school student?"

"He's only fifteen," Corey said. "He was interviewed by *Baseball America* a month ago, and claimed that it is his dream to pitch in the MLB. There is even some speculation that his father bought SJC only to bring his son here to be exposed to American baseball."

"And you want him playing for Farmington?" Connor gathered.

"Don't you?" Corey scoffed. "He'd be the ace of any high school team in the country. You still have some connections at Stanley Jalbert, I would assume, and might be able to open the doors to having Osamu play here."

"Recruiting, Corey," Connor said. "This is dicey."

"His father has not committed to a school yet. Why can't he decide to send his son to Farmington? It's a school of choice."

Connor sighed. First Dom with his desire for a power hitter, and now Corey with a Japanese pitcher. If the league ever investigated their activities, he wondered if they would think they crossed the line with these players. It was definitely touchy, and he did not want to break the rules. But, Osamu did have to pick a school.

"I'll make some calls," Connor said.

"Really? Great!" Corey said excitedly. "I can see him in one of our uniforms already!"

Connor had a good chuckle at that. He wished he could see any of the players in their uniform. The final design still had to be decided, so what it looked like was anyone's guess.

"I'll give you a call back when I know more," Connor said.

"Talk to you then, bye."

"Bye," Connor replied. As he hung up the phone, he stared at his computer and the RPG materials. So much for getting some work done. Closing the document, he quickly cleared his desk so that he would not have any distractions. Then he opened his phone directory and dialed Hobbes. Since he was still at SJC, maybe he could arrange some kind of meeting with the new owner.

❖ ❖ ❖ ❖ ❖

Hobbes proved to be quite resourceful. As a former pitcher himself, as well as someone who had always been fascinated in Japan and Japanese culture, he was able to speak the language that Satoshi Ishikawa wanted to hear. He got Connor and Corey a fifteen-minute window to speak with the new president, and though it was not much time, it was an opportunity.

Connor went through security and stepped into the elevator he recalled using all too well. The top floor was where the boardroom and the president's office was. Every quarter, Connor had been in the boardroom with the rest of the Continuity specialists in the company. There was also a library and a sitting room that was quite luxurious. He enjoyed his time on the top floor.

When they reached the top, Connor directed Corey to the right and down the hall. He stopped at the receptionist before the President's office and announced their arrival. She told them to rest in the library and would get them when Ishikawa-san was ready.

The two sat on comfortable chairs and waited, nearly in silence. Corey really hoped that things worked out, and was trying to hide both her enthusiasm for success, and her fear of failure. Connor was approaching this realistically: they had pitchers in the mix already and would make do with what they have. A kid who could throw in the 90's was impressive, but their season would not be won or lost because he was pitching once a week.

The receptionist walked out, bowed, and said, "Mr. Ishikawa-san will see you now."

Connor and Corey stood up. Both were wearing suits for the occasion, and followed the receptionist. Connor had been to this floor, but never in the office of the President before. It was spacious; almost intimidating with all grand mahogany furniture that looked like it cost more than the money he brought in from a bestseller. On one wall Connor saw—from ceiling to floor—Japanese katana blades. Since Ishikawa was a billionaire, he suspected that the swords were all hand-crafted specifically for him.

Standing behind his desk, looking out the window and speaking in Japanese over a headset, was Satoshi Ishikawa himself.

"Have a seat," the receptionist said.

Connor and Corey both sat down in chairs before Ishikawa's desk. They waited several minutes as Ishikawa did not even turn around. Then, he pulled the headset off, turned around, and in perfect English, said, "You wish to speak of my son?"

"We do," Connor said, standing up and bowing in what Hobbes had told him was proper Japanese culture.

"I am a very busy man," Ishikawa said. "Speak quickly and clearly."

"We know your son is interested in pursuing baseball in the United States, and that he has hopes of becoming a Major League Baseball player. We would like to present the opportunity that exists for him doing so at Farmington."

"No, impossible," Ishikawa said. "My son is going to Quallin Regional, a private school."

"I see," Connor said. "I'm sorry to hear that."

"I'm sure you are," Ishikawa said. "Well, if that will be all?"

"You misunderstand," Connor added. "I'm sorry for your son."

"Why is that, exactly?"

"Quallin Regional is a fantastic school. If you want your son to follow in your footsteps and run companies, that's the place for him. Most Quallin graduates find themselves in Ivy League schools, and have very bright futures before them."

"This does not sound like a problem," Ishikawa said.

"Yes, true," Connor nodded. "But your son wants to play baseball, not run a company, correct?"

"Correct," Ishikawa said, sitting down and watching Connor closely.

"Do you wish him to have that which he desires?"

"I do," Ishikawa said.

"Well, Quallin is a good school. It has a *good* baseball team. Add your son into the mix, and they'll probably be a great baseball team. But then your son will go to an Ivy League college and wind up here with you."

"You have a counter-proposal?" Ishikawa asked.

"Farmington has never had a baseball program. I will not lie to you, that is a fact. But, it is a program in its first year and established by the Governor. Due to this, Farmington has been receiving quite a bit of public attention. Reporters have been calling daily and are hovering around the school just to see how the Governor's program is working.

"Then there is the addition of myself as coach. If I were just a son trying to honor his father—a phenomenal baseball coach—it would be a human-interest story and attract attention. But, I'm also a best-selling author who is leaving that to coach. Just like the school, my phone rings off the hook with people looking for interviews and updates.

"All in all, if you want you son to have a great education, have a decent high school baseball career, and then go to college to become one of the business leaders of tomorrow, then stay at Quallin. If you want him to have constant exposure, to be in the highlights in a school and program that is already receiving publicity, and have scouts and Major League Baseball teams take notice, then Farmington is the choice for you."

Ishikawa pushed a button on his phone. Connor heard the door open behind him. "Your argument is quite persuasive, though I feel the best education possible for my son, paired with his sports excellence is the way to go. However, I shall discuss what you have said with him. That is all I have time for now. Thank you for stopping by."

"Thank you for granting us an audience," Connor said, bowing again.

"Yes, thank you," Corey said, bowing as well.

They then headed out of the office, where the receptionist was holding the door open. She escorted them back to the elevators, and when they were in it, she returned to her desk.

"You did your best," Corey said.

"Yeah, but was it good enough?" Connor said.

"I guess we'll find out," Corey replied.

❖   ❖   ❖   ❖   ❖

It did not take long. Connor and Corey had not even gotten out of Boston before his phone rang and Ishikawa's receptionist was on the phone. She informed him that Ishikawa-san has discussed the matter with his son, and that Osamu was interested in the added publicity possibility. She then told Connor that Ishikawa would be contacting him over the next couple of days to discuss the official enrollment at Farmington, and his son's future with the team.

Connor told Corey as soon as he hung up the phone, and had never seen her so excited in his life. Neither had seen Osamu pitch, but if what was reported was even partially accurate, they just found their ace for the season.

CHAPTER 19

Connor sat patiently at his desk. His coaching staff and Bob Sullivan were in the office with him. Another fifteen volunteers that Bob had acquired were just outside of the office, waiting. They had come a long way already, and the moment they had all been anxiously waiting for was finally upon them. It was March 19th, the third Monday in March, and the first official day of Spring Training.

The fields were already set up. The equipment was lying in wait for them. Connor also had created detailed progress reports for each student that they would be filling out as they went through the Spring Training drills. The forms were divvied up amongst the coaches in folders and with clipboards. Each of the volunteers also had clipboards and were ready to record what the coaches asked them to.

The past few days had been full of changes. When Connor and Corey had gone to Boston to meet with Satoshi Ishikawa, they had hoped to come away with a new pitcher. They did that and more: Ishikawa was aware of the sports department's budget, and through SJC made a sizeable donation to the Farmington School System. With it, Connor and each of his coaches were actually going to receive a fair compensation for their time. Even more importantly, they were able to purchase an ample amount of supplies and equipment for the team, including some of the best bats on the market. The quality of uniforms that Connor was looking at was also possible now—he had been dreading having to decrease the quality to t-shirts, but had thought that it was something they may have had to do for the first year.

It was an unexpected and generous offering. Connor also heard that Ishikawa had personally offered to build a new baseball stadium for the team. The four fields that were currently there, Ishikawa claimed could be practice fields, but he thought the team needed something more for games. He offered to make an identical replica of the stadium his company had once built for a team in Japan. Details of that were left up to the Principal, Superintendent, School Committee, and the Governor. For now, Connor was fine with the fields he had available.

His eyes focused on the Red Sox clock on his desk, Connor saw it turn to 2:50. "Okay, let's go."

"Yeah," Dom said in an exaggerated exclamation.

Connor led the coaches and volunteers out of the locker room and to the fields. They found the team already assembled. Some people were playing catch, some were jogging, some were swinging bats, some were talking, and others were off by themselves.

His watch read 2:54, and as the second hand reached the 12, Connor picked up his father's whistle—he and his mother had found it when going through his father's things; it had a white bottom and green top, representing the school colors of the team he had coached—and blew it three times, signaling everyone to come together by him.

"We currently have ninety-eight students trying out for this team," Connor said, taking into account the addition of Lamont Aronson and Osamu Ishikawa. "Between now and opening day, we have fourteen days worth of practices to take ninety-eight and bring it down to eighteen. Intensity, hard work, and determination will help you to be amongst those final eighteen.

"For those of you who are asked to leave the field, you may report to Coach Sullivan to determine your new schedule for try-outs for the JV team if you remain interested. Coach Sullivan has volunteered his time to assist us until we get to the point where some of you will be shifted to his focus specifically. Since we only have fourteen days, I would expect that to come no later than Wednesday."

Connor glanced at his watch and saw that it was 2:59. "Practice begins every day with two laps around the four fields. If you are not running by 3:00, your laps are doubled. Every minute you are late from that point on, your laps are doubled again. Begin."

The prospects began their laps, jogging around the field. Most had gloves and balls and dropped them right where they had been. Connor watched as they got halfway around, seeing some people clearly in the front—nearly sprinting—some taking a more leisurely pace, and others already beginning to fall behind.

Connor turned to the volunteers. "Get the bats back where they're supposed to be and have the fields ready for the first drill." He then lifted his clipboard and began flipping through the names of the people he was watching today. As the kids finished their second lap, many huffing and puffing, Connor said, "Rickey, you're up."

Rickey blew a whistle of his own, and directed the prospects to line up for calisthenics and stretching. To finish, he had everyone line up leading to home plate, and instructed them on a series of drills. He told them that this was their cool-down period, as they were waiting. Each player would then run the bases three times, each time doing something different. The first time they were to run backwards, the second time they were shuffling to the side, and the third time they did a leg-over-leg exercise. Rickey blew his whistle to begin the exercise, and blew it when the runner was a third of the way down the line to signal the next student to go.

Connor pulled his other coaches together. "The laps, directed warm-ups, motion exercises, and fence sprints will be the daily routine. We're doing it all together today so the kids see what needs to be done, but starting tomorrow, we'll be using all four fields to speed things up."

The motion exercises for ninety-eight students took a while. The players would line up to run around the bases, but rather that running normally, there was one of three motions that they were to take—the first time around the players ran backwards, the second time the shuffled to the side, and the third time they had a leg-over-leg motion. Once everyone was done with that, Rickey had them line up along the left-field line. He instructed them to jog out to the cones placed in center-field, and then sprint all the way back. After this session, it will be from home plate to the right field fence, but for now, with so many students, the cones would work.

Once that was done, Connor blew his whistle to bring everybody in again. "For the remainder of practice, we shall be using separate fields. Coaches Forester, Petrioli, Urban, and Lane all have twenty-four or twenty-five names. Listen for your name and go with the appropriate coach.

"Every field will be running the identical drills. Coach Sullivan and I will be stopping at each field, and conducting a specific drill today. You will all go through this drill before the end of the day. Now, listen for your names and go to the appropriate field."

Corey stepped up first and went through her names. Then Dom did his list, then Rickey, and finally Joe. The student-volunteers split up amongst the coaches as well, three going with each assistant coach, and three more remaining with Connor and Bob Sullivan.

The field he was at now was Corey's. He would begin the fielding exercise with them. Every other field, while he was doing fielding exercises, would be going through a variety of drills. The first was a timed sprint drill, where every player, one-at-a-time would sprint from home to first and be timed. They would all do this five times individually, and three times with a partner to see if their timing was improved in what they considered a race.

The second drill was a simulated base running drill. The first player would run through first as if they just had a hit. When the coach blew the whistle, the second player would run through first, while the first player goes halfway to second, stops—simulating their waiting to see if a fly-ball has been caught—and then run the rest of the way to second. When the coach blew the whistle a third time, the third player would go through first, the second player would pause and then go on to second, and the first runner would go as fast as they could to third and slide—head first or foot first was up to the individual. With the fourth runner, all activities were the same, and the first runner would just jog home. Once a runner scored three times, they were done unless the coach thought the base runner had not put their best effort into the drill.

The third drill finally allowed the players to use their gloves. Players would break down into pairs and roll the ball back and forth to each other. They were instructed to do so lightly at first, making sure that each fielder knew how to properly field a ground ball. Partners would then gradually increase how hard they were throwing the ball, and then also begin doing so to the sides instead of directly to the fielder. The fielder should use a shuffle or side-step to always keep the ball in front of them. The idea was to master the fundamentals before just letting the players field hits.

The fourth and final drill that was being run on each field was the foundation for a pickle—a situation when a base runner is caught between fielders who have the ball. The players would line up, and when the coach blew the whistle, they would run as hard and as far as they could. When the coach blew the whistle again, they would try to immediately stop, turn, and change directions, heading back the way they had come. Every time the whistle blew, they would do the same thing, whether the whistle was blown after a few seconds or the coach waited until they got most of the way to the other side of the field.

Whichever field Connor was at though, became a live-hitting field. Nine players took the field, and Connor hit to them with the volunteers recording who was hit to and how often. Every player rotated, and once a player fielded five balls in a position, they were done with that position and moved on to another one. While the volunteers were keeping the records accurate of who needed to field what and where, Bob Sullivan and the assistant coach monitored and recorded how well each player did. This became a quantitative number at a position, such as 4 out of 5, or 80% fielded cleanly at a specific position.

The intentions of the drill was to gain some perception of how good of a fielder the player was on Day One, and to see where the player did the best. Some people thought that they were infielders, but really did better in the outfield. Connor also recalled having a leftfielder in softball who never missed a ball. Put the same fielder in right, and he dropped everything hit to him. This drill quickly got some kind of handling on the situation.

Things would speed up the next time they did this as well. Every player would be given the opportunity to field a position until they did so cleanly. The fewer times it took them to field the ball, the better. That was a drill for tomorrow, though. Today, Connor wanted to give everyone the same number of hits and tries.

It seemed like before they knew it, practice was over. Connor had everyone run two more laps, and then pulled everyone together for a few closing remarks and discussions.

"You all did good out there today," Connor said. "I saw a lot of effort and hard work. We'll see much of the same over the next few days, and you'll also begin to have more baseball-oriented activities included in the drills. For now, we're focusing on fundamentals, endurance, and building the foundation for what we will be working on over the next couple of weeks.

"Tomorrow, by 3:00, you will all be running your two laps. When you are done with your laps, you shall immediately go to the field you were practicing at today. The coach at that field will give you your instructions from there. Good job again everyone—get a good night's sleep and we'll see you all tomorrow."

Connor recalled in softball how much people just wanted to bat. He could see that on the faces of these kids as well. They did a lot of running today, and would do even more tomorrow. They would not, however, bat for a few days yet. They did so in the batting cages, and should be able to go a few days without focusing on batting drills. Now was a time to show what they could do in the field, and see how well they can hold up to the exercises. Speed and endurance were key, even if this was baseball and not a sport like basketball or football where players are running far more.

Connor met with the coaches after practice to go over observations from the day. They all also went over each and every progress report, filling in comments and results from the drills. The players did not have to be perfect on Day One; they just had to show the desire and ability to keep going. In fact, it was a starting point. Connor used these reports to look for progress over time. If they did not have a fourteen-day deadline to cut eighty players, he would do this gradually over a couple of months. They did not have the time though. By Wednesday, the players who are struggling would be sent to a field designated as JV with Bob Sullivan. With fewer players remaining, the pace would pick up even faster, and the roster would narrow down quickly.

Once their review was done, the coaches called it a day, and headed home. Connor remained behind to make a few modifications to his plans for Tuesday's practice. The sped-up fielding drill would be the next opportunity to see how players do in each position. By tomorrow night, he would know where he wanted players to play. It was a quick evaluation, but students had an equal opportunity to show what they can do.

CHAPTER 20

The second day was much like the first, with a few new drills added in on each field. The normal timed sprints were recorded, but then later in practice, they did them again swinging the bat and then running. The normal instinct of a batter is to watch their hit and see where it went. Connor wanted to drill that habit out of them: whether the ball is a home run, a dribbler to the pitcher, or a foul ball, he wanted them running to first immediately upon contact.

The times recorded were obviously considerably slower than the ones for the straight sprints, but after five tries, the batters did cut their times down after their swings. The next variation of the drill was actually hitting a ball and running, but that was still a few days away.

There was also a base coaching drill added. Coaches would bark out instructions to base runners, telling them to go, go back, slide, get in a pickle, and more. The goal of the runner was to score five times, and keep going until they did. Those players who made mistakes and were considered out had to do it again until they did score.

The final activity was similar to rolling the grounders to each other, but this time people threw pop-ups to each other in the outfield, making sure each fielder called the ball clearly, got under it, and caught it with the proper fundamentals.

All of the drills were quite simplistic, and a few times one of the coaches heard a player complain about having to do something so easy. Those players found themselves running extra whistle drills, with the whistle blaring for the player to turn until they practically collapsed.

By the end of the second practice, Connor and the coaches took both days worth of data and used several poster boards to identify who should be able to play where. The positions were listed on the boards, and one-by-one, names were added under the positions. Some players were listed under numerous positions, some were placed only under one. A fielding percentage based on how they had done in the two fielding tests was listed next to each player, showing who was better at the position.

When they were done, they had a breakdown of players who were considered eligible for each position. They compared the results to the original questionnaires, and saw that some were similar, but a few had positions other than what they wanted where they were better suited.

With new positions ready to go, the coaches reorganized the players at the fields so that each field would be able to field at least two full teams defensively. They then went through the drills and coordinated the game plan for the next practice. The biggest deviation other than allocating people to different fields was pitching: tomorrow, pitchers and catchers would begin to work specifically with Corey.

❖ ❖ ❖ ❖ ❖

On Wednesday, the routine began the same, with the laps, the separation to the four fields, and then the calisthenics, sprints, and motion exercises. Once those were done, all of the players of each of the fields were pulled back together at field one, where Connor was waiting.

"We're going to do something a little different today," he said. "All prospective pitchers and catchers will be reporting to field four. Coach Forester has a list of names."

Corey held up her clipboard and called out the names of fifteen people who indicated in their questionnaires that they either could or would like to pitch. She then called another fifteen names as catchers.

"Hey wait, I'm not a pitcher or catcher," one kid protested.

"That's okay," Corey replied. "We need a few extra catchers today, so you're coming with me."

Once they headed off, Connor told the rest of the players what was going to happen. "After the last couple of days, we have selected positions for each of you based upon what you showed us. We will be going to the different fields to begin working on drills that will test you at those positions. Once you hear your name, go with the appropriate coach."

The players separated as called, going to the three unused fields. The infielders began with the outfielders assisting. Each infielder had two outfielders with them, along with a volunteer to record their progress. One outfielder would throw a grounder to the infielder, and when the ball got ¾ of the way to the fielder, the next outfielder threw a ball. Each outfielder had a bucket of ten balls with them. The purpose of the drill was to test reflexes and ability when a fielder was unable to think about what they were doing. The infielder would throw all balls successfully recovered to the side where a fourth fielder was waiting to collect them. Their average was based on however many balls the final fielder had at the end. The coaches also made certain that the players throwing the balls did not slow down, even if the fielder missed a ball and could not recover in time to get the next one.

The outfield drill was a bit different. The outfielder began in position, and had an infielder throw the ball over the outfielders head. The outfielder was supposed to run and try to catch the ball. The second infielder would then throw the ball shallow to make the outfielder run in on it. Like the infield drill, there were two buckets of ten balls in each.

While the players were broken up into their respective groups, the coach of the field also had a live fielding drill, where they would designate a specific position—making sure that the drills would not intersect with each other—and hit fifteen balls at the fielder. Another player caught the balls that the fielder threw back, and a volunteer recorded how many of the hits were fielded cleanly.

The activities were far more strenuous than the prior days, with more activities going on at once and everyone involved at all times rather than having some people standing around and waiting for their turns. When these three drills were done, the entire field was put to use, with the coach batting, the players fielding, and base runners running as appropriate. Each base runner was to score three times, and then rotate into the field in their position.

Shortly before 5:00, Connor made his way to field 4 to see how the pitchers were doing. When he arrived, Corey did not look too happy.

"What's going on?"

"Billy Knight," she said, lifting her head to point the kid out. "He's definitely *not* interested in being a team player."

"Knight," Connor shouted. "Over here, now."

Billy ran over, all smiles, "Yes Coach Blake?"

"Give me four laps around the baseball field."

"Yes, sir," he said, almost enthusiastically.

After he was running off, Connor looked at Corey. "I don't get it?"

"He hasn't been doing a thing I've said all afternoon," Corey shrugged. "He's been disrespectful, disobedient, and insulting."

Seeing Knight making his third lap, Connor said, "Call him back."

Corey blew her whistle. "Knight, over here."

Knight ignored her, continuing his lap.

"Knight!" Connor shouted.

Billy looked up, and when he saw Connor beckon him, ran over. "I still have another lap, Coach."

"Why didn't you answer Coach Forester?"

"Oh, come on Coach," Billy said, grinning.

"I'm waiting."

"You told me to do the laps, so I was doing them."

"But she called you over," Connor said.

"You can't expect me to really play for a woman, can you?"

"Excuse me?" Connor said, glaring at Billy. "She is a coach on this team and deserves your respect."

"Women have to earn my respect," Billy said. "There's no way I'm listening to her."

"Fine," Connor said. "You're gone."

"What?" barked Billy. "You can't get rid of me. I was in the State Tournament last year. I won MVP. I'm the best pitcher you've got."

"And you're gone," Connor said. "If you can't respect your coach, you have no place on this team."

"You'll be sorry," Billy growled. "You and all of your stupid softball coaches. You know nothing about this game and how to build a team!"

"Have your locker cleaned out and be gone before practice is over," Connor said.

Billy shouted in frustration and stormed off.

Connor watched him go, wondering if Billy would trash the locker room on his way out. If anything was out of place, he knew who was at fault.

"You didn't have to do that," Corey said.

"Yes, I did," Connor said. "There's no room on this team for sexism, prejudicism, or bigotry. How has everyone else been?"

"Good," she said. "Osamu is definitely as advertised. There are some other pretty big egos over here, and some people who might have confidence issues, but it's a good start."

"Do you think they are ready to pitch to batters?"

"Sure," she said. "They'd enjoy that."

"Good," Connor said. "Let's head back to the main field."

At 5:00, Connor reached the main field and blew his whistle to summon everyone over again. Once all of the players and coaches arrived, he said, "We have the entire team split up into the four fields, broken down into what could amount to eight miniature teams. Listen for your name, and report to your designated field. Once you're there, wait to hear your position and lineup. Then, for the next hour, enjoy yourselves and play a game."

Connor heard a few cheers at the announcement. Everyone loved playing scrimmages almost as much as batting. The names were called out and the fields were divided. Connor stayed at field one, and then moved around so he could spend a little time watching each game.

At 6:00, he blew the whistle to end practice for the day. Other than the incident with Billy Knight, it had been a great practice. Now, with even more drills and specific position fielding stats, as well as progress in the scrimmages, it was time to make the first round of cuts. Along with his coaches, Connor remained until nearly 9:00 before twenty names were removed from contention. All twenty would report to Bob Sullivan at field four from then on, with the other three fields and coaches working to cut the number down even more.

CHAPTER 21

By the end of the double-practice on Saturday, the team was really beginning to take form. Of the original ninety-eight players, forty-two of them still remained in contention for the final roster. Throughout the week, they had played in scrimmages, did more running and physical training than any player ever could have expected, worked on base running and fielding fundamentals, began batting practice, and continued working on pitching.

After the first round of cuts, Connor began an "error penalty" program, where every error, whether it be a bad throw, a bobbled ball, a dropped ball, or a misplay, resulted in a lap around the baseball fields at the end of practice. This made the players more mindful of taking their time and making the play properly, but that did not stop most of the team from having to run double-digit laps, some as high as fifteen or sixteen.

One player who stood out was Roger Nauth. He was a solid defensive catcher with a decent, not great, bat. What made him stand out though was his attitude. One practice, he earned himself seven laps, but ran the full fifteen with Domingo Milas, an outfielder who had a particularly rough practice and probably could not catch a cold if his life depended upon it.

Connor and Joe were quite impressed by Roger's willingness to do more along with his team. Domingo looked like he was ready to collapse at times, but Roger slowed his pace to help his friend up and keep him moving. When they were done, Domingo looked like he was mere steps from passing out, whereas Roger was not even sweating or breathing heavily. He had paced himself and could probably keep go-

182 • CLIFFORD B. BOWYER

ing for another fifteen laps if he were asked to.

Connor spoke with Roger as Joe made sure Domingo got a drink and into the locker room without any problems. Roger told Connor that he was looking to go to West Point, had the grades for it, the mental and physical dedication and commitment, and specifically chose Farmington because it might give him a better chance for a recommendation by being at the school known as Governor Shilalie's "baby."

If Connor took the time to admit it, there were probably better catchers currently trying out for the team. Players who could hit better than Roger, and have comparable defensive abilities. However, a player was more than just a batting average and fielding percentage. Who the player was, what they brought to the team, and how their attitude impacted themselves and their teammates were all considerations. Taking the entire prospect into account, Connor saw little doubt that, when the final rosters were determined, Roger would be amongst the final team.

An added bonus, Connor thought, was that Roger would have been the kind of man that his father would have liked. He was dedicated, hard working, determined, willing to go above and beyond what was asked of him, and someone who loved both baseball and the military.

The complete opposite argument could be said of Ryan Wolf. He had the strongest arm of every fielder; could play first, second, and third with exceptional skill; had pure power down the left-field line; and could even pitch. Rickey loved him defensively, Dom loved him offensively, and Corey loved the option of an extra pitcher that she could call upon if she needed it. But, unlike Roger, his attitude was horrendous.

Ryan consistently came late to practice, and even though he ran his penalty laps, he did so slowly and without much consideration or effort. He conveniently did not hear instructions given to him if it went against what he wanted to hear. He also had the strong belief that if he was there and ready to play, he should be given the opportunity to do what he wanted because he was the best one on the field.

Ryan Wolf, Connor knew, was going to be a thorn in his side all season long. Presuming he kept him, Ryan would continue with his bad attitude all season and be like a canker on the team. At the same time, if he cut him for that attitude, then everyone else on the team—not to mention the Governor, press, parents, and everyone else who has been paying attention to everything they have been doing—would wonder whether Connor was serious about winning or not. Ryan Wolf was a winner, and he knew it. That was the problem.

In softball, Connor had someone very similar to Ryan Wolf on his team. He came to maybe a third of the games, and when he was there, the team definitely had a better chance at winning. But, what kind of message was it to the rest of the players to say that a guy who did not come to practice, and did not come to most of the games would automatically be inserted into the lineup? Every year Connor did his best to replace that player, and every year he found that it was easier said than done.

With the first full week done, though, Connor definitely did see some promising players. One outfielder, who Connor saw as being the centerfielder, Alejandro Izquierdo, was probably the best center fielder Connor ever saw play the game—including Major League Baseball talent. He had speed, he had defense, he could run to the left- or right-field line and catch a pop-up even though he was playing center field. His bat was fantastic, as were his baserunning skills and awareness. The only possible detriment to Alejandro was that at times he seemed to try to hit for power, and when he did, he came up short.

For a senior, Alejandro would have been an unrivaled and impressive player. For a freshman, his talent was awe-inspiring. The fact that Alejandro could be the center fielder for Farmington for the next four years was something that Connor, and all of his coaches, was excited about.

Alejandro was not alone in the speed and defense department. The Dillingham twins, Marty and Pat, were both seniors and Connor thought locks to make the team. Marty played either shortstop or third and was clearly the best defensive shortstop on the team—even over Robert, who Connor was thinking of moving to second. Marty's biggest flaw, if he had one, was that he threw almost sidearm, and the ball often was trailing up and away from first base. A few adjustments though at first, and this wouldn't be a problem at all.

Pat, if it was possible, was an even better defensive player than his brother. Connor got to the point that when a ball was hit to left, he did not even have to watch anymore: Pat caught everything. An outfield with him in left and Alejandro in center was a solid foundation of speed and defense.

The list of potential players went on and on. He was looking at a right fielder, Tyrell Witham, who was just as fast as Alejandro and Pat, but a step below them defensively. He did, however, have a great arm, which is important in right field. With the speed of the three combined, their outfield would be a strength.

There was also Julio Diaz, a sophomore middle infielder who could run and field with the best of them, but had trouble getting the ball out of the infield when batting. Karlic Kulin, another middle infielder, had a great bat, but was not nearly as good defensively. His biggest benefit, and Connor was quite pleased to see it, was the fact that he could placement hit. He tried to send the ball down the right-field line, and if he had two strikes on him, he sent it right down the middle instead. Especially for a high school ballplayer, and a junior, that was an impressive ability.

Dom had been right, though, about the power situation. Ryan Wolf had power to left, and by the time Alejandro was a junior, he would probably be a power hitter, but other than that, there were very few guys who were able to knock the ball out of the yard. There were some guys who got close, but nobody who was able to do so consistently.

Dom's player though, Lamont Aronson, was a dream come true for Connor. Whatever was thrown at him—fastball, changeup, curve, or some other kind of breaking ball—he could nail it, sending the ball for some record rides. One time, his ball landed on the pitcher's mound of the field across from the one he was batting on. He had power to all three sides, and, unlike Ryan Wolf, did not have a cocky or conceited bone in his body.

Pitching was moving a little more slowly, but that was beginning to come together too. Corey was no longer being referred to as Coach Forester, but Coach Corey, and she seemed perfectly content by that. Of her eight pitchers still remaining in camp after the first few cuts though, who was going to make the final roster was anybody's guess.

Osamu Ishikawa was a lock, earning the opening day start. He was definitely as Corey had advertised, in every way possible. His work ethic was also unparalleled, though Roger Nauth probably came close. After Osamu though, Corey had not made up her mind about the pitchers.

The one name that kept coming up was Dane Olney. He was thin, wiry almost, and had tremendous confidence issues. However, Corey liked him. When Dane was pitching and was confident, he could pitch just as effectively as Osamu Ishikawa. When that first moment of self-doubt crept in, he had a complete breakdown and would begin hitting and walking batters and losing all control.

Corey felt confident that she could keep Dane feeling good about himself, and if so, he was clearly the best pitcher for the rotation. He did not have a great fastball, barely reaching the 70s, but he had a devastating curveball that made batters buckle at the knees, an effective changeup, and, surprisingly, he could throw a slider, too. He was also a lefty, which Corey liked as well.

Jimmy was still very much in the mix, and Corey had told Connor that his nephew had definitely impressed her. He threw hard and he threw accurately. Like Dane, he was a lefty. In a conversation with Corey, she had said that Jimmy might very well be the second best pitcher on the team, but Dane was either a starter or he was not on the team. Jimmy had some flexibility: he could be a starter, or he could be a closer. That left the third rotation spot open between three seniors and two juniors, who were all vying for spots.

Connor spent the weekend going over the reports, opinions, and analysis of every player. He wanted to narrow in on the starters quickly, and then have a few practices with only the players who were going to make the team. If he could do so by Wednesday or Thursday, he felt that would be ideal. It would also give Bob Sullivan a week with the players Connor thought was the best but not quite what he wanted for varsity at the JV camp before the season began.

Circling Wednesday on his calendar, he decided that one way or the other, he would have his roster set by then. In the meantime, he continued scrutinizing the materials in front of him. Everything a player did, he had stats for. With batting practice, everyone was given ten pitches. A swing and a miss was a strikeout. A fielded ball was an out. A foul ball was an out. A hit was a hit. This, plus the stats from the actual games, gave batting stats to go along with the fielding records they had been keeping all along.

The roster looked very much like Connor had been expecting: a lot of speed, solid defense, and hopefully decent batting. One big benefit going forward—to this point, Corey had been pitching batting practice; now, they were going to use live pitching for all drills. With a pitcher like Osamu Ishikawa throwing to his batters, it could only make them better. If they got accustomed to hitting Osamu, and then faced other pitchers who were nowhere near as skilled in games, then the pitches would look like they were moving in slow motion.

The phone rang, interrupting Connor's thoughts. Marina was out for the night with her friend again. Connor picked it up, "Connor Blake."

"Connor, this is Principal Bill Murphy of Corinth, how are you?"

"Good Bill, thanks," Connor said.

"How is Farmington doing?"

"I'm liking what I'm seeing," Connor said. "We've got a good group of kids, some solid support from the community and parents, and you know I couldn't have asked for a better opportunity than being head coach."

"Great, great," Bill said. "Well listen, I had a proposal for you and thought maybe I might be able to help you out a little."

"I'm listening," Connor said.

"You know the competition in this league is quite rough. I've seen the teams you're going up against, and it's not going to be easy. So, I thought, maybe you could use a little pre-season scrimmage time."

"I'm interested," Connor said.

"Great, great," Bill replied. "How about bringing your team down to Corinth on Thursday, a 4:00 game?"

"Thursday, eh?" Connor said. "We'll be there."

"Perfect," Bill said. "I'm looking forward to seeing your team in uniform."

"Me too," Connor said, realizing that they still did not have uniforms since the final names and numbers had not been determined. That would be his next order of business on Monday morning.

"Bye," Bill said.

Connor hung up, looked at his calendar, and thought: maybe Thursday would be the final cut day instead of Wednesday.

CHAPTER 22

The first thing Monday morning, Connor called Custom Sports about the uniforms. The uniform design had been finalized, and Connor had an order in for the shirts, but Kenneth Carlson was waiting on final details for sizes, names, and uniform numbers. Connor made sure everything was as close to being ready as possible, and thanked Kenneth again for squeezing the uniforms in with the season deadline quickly approaching.

The varsity and junior varsity teams were both having slight variations to the uniform. Connor, along with his RPG graphic designer, had created both uniforms for the team together. Farmington, being the political creation that it was, had the mascot of the American Bald Eagle, and had the colors of the American flag. It was quite patriotic, even if the baseball team would be the first one to display the colors.

The varsity team would be wearing blue button down shirts with a red stripe around the collar and down the front alongside the buttons. The left sleeve had a picture of an eagle for the mascot. The front of the shirt said Farmington in red letters with white outlines, in an Old English font that looked like it belonged on the Declaration of Independence or the Constitution. Just beneath the town name on the left-hand side was the player's number. On the back, in the same red with a white border, though block letters instead of the fancy font, was the player's last name and directly beneath it was a large uniform number.

The pants were all white with a single red stripe down each side. The socks were a blue-stirrup, and cleats were whatever color each player desired. Connor had given a lot of thought to the hats. He could go with an all red, an all blue, or an all white, but none of those worked for him—though the all-blue with a red "F" with a white border was the one that he kept going back to the most. He then thought of the hat and beak being different colors, looking at the red hat with blue beak and the white hat with blue beak. The white hat had the red "F" with a blue outline to it, and as Connor kept going back and forth, he liked it the most, so that was what he went with.

Farmington jackets were also available, which were blue and glossy, button-down jackets that said Farmington on the front the same as the shirts, and had the eagle on the left sleeve. The collar had a pair of red stripes with white borders on it.

Connor recommended that every player get a pair of pants and socks, at least one hat, and at least one shirt. Some players wanted the jackets, some did not care. Kenneth Carlson also offered practice jerseys, which were blue tee shirts with the Farmington name on it and numbers on the back. For the scrimmage, the tee shirts, pants, and hats would be all that Connor would have his team wear.

The junior varsity uniforms were slightly different. Rather than the blue shirts, they had red shirts. Everything that was red on the varsity uniform—the letters and the stripe around the collar—became blue. The white remained the same on both shirts. The pants were identical, but the socks were switched to red instead of blue. The hats also were the all-blue ones with red writing and a white outline. Jackets, if players wanted them, were the same regardless of team.

Connor drafted up a quick uniform order form, asking players for their desired numbers and sizes. There were certain players he knew were going to make the team, and they would definitely be able to have their order put in. The players on the cusp though, would get practice shirts and pants, and have their game jerseys only ordered if they made the team. He wanted his team to look presentable, but he also did not want to waste any of the sports budget just because of a single scrimmage.

With the form done, he had a message delivered to Edna Barrows in the office who announced at the end of the next period that all players should see Coach Blake before the end of the school day. Connor then handed out the forms as people came to see him, and told them all to return it the first thing at practice. When practice was over on Monday, Connor told the team about the scrimmage. He also said that the second to last roster cut would be Wednesday, and that maybe twenty-five kids would be on the bus on Thursday.

The announcement was exciting. Playing each other in scrimmages and practice was one thing, but playing against a team that was picked to become the next state champion was something else entirely. The feeling was infectious: it would be good to test themselves against another team.

CHAPTER 23

Wednesday came and went, and the roster was cut down to twenty-five players. Those twenty-five were all guaranteed a spot on either the varsity or junior varsity teams, and Connor said that he would have their pants, practice shirts, and hats before they got onto the bus the following day. Those seven players who were sent down to JV would have an extra hat, but Connor felt that this was the best way. He did not mention the socks so that there would not be an added expense for those seven players.

Connor himself was wearing blue shorts, a team practice jersey, the team jacket, and a team hat. Connor always wore shorts whenever possible, even at times in the winter when it was already cold, he would have them on. He just always preferred shorts. At SJC, he obviously wore suits every day, which was something else he loved. But, if he wasn't in a suit, he preferred shorts, and as a writer, that was certainly a viable wardrobe.

Of the players remaining on the roster, he had eleven infielders—Roger Nauth and John Turner at catcher, Lamont Aronson and Dan Tripp at first, Julio Diaz and Greg Koras at second, Brian Dickson and Ryan Wolf at third, and Marty Dillingham, Robert Griffin, and Karlic Kulin at shortstop; seven outfielders—Pat Dillingham and Jacque Jennings in left, Alejandro Izquierdo and Preston Reilly in center, and Gary Gillander, Domingo Miles, and Tyrell Witham in right; and seven pitchers—Andre Borga, Ramon Diaz, Osamu Ishikawa, Troy Kane, Jimmy Kerrigan, Dane Olney, and Dean Rubin. Of these twenty-five players, seven would be cut after the scrimmage.

To help determine exactly who would be cut or not, Connor decided to start his borderline players. He would do his best to get every-one into the game, but certain people, like Lamont Aronson, the Dillingham twins, Roger Nauth, Alejandro Izquierdo, Osamu Ishikawa, Dane Olney, and Jimmy Kerrigan were all locks for the roster. That meant Connor wanted the other seventeen players to have a chance to show what they could do.

He put the preliminary lineup together, knowing full well that it was not anywhere near the best lineup, or even one that made sense. He did not put two speedy guys near the top, or a power hitter third or fourth. He put together the lineup the way he wanted to test the players in the pre-season, not in an attempt to out-strategize the opposing manager.

The only hole he had in the lineup was pitcher. With Osamu and Dane out of the mix for starter, that left Troy Kane—the senior with the fluorescent orange hair which was currently in dreadlocks—and Andre Borga, a junior. Ramon Diaz and Dean Rubin, both righties, were considered bullpen pitchers. Connor wanted all four to have a chance at pitching in the game, but which one actually started it was the question.

As for the rest of the lineup, Connor did find it difficult. Especially in the infield, there were several players Connor wanted to give considerable playing time to. The lineup he ended up with was Karlic Kulin batting leadoff and playing shortstop, Domingo Milas batting second and playing center field, Gary Gillander batting third and playing right field, John Turner batting cleanup and catching, Dan Tripp batting fifth and playing first, Brian Dickson batting sixth and playing third, Jacque Jennings batting seventh and playing left field, whoever Corey wanted as pitcher would bat eighth, and Greg Koras batting ninth and playing second base.

Of the group, Koras was probably the least likely to stick around. The depth of middle infielders was too much on this team. Koras had a great glove, but not the range of some of the others. He also had a great attitude, but his bat just wasn't enough to win him a spot on the team. He was a very solid defensive second baseman or utility man if the team did not already have three shortstops who could all start for him, and another second baseman in Julio Diaz who was faster and had more range than Koras.

Brian Dickson and Dan Tripp were also going to be given every opportunity to win roster spots today. Both could play third, though Dan was definitely better at first. If they won a roster spot, it would mean cutting Ryan Wolf free, which was a thought Connor was still entertaining. However, in terms of talent, Wolf clearly was the best of the three, and with Lamont Aronson firmly entrenched as the starting first baseman, the chance of Brian or Dan making the team were probably pretty slim.

The outfield was also full of question marks. Pat Dillingham, Alejandro Izquierdo, and Tyrell Witham were by far and away the starters on opening day. That left four players in contention for the backup outfielder roles. The three starters in this game, and Preston Reilly who had the best glove of the quartet but also no plate discipline at all, were vying for two slots. All four, Connor expected, would be in this game today.

As they were driving to Corinth, Corey decided to go with Troy Kane to start, and Connor wrote his name in. He then passed the lineup around to his coaching staff and explained that he wanted the backups and players on the cusp to be in the game today. Dom cautioned that they were probably going to get killed with this lineup, but Connor was fine with that. It wouldn't hurt to build a false sense of security in the minds of the teams in the league, either. He was here to test his players in a live-game situation. Winning or losing, today, was not a concern.

As the bus pulled into Corinth High School, Connor watched as they approached the field his father had been a fixture of for so long. This was the field he won State Tournaments at. This was the field where he became a legend and earned a spot in the High School Baseball Hall of Fame. It was only fitting that this was the field Connor's team would take on live-competition for the first time.

CHAPTER 24

"All right people, bring it in," Connor said after blowing his whistle. As the players came together, he continued. "We have all been working hard not only for the past couple of weeks, but since we first met back in January. The physical training, the batting cages, the captains' practices, and the spring training have all been a long journey to prepare us for what we have today: a game.

"Of course, this is just a scrimmage, and we won't have our real season opener until next week, but we have come further in a short amount of time than most people thought we could. We all heard the arguments: a new school, it takes time to build a system, and we're destined to fail. Well, the fact that we are here, we have succeeded. We have come together, and we will continue coming together.

"That said, this is also still part of the pre-season, and the lineup we're going with today is not the one we'll be using in the season. In fact, we're going with a lineup that will help us practice and improve, but whether you are starting, subbing in, or just watching today, each and every one of you will be rooting for your team and trying your best to win. Don't worry about the cuts that are coming between now and next week. Don't worry about being perfect tonight. Just play Eagle-ball, and we'll do fine."

Dom stepped forward. "Okay everybody, listen up." He then read through the lineup and batting order for the day.

Connor watched the players. Some were excited, some were disappointed. Only Ryan Wolf outright protested, saying that if they wanted to win, he should be in. Joe directed him to the bench and threatened him with laps for not being a team player.

As his team got ready to bat, Connor watched as Corinth took the field. They wore the same green and white uniforms that they had when his father had been here. It was familiar, very familiar.

The umpire put his mask on and shouted, "Play ball!"

"Okay, okay," Connor said, "Karlic, get us going."

Karlic Kulin stepped up to bat. His stance was angled, his left foot angled toward right field. The first pitch came in, and Karlic swung, hitting the ball down the right-field line, but foul. He swung and missed the second pitch, a changeup. As Connor watched, he thought that the next week would need more time with batting. By having everyone get accustomed to swinging because they only had ten pitches, he probably had made it so that his players swung at everything and had no plate discipline.

The third pitch was a ball, the pitcher trying to get Karlic to chase a bad pitch. The fourth pitch, Karlic hit down the middle, and sprinted as fast as he could to first base for the first hit of the season. The Farmington bench erupted into cheers as if Karlic had just got the winning hit at States. The enthusiasm brought a smile to Connor's lips.

Domingo Milas got up to bat, and took the first two pitches, both strikes. He then swung at a pitch in the dirt, striking out. Domingo threw his helmet in frustration, and Connor beckoned Dom to go talk to him.

Gary Gillander went to bat, and on the first pitch, hit a blooper over the head of the shortstop. Again, the bench was cheering as Karlic sped to third, sliding safely as Rickey signaled him to come in to the bag hard. Gary, one of the slower outfielders left on the roster, stopped at first without trying to go further than that.

John Turner stepped up to bat, and Connor watched the Corinth fielders closely. John was huge and looked every bit like a power hitter. The fact that he could not hit that well was tragic, but if the fielders all backed up seeing such an enormous batter coming to the plate, even a shallow pop-up could be a bases-clearing hit. Especially with the speed that Connor was thinking of having bat first through third on the final roster, a hit by John Turner could be huge in normal season games.

As he hoped, the Corinth coach signaled the outfielders to back up. The first pitch was up and outside, and John held off, though Connor saw that he had been severely tempted. The second pitch was right over the plate, and John swung and missed. Seeing his stance, Connor thought that Dom was right: even with the pre-season, John seemed unable to learn how to get into a stance properly.

John made contact with the third pitch, sending it just over the heads of the infield. The outfielders ran in as the infielders covered their positions. Karlic scored and Gary made his way to third. John tried to stretch his hit into a double, and was thrown out at second. Baserunning decisions notwithstanding, Connor had to be happy that his thought of John batting fourth was not entirely a bad one.

Dan Tripp then took the count full, fouling several balls off, and finally struck out. One run and three hits in the first wasn't bad, Connor thought. Overall, it was a great start to the game.

"Okay, you know your positions—play tight defense, back each other up, hit the cutoff man, and play sound fundamental baseball."

Troy Kane took the mound and began his warm-up tosses. Between him and Andre Borga, Kane probably had the inside track on the third pitcher in the rotation just because he was older. Borga could begin at JV and become a starter next season. Kane also was a cross between Osamu Ishikawa and Dane Olney. He had the confidence of Osamu, but his ability fell between them: his breaking balls were not as good as Dane's, and his hardballs were not as potent as Osamu's. Regardless, he was a good pitcher, though Corey had reported that he was very emotionally charged.

With every out, especially a strikeout or third out, Connor could see what she meant—Kane pumped his fist and began whooping out loud. When the ball was in play, he barked instructions to his fielders. When an error was made, he screamed at the offender. He was definitely emotionally charged, but through three innings, he allowed only a trio of base runners and gave up no runs. He definitely had skill.

In the fourth, Connor pulled Troy Kane and had Andre Borga go in. Borga was not as emotional or excitable as Troy. He went about his work without so much as a comment, his focus only on the batters and the situation at hand. Connor was impressed by his poise. Even when Borga walked a batter, had an error that got two on instead of getting him out of the inning, and then gave up a home run, he remained calm and composed. He did come back and struck out the next batter to get out of the inning.

By the fifth, Connor began making some roster moves. Karlic Kulin had two hits and a walk already, so when he went to leadoff the fifth, Connor had his nephew, Robert replace him. Robert hit a shot into left field for a double. With Domingo coming up, after striking out three times, Connor was ready to switch him with Preston Reilly, but decided to give Domingo one more chance. It proved to be well founded as Domingo hit a two-run in-the-park home run to tie the game.

Connor then pulled Gary Gillander for Preston, figuring that Domingo could move to right field and Preston could take center. Preston swung at the first three pitches he saw, hitting the third one as a slow dribbler to third. To Connor's delight, Preston beat it out.

John Turner was pulled for Roger Nauth. Roger took the first pitch, and Preston stole second. The second pitch was a ball, and Preston stole third. The third pitch was in the dirt, getting away from the catcher, and Preston flew home and scored, putting Farmington up by one. Roger put the ball in play, but was beat at first by half a step.

As the fielders went to take their positions, Connor made a few more changes. Julio Diaz replaced Greg Koras, while his brother, Ramon Diaz came in to pitch. Randy Wolf also came in to play third, replacing Brian Dickson, who had made a pair of fielding errors but also had a couple of hits on the day. He also pulled Jacque Jennings in left field for Tyrell Witham.

That left only the Dillingham twins, Lamont Aronson, and Alejandro Izquierdo as position players not to get into the game. Connor would try to get them at least an at bat if possible, but he really wanted to see the others play.

With Ramon Diaz taking the mound, Dean Rubin and Jimmy Kerrigan were the lone bullpen pitchers remaining. Connor could always put Osamu Ishikawa or Dane Olney into the game, but he had no intention of doing so. There were four innings to go, and three pitchers, including Ramon, ready to pitch.

Ramon gave up a couple of hits, but Corinth did not score. When Ryan Wolf got up to bat, he belted a home run over the left field fence. He made an exaggerated home run trot, and when he got back to the dugout, Connor heard him say, "See what happens when you let me play?" The fact that Wolf made two solid plays defensively saving a run from scoring made the decision all the harder. Wolf was a great player with a horrible attitude.

Dean Rubin pitched an inning where Farmington's defense must have forgotten how to play. Everyone struggled in the field, with throws going wild, trying to catch advancing runners that they could never catch and allowing other base runners to advance, and bobbling more than one ball. Since the field had players Connor saw as potential starters, it upset him a great deal to watch the collapse. When the inning was over, they went from winning to trailing by seven runs.

The seven-run-deficit was how it ended. Jimmy pitched the eighth, and since Corinth was winning, they did not bat in the ninth. The Farmington bats also quieted down, with strikeouts or grounders right to infielders for easy outs. As the players shook hands with their opponents, Connor spoke with the Corinth coach and thanked him for the game.

The loss was not upsetting. He had not really expected to come to Corinth and win by putting a group of backups and cusp players into the game. In fact, there had been a lot of positive signs that he took away from the game. Pitching was better than expected for the most part, and other than patience at the plate, his team could definitely hit and run. The late-game defense was troubling, especially since most of the backups were out of the game by then, but they would work on that. Overall, it was a good experience.

The final cuts, however, just became even more difficult; nobody really played themselves out of contention for a roster spot. Sure, there were things like the three strikeouts by Domingo Milas, but he also came through with a big game-tying hit and also preformed adequately defensively. The final seven cuts were going to be difficult ones.

CHAPTER 25

Without any of the seven cuts made by the end of the double-session on the Saturday before the season began, Connor instructed his staff to stay behind after practice to go over each and every player until a final decision was made. He needed to give the final uniform orders to Kenneth Carlson if they wanted uniforms for opening day, and he had every intention of posting the final roster in the locker room on Monday morning so that the team would know who belonged where.

They wheeled a blackboard into the office and Connor drew a baseball diamond. On the side, he wrote down the name of each player still on the roster based on their position. Once he was done, he turned around and looked at his staff. "Everyone ready?"

"Let's do it," Dom said.

"How about we begin with pitchers?" Connor suggested. "There are five roster spots for pitchers. Three starters and two relievers. Corey?"

"Osamu Ishikawa and Dane Olney for the first two rotation spots, and Jimmy Kerrigan as closer," Corey said.

Connor wrote them onto the board in the location of the pitcher's mound. "Who is your final starter?"

"Between Troy Kane and Andre Borga, I'll go with Troy," Corey said. "He's older, a bit better, and a lefty."

Connor paused. "That's three lefties."

"Isn't it wonderful?" Corey said, knowing that there were far more right-handed pitching in the league than left.

"Does everyone agree?" Connor asked.

"Sure," Joe shrugged. "Let Andre play at JV this year. He'll be the ace there, and then come up to replace Troy when he graduates."

"Sounds good," Connor said, adding Troy's name to the board with the rest of the pitchers. "That leaves one bullpen pitcher."

"You have to go with Dean Rubin," Rickey said. "He's a junior, and his bad inning in the scrimmage was more for fielding than pitching."

"I don't know," Corey winced. "Dean is good, I'll give him that. But I think Ramon is better."

"He's a freshman," pointed out Joe.

"He is," Corey agreed. "But his stuff is just as good as Dean's, and we'll have him for four years. He's ready for varsity."

"That puts two freshman in the bullpen," added Dom.

"I know," Corey said. "But we're looking for the best team, not just the oldest one, right?"

"Right," Connor agreed. "Ramon it is."

"Two freshman, two sophomores, and a senior," whistled Dom. "You cut a lot of seniors over the past week. That's gutsy."

"These are the best," Corey said, certain she was right.

"But it's not like the cut seniors are going to go play JV," Dom said. "You cut a senior, they're gone. You send a pair of freshmen down, they come back next year with more experience."

"Playing against lesser talent," Corey said. "These five are good-to-go. These five will help us win now, and since four of them will be here for at least the next three years, I'd be willing to bet we'll have a decent rotation for at least that long."

"I'm sold," Joe said.

"Me too," Connor agreed, writing Ramon's name in with the pitchers, finishing the position off. "How about we fill in the guaranteed players next?"

"I'm fine with that," Rickey said.

"Someone stop me the moment you disagree," Connor said as he began writing. He put Lamont Aronson at first, Marty Dillingham at shortstop, Pat Dillingham in left field, Alejandro Izquierdo in center field, and Tyrell Witham in right field. "So far so good?"

"No objections yet," Rickey said.

"I'm looking at keeping both John Turner and Roger Nauth," Connor said, indicating the catchers.

"That freshman you sent down on Wednesday, Jeremy Oulevay, he can out-hit both of those guys," Dom said. "Easily."

"I know," Connor said. "And you can make the same case as we did with the relief pitchers, but Jeremy can be the starter in JV and play every day. I like the attitude and effort I saw from Roger, and I've found John to be one of the most loyal and ardent supporters of the team. His ceiling is also huge with his potential if he can begin hitting like he should."

"Yeah, but for now, both of those guys give us a fairly consistent out in the lineup," protested Dom.

"Roger already has learned how to call a game," Corey interjected. "Jeremy will learn, but right now he is just catching what people throw, not thinking about what he's doing."

"That doesn't matter," argued Dom. "You and Connor will be calling the gameplan from the bench. Jeremy doesn't need to be someone who can figure out what to throw. He just needs to be someone who can turn his head to the side, see the signal, and then relay it. Besides, we all know Connor: he may talk about defense, but in the end, he's an offensive-minded coach. Jeremy will give better offense."

"He's right," Joe agreed. "You could have the best player on the team go 0-for-3, and then Connor takes him out. We may get a hit, but defense dips a bit in late innings."

"That's softball, not baseball," Connor said. "Softball is all about hitting. That's why our averages were well-over .500, and some in the .600 range. If someone didn't hit in softball, they were no good to us. In baseball, you don't hit nearly as much, and defense becomes even more important, especially late in games."

"We'll see," Joe said, grinning knowingly.

"Move on," Rickey said, ending the debate. "They're the only catchers still in camp, and two catchers make the team: they're locks."

"Fair enough," Connor said, writing the two names on the board. "We need two utility outfielders. I think after what we saw of Preston Reilly on base in the scrimmage that he's earned one of the spots. Anyone else?"

"That *was* impressive," Joe said. "He's got my vote."

"He can field, too," Rickey said. "I like him."

"I'd like him better if he didn't swing at everything," Dom shrugged. "But when he connects, he connects."

Connor wrote Preston's name in the outfield under Alejandro's as a utility fielder. "That leaves one more spot between Gary Gillander, Jacque Jennings, and Domingo Milas."

"Not Jacque," Rickey said.

"Why not?" Connor asked. "He's probably the best defensively of that group."

"I agree," Rickey said. "But he's young and should be playing every day. When Pat graduates next year, Jacque is probably our starting left fielder. But if he sits on the bench and doesn't play this year, then he might not be as good next season. It happens."

Connor knew that to be true. He had decided to play volleyball instead of baseball in high school. The decision was more because his cousin was coaching the team and he did not want people to think he made the roster because of a family connection. In volleyball though, he made varsity in his sophomore year, and by the time the seniors graduated, a lot of the JV players were suddenly starting over him. It was great being on varsity before his peers, but they all continued playing every day and meshing together as a team whereas he sat on the bench and took stats for his coach.

"Jacque goes to JV," Connor said. "I agree with your argument."

"Whoa, wait a second," Dom said. "He's the best of the group, he should be here."

"Rickey is right about being a backup and wasting his talent. Let him play every day and then come back next season as a starter," Connor said. "So between Gary and Domingo, who do we like?"

"Gary is more consistent," Dom said. "He's a good batter. Not with power, not flashy, not speed, just consistent."

"His fielding is about the same," Rickey said. "He knows what he has to do and he does it. Other guys are faster, have better arms, and are more aggressive, but he knows what he needs to do and does it."

"I would like a bit more," Joe said. "If he were starting, then that's all great. But what will his role be? A defensive replacement? Certainly not over any of the three starters we have in the outfield. A better bat? Again, I wouldn't put him in over those three. How about pinch running? He's one of the slower outfielders we have. Consistent, but as a backup, I don't see much value."

"You see more in Domingo?" asked Rickey, almost laughing.

"I do," Joe said. "Domingo is faster. His glove may not be as good, but his range is better. He could be a pinch runner, and he may not hit consistently, but when he does, it's usually a big hit."

"Domingo's a junior, Gary is a sophomore," shrugged Corey. "We could go with seniority. Plus, it's the same argument as with Jacque. Let Gary play everyday."

"Not quite," Connor said. "Tyrell is also a sophomore, not a senior like Pat, so sending him to JV for a year doesn't mean we have a roster spot for him. Besides, Tyrell's bat, speed, and range are all better than Gary's, but we might be able to use Gary and Tyrell in a platoon since Tyrell seems to overrun some routine plays and make little mental mistakes."

"So you want Gary?" Rickey asked.

"I'm just making a comment," Connor said.

"Then let Gary play every day at JV. With some polish, he could be a starter. Domingo never will be. He'll always be a fifth outfielder and backup. So let him fill his role," Rickey suggested. "Besides, if we decide that either Domingo or Tyrell aren't doing what we expected, we can bring Gary up then."

"Anyone else?" Connor asked.

"Yeah, fine," Dom said.

Connor wrote Domingo's name under Tyrell's in right field. "That's fourteen out of eighteen. Four more—all infielders—to go."

"Put Ryan Wolf down," Dom said. "You know he's a lock."

"With his attitude?" scoffed Joe. "Dump him."

"Okay, what would the lineup look like with him?" asked Connor.

"Wolf at third, Marty Dillingham at short, and either your nephew Robert or Karlic at second."

Connor saw Corey, Joe, and Rickey nodding that they agreed. "What if we didn't take Wolf?"

"That's crazy talk," Dom said.

"Just do it," Connor prompted.

"Marty would shift to third, Robert would go to short, and Karlic would play second," Rickey said. "The defense wouldn't be quite as good, but it would get all three of our top middle infielders into the game."

"Defense wouldn't be as good, and offense would suffer too," Dom added. "Wolf gives us another big bat. That drives in runs."

"It's not his skills on the field, but his attitude," Joe argued.

"We got rid of Billy Knight because of his attitude," reminded Corey. "Do we want Ryan Wolf on this team?"

"You may not want him, but we may just need him," Dom said. "Without him, the defense is fine, but the offense is just so-so. But, have Wolf and Aronson in the same lineup, and I'd put our lineup up against any team in this league."

"I want him on a tight leash," Connor said.

"We're keeping him?" Dom asked.

"Reluctantly," Connor said as he wrote Ryan Wolf's name at third. "So, based on the prior suggestion, that puts Karlic and Robert onto the roster as well? Second base and utility infielder?"

"They belong there," Rickey said.

"They do," Dom agreed.

Connor wrote Karlic's name at second and Robert's under Marty's. "That leaves one slot open, and four players left. Dan Tripp at first,

Julio Diaz and Greg Koras at second, and Brian Dickson at third."

"Lose Koras and Dickson," Rickey said.

"Why?" asked Connor.

"Koras is dependable, but there are players who are better. He'd never see playing time unless there were injuries. As for Dickson, he's got a nice bat, but his defense is atrocious," explained Rickey.

"A nice bat could be a good pinch hitter late in a game though," Dom said.

"But if Connor is really going with speed and defense over offense, having a bat replace a defender—a defensive-downgrade—might not be the best option," said Joe.

"But a pinch hitter could win the game," Dom countered. "I'd rather his bat than Koras."

"Everyone agrees on Koras?" Connor asked.

"I agree," Corey said.

"Okay, Koras is down—that leaves three for the last spot," Connor said.

"We have to go with Tripp," Rickey said. "A backup for Aronson."

"You telling me nobody could backup first base if Lamont needed time off?" Dom scoffed.

"Since Ryan Wolf is on the team, he can play first," Connor said. "We can also have one of our catchers move over to first if needed."

"I guess," Rickey said.

"Who is the best defensive player of the group?" asked Connor.

"Julio Diaz, no doubt," Rickey said.

"Who is the fastest?" Connor asked.

"Julio Diaz," Joe said.

"Who has the best bat?" Connor asked.

"Brian Dickson," Dom said. "But Diaz did better than Koras with the bat, and also shows good ability with bunting. He is third on our list for hitting though."

"If we go with Julio, at least he and Ramon can play together," Corey said. "It would be pretty sad if the freshman pitcher made the team and the older sophomore brother was in JV."

"It may be sad, but that's not a concern," Connor said. "Who would be best for the final spot is all I care about."

The debate for the final spot went back and forth. Rather than going solely on opinion, Connor pulled out the scouting reports for the past couple of weeks and went over the three finalists with his staff. In every speed and defensive category, Diaz was well ahead of the other two. His bat was definitely his downside, whereas the others could be a potent pinch-hit, but Diaz gave them a solid defensive replacement, pinch runner, and potential sacrifice bunt when needed. In the end, the final spot was given to Diaz.

The roster was full of youth, which Connor knew both Dom and Rickey were concerned about. Of the eighteen players on the team, they had six seniors, five juniors, four sophomores, and three freshman. Four of the freshman and sophomores were being counted upon for major rolls on the team. It would be a lot of pressure, but Connor was confident that he and his staff had made the right decisions.

Connor typed out the roster, putting the players in alphabetical order, and taped it to the locker room door before calling it a night. For better or worse, they now had their team. There were two more practices before opening day, and that meant two days for the team to become accustomed to practicing in the positions and lineups they will be staying in for much of the season. His team was fast, it had solid defense, incredible range, and a little taste of power, too. Connor liked it, and looked forward for the real season to begin.

CHAPTER 26

For years, Connor and his sister, Lauren got together to have break-fast. Their location changed from time to time, going from small diners to local restaurants, even to chains that had some decent breakfasts they were in the mood for, but overall, they typically met anywhere from once a week to once a month. The only time that tradition really stopped was shortly after Connor and Marina met, when Hobbes, Connor's roommate at the time, moved closer to work in Boston and Connor moved in with Marina near the Cape, in Marion. With the added commute, Connor and Lauren gave up their morning rituals.

After Connor and Marina moved again, choosing a location that was about halfway between where he had been and where they were then, he tried to begin their breakfast mornings again. They were no longer as consistent as they had been before—sometimes going a month or more without getting together—but they did still try, and it was something Connor truly enjoyed and looked forward to.

When Connor was a child, he had spent much of his time visiting Lauren in the hospital during her cancer-treatments. With scares and constant monitoring of her condition throughout her life, Connor took the role of the protective little brother, who did his best to make her laugh and enjoy herself. In the times when there were test-results to worry about, this was more important than ever. For the rest of the time, it was an easy role for Connor to maintain, and he lived by it.

He recalled one day being at work and receiving the call that her cancer was back. It was the first time it had returned since Lauren had beat it as a child. Connor stared at his desk phone for a good fifteen minutes, ignoring the constant ringing phones and chatter of the financial sector, and then stood up to tell his boss, in no short terms, that he was leaving. He did not give a reason or explanation, just in a very solemn voice said he had to go, and then was gone.

It took him nearly forty-five minutes to get back to his parents' house, where he walked out back and saw both sisters and his mother sitting in chairs and watching his nieces and nephews by the pool. The kids were sitting around a table at the pool, all quiet and deflated, not even talking as they ate. Connor's father was the only one seeming to be doing much, bringing food out and seeing if anyone needed anything. The sight broke Connor's heart.

He sincerely believed that positive feelings and well-wishes could overcome hardships. If someone gave in to their disease, surrendered to it, then they were lost. If they fought, continued the struggle, then they could overcome anything. It went along with his second philosophy: laughter was the cure to all evils.

With this in mind, Connor took a deep breath before announcing that he was there, and all sadness and fear was gone—or if not gone, at least masked. As "The Uncle" began playing with the kids, getting them to laugh, joke, run around, throw each other into the pool, and have a good time, Connor caught an occasional glance of his sisters and mother, smiling and laughing as well.

In the grand scheme of things, Connor did not know whether or not he helped that day. But the kids all had a good time, forgetting for the moment what was happening. Rather than them going home and facing reality, when it was time to go, Connor took them all to the movies and they saw *Small Soldiers*.

When Connor had dropped them off that night, his mother told him that he had really helped. That the mood had been lifted, and that even Lauren was enjoying herself in light of her diagnosis. She miraculously beat that round of cancer, too.

On this morning, Lauren had called Connor and asked him if he could squeeze a breakfast in. Connor rearranged his schedule to accommodate, and met with his sister in Milford, at the small restaurant that they had been frequenting the past few times. As usually, Connor ordered a French toast breakfast that came with bacon and eggs, along with a hot chocolate, and Lauren ordered a mushroom and ham omelet, a cinnamon bun to fulfill her craving for something sweet, and an orange juice.

The two had a little small talk while they waited for the food, discussing things going on with the family, the Red Sox, Connor's books, and plans for a summer get-together. When there was a lull, Lauren looked Connor directly into the eyes, and said, "Well Brother, how is my son doing?"

"Jimmy? Fine," Connor said. "He's our closer."

"I know that," Lauren said, and she would. One thing Connor always marveled at with Lauren was the fact that every day when the kids got home from school, the first thing they did was sit down with her and talk about their days. If there was an incident with another student, they told her. When Chrissie had a crush, she talked about it. They discussed their classes, all of their assignments, and anything else that they needed to do or worry about. Connor had been there a couple of times when the kids got home, and could not believe how much the kids were talking about their personal lives with their mother. But they all got along phenomenally, rarely had the problems Connor would associate with most teens and parents, and they all enjoyed their daily talks. "But he transferred to your school to play ball with you and to honor Dad. Is he in over his head, or is he okay?"

"He's doing great," Connor said. "Regardless of him being my nephew, and transferring to Farmington, if he did not belong on the team, he wouldn't be there. Corey had about 95% of the decision in terms of pitching, and she wanted Jimmy."

Lauren took it all in and nodded. "Thank you," she said. "Well, Brother, I have to tell you, this schedule of yours doesn't make me too happy."

"Oh?" Connor replied, not very pleased with how far they would be traveling himself.

"Twelve away games, and going all over the place," Lauren said. "The Cape Wednesday, then all the way out to Mondale on Monday? I need a map just to figure out where these places are, and will probably still get lost going to the games."

"You're coming to the games?" Connor asked, shocked for a moment, but then realizing that he shouldn't be.

"Cindy and I are planning on driving together," Lauren said. "Driving an hour and a half Wednesday in hopes that we're winning so my son can pitch for one inning. Will we be winning?"

"We have a good team," Connor said. "I really like it. Of course, don't let Jimmy know I said so. We are a first-year team going up against schools who have been playing together and had programs for years. Little league all the way up to varsity. Those kids know each other, know how to play with each other, and have won or lost with each other. Our team is still trying to remember each other's names."

"Seriously?"

"An exaggeration," Connor shrugged. "But not too far off. The team is young though, so even if we don't do that good this year, by the time Jimmy is a Junior or Senior, I'd say we have a very good chance of at least making the playoffs if not going to States."

"What about this year?"

"The talent is there," Connor said. "The coaching determination is there. The effort for the players who made it is there. It will all come down to how well the team meshes together, and both how much they think they can do it, and how much they want it. Going up against some of the schools on our schedule can be pretty intimidating. If our guys think that they'll lose, they will. I don't care how talented they are."

"Do you see that when you work with them?" asked Lauren.

"I see a group of guys who started with nothing and have worked harder than any other school and team in this state," Connor said. "If they can pull together, and keep their spirits up, the sky is the limit."

"Is Jimmy going to remain a captain?"

"A good question," Connor said. "We just got the final roster put together Saturday night. I'll meet with the other coaches again after practice and name the official captains prior to the game." Connor paused, and watched his sister closely. "Does he want to be a captain?"

"He's enjoyed it," Lauren said. "Says it makes him more like his Uncle."

"Heh," Connor grinned. "Flattery will get you nowhere."

Lauren shrugged. "Brother, I don't have the slightest inkling about what you're talking about."

"Sure you don't," Connor sarcastically replied.

"Seriously though, good luck this season."

Luck was not necessarily what they needed. They needed chemistry. They needed confidence. Connor saw it, saw the potential, but was afraid that it would be just outside of their grasp. On Wednesday, on opening day, he would do his best to see them through a cloud of obscurity and uncertainty, and guide them to success.

CHAPTER 27

There is nothing in the world like waiting until the last minute and cutting it close. All his life, Connor was someone who liked to plan things in advance. He liked to consider himself flexible, and willing to be spontaneous if he had to be, but deep down, in reality, he was the furthest from a spur-of-the-moment kind of guy. He planned everything, well in advance. Whether it was a book he was writing, vacations, business, or even time set aside to do something like watch a movie or play a video game, he adhered to the schedule. The biggest thing that got him upset in life, the thing that made his heart pound and his temper waiver, was when things interrupted his plans.

Not all the time, but often enough. He scheduled things tight, but allowed for some leeway. However, if he had agreed to meet someone at 3:00, and allocated 45 minutes to get there, when it was really only a 30 minute trip, and hit traffic, his mood became most foul. His eyes would glance at the clock every few seconds, his imagination swirling into the abyss of being late for a meeting or appointment. Usually, he did arrive on time, his leeway sufficient; but the times he was late, he truly beat himself up over it.

The same was true with most things in his life. He could manage fifteen projects more quickly and efficiently than someone else could handle a mere fraction of that. At SJC, that was one of his attributes that helped him rise through the ranks. Connor had the ability to prioritize, rearrange his schedule to accommodate a larger workflow, and get it done. He never lost his cool or got frustrated. One task or fifteen, he faced it with equal fervor and determination. But, when the clock began to tick closer to a deadline, if he was not done, he was in overdrive trying to beat the clock.

The miracle of his clock-dilemma was the fact that he was ultra-organized, efficient, productive, and focused. In work, in only the rarest of occasions did he find himself racing against the clock. In his personal life as well, he did his best to do things well before they were due to make sure it was not a problem. His books, for instance, were written three years in advance of their release to the general trade. There was no deadline to worry about when you were three years ahead.

But times did present themselves—where the clock seemed to pound and every second was like an eternity, and at the same time, moving like quicksilver—when Connor was not done. He knew, deep down, that even if he was late for something, usually people would understand, but that did not stop him from watching the clock and cringing as time was running out.

On the morning of Tuesday, April 3rd, Connor was watching the clock with great desperation. He and his coaching staff had finalized the roster, and on Monday after practice, announced the official team captains as Roger Nauth as well as Connor's two nephews, turning their "interim" title into official team captains. They also determined the starting lineup for Wednesday's game, which was particularly difficult in determining who would start between Robert Griffin and Karlic Kulin at second base. Both boys were shortstops, but Marty Dillingham was the clear starter there. Karlic had the ability to placement hit, which was incredible, but Robert had a little more pop to his bat, and also better defense. In the end, Robert got the opening day nod—barely.

But the thing that was worrying Connor wasn't the captains, the upcoming game, or the lineup, but the uniforms. He had spoken with Kenneth Carlson nearly a dozen times since Monday, and thus far, the uniforms were not ready. With the contribution of Satoshi Ishikawa, every player was receiving a fitted hat, two shirts, two pants, two pairs of socks, and even matching cleats. The only thing the players needed to provide themselves were their athletic cups, gloves, and batting gloves. Each player was also getting a white mock turtleneck with the name

"Farmington" on the collar, and a blue team jacket. Neither of these were required parts of the uniform, but Ishikawa felt that they would look good for the players, so everyone was able to get them.

During Connor's last call with Kenneth, the shirts were being finished as they spoke. However, Kenneth still hadn't been sure that he could have them to Connor before the school day was over, which meant the team might get their uniforms on the bus to the Cape for the game. He wanted every player to have their full uniforms before leaving tonight.

They already had portions of their uniforms. For the scrimmage, Connor had picked up pants, one pair of socks, a hat, and the practice jerseys for each player. If worse came to worse, they could wear those for opening day, but Connor wanted everything to be perfect, and that included their actual uniforms.

To make matters worse, he received a call from Governor Shilalie, who indicated that he was planning to make the trip to see the team play their first official game. Along with the Governor, Connor expected a contingent of both sports and political reporters to cover the story. The last thing he wanted was for the story to be covered and the Governor's team looking shoddy with cheap t-shirts and without official uniforms.

Glancing at the clock again, Connor had nearly two hours before practice. With two hours, he could still get to Custom Sports, pick up the uniforms, and get back in time. If only the phone would ring. And just like that, it did.

"Connor Blake," Connor said.

"Connor, good news," came the reply, one Connor recognized instantly as Kenneth Carlson. "The uniforms are all done."

"They're done?" Connor asked, making sure he heard correctly.

"Done," Kenneth repeated. "I'll have everything boxed and ready to go within fifteen minutes."

"I'm on my way," Connor replied, hanging up the phone and exhaling in relief.

Connor left the gym, putting a note on his office door in case anyone was looking for him, and made his way to his truck in the parking lot. As the truck roared to life, Connor glanced at the clock. There was plenty of time. Even if he hit traffic, he would be back about twenty minutes before practice began, and, he would have the uniforms with him.

The uniforms were not only for the varsity team, but for the JV as well. Bob Sullivan had taken the latest cuts from the varsity roster and gave them all spots on the team, and also narrowed his roster down to the best twenty-five players. They were mostly freshman and sophomores, giving a younger group some time to develop and grow together.

Putting his truck in reverse, Connor headed out. Everything was coming together. The final practice today, and then Opening Day tomorrow. It was finally time to play a game, and coach as his father had before him.

CHAPTER 28

In what had to be the biggest mishap of mishaps, Connor led his team out to the school bus for the trip to the Cape for their game against Dennis-Yarmouth, and found Andre, the janitor sitting in the driver's seat. Connor made a quick call to Principal Daniels, and she calmly told him that the school bus drivers were all taking the students home to their various locations around the state, and that Andre was to be their team's official driver.

Connor accepted the news and handed Andre an extra non-fitted baseball hat that he had ordered in case anyone lost theirs or needed a new one. Andre put it on with pride, and pulled out of the parking lot. He was friendly and sociable, but as they would learn throughout the season, he did not necessarily know where any of the schools they were driving to were located. They arrived at their opponent's field five minutes before game time, after going around a pair of rotaries several times before choosing the right way, and found the bus mobbed by parents, reporters, and even other students who had beat them there by driving themselves.

Connor led the team off of the bus, rather surprised by the turnout. He knew with Governor Shilalie in attendance that there would be reporters covering the story and game, but he saw dozens of people with tape recorders, cameras, and even television crews. He also saw half a dozen Japanese reporters, talking to none other than Satoshi Ishikawa, and running over to the bus the moment that Osamu stepped down, bombarding him with questions about fulfilling his dreams by playing ball in America.

As they made their way to the visitors' bench, Connor saw Lauren and Cindy in the bleachers, ready for the game. They were not alone, as Connor recognized quite a few students and saw people waving to his players—people who he assumed were their parents. It was a tremendous turnout, especially since they had to travel so far.

Taking in all of the attention, Connor glanced at his players. Some seemed mesmerized by all of the attention. Others were staring at the players practicing on the field, and looking quite anxious. Connor followed their gaze. Each player on the field looked like a football linebacker more than a baseball player. If he was willing to make a quick guess based on looks alone, Dennis-Yarmouth featured a strong and powerful lineup.

The umpire walked over, pointing at his watch. "I'm sorry, Coach, but we need to get started."

"Can we have a few minutes to warm up?" asked Connor.

"A few minutes, but no fielding or batting practice," he said, checking his watch again.

Connor turned and pointed at Joe, who began calling out to the players: "Okay everyone, start warming up and playing toss. The game is going to start in a few minutes."

Corey frowned, and walked over to Connor. "Osamu needs ten to fifteen minutes to get ready."

"We bat first, so get him throwing now and keep him at it until we have to take the field," Connor said.

Corey beckoned Roger Nauth to play catch for Osamu, and after they stretched, the two began with short toss and then gradually took a few steps back until they were at the appropriate distance. Corey watched as Osamu began throwing some light pitches.

When Connor saw the umpire heading his way again, he waived that they were ready. "Okay everyone, bring it in."

Joe, Dom, and Rickey all shouted for the players to bring it in, and hustled the few stragglers along. Before Connor began speaking to the team, he handed the lineup to Dom who went over to exchange lineups with the other team's coach.

"Okay everyone," Connor said. "Opening day is finally here. The day we've worked so hard for, prepared so long for. Today is the day we go out and show not only this team that we're not to be overlooked, but the entire state.

"Ignore the circus that you see around you—it's a distraction. We knew that playing on this team was going to bring some definite publicity with it, but we have to play our game and not worry about how we look on camera. Play hard, do your best, and everything else will fall where it supposed to."

Connor saw Alejandro and Julio whispering to themselves. "Alejandro, Julio, what is it?"

"They're big, Coach," Alejandro said.

"Real big," Julio agreed.

"That they are," Connor said. "But let me tell you a little something about Dennis-Yarmouth. When I was in high school, we were a Division Three football team. Every year we played a Division One school, and in my freshman year, that school was Dennis-Yarmouth. Their team was huge. Their band-members alone were the size of our football team. Their side of the field had standing-room only.

"But you know what I remember most about that day?" Connor asked, rhetorically. "I remember the Panthers winning forty-something to three. It doesn't matter how big they are, or how formidable they look. This is a game, and when it comes to game time, anything can happen.

"This team, our team, the Eagles are fast, have solid defense, can hit consistently, and are ready to show everyone just what we can do. I don't care how big or strong they are, we're the Eagles, and we're going to win!"

Connor saw the cheers of his players, and the enthusiasm. The fear of playing a bigger and stronger team may still be there, but it was buried beneath confidence. They could play against any team, and they would always have a chance to win. The Eagles were ready for the season, and it was time to prove that.

"Okay, we have to make this quick since we were late, but the lineup shouldn't have too many surprises to begin with," Connor said, handing a folded piece of paper with the lineup on it to Rickey.

"Listen up, I'm only saying this once," Rickey said. "Batting leadoff and playing left field—Pat Dillingham; batting second and playing right field—Tyrell Witham; batting third and playing center field—Alejandro Izquierdo; batting cleanup and catching—John Turner."

"What?" growled Ryan Wolf. "Turner can't hit."

"Pipe down," Joe said, glaring at Ryan.

"Batting fifth and playing first base—Lamont Aronson," Rickey continued, glancing up and seeing Ryan Wolf scowl at the fact his name still wasn't called. "Batting sixth and playing second base—Robert Griffin; batting seventh and pitching— Osamu Ishikawa; batting eighth and playing third base—Ryan Wolf."

"Eighth?" shouted Wolf. "I should be third or fourth!"

Connor grabbed Ryan by the shirt and pulled him away from the team. "Sit down and shut up," he said. "You are batting eighth because I want you to bat eighth. If you don't like it, you can always sit on the bench and I'll have Karlic go in."

"Why eighth?" protested Ryan. "If you want to win, you need me near the top driving in runs."

"It's called strategy," Connor said. "I want you driving in runs at the bottom of the order. Now do you have a problem with that?"

Every inch of his face and demeanor was screaming yes, but Ryan replied, "No Coach. No problem."

"Then go get ready for the game," Connor said. It was his father's strategy, putting a power hitter eighth so that if the pitcher eases up at all, you can capitalize on it by having one of your best hitters at the bottom. He knew that it probably meant only three or four at bats instead of four or five, but having a power hitter eighth meant more runs that could be driven in that may not have scored otherwise. He liked his father's strategy, and he would follow it. If Ryan Wolf couldn't handle it, Connor would find someone else who could.

Batting behind Ryan was Marty Dillingham, who had speed and consistency like his brother. If Ryan drove everyone in, then Marty acted like the new leadoff batter heading right into the top of the order. That was another strategy, and why his pitcher was batting seventh instead of ninth, like most teams did.

"Play ball!" the umpire shouted. The time for creating strategies and establishing plans was done. It was game time.

❖   ❖   ❖   ❖   ❖

Pat Dillingham put on his blue helmet with the red "F" on the front and headed up to bat. Connor liked Pat in the leadoff role. He was one of, if not the most patient batter on the team. Pat never swung until there was at least a strike on him, and even after that, he had tremendous judgment of the strike zone. Add in his speed and ability to both outrun infield hits and to then steal bases, he was the ideal pick for the top of the order.

Pat's way of watching pitches was somewhat unique, as well. Every pitch that was an obvious ball, Pat shifted his stance and body, bringing his head down to watch the pitch. By doing so, there was no way he could possibly recover and swing at the ball if he decided it was a strike after all, but it was his little mental crutch to make sure he watched the ball and kept his bat on his shoulder.

The first pitch of the official season was a ball, with Pat lowering his body and watching it. The second pitch was up near Pat's head, sending him dropping to the ground. Baseball was full of messages, and even two pitches into the game, that was the pitcher's way of telling Pat that he did not like the batter mocking him by watching a pitch the way he had.

Pat stood up and dusted himself off, and then got back into the batters box. The next pitch was right over the plate for a strike, a perfect pitch, and Pat just let it go.

"All right, you've seen it now," Dom shouted. "Be a hitter now, be a hitter."

Pat took the fourth pitch, shifting his body and watching just as he had with the first one, and got a called ball three. With the next pitch, he twirled his bat to the side and began jogging down the first baseline with the walk before the umpire even called the pitch, certain that the pitch was not a strike.

Connor and Dom, standing side by side, exchanged a glance. "That's not going to make him very many friends with the umpires," Connor said.

"Some of those close pitches might get called the next time around," Dom agreed.

Joe, the first-base coach, spoke with Pat. Dom signaled Rickey at third, who then sent the sign for the play to Tyrell Witham at the plate. The entire set of signals was only a few seconds long, instructing Tyrell to take the first pitch and try to let Pat steal.

Pat walked a few feet from first, nonchalantly, and watched the pitcher. As the pitcher got set, he took another stride, heading toward second. As the pitcher took his foot off of the rubber and began twisting around, Joe shouted on the top of his lungs, "Back!"

Pat dove back toward the first base bag, sliding head-first into it. The pick-off attempt was low, and the first baseman misplayed it, with the ball drilling Pat in the ribs. Pat shrieked in pain, but never took his hand from the bag.

Joe called for time when the first baseman recovered the ball, and the umpire immediately granted it. He then crouched down and spoke to Pat, then began gently touching his side. Pat winced as he stood up, but got up and waived Joe off. Joe then waived to Connor to let him know that Pat was staying in the game.

With the next pitch, Pat was off and running toward second. He did not seem quite as swift as he usually was, but still managed to slide in safely before the tag. Connor breathed a sigh of relief.

"Watch him closely," Connor said to Dom. "We might need to take him out today if he's hurt."

"He's tough," Dom said, shrugging. "But I'll watch."

Tyrell laid down a bunt, and was thrown out at first, but Pat managed to make it to third safely on the sacrifice. That brought up Alejandro Izquierdo, one player who Connor thought the sky was the limit for. Alejandro swung at the first pitch, sending a bullet back up the middle and into the outfield. Pat scored easily on the play from third. Alejandro ran full speed down to first, and though Joe was signaling him to stop, he went through the sign, sprinted for second, and slid in just under the tag.

"Ballsy," Dom said.

"He ignored Joe," Connor replied.

"People only listen to the first-base coach when they are standing at first," Dom said. "He probably didn't even see or hear him. It's not like third when you are looking right at the coach."

"I guess," Connor said, still not pleased that Joe had been ignored.

As John Turner stepped up to the plate, Connor was glad to see that the outfielders, just like in the scrimmage, took a few steps back. John struck out, but at least the fielders reacted the way Connor wanted them to. Lamont Aronson came up, and they stayed back for him since he was also big. For Aronson, it turned out to be perfect positioning since he sent a ball all the way to the fence for an out.

"Not bad, not bad," Connor said, thinking that a run was a good start, though if Pat were hurt and lost for any significant amount of time, that one run would prove to be far less significant. Connor then glanced at Corey who was monitoring Osamu Ishikawa warming up.

She said something to Osamu, and he began making his way to the mound. Roger Nauth went with him, playing catcher until John Turner finished getting his gear on. John had been very specific about his catching equipment, asking for a hockey-style helmet that was seen more often in professional baseball instead of the traditional catchers masks. He offered to pay the difference himself. On each side of the helmet was painted an eagle, and the top had a giant "F" on it.

When John was ready, he went in and replaced Roger, taking two pitches before the umpire said, "coming down." John shouted it as an announcement, with the fielders tossing their practice balls in and John sending the next pitch down to second to simulate throwing out an attempted base stealer.

With the warm-ups done, Corey walked over to where Connor and Dom were standing.

"How's he doing?" Connor asked.

"He needs about five to ten more minutes," she said. "He's not fully warmed up."

Connor did not like the sound of that at all. If Osamu was pitching before he was ready, it was far likelier that he could seriously harm himself. But, their bus was late and there was very little that they could do when the umpire was telling them to speed up.

Osamu threw to the first batter, sticking mostly with breaking balls and not his signature heat. His placement was good, even if his balls were not thrown very hard, and the leadoff man struck out. The second batter had little success as well, sending a line drive at Marty Dillingham, who caught the ball without even having to take a step.

"He looks like he's doing okay," Connor said.

"He's being lucky," Corey replied. "Until I see a fastball, I know he's not ready and doesn't feel comfortable up there."

"Hey, he's warming up while he pitches," pointed out Dom. "Two outs in two batters is a nice warm-up."

The third batter hit one hard, sending it into right field. Tyrell Witham ran in for the ball, then skidded to a halt and tried backpedaling. The ball went over his head and rolled to the fence. Tyrell began running after it, but Alejandro Izquierdo backed him up from center and threw the ball to the cutoff man. With the quick backup, the batter stopped at second.

The cleanup batter hit a shallow line drive to center. Alejandro played in on the bounce, and then began running in with it, watching the runner who circled third and took a few steps down the line toward home plate.

"Throw it to the cutoff!" Connor shouted from the sideline, knowing that the longer Alejandro held it, the more likely the runner would score.

Alejandro watched the batter, still coming in toward the infield, and then glanced briefly at first to make sure that runner was staying where he was. When his eyes shifted back to third, he saw the runner begin to charge toward home. With a perfect strike, Alejandro stepped into a crow-hop and gunned the ball to the plate. John Turner waited for the ball, then glanced at the baserunner to see how much time he had. In that instant of taking his eye off of the ball, he misplayed it, bringing his glove swinging down to tag the sliding runner before he had fully caught it. The ball tipped off of the top of his glove and ricocheted to the backstop.

"Safe!" the umpire called as the runner slid in and John fell on top of him.

From the pitcher's mound, Osamu ran to the backstop and collected the ball, spinning quickly and looking for the runner who had been at first. He was on his way to third.

"Hold it!" Connor shouted, but Osamu either did not hear him or the words did not register. He threw the ball to third, the throw was high, going over Ryan Wolf's head and into the outfield. The runner was able to jog home and score.

"Goddamn it!" Connor cursed.

"Calm down," Dom said. "It's only two runs."

"A team that throws together loses together," Connor said, quoting something his father had said to him quite often, since it was a lesson his softball team had never quite mastered.

Down by a run, Osamu retook the mound and got into his windup. He threw a pitch—a fastball—and the batter hit it cleanly, sending it over the center field fence. Alejandro jumped up, one foot on the fence and then propelled himself up to try and make the catch, but it was too high for him. A home run.

Connor glanced at Corey. "Fastball?"

"Not as fast as normal," she said. "But it was a fastball."

Osamu walked the next batter and then gave up a pair of hits to load the bases before finally having a grounder to second that Robert Griffin could field cleanly. It was not a great inning, and certainly not a good beginning to the season, but it ended with Farmington trailing only by two.

Connor greeted Robert as he came in and congratulated him on the play. Robert was leading off, grabbed his helmet and got up to bat. He hit the ball hard, but unfortunately it was right at the third baseman who caught it. Connor could hear Lauren shouting behind him. He turned around to glance, not surprised at all to see Lauren standing on the top of the bleachers and shouting. He remembered her doing this at every game he had ever been to with her, whether it was Chrissie's softball or volleyball games, or Jimmy's football, wrestling, baseball, or lacrosse games. She was definitely a passionate and ardent fan. Cheering for her nephew just went along with the spirit of the game.

In Connor's opinion, the innings started flying by. Osamu finally settled down—or warmed up, depending upon one's perspective—and did not allow even one more base runner for the next six innings. His efforts were admirable, and Connor would love to get him a win, but his team seemed to forget how to hit as well.

In the fifth inning, there had been some excitement. Alejandro did get another hit, as did John Turner, but Alejandro was stopped at third. They walked Lamont Aronson to load the bases, but Robert grounded into a double play to end the inning. When Connor glanced to see the reaction of his sisters, he was surprised to have seen Marina and his mother in the bleachers as well. He wasn't sure when they arrived, and certainly had not expected them, but they were there.

In the eighth inning, John Turner was leading off. Connor watched the outfielders closely and saw that they were moving in instead of back. Clearly, his pop-out to shallow left center and his hit in a similar spot were enough for them to decide that he wasn't going to be reaching the fences.

"Karlic—grab a helmet—you're up," Connor said.

Karlic, all excited to get into the game, took a helmet and a bat and ran up to the plate. He even forgot to put his batting gloves on in his enthusiasm. John just nodded as Karlic replaced him, and went back to the bench, accepting the decision without complaint or protest. One thing about John: he was a team player and loyal to the makeup of the team.

Karlic took a couple of pitches, one ball and one strike, and then sent the third one down the right-field line for a base hit. He rounded first, watching the right fielder make the play, and then retreated back to the bag for the hit.

Lamont Aronson came up next, and Connor slowly rubbed his hands back and forth, hoping that this was the time Aronson came up with the big hit. He had two balls that could have been gone already, and seemed just on the verge of hitting a home run. One now would tie the game.

Aronson sent the pitch soaring, heading to left field, well over the fence, but foul. The hit, even foul, got Connor excited. "Okay, straighten that out now, you've got it."

Aronson swung at the next pitch, sending it to the exact same location, only hitting it even further this time.

"That boy can *hit*," Dom said, grinning. "I *told* you."

"Don't jinx him," Connor said.

The third pitch was in the dirt, and Lamont managed to check his swing, for the first ball. The fourth pitch he sent into right center, between the right and center fielder for a hit. Karlic ran to third, Lamont stopping at first.

Connor clapped excitedly. It wasn't a home run, but there were also no outs, and his boys were finally starting to hit. If they could put something together right now, the way Osamu was pitching, the game was theirs.

Robert Griffin stepped up to the plate, hitless on the day. Connor knelt down, watching in a crouched position, practically holding his breath for each pitch. The bat cracked, and Connor leapt up cheering as the ball made it between the third baseman and shortstop for a hit. Karlic scored, making it a one-run game, with Lamont making it to second easily.

"That's it, that's it," Connor said, rubbing his hands together again in anticipation.

Osamu went up to bat, and on the very first pitch, was hit by the ball. Connor turned sheet-white as he watched his star-pitcher shaking his pitching hand. The boisterous crowd on the Farmington side of the field went deathly-quiet. Osamu was cringing, holding his hand in pain and looking like he wanted to scream.

Connor glared at the pitcher as Joe ran in from the first-base coach's position and began examining Osamu's hand. Corey also went over to see how Osamu was doing. Connor's gaze shifted from the pitcher, who was grinning, to the coach of the other team who was looking anywhere but at Connor. If the pitcher had intentionally gone after Osamu because of the game he was pitching, it was a definite sign of poor sportsmanship.

"What do you want to do?" Dom asked.

"He's done," Connor said, not even waiting to hear what Joe and Corey had to tell him. "It's opening day, he already had to start without a full warm-up, and now he's been hit on his throwing hand. I'd rather him be pitching all season than trying to force the last couple of innings now and maybe be lost from now on."

"I agree," Dom said. "What about retaliation?"

"What about it?" Connor asked, knowing that it was the general rule in baseball to protect your players by throwing at the other team after getting hit yourselves.

"You know what I always say. If you can beat 'em, then beat them."

"Nice," Connor sarcastically replied. Glancing over at the bench, his eyes settled on Preston Reilly. "Preston, you're pinch running."

Preston grabbed a helmet, waiting until Osamu officially came off of the field, and waited to head down the first-base line. When Corey and

Joe walked back to the bench with Osamu, Joe grabbing an ice pack for the pitcher's hand, Connor signaled Preston to go into the game.

"Dom, go take first-base coach," Connor said, having Dom replace Joe at first. Connor then walked over to the bench to see Osamu. "How is it?"

"I am fine to pitch," Osamu said.

"Not today," Connor said. "You pitched a hell of a game. Let us win this one for you."

Still down by a run, but with no outs and the bases loaded, Connor decided to go with his closer instead of Ramon Diaz. "Roger, start warming Jimmy up."

"Sure thing, Coach," Roger Nauth said.

Connor looked at Osamu again, and how red his hand was. If it wasn't broken, then the one good thing was the fact that it was opening day. This was the only game this week, and with a game Monday against Mondale and next Thursday against Newbridge, Osamu would not have been scheduled to pitch again until the home opener on Tuesday the 17th against Blackfield. That was almost two full weeks between starts. Hopefully enough time to recover.

Ryan Wolf was taking his practice swings, and then began making his way to the plate. Connor rushed to him. "Nothing fancy. A base hit scores two."

Wolf looked less than enthused, and walked the rest of the way to the batters box. The pitcher threw a ball, and Ryan Wolf stood at the plate, holding his bat in the middle of the barrel in front of his chest to signal that he was not swinging. Once he had a strike on him, in what was probably the lightest and easiest pitch of the day, he then got into his proper stance.

As the second pitch came in, Wolf swung, launching the ball down the left-field line, well over the fence. The umpire signaled that it was a fair ball, and a grand slam, making it six to three.

The fans erupted, forgetting for the moment that their ace had just been drilled and could be lost for the season. The cheers were raging for the Ryan Wolf home run. As Wolf crossed the plate and walked past Connor, he said, "Bat me eighth—screw that!"

"Wolf!" Connor shouted, angered by the fact that he just kept walking and ignored him. Connor shook his head. This was one kid who needed a serious attitude adjustment. The fact that he just hit a grand slam in the eighth spot of the order was exactly why he was in it. But if he was going to behave the way he had been, his role on this team would be short-lived.

Marty followed up with a hit, but his brother Pat knocked them into a double play. Tyrell Witham struck out to end the inning. With a few substitutions to make, Connor waited until Dom got back to the bench and had him make the announcement.

"Listen up," Dom shouted. "Preston Reilly is in right field, Tyrell, you're down for today. Roger Nauth is catching; Ryan—you're out."

"Excuse me?" barked Ryan Wolf. "You're pulling me for *him*?"

"We need a catcher," Connor said. "And you need an attitude adjustment."

"Just think of all the laps you'll be running tomorrow," Joe grinned.

"Yeah, whatever," Wolf said, grabbing his glove and walking onto the field as if he were still playing.

Dom watched Wolf go. "Wolf, on the bench, now!"

Wolf turned and glared at Dom, then made his way to the Dennis-Yarmouth sideline, where he sat down by himself outside of the field of play near third.

Connor shook his head at the spectacle. This was only game one, and Wolf was already a major headache.

"Marty Dillingham, you're shifting to third," Dom continued. "Robert, you'll take shortstop, and Karlic will stay in the game at second. Any questions?"

"Strong defense," Connor said. "Protect the lead."

Jimmy walked out to the mound and threw several practice pitches to the new catcher, Roger Nauth. He had a three-run lead, and two innings to get through to save the win for Osamu Ishikawa. The two innings proved to be quick and easy ones, with only one base runner—the batter who had hit the home run, who was drilled on the back by Jimmy in retaliation for hitting Osamu. After that pitch, the umpire warned both benches that another hit batsman would result in an ejection from the game. It didn't matter. Jimmy shut them down just as Osamu had done, and Farmington won the season opener.

❖ ❖ ❖ ❖ ❖

Once the game was won, and Connor had a few final remarks with his team, he found himself surrounded by reporters looking for comments about the game, his quest to honor his father, the status of Osamu Ishikawa, and just what happened with Ryan Wolf and why he was pulled after hitting a grand slam. Connor had been in quite a few interviews over the years, and had seen even more press conferences. With things that could be controversial, the best line was to say very little.

"I'm grateful that we won today, and feel that there were some positives out of this game, but, I also feel that we still have a lot to work on and a long way to go before the season is over," Connor said.

"Coach Blake, what is the status of Osamu Ishikawa?"

"Right now, we don't know very much," Connor admitted. "We'll have Osamu checked out at the hospital, take some X-rays, and then take it from there. He's not scheduled to pitch again until the 17th, and hopefully he will be healthy enough to make his scheduled start at the home opener."

"Coach Blake, why did you pull Ryan Wolf?"

Connor paused, knowing that his response could blow up in his face quite quickly. "Mr. Wolf gave us the opportunity to win with his hit, but we felt that mixing-up the lineup for the last couple of innings gave us the best chance of preserving that lead."

"Coach Blake, are you concerned about the fielding errors seen in the game?"

"Concerned?" Connor asked. "Of course I'm concerned. This is a new team working to grow a familiarity with each other, and to build team chemistry. There is a lot of work ahead of us—on all of our parts—before we will see that goal fulfilled."

Connor saw that his players were on the bus and the driver was waiting for him. "That's all the time we have for now," Connor said. "Thank you all for coming and supporting Farmington baseball."

"Coach Blake, one more question!"

"Coach Blake!"

Connor turned and headed toward the bus. He would have liked to have found his family to speak to them before leaving, but staying would mean more interaction with the media, so it was best to just get going. He also wanted to get Osamu to a hospital for X-rays as quickly as possible, so leaving sooner rather than later was his best bet.

Stepping onto the bus, Andre said, "Good game, Coach Blake."

"Thank you, Andre," Connor said.

Andre closed the door behind Connor and started the engine. Connor took a last look at his players before sitting down. They did make mistakes, and there were a couple of injury scares early on, but a win was a win. The season had begun, and they were on their way.

CHAPTER 29

Opening day ended at the hospital with both Osamu Ishikawa and Pat Dillingham going for X-rays. The good news was that neither player had any broken bones, but the doctors did recommend caution and time before either could be cleared to play again. Connor spoke with both players first, each of which said that they would be fine in time for Monday's game, but when he talked to the doctor, he was told that the game on the seventeenth should be the earliest either got back on the field.

Connor knew all too well about injuries and trying to rush back. He'd had his fair-share of sports-related injuries—from a fractured skull down to something as simple as an ankle sprain. He had always played the game hard, and doing so leads to injuries. However, very rarely, if ever, did he pull himself from the lineup. Playing through the pain was a sign of his dedication and reliability; but, looking back, he knew that his stats fell during those times, and his injury lingered. There was no better example than his ankle injury that plagued him all season long, but two weeks after the playoffs, one day he realized that there was no pain anymore. Those two weeks off could be crucial to getting back onto the field far more productively than playing through the pain.

Osamu was part of a rotation, and he would not be scheduled to pitch until the 17th anyway. Connor knew that around the league, third starters were often bumped and pitched out of the bullpen so that the first and second starter could pitch more often. However, Connor did not want to risk injury by having his players pitch too much, and he and Corey agreed that they would stick to the rotation unless they were forced to make some kind of switch for some reason.

The loss of Pat would be felt right away, though. He was a very important part of a speedy and solid defensive outfield. He was also a legitimate leadoff batter with a lot of patience. Taking him out of the game from either side would hurt the lineup, but Connor would give Pat the full two weeks before the home opener to have some time off to rest and heal. Then, if he was okay for the game against Blackfield, Connor would be glad to have him back in the lineup.

The likeliest scenario—and Connor would run it by the other coaches before making a final decision—was to move Tyrell Witham from right field to left, and have Preston Reilly play in right. They were both quick, and Reilly definitely had a great glove, but his arm was stronger than Tyrell's, so if both were playing over Pat, it only made sense for Preston to play in right since there was a chance for longer throws from that position.

The batting order, however, was a completely different problem. Reilly was a free-swinger, and certainly not the type of player to put at the top of the batting order. The best leadoff option, Connor thought, would be Karlic Kulin, which meant the infield would also have to be tinkered with for the next week. With Ryan Wolf's outburst, Connor had no problem with making the star sit for a couple of games to try and humble him. That would at least put Karlic's bat into the lineup, though Connor expected quite a fall-out from benching Wolf.

For one reason or another, that meant three starters would be gone for the next week. Sure, he could call upon Ryan Wolf as a pinch hitter, but if he was going to suspend the third baseman, he was going to suspend him and not let him in at all. Sometimes, the desire to win had to be balanced with what was the right and proper thing to do. Ryan Wolf had no respect for his teammates or coaches, and needed to learn that no matter how skilled he was, there were consequences to his actions.

As Connor was leaving the hospital, he managed to see himself on the television in the waiting room. Pausing to listen, he heard himself say, "Concerned? Of course I am concerned." The sound bite ended there, with the news anchor taking over.

"So Farmington manages to squeeze out a win, but you heard it directly from Coach Blake—he's concerned."

"That's right, Jim. I don't think we'll be seeing too many more wins from the Eagles this season."

"Luck," Jim said with a chuckle. "Good luck Eagles. This should be an interesting season to watch."

"Great," groaned Connor. They cut off his statement and turned his comment from a positive one to a look of lunacy. Now, he sounded like he had absolutely no confidence in his team or his players. "Just great."

❖   ❖   ❖   ❖   ❖

The week went by in a blur to Connor. The news report was soon forgotten as the team worked to get ready for the next game. His staff had agreed and put Karlic in over Ryan Wolf and let him bat leadoff. Preston Reilly took over the eighth slot in the order vacated by Wolf. They managed to win both games of the week, but neither were what Connor would consider to be good games.

In Monday's game against Mondale, Dane Olney pitched four flawless innings, and then after giving up a leadoff homer in the fifth, completely broke down, walking the bases loaded and two runs in before giving up his second home run without recording a single out in the inning. He left the game with Farmington down by two, with Ramon Diaz coming in to relieve him. Diaz gave up another pair of runs over three innings of work, and gave the ball over to Jimmy Kerrigan in a non-save situation. Jimmy pitched the last two innings without giving up a single hit, giving the offense a chance to tie the game and go into extra innings. With Osamu Ishikawa hurt, and only Troy Kane—Thursday's starter—left in the bullpen, Connor had been afraid that the extra innings would find him out of pitching options. But, in the eleventh, Lamont Aronson hit his second home run of the game, and Jimmy finished the bottom of the eleventh for the win.

After that game, Connor and Dom had a long discussion about the cleanup slot in the batting order. The first couple of bats, everyone did back up for John Turner, but he was just not a good enough hitter to always take advantage of it. He was striking out frequently, popping up to the infielders, and occasionally getting the ball hit into the outfield. It also became quite apparent in an extra-innings game that having a less-skilled batter fourth was a gaping hole in the lineup.

Connor still liked the idea of a power hitter, or at least one of the better batters, batting eighth, and even when Ryan Wolf served his suspension, Connor did not consider it an option to move Wolf up into the fourth slot. However, Connor did agree to move Lamont Aronson up to cleanup, batting behind Alejandro Izquierdo, with his nephew Robert batting fifth and Roger Nauth taking over the sixth slot and becoming the starting catcher. The pitcher, whoever it was, remained seventh in every game.

In Thursday's game against Newbridge, Connor tested the new lineup out, and quickly saw that the back-to-back combination of Alejandro Izquierdo and Lamont Aronson was a very formidable pairing. The two were leading the team in average—both batting well over .400 this early in the season, and had five home runs between them through three games.

Troy Kane pitched a good game, giving up three runs through seven innings before turning the ball over to Ramon Diaz, who finished the game in a non-save situation. The game itself was a complete blowout, with Farmington winning twelve to three. Connor even managed to make a few switches in the lineup so that the backups could get some playing time in. Julio Diaz made his first appearance, replacing Robert; Domingo Milas was able to give Alejandro Izquierdo a few innings off; and John Turner got his first attempt at playing first base—which was an adventure in itself since he decided to tag every player running to first rather than just stepping on the bag. Connor spoke with him after one particular play, where John held his glove out at arm's length at the runners head, daring them to run into him. His words: "They'll stop,

236 • CLIFFORD B. BOWYER

Coach—oh yes, they'll stop."

Connor had thought that the media presence surrounding the team would die down after opening day, but the fact that they were 3 and 0, beating three teams that were projected to be better than they were, got some reporters still coming and asking questions. For a high school team, he thought it odd, but accepted the press conferences as a way to promote the school and his team. He was just far more cautious with what he said after the opening day interview.

When they arrived back at Farmington High after the Newbridge game, every coach and player was a little shocked to see construction trucks in the parking lot and portions of the grounds blocked off by orange-plastic fences. A big sign stood before the fence, announcing that it was a construction site for a baseball stadium.

Connor knew that Satoshi Ishikawa had mentioned his desire to make a real stadium where his son could play, but he never thought that the school committee and town would allow it. It looked like they would be having a real baseball stadium in the near future. Probably not for this season, but definitely in time for the home opener next year.

With three days of practice, the team was ready for their first long week. They had the home opener against Blackfield on Tuesday, another home game against Rockton on Wednesday, and then were on the road again Friday against Millwood. Connor had both Osamu and Pat visit the doctors again to each get a permission form that let them back on the field. They were undefeated in their first couple of weeks, and were finally back to full strength. The suspension of Ryan Wolf was also served—begrudgingly—and they were ready for Blackfield.

CHAPTER 30

The day of the home opener, Connor took the day off from school to head back to Holliston and spend it with his mother. Since he had begun coaching, he had not spent as much time with her as he wished that he had. Not only did he want to honor his father's memory, but when he saw his father on the ground the way he was, and held his cold hand and crying, Connor had promised his father that he would look after and take care of his mother. That was something he was not living up to.

His mother had a doctor's appointment at 11:00 with her primary care physician. It wasn't that anything was wrong and she needed his support, but she still did not like going certain places without someone with her. Cindy had taken her the last time she had to go, and this time, Connor heard his mother's voice quivering every time she mentioned that she was going to go alone. He did not want her to have to do that, and cleared his schedule to bring her.

He picked her up at 10:00, stopping first to make sure that Chip and Dale had a chance to go out while his mother finished getting ready. When he let the dogs in, he checked each door and window to make sure everything was locked, and then took his mother out to the truck, opening the door and holding it for her.

"Thank you," she said. "You know, your father used to always hold the door open for me."

"I learned from the best," Connor said, doing his best to sound up-beat, but still seeing the pain in his mother's eyes and feeling it himself.

As they were driving, his mother began talking about what she was going through. She always said it with an apology, as if she should not still be suffering and letting others know about it. She was afraid more than anything about being a burden to others.

"I realized the other day that I used to wear makeup only for Dad," she said.

"Oh?" Connor asked, turning his directional on and pulling out into traffic.

"I always thought it was for me," she continued. "But now, I just don't care."

Connor listened, staring straight ahead at the cars in front of him. He never had a response for conversations like this. He never knew what the right thing to say was, if there was a right thing. He only prayed that his presence was enough. To be there for her to talk about his father, share her grief, and know that he loved her and was there for her.

"I go to the bank, the post office, even to these doctor's appointments without putting anything on," she kept going. "It was definitely for Dad, not me. He used to always tell me how beautiful I was, and that was why I tried to always look good."

"You've always been beautiful," Connor said, knowing that it did not mean as much coming from him as it would have from his father.

"Thank you," his mother replied. "You know, Dad did leave me one thing, a true gift."

"Oh?" asked Connor.

"He left me you," she said.

The conversation continued while they drove, and again after the appointment when they went out to lunch. They decided to make it simple, with an appetizer of mozzarella sticks, and an order of chicken parmesan, for each of them, and glasses of water. Connor stopped eating when he ran out of meat, leaving some of his penne behind. His mother took about half of hers to go, having the waitress put Connor's extra pasta and bread into her container as well. It wouldn't be dinner that night, but it certainly was enough for one night this week.

It was beginning to get late by the time they finished lunch. The game was scheduled for 3:45 that afternoon, and Connor would be cutting it close to get back to his office by 3:00. He considered asking his mother if she wanted to go with him. Cindy and Lauren had been to all three games, but his mother and Marina had only come to the first one. He decided against asking, realizing that if she did, she would be stuck at the school with nothing to do until game time. If she wanted to come, perhaps Lauren would pick her up and at least they would have companionship both before and during the game.

Connor dropped her off, taking the time to come inside, take the dogs out again, and make sure his mother was settled and had an opportunity to feed both the dogs and cats before he left. With a last glance at his watch, he hugged her goodbye, and was on his way to the field.

CHAPTER 31

If Connor had thought that opening day was a circus, it paled in comparison to the home opener. When he pulled into the school parking lot, there wasn't a single space to be had. The street leading up to the school was full of vehicles parallel-parked as well. Across the street was a line of media trucks and news crews.

By the time he found a space, well-down the road from the school, he had just enough time to get to his office and change into his uniform before he was supposed to meet with his players. The team was in the locker room, waiting to go out and show their new school what they could do on their home field for the first time.

"Cutting it a bit close, aren't you?" Dom asked softly so that only Connor could hear as he walked into the locker room.

"Today is our home opener," Connor said, indicating the obvious. "We had a good road trip, winning our first three games. Now we come home where we have the most support and the people who want to see us win."

It definitely was not far from the truth: with the amount of cars around the school, it looked like every student, every member of the faculty and staff, and possibly even every parent were at this school right now. If this would be the normal crowd that the baseball team should expect, then the new stadium being built would be a blessing.

"The good news is that Pat and Osamu have been cleared to play," Connor said, hearing a few cheers from the team. "Ryan, you're also back in."

Ryan Wolf looked like he desperately wanted to say something, but wisely only nodded. Connor expected some kind of retort like, "It's about time," but surprisingly nothing came out of the player's mouth.

"That means today's lineup will have Pat back in left and batting leadoff, Ryan playing third and batting eighth, Marty and Robert both get shifted back to your positions from opening day, and Roger is in at catcher and batting sixth." Connor announced only the changes to the lineup expecting that by now the regular lineup should be apparent since he was not making many changes at all. "Any questions?" Seeing none, he finished with, "Then let's go show them whose field they're on!"

"You heard him—let's go win this one!" Joe shouted as the players cheered and ran out of the locker room toward the field.

Corey, leaning against the office door, waited for Connor. "Do you know who we're up against?"

"Blackfield," Connor said. "They are also undefeated."

"Yeah, because of one kid," she said. "Roger Collins, a senior who is scouted at every game and is expected to go in the first round of the MLB draft this year."

"That good?"

"That good," Corey replied. "They had him pitch all three games so far."

"That's insane," Connor replied, shaking his head in disbelief.

"With the schedule broken up a bit at the beginning of the season to ease the teams into it, he was able to have enough days off. He's pitched three complete game shut-outs for three wins."

"Impressive," Connor said.

"Today is day four," she added.

"Well, we have an ace of our own in Osamu, and our guys got used to batting against him in practice, so I'll take our lineup against this kid any day."

"Just letting you know," Corey concluded. "Let's get going."

The two walked out of the gym and followed the team and other coaches to the field. As they made their way to the field, they passed the construction site of the new ball field, which, remarkably, was already beginning to take shape—Satoshi Ishikawa must really be pushing the construction company and paying a lot to get them to work this quickly. A large gathering of reporters and television crews were by the construction site, with Ishikawa by the sign announcing the construction and speaking to them. The publicity and press he was receiving for building the field and helping the school would probably pay off huge for him. It could have quite an impact on Osamu's recognition as well.

Once they reached the field, Connor saw that the bleachers were entirely packed and had no room for anyone to sit. The outfield fence separating the four fields were also full, with people sitting on lawn chairs or standing by the fence. The Farmington side had an overwhelming outpouring of support, with students all garbed in the Farmington red, white, and blue colors—quite a few even wearing face paint.

Standing before the crowd, oddly, was a group of cheerleaders wearing the Farmington colors and pumping the crowd up. There was also someone dressed like a giant Eagle, the mascot.

"Cheerleaders? At a baseball game?" Corey asked, shaking her head.

"Hey, it works for the Florida Marlins," Connor said, thinking of a picture he saw of the Marlins cheerleaders at a game.

"Coach Blake, can we have a moment of your time?"

Connor turned around and saw half a dozen reporters who were becoming quite familiar to him since announcing his role as the head coach. To Corey, he said, "Why don't you go and make sure everyone is ready."

"Good luck," she said as she headed off.

"I only have time for a question or two," Connor said, waving his hand at the field to show that he had a game to coach.

"How do you feel your chances are against Blackfield and Roger Collins?"

"I feel our chances are quite good," Connor said. "We have our own ace, Osamu Ishikawa back to pitch today with a clean bill of health, and I anticipate a real good pitcher's duel between the two."

"What is your strategy against Collins?" another asked.

"Well, since I was a child, my father used to tell me that baseball was a game of mistakes. Both teams potentially have good pitching, good fielding, and good hitting. That puts us on an even playing field. Some teams excel in certain areas, but for nine innings, it all comes down to who makes the most mistakes. At the end of the day, if our team is focused and determined enough, hopefully we've made fewer mistakes than our opponent."

"Will your players feel the added pressure of playing before Major League Baseball scouts?"

"Scouts?" Connor asked, his eyes scanning the crowd again and settling on a dozen people with notebooks, cell phones, and various other little devices and equipment to monitor the game. They were all on the away side of the field, and probably here to see Roger Collins.

"Scouts are part of the game," Connor said. "Our team will relish the possibility of showing just how good they are before scouts. Thank you, gentlemen—that's all the time I have until after the game."

Heading over to his team's bench, Connor decided that mentioning anything about professional scouts being at the game was the last thing that he should do. He did not want anyone to try and show off for the scouts, potentially causing mistakes and weakening the team structure overall. He was sure scouts would come to see some of his players throughout the season, but for now, what the team did not know did not hurt them.

"How did it go?" Corey asked when Connor got to where the coaches were waiting.

"I'll tell you later," he said, his eyes shifting back to where the scouts were waiting. "Now, we have a game to play."

❖ ❖ ❖ ❖ ❖

If William Blake was right, and baseball was a game of mistakes, then the home opener against Blackfield was a flawless display between two teams. Roger Collins was everything that his hype billed him to be. Through eight innings he had not allowed a single batter to reach base, and also struck out fourteen players while doing so.

As Connor watched and tried to break-down the player that was Roger Collins, he realized that Collins did not really hide what he was going to do very much. He threw fastballs, and only fastballs, but he managed to change the speeds of the pitch and had tremendous control for a senior. If a batter was behind the first pitch, he would reduce the speed of his fastball and then they were ahead the next pitch. He seemed to throw everyone off balance—even Alejandro Izquierdo and Lamont Aronson, both of whom looked almost foolish against the Blackfield pitcher.

Fortunately, Osamu Izquierdo was just as dazzling. He had only struck out nine through the first eight innings, but the defense behind him had been phenomenal, and with only a pair of hits against him, the score was zero to zero.

It was a real pitcher's duel, and Connor thought it was certain that either kid could be in the major's one day and replicating their efforts here today. Both knew what was going on, had a good grasp of the game, good command, and were on the top of their games. If Osamu had any lingering effects from being hit in his pitching hand, he certainly did not display that in this game.

Connor's recognition of Osamu Ishikawa as being a benefit to playing for Farmington was also coming true in this scoreless game. The press had been around since the beginning, and the fan support was tremendous. But, even more important to Osamu's future, the scouts that were here to monitor Roger Collins were seeing a sophomore pitcher being just as impressive and proving to be someone worth watching.

"Strike three!" the umpire shouted as Roger Nauth struck out to end the inning.

Connor walked over to Osamu, who was picking up his glove and getting ready to take the field. Corey was standing behind him. "How are you feeling?"

"I good, Coach," Osamu said.

"Your hand okay?"

"No problem, Coach," Osamu added, flexing his fingers and waggling them for Connor to see.

"Okay then, see if you can finish this one off," Connor said.

"I shall not let you down again, Coach," Osamu said as he hustled to the mound.

Connor glanced up at Corey. "He thinks he let me down?"

"It's an honor thing," she said. "He felt like coming out of the game after being hit by the pitch was akin to letting the team down."

"He didn't let us down," Connor said. "He pitched a hell of a game. Then, and today. I should talk to him more later."

"Later," she agreed, with the hidden suggestion that while Osamu was in the pitching zone, he should be left alone.

Osamu struck out the first batter, had the second batter ground out to Robert at second, and then the third batter drove the ball to deep center field, where Alejandro Izquierdo leapt onto the fence and kicked himself up to make the catch in what was quickly becoming his signature way of saving the big hit and dazzling the fans.

"We got luck there," Dom said to Connor.

"Yeah," Connor agreed as his team brought it in.

"What do you think—Karlic pinch hitting for Osamu?" Dom asked.

Karlic Kulin was definitely the best bat on the bench. With Osamu Ishikawa leading off, and after pitching nine full innings, he would not be going back in to bat—it was definitely the best option. Karlic also was a solid leadoff batter, making him the perfect choice.

Osamu grabbed his helmet and bat and got into the batters box. Connor watched, curious to see the pitcher eager to bat. "Give me a second," Connor said to Dom. "Osamu, you pitched a good game today. We'll win this one for you."

"No, Coach," Osamu said. "Please, if it agrees with you, I wish to try and defeat my opponent."

"You want to bat?" Connor asked. "I won't put you back on the mound again today. We could have someone else bat for you."

"I wish to bat," Osamu said, full of conviction. "Please."

Connor looked into Osamu's eyes, and nodded. "Okay, you've kept us in this game. The least I can do is let you finish up."

"Are you crazy?" Dom asked, shaking his head. "Karlic is a much better batter. Besides, we lost Osamu for two weeks in the last game because he got hurt batting. If he gets hit again—against *this* guy—we could lose him for the year!"

"Let him bat," Connor said. "He's determined. He's not afraid of Blackfield's pitcher. Let's see what he can do."

"Batter up," the umpire shouted.

Osamu Ishikawa stepped up to the plate, every inch of him was bristling with confidence and certainty. Moving into his stance, he stared out at Roger Collins, ready for whatever the pitcher had to offer.

Collins got into his windup and threw his signature heater right down the middle of the plate. Osamu was a little behind the pitch, missing it for strike one. The second pitch, the velocity slowed down, and this time Osamu was ahead of it.

"I can't watch," Dom groaned. "Tell me when it's over."

Connor beckoned Corey, signaling her to begin warming Jimmy up. It was not a save situation, but he was the better pitcher to go into extra innings with. If they did not score again this inning, it would be a battle of the bullpens.

Collins got into his windup and threw one last pitch to Osamu Ishikawa. The last pitch he had taken something off of; this one he threw with all of his might. Osamu, aware of pitching strategies and trying to throw batters off balance, was waiting for it and struck the ball soundly, sending the first hit of the day into left center.

Osamu was running almost the second his bat hit the ball, darting down the first-base line and into second, where he slid before the cut-off man got the ball back to second. The Farmington side of the stands erupted in cheers at the hit, the cheerleaders quickly jumping up and down and twirling their pom-poms as well.

"Are you watching yet?" Connor asked Dom.

"Well I'll be," Dom said. "He got a hit."

As Ryan Wolf made his way to the plate, Connor signaled Rickey at third base to have Ryan swing away. It was what he knew Wolf wanted to do, and if he got a base hit, Osamu should be able to score.

Collins got set, glancing back at Osamu, and then throwing the ball home. Ryan Wolf swung and missed, but Osamu was off on the pitch, darting toward third. The catcher gunned the ball to third, Osamu slid, the tag came down, the play was close, too close.

"Safe!" the umpire shouted as he spread his arms out to signal that Osamu had made it.

Connor let out a long breath, unaware that he had been holding it. With Osamu at third, and nobody really touching Roger Collins all day, Connor decided to try something a little different. With no outs, a deep fly ball would win the game as long as one of the next two batters hit it. A base hit would win it as well. But against this pitcher, there was no guarantee that Ryan Wolf or Marty Dillingham would be able to hit a fly ball.

Making the signal to Rickey, who then relayed it to Ryan Wolf, Connor could see that his player was not happy at all with what Connor decided. As long as he listened and did it, he could be as unhappy as he wanted to be.

Collins glanced at Osamu at third, and then threw the pitch to Ryan Wolf. Wolf extended his bat, bunting, and knocked the ball down the third-base line. Collins ran to try and get the ball, the third baseman ran in as well, with the catcher, who had been closest, staying behind the plate to field his position with Osamu running home. Osamu, who had a decent lead, was off with the pitch and heading home. He passed the ball and kept going.

Collins got to the ball first, and had to step over the foul line so as to have a clean line of sight with his catcher. He threw the ball home, with Osamu sliding. The catcher caught it and brought the glove down, tagging Osamu on the shin, but again, the umpire shouted "Safe!" His foot had touched the plate before the catcher tagged him. He was safe, and the game won!

The cheers of the hit paled in comparison to the cheers at the game winning bunt. Even Ryan Wolf jumped up and down excited by the win. Osamu stood up, bowed to Roger Collins, and then ran to the bench, jumping and pumping his fist as he did so. His catcher, Roger Nauth was waiting, who grabbed Osamu and lifted him up. The team circled around their pitcher, lifting him up onto their shoulders and cheering for Osamu's achievement.

The moment was jubilant. Connor could feel the intensity and excitement of the game washing over him. It may only have been a single game, the home opener, but the hype of Roger Collins and the pressure of the scouts at the game was more than enough to make this one a nail-biting experience. The win was well-received and well-deserved. His team played hard and never quit.

"Okay, okay," Connor said after the team kept cheering. "Settle down." The players let Osamu down and circled around Connor. "I think this one is obvious—the game ball belongs to Osamu Ishikawa."

Connor tossed the ball to Osamu, and the players all began cheering again, reaching in and hitting him on the shoulder, the back, or whatever they could get. The excitement was contagious.

"Coach Blake, Coach Blake—any chance we can talk with your pitcher?"

Connor turned his attention away from his team for a moment. The reporter's request was not uncommon. They wanted to talk to the players who did a good job. Connor wasn't sure he wanted to risk team chemistry and harmony by signaling any one player out though.

The last thing he wanted was for his players to grow big egos thinking that they were superstars that needed attention. He wanted them to have the exposure to the scouts and potential baseball careers, but he wasn't as certain of having them individually being exploited.

At the same time, the interest in the team, the players, the school system, and ultimately the Governor's program also had to be taken into account. They were not just any high school with a good pitching performance, they were a political vehicle that needed to consider public opinion. It was not the way he wanted to address the concern. He would rather only consider what he felt was best for the team, but ultimately, what was good for the program was good for the team and individual players as well.

"Just a few minutes," Connor conceded.

The reporters needed no further invitation. They swarmed in, circling around Osamu Ishikawa and began bombarding him with questions. Questions about coming to America and his dream to play in the Major Leagues. Questions about his thoughts of defeating a player expected to be highly-drafted this year. Questions about whether he felt intimidated by being before so many scouts.

Connor let him answer the questions however he wished, and stepped away. The questions about the scouts would come as a surprise, but the game was over. He was going to tell the team about the scouts now anyway.

He saw a few reporters go over to talk to other players as well. Some spoke with Alejandro about his dazzling catch in center field. A couple spoke with Ryan Wolf about his game-winning bunt, and also a few questions as to why he had not been in the lineup the past week. Connor closed his eyes and wondered if the battle of public opinion was one he was now going to have to rage as well. If Wolf said that he was suspended, then it was no longer just the respect of his team, but the newspaper readers' as well. Why—when the success of this program was so vital—had the best player been suspended for two games after hitting a home run?

It was not a question he was looking forward to fielding. He would tell the truth, indicating that respect and being a team player were more important than individual efforts and poor sportsmanship, but he grew up a Red Sox fan: people in this area wanted wins and criticized every move made. Fortunately, Farmington was winning. What would happen, he wondered, when they lost?

CHAPTER 32

Driving home, Connor listened to Sports Radio like he normally did. He was expecting to hear all about the Red Sox, but was shocked to find them talking about the Blackfield-Farmington game. The discussion was centered around Roger Collins, with one of the hosts clearly a fan of the Blackfield pitcher.

"This is a complete outrage," he shouted. "Some kid from Japan manages to beat Roger Collins? They shouldn't let hired guns into the country!"

"I don't know—if Collins is as good as everyone says, he'll be going up against big talent soon."

"Oh, he's that good," the first speaker said. "To think otherwise is just plain stupid. This guy is going in the first round, and if the Sox don't go after him, then I don't know what they are thinking!"

"The local boy for the local team is always a good story."

"But this guy could probably get drafted and maybe even make it to Fenway this season!"

"This season? That's setting expectations awfully high."

"You can say that again," Connor said, shaking his head at the absurdity of the prediction.

"Trust me, I've seen this kid pitch. If the Sox know what is good for them, they'll find a way to get him and have him play this year."

"You know he lost tonight, right?"

"Who cares about that? Farmington isn't even a real school. That Japanese kid—Igawa-whatever his name is—is a fluke. He doesn't even have the ability to carry Roger Collins's bags! Collins is great! He's going to be one of the best."

"Don't put him in the hall of fame just yet," the co-host said.

Reaching home, Connor shut the radio. The reporters who come to the games may be supportive, but obviously it is going to take quite some time to convince the rest of the sports world that they meant business.

Connor got to the door and stepped inside. Rose petals greeted him at the door, and Connor followed them into a candlelit atmosphere. The table was set up with candles as well.

Marina saw him, smiled, and came over to kiss him. "Welcome home."

"I thought this was usually *my* routine," Connor said, indicating the candles, the romantic dinner, and the flowers in the center of the table.

"I heard about your big win and thought that maybe we would have a little celebration of our own."

"Oh?" Connor said, grinning happily.

"I made all of your favorite things," she said.

"I can hardly wait," Connor replied, sitting down at the table.

Marina brought the food out on platters and set them down. She had gone to considerable effort, and Connor truly appreciated it. They dined, laughed, and made love by candlelight. It was the perfect ending to the day.

CHAPTER 33

Over the next couple of weeks, it seemed like nothing could go wrong for Farmington. They had three home games—Rockton on Wednesday, Andon the following Monday, and Tynesfield that Wednesday—and two away games—Millwood on Friday, and Stonington the following Tuesday. All five games were wins, and after nine, Farmington remained undefeated.

Dane Olney pitched the Rockton game. His confidence had wavered after struggling against Mondale, but pitching before the home crowd seemed to really reinvigorate him, and he pitched a solid game. In his next appearance, on the road against Stonington, he pitched every bit as effectively as Osamu Ishikawa, showing exactly why Corey wanted Dane for her rotation over some of the other harder-throwing pitchers.

Osamu himself picked up another easy win against Andon, shutting them out while the Farmington offense scored eleven runs. In that game, both Lamont Aronson and Ryan Wolf had a pair of home runs apiece, and Robert went five-for-five, with Alejandro doing almost as well getting four hits in five at bats.

Troy Kane also pitched two great games. His flair and passion on the mound was becoming infectious, as Connor began seeing quite a few students coming to games with t-shirts that had Troy's uniform number—number 9—and hair dyed the same fluorescent orange shade as the pitcher.

The press was also beginning to look for more opportunities to speak with the players, and to accommodate, Connor said that at every home game, after the players had a chance to take their showers and get dressed, they would come back out for fifteen minutes to give the press the chance to speak with whomever they wanted.

When Governor Shilalie heard that the press actively wanted to speak to the players, he made a few calls and the press conferences were switched to the auditorium, with the players coming out on stage to meet the media below. With almost a month into the season, quite a few members of the Farmington team were in high-demand, including the three starting pitchers and Jimmy, as well as Ryan Wolf, Lamont Aronson, Alejandro Izquierdo, and Robert Griffin.

The Dillingham brothers were far-more quiet than the rest of the lineup, and did not get as much publicity, but Connor had already fielded multiple calls about the seniors and their desire to enter the draft. The twins quietly and competently were becoming a pair of examples of what real baseball players should be. They had speed, phenomenal defense that in Major League Baseball games would make highlight reels as the plays of the week, and both steadily batted a little over .300. They were a pleasure to coach, and Connor would be surprised if there wasn't life in baseball for them if they wanted it.

In fact, he found himself quite fortunate with the team that he had. Most towns had a star, maybe two. A few towns were fortunate to be well-balanced with several players who could be stars. He had a team of stars. If they were seniors, Alejandro Izquierdo, Lamont Aronson, and Osamu Ishikawa would probably all be high first-round draft picks. The Dillingham boys were solid and would be drafted, though he doubted they would go in the first round. First-round players seemed to be the flashy players—especially if they were coming from high school and not College. The Roger Collins and Ryan Wolfs of the world.

If Wolf wanted a career in baseball, Connor was sure that one would be handed to him. He definitely had the talent and ability to play beyond high school, though he was the prototypical case of a high-maintenance star. Whoever got him would have to cater to Wolf's will, or else he may shut himself down and stop trying. That in itself could hurt his chances, but the press seemed to love Ryan Wolf.

Neither of Connor's catchers had a career in baseball. Roger Nauth, Connor suspected, would be a fine addition to the military academy, and excel in that role. John Turner was more interested in football than baseball, but the fact that there was no Farmington football program most likely would hinder his recruitment in college. He would have to find a school that he could try out for, and try to earn a spot. Perhaps after a year of proving himself he may find a scholarship. If not, college would probably be short-lived—John's parents weren't able to help him with college, and John was already working part-time collecting leaves, working on dump trucks, and driving around as a tow-truck driver to finance at least his freshman year.

Connor's phone rang. Without thinking or checking caller ID, he answered.

"Connor Blake."

"Coach Blake, this is Brian Jordan of WTB Radio, Boston. I was wondering if I could have just a few minutes of your time."

WTB was a well-known radio station. Not just sports, but serious news. Connor had an interview on WTB once for his novels that his publicist set up for him. "Sure, Brian, what can I do for you?"

"Do you mind if we record this to air Monday morning?" Brian asked.

"I'm fine with that," Connor said.

"Wonderful. Then on three," he said. "One, two, three...Good morning, this is Brian Jordan of WTB Radio, Boston, and I am on the phone with a very special guest this morning, Connor Blake. Good morning Connor, how are you today?"

Connor glanced at the clock, 5:15 PM, and hoped that he did not make any mistakes by alluding to the fact that it was not the morning. "I'm good, Brian, thank you."

"For those of you who do not know, Connor Blake is a best-selling novelist of fantasy and science fiction books. But, we're not here today to talk about his books, but instead about what he has been doing lately. Last October, Connor lost his father, a man who he looked up to and cherished. Since that time, to honor the memory of his father, Connor has given up his writing career and has become a high school baseball coach. Connor, why don't you tell us a little bit about that?"

"Well, I don't know if I've given up my writing career, per se, but I am coaching baseball in honor of the memory of my father."

"Have you written anything since you began coaching?" Brian asked.

"You've got me there, Brian," Connor admitted. "However, I am three years ahead in my writing, so at least for the next three years, my books will come out as scheduled."

"I'm sure your fans will be pleased to hear that," Brian said. "How can they get more information about your books and future releases?"

"They can visit Connor-E-Blake-dot-com," Connor said.

"Great—now, about coaching: how is that going?"

"I could not have asked for a better experience," Connor said. "I was fortunate to have found a team in Farmington that would allow me to be the head coach and try to honor my father the way I wanted to. It was a new program, fairly low expectations all around, but we have really pulled together and have done phenomenal."

"So phenomenal that your team is undefeated," Brian said.

"We are," Connor concurred. "We have a great group of boys on the team. They all try really hard, and considering the amount of press and scrutiny the team is under because of the school being a state project, they are really handling it quite well."

"You sound proud of them," Brian said.

"I am proud," Connor replied. "Of each and every one of them. We have all come a long way."

"Now, you used to play and coach softball, is that correct?"

"It is," Connor said. "For nine years."

"And all of your assistant coaches were also from that softball team?"

"They are," Connor said.

"Tell me, how do a bunch of softball coaches adapt and turn into a winning baseball team?"

"We may have played softball, but each of us are well aware of the fundamentals of baseball and have had a passion for the game. Even playing softball, I coached the team like a baseball team. We even had a pitching rotation and a closer. Who has a closer in slow-pitch softball?"

Brian laughed. "That's a very good point. Well, it is definitely working for you. Tonight though, everything comes together for you: you have your team, your undefeated team, and you are going up against Corinth, the team your father coached, and also another undefeated team. How do you feel going into the game? Do you feel added pressure to do well tonight?"

"I think we feel pressure to do well every night," Connor said. "But this game is of particular importance to me, yes. It was actually Principal Murphy of Corinth who led me to Farmington and to the job I have today. The Corinth school system has been nothing but helpful to me in the pursuit of honoring my father, and I recall them always being respectful and taking care of my father as well.

"This is one game I wish we did not have to play. I would love for both of our teams to go undefeated all year long, but Corinth is on the schedule, and my respect for the school and program will not in any way impact my leadership and coaching of my own team. One team will remain undefeated, and one will not. I will do everything in my power to make sure Farmington remains undefeated."

"Well, good luck with that," Brian said. "You have Japanese sensation, Osamu Ishikawa, son of billionaire Satoshi Ishikawa pitching, correct?"

"We do," Connor said. "Some teams shift their rotation to let their best pitchers go more often, but I like to stick to the rotation for the sake of all players involved. Everyone gets into the game, everyone is a little more rested, and this also hopefully helps to prevent injuries."

"A wise precaution and decision," Brian said. "Since this game will be in Corinth, do you feel, since the field is where your father coached for so long, almost like he would be there, watching?"

"It would warm my heart considerably if that were true," Connor said.

"Well, Coach Blake, again, I want to wish you luck at the game tonight, and in your quest to honor your father."

"Thank you, Brian, I appreciate it."

"That was Connor Blake, best-selling novelist and current baseball coach of the undefeated Farmington High School Eagles." After a short pause, Brian added, "That was great Connor, thank you."

"No problem," Connor said. "Thanks for the interview."

"This will be on the air Monday morning, probably at 9:00."

"Sounds good," Connor replied. "Have a good one."

As he hung the phone up, Connor glanced at the clock again and decided to call it a day. He would head home, and if Marina was up to it, maybe they would go catch a movie or something. The Corinth game would come when it came. There was no need for him to obsess or go over countless lineups when he already knew what he was putting against them.

CHAPTER 34

Corinth High School was a place that Connor would always look at and hold in high esteem. He had only been here a few times when he was younger, on the days when his father brought him to practice or games. He was so young that he probably would not recognize a single thing, but little images of the locker room, or sitting on the bench with the team manager and learning how to score a game crept into his thoughts now and again.

When he was older—before starting at SJC, but after his father had retired—the two used to come and substitute teach. Connor only came when his father did, and they were a welcome call since one phone call netted a pair of subs. Connor learned the school a bit better during these times, remembering meeting his father for lunches in the teacher's room or seeing his father sneak into the back of the class-room just to make sure that Connor was all right.

Since they drove together as well, Connor recalled the numerous little side-trips. First, he learned the back-roads that he would later drive going back to Holliston from Hobbes and his first apartment. Second, his father had little spots he enjoyed stopping at and showed Connor where they were. There were donut shops, sub-sandwich shops, and even a florist that he stopped at every other week to bring fresh flowers home for his wife.

While driving, they also spoke at length. It could be about anything, centering around baseball, life in general, or simply the day at school. Connor's father also pointed landmarks out as they drove, including one house where a kindly couple let him come in and warm up by a fire in the midst of a snowstorm when his car got stuck, or the spot where he had found a box of puppies. Wherever they had been, he was full of stories and memories that he shared with his son.

Brian Jordan had asked on the radio if Connor thought it was like his father was here. As he stood on the baseball diamond, going over the final details with his team about the game, he realized that his father *was* here: a very strong presence that he could feel just as clearly as if his father was next to him, holding and gently caressing him as a child. His father was here, and he was aware of what Connor was doing for him.

"The last time we were here, we were testing out players to find out who belonged on this roster," Connor said. "We had a lot of players in the game who are not on this team. So, put it out of your minds that we lost by seven runs, because we're not the team that Corinth faced before. Now we're one of the best teams in the league. An undefeated team that is causing quite an upset.

"Corinth is undefeated, too," Connor continued. "But I'll tell you what, they expect to play the same team that they beat before the season began. They don't know who we are now or how we play the game. It's time for us to go out there and show them just who the Farmington Eagles are. Is everybody with me?"

"We're with you, Coach," Roger Nauth said.

"Farmington on three," Connor said. "One, two, three, Farmington!"

The entire team shouted the school name, and then made their way to the bench, with Pat Dillingham getting his helmet on and swinging a few practice swings. Tyrell Witham got on deck, picking up a bat as well.

Rickey and Joe jogged out to the base coach positions, Dom sat with Connor on the bench, and Corey was with Osamu Ishikawa and John Turner warming the pitcher up. The coach of Corinth made his way over, pausing at the bench.

"Coach Blake—have a good game tonight."

"You too," Connor said.

The opposing coach, his father's replacement, returned to the Corinth side of the field. Connor was cordial, but this was the man who did replace his father. When his father had retired, it had been earlier than he wanted because the school was going to be forced to lay several teachers off. Part of his agreement was to remain with the school and continue coaching the team even though he was no longer teaching. They did that for a season, and then asked him to step down for a younger coach, acting instead as the assistant coach to help guide the replacement into a smooth transition. Connor's father had not been willing to step down and still travel with the team like some kind of third wheel or hall of fame mascot. If the school no longer wanted him, then he was willing to walk away rather than trying to stick around.

"Let's go, Pat, let's get us started," Connor shouted, standing up and beginning to pace. This game was important to him. Very important. Glancing into the stands, Connor saw his sisters and mother sitting there. Lauren had picked their mother up and brought her to this one.

The Eagles jumped out to a quick start. Connor didn't care whether it was because they did underestimate Farmington, or whether their pitcher just was not as skilled. The point was that they grabbed an early lead. Pat Dillingham was walked, and then Tyrell Witham got a triple. Alejandro Izquierdo then got a hit, driving Tyrell in. He stole second and third before Lamont Aronson hit a ball so hard that it went through the shortstop's mitt, forcing the player to use someone else's glove for the rest of the game. Robert followed that up with a double, scoring Lamont, and then Roger got a base hit as well. Osamu grounded into a double play, but then Ryan Wolf hit a shot down the left-field line for a home run. Marty Dillingham got a hit to right, bringing Pat back up for the second time in the inning. Pat grounded out to the pitcher to end the inning, but Farmington had a quick six runs to start the night.

The six runs, though they were not the only ones that Farmington would score, proved to be more than enough. Osamu Ishikawa gave up three hits and one run over six innings before Connor decided to give the rest of the bullpen some work. Ramon Diaz pitched the seventh and eighth, and then rather than using Jimmy in a blowout, Connor decided to give Ryan Wolf a chance on the mound, who gave up a single hit but struck out three batters to end the game.

The final score was fifteen to three, and the town his father had coached, the team that was projected as this year's state champions, fell like they were a bunch of amateurs against a professional team. Tyrell Witham earned the game ball by going five for six, having four stolen bases, scoring four times, and playing flawless defense in right field.

It was a great night, for everyone. The bus ride home was festive. The players were all excited. They beat Corinth, and finished their first month without giving up a single loss. Connor shared in the mood, but none of them expected that the following day things were about to change.

CHAPTER 35

When Connor arrived at school on Tuesday morning, he found two things in his in-box in the office. The first were the academic progress reports of the players, and the second was a Post-It note with a comment to see Principal Daniels. Placing the progress reports under his arm, Connor walked over to the principal's office and knocked on the door.

"Is it a good time?" Connor asked.

"Coach Blake—please, come in," Rhonda Daniels invited.

Connor stepped into the office and went to sit down.

"Close the door behind you."

Connor paused and reached back, closing the door. "What can I do for you?"

Principal Daniels stared at Connor a moment, as if struggling with how to tell him what she was about to. "There is no easy way to say this, so I am just going to come out with it."

"That's always the best way," Connor said, thinking that clear communication was far better than anyone remaining in a form of limbo.

"There was an incident last night," Principal Daniels said. "An incident involving gangs."

"Okay," Connor said, bracing himself for the worst.

"One of your players, Domingo Milas was shot."

"My god," Connor gasped.

"His younger sister was with him. She did not make it."

"Oh god," Connor said again. "What happened?"

"There was a drive-by shooting. Domingo and his sister look to be victims of being in the wrong place at the wrong time. Domingo tried to shield his sister with his own body, but they were both hit."

"How bad is it?"

"I don't have all of the details, but it sounds like he may never walk again," Principal Daniels said.

Connor was absolutely stunned. Domingo Milas was one of the liveliest players on the team. He may not play all that often, but he was the first to cheer a teammate, spread words of encouragement, and offer his support. Fate was often cruel, and Domingo Milas was the victim of that.

"Thank you for telling me," Connor said.

Connor headed to his office and dropped the progress reports on his desk. He put a note on the door that practice was cancelled, and then went to the hospital, where Domingo was with his mother, who was crying profusely. Connor spent the day with the Milas family, learning that Domingo's father had also been a victim of gang violence—beaten to death over his wallet, which had less than twenty dollars in it.

Domingo was the head of the family, looking after his mother and little sister. As Connor spoke with his player, he realized how little he actually knew the boys that played for him. Domingo could have been Connor: they shared many of the same ideals and outlooks towards family. Domingo had lost his father and little sister to gang violence, and now may never be able to walk again. Even facing that reality, Domingo's spirits were fairly high—though Connor wondered if it was an act for Mrs. Milas—and he was determined to make a complete recovery.

When Mrs. Milas was not in the room, Connor saw Domingo become all stern and serious. His hatred of gangs, and his desire to get out of that lifestyle, was what had led him to Farmington in the first place. The fact that this happened, he feared, was a sign that people could never truly escape their lot in life.

After staying with Domingo for most of the day, Connor returned to Farmington to go over some paperwork and consider who would be called-up to replace Domingo on the team. He did not want to appear heartless, and certainly did not want to make a move so quickly that it looked like Domingo Milas had not been an important member of the team, but he also knew that Domingo was not coming back to play this season, and sometime over the next week, a replacement player would have to be brought up.

Not wanting to face the decision and the discussion with the team, Connor began flipping through the academic progress reports. Report after report was positive. Some of the grades were borderline, but each he went through so far remained eligible to play. Connor was particularly pleased to see that Lamont Aronson had mostly A's with the exception of a B in Chemistry. His promise that day that Connor and Dom met him has been kept. Connor was proud, and fully believed Dom now in thinking that Lamont had nothing to do with why he was locked up. He was nothing but respectful, thoughtful, hard-working, diligent, and a great team player.

Connor also took special note of both of his nephews, who were also doing quite well. The last thing he wanted was to have to explain to his sisters why their sons were suddenly struggling in school after transferring. They were both excelling, as he expected.

He had been going through them alphabetically, and with only a pair left, Tyrell Witham and Ryan Wolf, Connor thought about calling it a night and heading home. These last two, and then he would go. As he opened Tyrell's file, on top of what happened to Domingo, Connor felt his spirits sink even more. Tyrell's teachers listed him as being below the academic standard that Connor specified, indicated that he appeared distracted, and one teacher even called him lazy.

His grades marked him as eligible based on the league rules, but not on the standards that Connor had implemented for Farmington. In light of Domingo, it seemed like such a minor point. How important were a few Cs and a D when a teammate was lying in the hospital with a bullet lodged against his spine? But rules were rules, and the team needed to know that even in the midst of tragedy, life moved on.

Opening the last file, Connor saw that Ryan Wolf remained academically eligible. Only Tyrell Witham had failed to maintain the academic standards. He had been having a phenomenal season, capped by a career-game against Corinth. The removal of him from the lineup, especially now, would not go over well with the team at all.

Writing a quick memo, Connor brought it to the office for Edna Barrows and requested that Tyrell Witham be called down to the baseball office in the morning. He had to be stern, and he had to be swift. Tomorrow was a home game against Weirfield, but it was also a day when Connor would have to address the team about Domingo Milas, and he would be doing so with new additions to the roster. It was not a day he was looking forward to one bit.

CHAPTER 36

The first week in May, a week when Connor would be celebrating his birthday, was proving to be a miserable one. The crippling shooting of Domingo Milas, combined with the death of his younger sister; the academic suspension that needed to be taken against Tyrell Witham; and, to top it all off, Connor's tire blew as he was driving to work, and—on a rainy day like this one—he was soaked through and through by the time he made it to Farmington High.

Connor slouched down in his chair, drenched, and thought about the day ahead. He had a morning appointment with Tyrell Witham, and then at 11:00, Dom was coming and bringing Rickey with him. Connor had spoken with Dom while driving home the night before, and they agreed to have a strategy session to discuss what to do with the lineup.

At 4:00—if the weather let up—was a home game against Weirfield. At least, Connor thought, the game was here and not in Weirfield. He had no desire to sit on a bus for forty-five minutes today to drive to their opponents' school.

Deciding to take a shower and get into his uniform early—his only dry clothes at the school—Connor got up to go. Tyrell Witham beat him though, just about ready to knock on the office door.

"Coach Blake, you wanted to see me?"

"Come in, Mr. Witham," Connor said, dropping back into his chair and pushing all sign and concern of everything other than Tyrell Witham out of his mind.

Tyrell walked in and sat down in the chair opposite Connor. "You got stuck in the rain?"

"I did," Connor said, standing up and getting himself a towel to dry himself off better than he was. When he was done, he picked up Tyrell's file. "Do you know why I've called you here?"

"Is it about Domingo?" Tyrell asked, hesitantly, as if he really did not want to know what happened to Domingo Milas.

"What do you know about what happened to Mr. Milas?"

"I heard that there was a shooting," Tyrell said. He let the words trail, as if he had obviously heard more, but left it at that. Connor could only imagine what the rumors may be.

"Your teammate, Mr. Milas was involved in a shooting, that is correct," Connor said. "His spirits are good, and he should make a complete recovery, though it will take time." Connor knew that the doctors were skeptical about Domingo walking again, but Domingo himself was definitely a hard-worker and determined. Connor would not bet against the boy. "That, however, is not why I called you down here."

Tyrell sat, expectantly.

"How are your classes going?" Connor asked, deciding not to just show the file and confront him directly.

"My classes?" Tyrell asked, wincing. "I'm... I'm doing all right, I guess."

"You don't sound so confident," Connor said.

"I have... trouble," Tyrell said. "It's hard for me."

"Why do you think it's hard?"

"Do you want me to be honest, Coach?"

"Please," Connor prompted.

"Well, sometimes I'm reading along with the class, and I'm not reading things the same way. What they say makes sense and all, but I just don't see how they got it."

"Have you always had this problem?"

"As long as I can remember," Tyrell said. "Honest, Coach—I try real hard. I do my homework, I study every night, but I just don't seem to get it right."

Connor opened the file and tabbed through Tyrell's materials. It did not have all of his records, but it did have a transcript of his grades prior to coming to Farmington. "It says you were a good student at your old school."

"They didn't care," Tyrell said. "They passed me because I was playing basketball."

"Basketball?"

"If you're on the team, the teachers looked the other way," Tyrell said. "It's why I wanted to come here. I wanted more than just basketball—I wanted to learn."

"I can appreciate that," Connor said. "Well, Tyrell, I'm no specialist, but it sounds like you have a learning disorder, probably dyslexia or some kind of comprehension problem. If so, this is something that should have been identified when you were much younger, and you should have gotten help."

"I never knew," Tyrell said.

"We can get you help here," Connor said, assuming that the school would provide the necessary services. "But, your grades are below the academic requirements for playing baseball."

"Coach, all I want to do is play. I can play. I'm good at it. Let me play. I'm doing my work, I'm trying real hard. You can't take baseball away from me because of some disorder, can you?"

"I'll tell you what, if you do have a learning disorder, then that will be taken into account with my decision. Your grades have dropped below the eligibility requirements, so I am pulling you. But," when Connor saw how upset and worried Tyrell looked, he held up his finger and continued, "but I am not giving away your roster spot. You are still on this team. I'll see if I can have your teachers give you an oral exam over the next couple of weeks, and if your grades show improvement, then you'll remain on the team and get your starting position back. Fair enough?"

"Fair enough," Tyrell said. "I'll do real good with the oral exam. You'll see, Coach. Real good."

"I'm glad to hear it," Connor said. "Why don't you head back to class now. I'll make a few calls and see what I can do. If you need extra help beyond what you are getting in class, or what the school can provide, I'll be happy to work with you, too. This be in addition to your normal school and baseball obligations."

"Thank you, Coach. I appreciate that," Tyrell said. "I promise, I'll do good. I won't let you down."

"That's good enough for me," Connor said. "I'll see you after school for the game."

After Tyrell left, Connor checked his clothes and decided to just stay as he was. He was already drier than he had been, and it seemed foolish to take a shower and change into his uniform now. He had a couple of hours before Dom and Rickey would arrive, and spent it researching dyslexia on the Internet, and then making a few phone calls. The school was required to provide services, he learned, and Connor intended to make sure that Tyrell got exactly what he needed—not just so he would be academically eligible to play baseball, but so that he could also learn to read properly and have the education that he deserved. He tried way too hard to not be successful in life.

By the time Dom and Rickey arrived, Connor had already managed to secure a private tutor for Tyrell, and got three of his teachers to agree to an oral exam within the next two weeks to see what Tyrell knew and understood compared to what he was able to read and write. The last two teachers were thus-far resistant, but Connor was determined and would keep at it.

"At least the rain stopped," Dom said as he sat down in one of the chairs. "It was pouring earlier."

"I know that all too well," Connor said, rubbing his hands through his now-dry but very messy hair. "Well, gentlemen, we have a decision to make. Domingo Milas will be out for the rest of the season, and Tyrell Witham will remain on the team, but will be ineligible to play for probably the next two weeks."

"How is Domingo?" Rickey asked.

"Maybe in denial," Connor said. "He just lost his little sister and is faced with possibly never walking again, but his spirits seem high. We'll see over the next few weeks."

"Can we visit him?" Dom asked.

"I would encourage it," Connor said. "I was hoping maybe some of the guys on the team would send some things over. Flowers, an autographed ball, team picture, things like that."

"And you want the idea to be theirs?" Dom asked.

"Exactly," Connor said.

"I'll see to it," Dom nodded. "So what's wrong with Tyrell?"

"His grades have dropped below academic eligibility," Connor said. "It could be because of an undiagnosed learning disorder. I told him that I was inactivating him for two weeks to try and get his grades up, and if he shows progress, he'll be back. He'll still practice and participate in all team activities while doing this, since he remains a member on the roster."

"That leaves us a man short," Rickey said. "Outfielders grow on trees. We should just bring up a replacement so we don't risk being short a player in a game."

"We'll make do," Connor said. "I want to show Tyrell that we have faith in him and believe in him. If we replace him, he may lose his motivation, and his desire to improve himself academically is legitimate. I want him to maintain that desire."

"So one replacement then," Dom said. "An outfielder?"

"An outfielder," Connor agreed. "Right field specifically. Whoever we bring in will become the starting right fielder."

"That's simple, then—Jacque Jennings," Dom suggested. "He's the best defensive player, and he could also probably take over Tyrell's spot in the batting order. He fits."

Rickey shook his head back and forth. "Not Jacque."

"Why not?" Connor asked.

"He's great in left field, and next year when Pat graduates, I have no doubt in my mind that he will be starting. But right field just isn't for him," Rickey said.

"What about moving Pat to right?" Dom suggested.

"Pat can't catch a cold in right field," Rickey said bluntly. "I don't know what it is, but both of them struggle when seeing the ball from an angle other than left. Besides, if Tyrell does come back in two weeks, then Jacque would become a backup again, and we said before the season began that we wanted him playing an entire year in JV. Batting every day."

"We did," Connor agreed. "So Gary Gillander, then?"

"He doesn't inspire me, much," Dom shrugged. "I'd rather Jacque."

Connor pulled up the spring training notes for each player on the computer. Jacque definitely was faster, had more range, and had a more consistent batting average, but Gary was more than one hundred points higher in fielding percentage in right field than Jacque. That was a tremendous difference. Gary's batting was also consistent, even if he was not as flashy as Jacque.

"The numbers support him defensively," Connor said.

"But where does he bat in our lineup?" Dom argued. "Jacque fits into the number two hole. What is Gary? Certainly not a number two batter. So who do we move around?"

"If Karlic plays, he can bat second," Connor said. "On the days he doesn't, we can move Robert second and have Gary bat fifth."

Dom cringed. "Gary, Roger, and then the pitcher in the five through seven slots of the batting order. That's weak. Real weak."

"That still leaves six solid producers in the lineup," Connor said. "How many teams have that?"

"Are you sure we can't bring up two players?" Dom asked. "Fine, have Gary play right, giving us a decrease offensively, but then bring up Jeremy Oulevay to catch over Roger Nauth. I checked with Coach Sullivan: Oulevay is batting third in the order and is over .400!"

"Good thing he's next year's starter," Connor said. "No, I'm leaving Tyrell's roster spot open for now. We'll bring Gary up and go with it from there. Another four wins probably makes us a lock for the playoffs, and one player shouldn't make that big of an impact to our lineup. It's all about nine individuals playing well together anyway. We'll just do that with Gary instead of Tyrell for a couple of weeks."

"If you say so," Dom shrugged in defeat. "Me though? I'd take the best player available, and that means someone who can hit."

"There's more to a player than offensive numbers," Rickey said.

"Not much more," Dom concluded.

Connor had always been an offensive coach in softball. If a player did not hit, he did not play. But baseball was different. There were far more factors involved in choosing the right player for the team. Gary had solid defense in right field, and would give them a legitimate alternative. He may not be as fast or have the range that Tyrell had, but with Alejandro Izquierdo in center, there really would not be that big of a drop-off with defensive range. Gary also had a good arm, which was beneficial in right field. Above all else, he was level-headed, consistent, and steady: something this team could definitely use when the news of Domingo Milas was given to them.

CHAPTER 37

Gary Gillander was to become the newest member of the varsity team, but it would not be against Weirfield. When Connor sent a message to Edna Barrows to have Gary called down to the athletic department, she told him that Gary was out sick for the day. That left them with sixteen players for the game that night.

Connor discussed alternatives for the lineup with Dom and Rickey. The logical choice was to have Preston Reilly, the only remaining backup outfielder play right field. He had speed, a great arm, and solid defense, but Dom said that the pitcher going against them threw a lot of balls around the strike zone, and as a free-swinger with no plate discipline, that was not the time to put Preston Reilly into the game.

They decided instead to take Karlic Kulin and give him a game in the outfield. His bat would definitely fit in nicely second between Pat Dillingham and Alejandro Izquierdo, and although his spring training infield numbers were better than his outfield ones, he did not do that terribly in the outfield.

With the lineup decided, the two other issues for them that day were the weather and talking to the team about Domingo Milas. The weather could not be controlled. It had stopped raining, but Connor, Dom, and Rickey took a walk along the field and saw that it was wet. Probably not so wet that the game would be cancelled, but definitely wet enough to make the game interesting. Balls would not roll as well on the grass, and in places on the dirt there were actually puddles. They would also have to watch Dane Olney closely on the mound and make sure he wasn't losing his footing at all under these conditions.

The forecast indicated that there was an 85% chance for the rain to return in the evening. If the game was played quickly, they should get through the game before the rain started up again, if it started up again. Even knowing that, the sky did look dark and ominous.

The other matter was the one that Connor was dreading more. What happened to Domingo had to be relayed to the team, and the announcement could crush them. He considered himself a straight-shooter most of the time, but telling the team that Domingo may never walk again could be akin to tearing the spirit right out of the team. He had to tell them the truth, but try to sound enthusiastic and encouraging.

Even as the clock kept ticking, the school day ended and his players arrived, Connor was not sure exactly what he was going to say. Finally, the moment was upon him, and without a preconceived notion, he decided to just begin speaking from his heart.

"Good afternoon," Connor began. "There are a lot of rumors swirling right now about what happened to Domingo Milas. I'm going to end those rumors right here and now: the other night, your teammate was with his younger sister, Alexis, and they were shot. They were not the intended targets, but were innocent bystanders.

"Domingo tried to shield his sister, but one bullet passed through Domingo and into Alexis, killing her. Another bullet is lodged against Domingo's spine, and they are trying to decide whether to operate or not based upon where it is." Connor stopped, seeing the faces of his players. Perhaps he was telling them too much of the truth, but he wanted them to know.

"Whether they operate or not, there is a good chance with rehabilitation that Domingo will manage to get on his feet and walk again. He is not in critical condition, and they do expect him to make a full-recovery. For those of you who are interested, he is alert and would probably welcome visitors."

"Whether you go or not, everyone see me and drop five bucks in my hat before you leave tonight for flowers," Dom added. "Anything else you want to send would be appreciated, too."

"Thank you, Dom," Connor said. "I'm sure you all have questions, and Domingo's best interests at heart. Therefore, I want us to all share a moment of silence for Domingo and Alexis."

Connor lowered his head, closed his eyes, and let out a little sigh. It was not the best speech, but it was sincere. Players on a team look after each other—at least that was something Connor strongly believed in. Hopefully they did not let Domingo down by abandoning him in his time of need. Too many people seemed to vanish when a friend was seriously injured. Too many people vanished in times of pain, regardless. Connor knew that when many of the people he considered friends never even sent a card or even an email expressing their sympathies when his father died. It was like people didn't know how to handle these things.

"Okay," Connor said, ending the moment of silence. "Now, I'm going to ask you all to do something very difficult: I'm asking you to push this out of your mind. We have a game to play, and that is what we all need to be focused on. Domingo would not want us to lose because we were distracted thinking about him. So let's go out there and win this one for Domingo!"

It was not an ending he liked. The whole "let's win this one for Domingo" seemed rather cliché to him, but the team seemed to respond, heading out of the locker room and to the field. As he picked up his clipboard and followed the team, the one truth about life kept circling in his mind: life goes on. Whether it is the death of a father, or the loss of a teammate, life does not stop to let you grieve or take the time you need to recover. People have responsibilities, expectations, and obligations, and whether they are ready or not, they have to face them.

❖ ❖ ❖ ❖ ❖

The team may have left the locker room in good spirits, but they played like a team that wasn't there at all. It began with Dane Olney, surrendering four runs before getting an out, and then giving up five more before Connor had Corey begin to warm Ramon Diaz up. Two runs later, Ramon was brought into the game with two outs in the first inning and down by eleven.

It was not only Dane's fault: balls were hit to fielders that should have been routine and played with ease, but players were dropping them, missing the bounce and having to run after balls, or watching balls go through their legs. The wet field conditions didn't help either, with Alejandro Izquierdo making the second out, slipping, and then sliding halfway to the infield on his back.

To their credit, the cheerleaders did their best to keep the spirits of the crowd up and lift those of the players, but it was to no avail. The home side of the field was so quiet that you could actually hear the whine of the ball as it was being thrown.

The offense was little better, with an occasional hit followed by a poor base-running decision. Connor would never have believed it, but he watched as Alejandro got the team's first hit, rounded first toward second instead of heading to the right and sideline, and being tagged out for attempting to "advance" to second when it had been an infield hit.

Every play was like that. Pat Dillingham tried to steal a base in the third inning, only to trip on his own feet and fall face-first onto the dirt halfway to second. Ryan Wolf hit a ball that he thought was gone, and began jogging around the bases. How he missed everyone yelling for him to run was beyond Connor, but he found the second baseman waiting for him with the ball in glove. There was not a single play made or attempted that even showed some remotely positive sign of a quality performance.

In the top of the fourth, with the score twenty-one to one, the rain returned. The 85% probability became a certainty. Connor glanced at his watch, realizing that the storm was not early: their game of blunders and mistakes was just making this game drag far too long. On a clear weekend day, with the team playing their normal game, they probably could have finished two complete games in the amount of time it took them to just get into the fourth inning.

In the fourth, Weirfield scored three more runs before the umpire decided to pull everyone off the field to see if the rain would slow down at all. For the next hour, players and fans were huddled under umbrellas, hoping that the rain would let up enough to get through at least five innings, making this despicable excuse for a game count.

With the rain letting up slightly, the umpire had the teams take the field again. Since Ramon Diaz had such a long layoff between pitches, Connor had Jimmy warm up and go in. On his third warm-up pitch, he slipped on the mound, landing on his back and feeling like he pulled something in his leg.

With Jimmy being escorted off of the field, Ryan Wolf came in to pitch, with Julio Diaz taking over at second base, and Robert and Marty both shifting over one position. Wolf got the next out, but he too was slipping and could not get his footing on the mound. When the inning was over, the rain picked up in ferocity again, and the field being in the condition it was, the umpire called the game.

It was a horrible day, everything about it. The team was obviously suffering, and an appearance like this one could send them spiraling down a one-way path to a complete and total team breakdown. The only positive they could take away from this at all was the fact that the game did not count. They would schedule a make-up game and play Weirfield again. A record was forgiving like that. Connor doubted that people's memories would be so lenient.

CHAPTER 38

That night was spent in the hospital with Lauren, Cindy, and Robert, waiting for news about Jimmy. The doctors were being thorough, having him go for X-rays just in case there was a break or a fracture. When they brought the family in to talk to everyone together, the diagnosis was a pulled hamstring that would cause Jimmy some pain for quite some time.

He was given medicine and instructions not to aggravate it. When Lauren asked about whether Jimmy could pitch or not, the doctor recommended at least ten days without doing anything strenuous, but then it was up to Jimmy as to whether he could play or not. The injury was one that could linger, or could go away completely. Jimmy could also play through the pain if he really wanted to, though the doctor advised against it.

Under that estimate, the earliest Jimmy could be ready to pitch was the only Saturday game on their schedule against Quallin Regional. Jimmy said he was ready to play right away, and could pitch the following night if needed. Connor promised Lauren that he would not risk Jimmy's health for baseball.

When he arrived home, Marina was sitting on the couch and waiting for him. She did not look pleased at all.

"Long day?" he asked, wondering if her day had been as bad as his.

"Too long," she said. "Made even longer by the phone calls."

"Phone calls?" Connor asked, afraid of the answer.

"You wondered what would happen if the team lost. Now we know," she said. As she was talking, the phone began ringing again. "It's been non-stop, with questions about how bad the team looked, the complete breakdown of chemistry, asking whether you are able to coach through adversity, and even one demanding to know why a player who was academically eligible to play by league standards was being held out."

"Wonderful," Connor said. "Unplug the phone."

"You want the good press, you need to take the bad to go with it."

"I'll schedule a press conference after tomorrow night's game," Connor said. "For now, I just want some peace and quiet."

"You and me both," Marina said.

"So how was your day?"

Connor listened as Marina talked about her children misbehaving—one had even bitten her on the shoulder. Some days, she had to restrain the children, and this was one of them. Every inch of her body was in agony, and—not for the first time—she began wondering if it was all worth it.

Connor forgot about his own concerns and did his best to look after her. He rubbed her back and gave her a massage, applying pressure where she needed it and brushing his fingers lightly over the spots that did not. It wasn't much, but it was enough for the night. Their problems would still be there in the morning.

❖   ❖   ❖   ❖   ❖

Marina had thought she fielded a lot of calls at home; well that was nothing compared to what Connor had waiting for him the following morning. With so much correspondence, both on voicemail and in his in-box in the office, Connor decided to prepare a simple statement to give to everyone. He wrote it quickly, but thought that it was good enough:

> *This program and this school has brought a large degree*
> *of recognition and support to this year's baseball program.*
> *On behalf of everyone involved, your continued support*

and well-wishes are well-received, especially in light of these times.

In sports—and life in general—we are faced with many obstacles to overcome. The tragic events surrounding one of our esteemed players, Domingo Milas, and the grief his family is feeling now has had a profound impact on his teammates and this team. In last night's game, understandably, the team was distracted by this grief and concern, and I am proud of each and every member of this team for doing their best to carry on when all they really wanted to do was go and see their teammate and support him themselves.

In the spotlight of our success, last night's failure is escalated out of proportion. It was one dark and stormy night, in more ways than one. Farmington remains undefeated, but even if we lose every game from this point on, we have already achieved more than anyone ever could have expected. I do not anticipate losing every game from this point on. I anticipate the character, the sportsmanship, and the fiber of our players to shine through. I anticipate that this tragedy will not destroy us, but make us stronger.

Will we lose a game here or there? It seems only natural that a team loses at some point in time. We remain the only undefeated team in the league, and that is quite an accomplishment. Our team will rise above this experience, pull it back together, and persevere.

I ask you all to support the team by continuing to cheer the players on, to offer your encouragement and support, and above all else, by praying and keeping the Milas family in your thoughts. Thank you.

Connor read his statement over once, and then sent a mass-email in response to every reporter who had contacted him. The statement said everything that he needed it to say, so he decided to stick with that rather than hosting another press conference.

As the day continued, an umpiring crew came out to check the field. The rain was not as intense as the day before, but it had been steady. The field had no time to dry out, and rather than risking further injury, the game against Newbridge was postponed shortly after lunch.

Connor had Edna Barrows make the announcement on the afternoon announcements, and also gave the entire team the day off. Everyone needed it, himself included. Rather than sticking around, Connor headed out. It was his birthday, and at that moment, he wanted to be anywhere but at the school.

CHAPTER 39

That Friday morning, a damp, drizzly day, was the funeral of Alexis Milas. Connor attended the funeral, which began at the church before heading to the cemetery. Connor's father had not had a church ceremony, with just full military honors at the cemetery. However, sitting in the church, Connor could not stay focused on what was happening. Images of his father flooded into his thoughts. He saw his father lying on the ground the way he had been found. He saw his father in the casket when the family went to visit him. He tried to keep his attention on the tragedy of Alexis Milas, but only the vision of his father remained. It was suffocating, and Connor could barely get enough air to breathe.

As a man who was not very religious, most of the service was over his head. But people got up to speak, and Connor's heart opened for them. The support and outcry at what happened was overwhelming. Connor wished that Domingo could have been there for his sister's service, but the doctor's decided that he was to go for surgery to remove the bullet, and until the procedure was complete, they were not letting him out of the hospital.

When everything was over, Connor returned to Farmington, and spent much of the afternoon walking around the wet field, remembering the many games he had played on similar diamonds, and saw his father in various places offering encouragement to him. He was behind the backstop, in the bleachers, right behind the dugout bench. All of the places Connor recalled seeing him, he saw him that day, just as he had been.

"Choke up on the bat, son."

"Keep your body low to the ground."

"Watch the pitcher's foot pivot to know when you can run."

"You're part of a team. You can't do it all on your own."

The tips and advice flowed through his mind. He could visualize and hear his father clearly. If he allowed his mind to wander, he would be a child again, going up to bat in a Little League game with his father offering advice and tips along the way.

"Do you know?" Connor asked, looking up at the sky and hoping for some kind of answer. "Do you know what I've done?"

Raindrops striking his forehead were his only response. Connor sat down on the home bench, sitting in the rain and watching the field. The droplets of water striking puddles and the way water circled around it. A chill was coming in. In New England, one could never truly predict the weather, but Connor thought it a bit too cold for early May.

Their next game wasn't until Tuesday. It was an away game against Blackfield. Domingo's surgery was scheduled for Monday. At least they would know the outcome before they went to play the game. Three practices were scheduled between now and then, but the weather was certainly not very accommodating. Deciding against having practice in the gym, wanting to give the players some more time to find peace with what happened, Connor canceled practice until Monday afternoon. They would get back together, have one practice, and then head to Blackfield.

With one last look at the field, Connor saw his father standing on the mound, talking to him about how to get into a proper stance. Connor followed the pitch, and saw himself, as a child, swinging away. As he got a hit, his father cheered him on, picked him up and put Connor on his shoulder, and danced around as if it was the game-winning hit in the World Series.

Connor remembered it all, and for pretty much the first time since he received the call about his father being dead, the images of him lying on the ground were not taking over his memories. His mother had said to him often that she only wished she could see him the way he had been, not the way he ended up. Connor had offered her his support again and again, but his own memories were too-often flooded by images he did not want to see.

On this cold and rainy afternoon, with the images finally gone, and the memories all that remained, Connor looked up again, smiling even though tears were flowing down his cheek, and whispered, "Thank you."

CHAPTER 40

On the bus to Blackfield, Corey sat down next to Connor. "I have some good news."

"I could use some," Connor said. "What have you got?"

"Roger Collins pitched yesterday," she said. "That means he won't be pitching today."

She handed Connor a newspaper that had a picture of Collins with one finger in the air. Connor read the article, which indicated that before nearly thirty scouts, Roger Collins pitched a no-hitter to beat Stonington. The article had quotes from Collins, from the Blackfield coach, from a few Stonington players, and even a pair of scouts went on record to say that it was an impressive performance.

Connor also saw that Collins pitched on two days rest, with a game played on Saturday against Mondale as well. Two games in three days probably was a safe bet that the future first-round draft-pick would be sitting on the sidelines for the game. No coach would ever have a starter pitch back-to-back days after a complete game, and certainly not three games in four days.

"That is good news," Connor agreed.

After the first week in May, this week seemed to be starting off much better. Monday's practice had been normal, the players worked hard, and spirits seemed to be high. Gary Gillander had recovered from the ailment that kept him out of school the week before and really seemed motivated to do well in practice and in the games he was about to play in.

Connor also checked with Domingo's mother, who told him that the doctors were pleased with the surgery, and that the bullet was successfully removed from his spine. They were hopeful that with time and rehabilitation, he may actually be able to walk again. It was quite encouraging, and Mrs. Milas sounded genuinely hopeful.

The makeup games were also scheduled: the game that was cancelled Thursday against Newbridge was going to be made up on Friday, the 11th. Since they only had that day's game against Blackfield and then Saturday's game against Quallin Regional this week, the extra game wouldn't be an added strain. The second make up though was the following week, on Tuesday, which could add quite a bit of pressure—not to mention fatigue—on the team.

With the Friday game against Newbridge, the Saturday game against Quallin Regional, followed by an already-scheduled Monday game against Rockton, the Tuesday makeup against Weirfield, then another game Thursday against Millwood and finishing off the week Friday against Andon, they had one full schedule. The good news could potentially come with reinforcements. In the midst of those games, Jimmy potentially would be eligible to return from his injury, and if Tyrell showed progress in his classes, then he too would be back before the end of the next week.

But all of that was to come. For now, the only game that mattered was Blackfield. Since Troy Kane missed his start from the rain delay on Thursday, he was scheduled to pitch today. Gary Gillander was making his season-debut in right field, and Robert was moving from the fifth spot in the order to second with Gary batting fifth. The middle of the lineup was a bit weaker, but Troy Kane was also the best batting starter of the trio; so for at least today's game, the deficiency would be hidden somewhat.

"We're here, Coach Blake," Andre said as the bus pulled into the school parking lot. Like most Division One schools, Blackfield was quite large. To those coming to the field, it was relatively intimidating. Like the stadium that Satoshi Ishikawa was building in Farmington, Blackfield had a real baseball stadium on school property. It was used by the varsity team, as well as a Single A Minor League Affiliate—the

Blackfield Clippers.

The team made their way into the stadium, seeing students and fans already in their seats. The black and tan colors of Blackfield were everywhere. The students were wearing it, signs displayed the colors hanging around the stadium, and the opposing players wore black shirts, black pants, and had tan writing on their jerseys.

"Start warming up," Connor said.

Joe directed everyone into lines and began a guided warm-up and stretching session. When he was satisfied, he had everyone run two laps around the stadium. When they returned, the players began throwing light toss, gradually stepping further and further back.

Jimmy remained on the bench with Connor, watching everyone preparing for the day. He was still in uniform, but wore regular sneakers instead of cleats to show that he was not playing. Connor decided to let Jimmy handle the book for the day, letting him stay involved in the game that way.

One of the Blackfield players walked over to exchange lineups, which Jimmy handled. When Jimmy walked back, he looked somewhat pale.

"Uncle," he said, quietly.

"What is it?" Connor asked.

"They're pitching Roger Collins."

"On one day's rest?" Connor balked. "There has to be a mistake."

"That's what they told me," Jimmy said.

"What are they trying to do—blow his arm out?" Connor said, shaking his head in disgust. "Well, we'll beat him just the same."

As the umpire was making his way to home plate, Dom called everyone in and let the players know the lineup for the night.

Connor then walked over to address the team. "We had a rough week last week, but that is behind us now. Domingo is going to be okay, and the game against Weirfield didn't count, so forget about it. This is our second time against Blackfield, and the first was a great game.

"They have decided to pitch Roger Collins against us on one day's rest. That must mean they don't like the fact that we beat them the last time. Well, he's going to be tired, he's going to make mistakes, and we already beat him once when he was fully rested, so I have no doubt that we'll get him again. Let's show them why we're a team, and why we do not rely on only one player."

As the players cheered, the umpire shouted, "Batter up!"

"Okay, Pat—let's get us started," Connor said, clapping his hands. As Pat struck out on five pitches, Connor watched the pitcher. Roger Collins may be pitching his third game in four days, but he looked every bit as strong as he had the last time. This would be a challenge.

❖ ❖ ❖ ❖ ❖

Roger Collins began strong, but by the fifth inning, his shoulders were sagging and his fastball was slowing down. It was still a low-scoring game, three to two, with Farmington down by a run, but the chinks in Collins's armor had never been more apparent.

Robert led off the fifth with a double, and Alejandro Izquierdo grounded-out to the second baseman, but Robert managed to get to third base. Lamont Aronson, who hit a home run earlier in the game to drive in Farmington's two runs, was pitched to carefully, and he drew a walk.

That brought Gary Gillander to the plate for his third at bat. He struck out his first time up, and flew out to right field in his second at bat. With the tying run at third base, he was determined to make a contribution to the team. Roger Collins reared back, looking for a little something extra to put on the ball, and sent a fastball rocketing at Gary. Gary swung, shattering his bat, but hitting the ball.

The ball went dribbling down the first-base line. The head of his bat went spiraling out to the pitcher's mound, making Roger Collins leap out of the way from being hit. Robert was darting home with the hit, scoring easily. The first baseman came in for the ball, with the second baseman covering, but Gary reached first safely.

Connor pumped his fist, an emotion shared by the team. Troy Kane actually began jumping into the air, screaming, "That's it, baby! That's how you do it!"

Without throwing another pitch or having his coach come speak to him, Roger Collins walked off of the field and sat on the bench. Connor watched as the coach began talking to him, but Collins held his hand up to indicate that he did not want to hear it. Connor did not know if the pitcher was hurt from the head of the bat, tired for pitching too much, or just annoyed, but he was out of the game.

The relief pitcher came in, but after batting against Roger Collins, any replacement seemed slow. Farmington got three more runs over the next four innings, and drove home with the win, six to three.

CHAPTER 41

The biggest challenge to the schedule was six games in eight days. Farmington went into that portion of the schedule with eleven wins, and left it with seventeen, remaining undefeated. Osamu Ishikawa picked up two more wins, Troy Kane had a pair himself, Dane Olney had a win, and Ryan Wolf won a game in extra innings when pitching in relief.

Jimmy came back for the Weirfield game on Tuesday, three days after they had thought he might be ready. It was possible he could have pitched against Rockton on Monday, but the emotionally-charged starter, Troy Kane, pitched his best game and finished it on his own. Jimmy struggled a bit in his first inning back, but he settled down and pitched four solid innings over three games.

On Wednesday the 16th, Connor had a meeting with Tyrell Witham's teachers. Four of the five teachers had ended up giving Tyrell a verbal exam, and all four said that Tyrell passed it with ease. The fifth teacher refused to budge, keeping Tyrell's grade the way it was. With four potential "A's" on his report card though, it was enough to make Tyrell academically eligible to continue playing. He was overjoyed, nothing more apparent than a five-for-five performance in his return game at home against Millwood.

The season was winding down, but the playoffs were just around the corner. Connor knew that they had made it into the playoffs, something they achieved after their fourteenth win. Now, they were just playing out the schedule to see who they were going to play in the tournament.

They remained the only undefeated team in the league, and Connor had to grin when the same radio personalities who had been trashing his team on sports radio were now talking about Farmington as if they had been their pick to win States all along. In this town, opinions change with the box scores.

The last three games were against Stonington on Tuesday, the final home game of the season; Tynesfield on Thursday, a team that had fallen apart with a few injuries and were just looking for the season to end; and Weirfield the final Monday of the regular season. Farmington did beat Weirfield in the make-up game, but everyone still remembered the complete shellacking that they had received at Weirfield's hands in the cancelled game. To finish the season against them before going to the playoffs was perhaps a cruel twist of scheduling fate.

Whatever the outcome, nobody could argue with the triumphs that Farmington had made. They persevered over public opinion and injuries, and were playoff bound. Connor could not be more proud of his team. If he could have hoped for a dream team, or even constructed a team from his imagination, it would have paled to the team he had in Farmington.

CHAPTER 42

Going over his notes and the scouting reports from the first Stonington game, Connor was immersed in the strategy for the game. The first time around, the Dillingham boys both struggled against Stonington, going a combined 0 for 9 in the game. For the second time around, Connor was debating between letting them have another crack at the same pitcher, or switching to Karlic Kulin at second with Robert moving to shortstop, and Tyrell Witham in left with Gary Gillander in right.

Connor believed in loyalty. The guys who tried the hardest, and the one's who had been there the most were the players he went with. Of course, in softball, that was an easy distinction. Did you go with the superstar who showed up to eight games a year demanding to play, or the regular guy who was more than willing to sit for the superstar but came to every game and practice? More often than not, unless someone was missing or absent at that game, Connor went with the dependable player.

With the Eagles, every player had been here since day one. Whether it was on junior varsity like Gary Gillander, or with the varsity team, every player had been part of the program, working towards making the team and competing this season. To these players, the game is their afternoon priority. In softball, it was a hobby, with work, wives, and weather often deciding whether a player came or not. In baseball, everyone was there, regardless.

Still, the Dillingham boys were the starters, and the one's Connor perceived as the loyal, dedicated, and reliable players. To pull them out of the lineup because they had one bad day could be construed as a punishment or a lack of faith in their abilities. At the same time, Karlic

Kulin had only made five starts this season, and he had one of the best bats on the team and could fill in regularly for just about anyone.

Connor wrote down two lineups: the first was his normal one, and the second was what the lineup would look like with Gary and Karlic starting. He would run them both by his coaches, but especially with Osamu Ishikawa on the mound, he was leaning towards letting some extra faces see some playing time. Perhaps he would even give Alejandro Izquierdo, Lamont Aronson, and Ryan Wolf some time off too, especially if they got an early lead. He could put Preston Reilly in center, John Turner at first, and Julio Diaz at second, with Karlic Kulin shifting to third.

So engrossed in the possibilities for the game, Connor was startled when he glanced up and saw Satoshi Ishikawa standing in the door of his office. "Mr. Ishikawa, my apologies. Have you been waiting long?"

"It is I who must apologize to you for this interruption," Ishikawa said. "You are clearly busy and in deep thought."

"I was just finishing," Connor said. "What can I do for you?"

"There will be a press conference after the Stonington game this evening to announce the completion of the stadium that I have been building."

"I heard," Connor said. "It's remarkable that you managed to build it so quickly. I read one time that it takes up to forty-eight weeks to build a stadium."

"Yes, well, that is a professional stadium with underground and built in facilities. We have a stadium, with twenty thousand seats around the field and bleachers in the outfield that could conceivably sit another ten thousand people if they desired. It is an impressive field, but not as time-consuming as a professional stadium."

"I understand," Connor said, thinking of the capacity and marveling by how big the stadium really was. When had thirty thousand fans ever come to a minor-league game, much less a high school game? Some Major League Baseball teams would kill to have thirty thousand fans in their stadium each game.

"Before the press conference, I wish to show you the stadium," Ishikawa added.

Connor watched him for a moment, in his three-piece suit, and nodded. "I'd love to see it."

Satoshi Ishikawa bowed slightly, and then extended his hand for Connor to head to the field first. From the outside, the stadium was impressive. It looked just like a Major League Baseball stadium, an entire structure built onto the school property. How Ishikawa managed to get this project approved, and then completed so quickly, was beyond Connor, but it was exciting to see happen.

"This way," Ishikawa said, leading Connor into giant double doors that served as the entrance to the stadium. Once they walked inside, there was a foyer that was nearly half the size of the gymnasium. There were stairwells leading up to where the seats were, clearly marked bathroom facilities, even vendor locations where Connor was sure various booster groups would be selling things to benefit the school, and in the middle of it all something covered by a tarp.

Ishikawa led Connor to the tarp, where half a dozen people were waiting. Whatever was under it was easily fifteen-feet high, possibly even taller.

"We shall do this again tonight, but I would like you to be the first to see the unveiling," Ishikawa said. He said something to one of the workers in Japanese, who pulled at the tarp until it slid off of the statue underneath.

Connor could only stare in awe. It was his father and him, in perfect representation, as if Ishikawa had somehow plucked the memory from his mind and transformed it into a bronze statue. His father was holding a bat over his shoulder with his right hand, and was holding a young boy's hand—Connor's hand—with his left. Connor was holding a baseball glove in his other hand.

At the base of the statue was a plaque with an inscription, saying:

IN HONOR OF
WILLIAM EDWARD BLAKE,
A BASEBALL LEGEND, A COACH,
A HUSBAND, AND A FATHER,
YOUR GREATNESS IS CARRIED
ON IN THE ACTIONS OF THOSE
WHOSE LIVES YOU HAVE
TOUCHED.

Connor read the engraving twice, both shocked to see what was here, and touched by what had been done for his father. "I... I don't know what to say."

"Then say nothing," Ishikawa said, "and simply think of your father and honor him every time you set your gaze upon this statue and come to this stadium."

"Thank you so much," Connor said, not sure if the words were enough.

"There is more," Ishikawa said. "Come."

Connor was not sure what else there could be, but followed the Japanese billionaire. They went onto the playing field, walked to the mound, and then Ishikawa pointed to the structure behind the seats of home plate. Whether they were some kind of luxury boxes or a press box, Connor was not sure. But, as he studied the structure, his eyes moved up and he saw the name of the field, the William Edward Blake Memorial Field.

"Mr. Ishikawa... Satoshi," Connor said. "This is too much."

"It is not enough," he said, sounding almost solemn. "Your father must have been a great man to have a son like you. I only regret never having the pleasure of meeting him personally."

Connor sniffled, feeling as if he was on the verge of crying. Fighting to keep his emotions in check, he turned away and studied the rest of the field. It was beautiful. The grounds were well tended, the dirt of the infield were calling for him to run around the bases. The stadium was huge, and could be quite intimidating to people playing here, especially if it filled up completely.

Different from most stadiums that Connor had been to, the bullpen was only five feet away from the dugout, and was designed identically to the dugout by being down several steps and with a fence in front of it to protect the players from foul balls. It was a good setup to allow Connor and Corey to interact when needed throughout the game about the pitchers.

"Come with me," Ishikawa said after letting Connor thoroughly examine the field. He led them back inside and up the stairs. When they emerged, they were within the structure Connor had seen from the field. It did have a press-box area for the reporters who did want to cover the team, as well as a specially designed area for student media—both the Farmington Newsletter and the new local-access cable channel that was under development and being introduced as a class in the Fall.

The room Ishikawa brought Connor into was not the press area, but more of a luxury suite or an owners' box. One wall was covered with framed newspaper clippings, pictures, trophies, awards, and a baseball uniform. They were all of his father.

"How did you get these?" Connor asked.

"We found the faculty and staff of Corinth to be quite accommodating," Ishikawa said. "Old students and players of your father also came forward and contributed to some of the materials that are on the wall."

The wall on the adjacent side was of the Farmington team, including one of their uniforms, newspaper clippings, a team photo, and plenty of room to expand with more memorabilia.

The entire room itself looked like it could support somewhere between fifty and a hundred individuals. It was more than a luxury box, but almost a baseball shrine honoring the Blake family.

"What will this room be used for?" Connor asked.

"Families of the players, faculty, and staff," Ishikawa said. "Most will probably wish to be in the stadium itself, but this will be open to those who desire it."

It was a day of surprises. In his wildest dreams, Connor never would have visualized something like what Satoshi Ishikawa had created, but it was all perfect. This one place, this stadium, Connor could come and see his father as the legend he had been, and remember him that way. Then, on the field below, leading his team, Connor could take the lessons he learned and continue the legacy of his father.

CHAPTER 43

The year and season was an emotional roller coaster, but it had come to an end. After the win at Stonington and what seemed like a week-long coverage of the stadium opening, the Farmington Eagles finished the season on the road with a pair of games against Tynesfield and Weirfield.

Connor had been dreading the Weirfield game, but Troy Kane pitched with an exceptional fervor and shut their offense down, marking the inaugural Eagles season as an undefeated one. He did not do any research on it, but Connor felt pretty certain that what they had accomplished this season was a first time and landmark event. It was a season for the record books, and one that would be legendary in its own right.

After a successful surgery, Domingo Milas traveled with the team to Weirfield, cheering his teammates along from his wheelchair by the bench. His spirit and unyielding perseverance was an inspiration to his teammates, and Connor was glad that Domingo could be there as they finished the season that they had all begun together.

Once the press had settled down a bit about the undefeated season and the opening of the William Edward Blake Memorial Field, Connor brought his mother to the stadium to give her a personal tour. He had considered inviting the entire family to see what had been done for his father, but decided that it was better to just be the two of them.

Like Connor, she was genuinely touched by everything she saw at the stadium. The statue brought tears to her eyes, and the room with his pictures and memorabilia had her dropping into a seat, just staring and remembering each moment from her own perspective.

There were not that many people at the stadium, mostly some groundskeepers that Satoshi Ishikawa had hired to keep the field pristine, but they all stopped as Melony Blake walked by, as if they all knew her and her loss, and gently touched her shoulder as if saying "I'm sorry" in their own way. It made her cry even more, but a feeling of being loved more than a loss.

"That was beautiful," was all she said when they left the stadium. Connor had to agree, it was.

On May 30th, Connor had a meeting with the league to review the playoff schedule. The teams that made the playoffs were in single-elimination mode, and the winner of the State Tournament would do so by securing three victories. The winner of each game would move up, based upon the pyramid they built which was devised from season records, not geographic location.

The team that Farmington was up against first was Timberlin, a western Massachusetts team that had just snuck into the playoffs with a season finale win. Since Farmington had been undefeated, they got the lowest ranked team in the playoff schedule. Fortunately, the two-hour bus drive would be Timberlin's as well, since they would visit the champion school.

Connor knew absolutely nothing about Timberlin, other than their record and the roster, which was handed out in a three-ring binder to all of the head coaches covering every team in the playoffs. The rosters were listed as eighteen-man teams, but all coaches were reminded that they could expand to twenty-two players if they desired in the playoffs. These last four players would not be in the materials opposing coaches had, and should be provided prior to the start of the scheduled game.

The game was scheduled for Monday the fourth, not giving a lot of time, but still providing four days to prepare for the first game of the playoffs. Between the meeting and then, Connor had to determine who exactly would be added to the roster from the JV team as well.

The two no-brainers of the group were Jacque Jennings, the left fielder, and Jeremy Oulevay, the catcher. Both provided the most consistent statistics throughout the season, and shone in what was a dismal season for the JV team. Varsity may have gone undefeated, but Coach Sullivan and his JV team managed to win only two games all season.

The last couple of additions were the question. Since he was already thinking to add two fielders, Connor would prefer to look at pitching alternatives, but that meant ignoring corner infielders Brian Dickson and Dan Tripp, both of whom had good offensive seasons, just not quite as good as Jacque and Jeremy.

If he were to go with a couple of pitchers, then Connor figured that Andre Borga and Dean Rubin were the two to go with. Both had been last minute cuts from the varsity team and had done enough to impress both Corey and himself. They could be added to the bullpen in case a starter got into trouble in the playoffs and extra pitchers were needed.

Of course, in the playoffs, rotations were pretty much scrapped. An ace of a staff may be called upon as a reliever or closer. Especially in a single-elimination game, all that mattered was winning, and if that was the case, they already had five quality-pitchers on the team who had fought for the right to be pitching on the mound when it really counted.

After Connor met with his coaches, the decision was made to add three bats, including the two Connor thought, of as well as Brian Dickson. Dickson's fielding was not his strong point, but he could come in as a pinch hitter, get a big hit, and then have a defensive substitution when it was time to go into the field. The one pitcher they added was Andre Borga, the starter, who could give them more innings if they did need a long-relief effort.

The game would be exactly one week from their season finale. With that much time off, Connor could go with any pitcher to start the playoffs, but it was naturally Osamu Ishikawa's turn to pitch. He was the ace, the first pitcher, and it was his turn to go. Part of Connor wondered if they should skip Osamu, going with Dane Olney instead since Timberlin was clearly the team with the worst season record and would likely be the easiest win. But, thinking like that could get him into trouble, and Connor did not want to begin thinking of the second round of the playoffs until they successfully beat Timberlin in the first round. That meant going with the rotation he used all season long. If Timberlin was a really easy win, then perhaps he would pull Osamu early so that he could pitch again sooner, but the rotation was there for a reason.

With all decisions made, the Farmington Eagles, Coach Connor Blake, and the entire Coaching staff were ready for their first playoff appearance ever.

CHAPTER 44

Games in the playoffs always brought a higher intensity and fervor to the players, coaches, and fans. It was not just another game, but a battle between the best of the best for the championships. When Connor had first met with Governor Shilalie, Superintendent McGovern, and Principal Daniels, none of them expected to be here today, playing playoff baseball. But after a long journey, that was exactly where they were.

Connor had a little something extra for each of his players. It was not much, but the white and blue hats that they wore all season had become filthy. The decision to wear white hats would be forgotten in seasons to come, with the Farmington hats being all blue like those worn by the JV team. Since the roster was expanded though, not everyone had the same uniforms. With a little added assistance from Satoshi Ishikawa, they now had new uniforms for every member of the team.

The hats were blue, and on the side was a patch of an eagle holding a bat in its talons with the words "2007 Division Champions" encircling it. The players also had white mock-turtlenecks with the name Farmington on one side of the collar, and the same symbol on the other. The rest of their uniforms were the same as the one's the varsity team began the season with, though new and clean.

After some considerable pleading, Connor ordered a uniform for his niece Chrissie as well. She pointed out that, other than him, she knew the most about baseball in the entire family. Her game of choice may be softball, but she played year-round through both the varsity softball team, as well as a tournament-league team that she had tried out for and won a starting position on. Her love and passion of the game was obvious, and her knowledge was also unquestioned. For the playoffs, Connor decided to let her have a uniform and take over all duties concerning the stat book. Chrissie was ecstatic.

Every player, coach, and student assistant also now had Farmington baseball jackets, which also had the division champion symbol on it. Domingo Milas also had a new uniform, and remained with the team in his wheelchair. It was a bit warm to wear the uniforms, mock-turtleneck, and the jackets, but the players decided unanimously to walk out to the field in unity with all aspects of the uniform on. The unity of the team was what Connor liked to see, personally.

This would not only be the first playoff game, but it was also to be the official opening of the William Edward Blake Memorial Field. Satoshi Ishikawa had really pushed the contractors to have the stadium complete in time for the playoffs, and there was no better time to play there than now.

Rather than entering the field from the front, where the statue of Connor's father was, there was a back door that opened up in right field that was close to the gym. Connor had his team assemble in the locker room as always, and when they were ready, they then went out of the gym, through the doors to right field, and found themselves walking through a double line of the Farmington cheerleaders and to the roaring applause of the fans in the stadium.

When Connor heard how many people this stadium sat, he had been utterly shocked. Yet, looking around as he walked to the dugout, he could see very few seats unattended. Since the school was selling tickets to attend the game, even at only five dollars a seat, they probably made enough money on this one event to fund a full curriculum of sport teams for next year.

Behind the home dugout, Connor saw both of his sisters, along with his mother, watching and cheering the team on . He was glad to have them here, especially his mother. She did not look sad at the moment, but swept up along with her daughters and the other fans in the playoff atmosphere.

They were not the only faces he picked out of the crowd though. Behind home plate Connor saw the Governor sitting, not alone, but with a pair of Massachusetts celebrities. Having Hollywood actors coming to a high school championship game seemed almost absurd, but it was a tribute to all that they had achieved this year.

Apparently, Farmington had also been busy with beginning other extracurricular activities, because shortly after arriving, a band wearing the Farmington colors entered the same doors in right field. They marched into centerfield, and then over a loudspeaker came the announcement, "Please rise for the playing of our national anthem."

"Hats off, everyone," Connor said, making sure the team knew the proper protocol. The players stood on the top step of the dugout, took their hats off and held them over their hearts, and looked up at the flag blowing in the wind behind the center field bleachers.

The band played the national anthem, and then marched back through the right field doors. The doors were then closed behind them, ready for some baseball.

"Okay, everyone—take the field," Connor said. In the locker room he had gone over the lineup, and as the players took their positions, Chrissie rushed over to the opposing bench to exchange lineups with the coach of Timberlin.

The announcer came on again and went around the field indicating who each player was and where they were playing. When the announcer finished with the Farmington lineup, they then read off the batting order of the Timberlin team.

The umpire calling the game shouted to play ball. Rather than two umpires like they normally had at games—one behind the plate and one in the field—they had four umpires judging the playoffs.

Connor watched the first batter come to the plate. He was looking at the fans in the stadium, almost with a deer-in-headlights look on his face. Osamu Ishikawa threw three straight strikes, and the Timberlin batter looked completely overmatched as he swung wildly without ever even coming close to making contact.

"That's it, that's it," Connor said, clapping after the strikeout.

"They're intimidated," Chrissie said.

"Oh?" Connor asked.

"The field, the obvious attendance, the reputation of the pitcher, and the fact that we're undefeated," she explained. "They don't think they can match up."

"They can't," Dom said, grinning from ear to ear.

"None of that," Connor cautioned. "Get too cocky and we're liable to lose this one."

"Like we could," Dom said, enjoying what he thought was a joke.

As the game went on, Connor probably did not need to caution his friend. Through five innings, it was just as Chrissie said: they were intimidated. With fifteen batters faced, Osamu Ishikawa struck out thirteen, with ground balls to the infield for the final two outs.

At the same time, Timberlin looked amateurish in the field. They misjudged balls hit, overthrew their cutoff man, and made more errors in five innings than Farmington did all season long. Putting Osamu's dominance, Farmington's normally consistent bats, and Timberlin's fielding together, and through five it was a sixteen-to-zero game.

In the fifth, Lamont Aronson hit his second home run of the game, making him responsible for seven of the sixteen runs. Robert got a double, Roger Nauth popped out but Robert got to third. Osamu Ishikawa successfully bunted Robert home, and still beat the throw to first. Ryan Wolf hit a shot down the third-base line for a double, though Osamu was thrown out at the plate. Marty Dillingham finished the inning by lining out to the second baseman in a play that for a moment looked like it was going to be dropped, but with a snow cone diving catch, the Timberlin second baseman made what amounted to the best fielding play of the day.

As the players began to head out to the field, Connor called everyone back. "You all did a good job out there," he said. "But we're going to give everyone a chance to get into this playoff game today. Everyone is out."

He handed Dom a piece of paper, with a new lineup on it. Dom scanned it quickly, and then read out, "Karlic Kulin, you'll be leading off and playing short; Jacque Jennings, second and left field; Jeremy Oulevay, third and catching; Brian Dickson, fourth and third base; Gary Gillander, fifth and right field; John Turner, sixth and first base; Ramon Diaz, seventh and pitching; Preston Reilly, eighth and center field; and Julio Diaz, ninth and second base."

Chrissie was writing the changes as Dom was reading them, and then ran over to the other dugout to exchange the switches as the new players took the field.

The most obvious switch was Ramon Diaz in for Osamu Ishikawa, since Ramon had been warming up while Farmington was batting in the bottom of the fifth. The rest of the team, Connor saw, was excited by the prospect of getting into the game. Especially the players called up from junior varsity. Even though they had a rough season, an atmosphere like this could turn it all around for those players.

Over the last four innings, Connor left Ramon in for two innings, got Andre Borga an inning of work, and finished the game with an inning from Jimmy Kerrigan. In that span, Timberlin put together a small streak to get two runs, with the final score being twenty-three to two.

After the game was over, Principal Daniels had a small ceremony planned. She came out to the pitcher's mound where a microphone was placed for her, and presented awards to the players and coaching staff. Apparently, as every person entered the stadium for the game, they were asked to vote for various awards for the players. In the overall league, the awards did not count for much, but for the players, it was an honor and recognition worth receiving.

The cheerleaders joined Principal Daniels by the mound, bringing out a cart with trophies on them. If the voting was really done at the beginning of the game, then they must have completed the engravings in the trophies during the game itself.

"Thank you all for coming and supporting the team," Principal Daniels said. "When I first met with Coach Connor Blake, I saw a man who was in pain, looking to honor his father, but not sure whether he could do justice to the memory of the man. His father was a champion, and he wished to carry that on—not losing the meaning of the Blake name, but carrying on the legacy.

"This team, this field, and this championship would not be here today if not for Coach Blake and all of his dedication, hard work, and effort. He has been an inspiration to us all, and as we win the first game of the playoffs, remaining undefeated on this magical season, I hope that he feels that his goals have been achieved."

One of the cheerleaders handed Principal Daniels a plaque. "Coach Blake, for your service, we have a plaque in recognition of all you have done, and all that you have achieved. Congratulations."

Connor walked from the dugout to the mound, accepted his plaque, and shook Principal Daniels's hand. "Thank you," he said.

"No—thank *you*, Coach."

Connor held the plaque up to cheers from the crowd, tipped his cap in thanks, and returned to the dugout, his eyes meeting those of his mother, and smiling.

"Next, for an unforgettable season, we have trophies for every coach and player of the 2007 Farmington Eagles," Principal Daniels continued. One by one, she called the coaches and players up to get their trophies. They were wooden based with the symbol of an eagle behind a glove and ball with two bats crossed. The base said "2007 Division Champions," and also had the name of the recipient. On the top of the wooden base was a golden ballplayer holding a bat.

"We also have some personal awards for those players who have gone above and beyond, as voted upon by the people here today. The first is Rookie of the Year, awarded to the student who is below the grade of Junior and made the largest impact on the team. This season's Rookie of the Year is Jimmy Kerrigan."

"Me?" Jimmy asked, dumbfounded, glancing over at Alejandro Izquierdo, also a freshman.

"Go get your award," Corey said, giving him a congratulatory pat on the back.

Jimmy walked up to the mound and accepted his award, holding it up for everyone to see.

"The Impact Player of the Year award is presented to a member of the team, regardless of grade, who made an impact on the field and with the team," Principal Daniels continued. "This season's Impact Player of the Year is Lamont Aronson."

Connor could see Lamont Aronson, the big man who he had found behind bars, with tears in his eyes. Over the season, Connor had begun to see that Lamont's heart was just as big as his swing, and that was saying a lot.

"The Batting Title is not a voted category, but a statistical one," explained Principal Daniels. "For batting .498 on the season, and accomplishing that as a freshman, this year's batting title goes to Alejandro Izquierdo."

Alejandro was grinning as he rushed to the mound for his award. The fans began cheering, widening his grin considerably.

"Next, we have a pair of Gold Gloves," she said, holding up two trophies with golden gloves replacing the batter that was on the team trophies. "Our infield gold glove winner is Marty Dillingham, and out outfield gold glove winner is his twin brother, Pat Dillingham."

The two brothers both went up, accepting their trophies and shaking Principal Daniels's hand.

"This year, this team had suffered some heavy losses, none more apparent that the death of a child so young as that of Alexis Milas, or the injury sustained by her brother, Domingo as he tried to save her life. I know that this next award pales in comparison to what the Milas family has suffered through this season, but this year's Most Inspirational Player is awarded to Domingo Milas."

Every fan in the stadium got to their feet as Domingo wheeled himself out to the mound, clapping and showing their support. Domingo accepted the award and a hug from Principal Daniels before turning around in his chair, holding the trophy up, and then wheeling back to the dugout.

Principal Daniels waited until the stadium was quiet again, letting the cheers for Domingo continue as long as people wanted them to. Once the crowd simmered down, she took the next trophy from the cheerleaders. "Our next award should bring no surprise at all. This year's Pitcher of the Year dazzled us all season, shut down opposing offenses, went a perfect seven-for-seven with an earned run average of a remarkable 0.84 on the season. This award goes to Osamu Ishikawa."

The cheers for Osamu seemed to shake the very foundation of the stadium, as every fan in the seats acknowledged just how amazing his first season in America truly was. The future for Osamu and baseball was bright indeed. Connor was just glad that he had some part of that by having the opportunity to coach the superstar at the beginning of his career.

"Lastly, is the award for the Most Valuable Player. This was one of the closest votes of the day, with quite a few players receiving a significant amount of the votes. The closeness of the vote truly is a tribute to just how good the players on this team have been this year. However, the Most Valuable Player is an individual, not a group, and as such, our winner this year is none other than Alejandro Izquierdo."

"What?" sneered Ryan Wolf, something Connor heard but was glad to see that Wolf quickly began clapping and being supportive of his teammate.

Alejandro Izquierdo walked up again, picking up his third trophy of the day.

"In recognition of this season, and the accomplishments achieved, congratulations to you all," Principal Daniels added. She then looked out to the fence behind the right field bleachers, directing the attention of the fans in attendance, and they all watched as the Division Champion banner was unfurled and lowered into place.

Connor stared at the banner with pride, and hoped that it would soon be joined by a state championship banner. The victory against Timberlin advanced them into the next round of the playoffs. Within the next day or so, he would know for certain who their next opponent would be, and where and when they would be playing. Based upon the materials he had been given, it would be the winner of the Quallin Regional and Farmington-North schools.

They had played Quallin Regional already this season, beating them on the road. Farmington-North was a different story though. The school was only fifteen minutes away, on the other side of town, and they had outright refused to play the Farmington School of Choice when the schedule was being designed. Not everyone favored the Governor's program, and the people who came from Farmington, based upon the firmness of their response, were of that mindset. If Farmington-North won their game though, they would have no choice. It would be Farmington versus Farmington-North. It most likely would not be billed as a grudge match, but Connor suspected that that is precisely what it would be.

CHAPTER 45

When Connor arrived at his office in the morning, a newspaper was left by his door, and he also saw the light on his phone flashing indicating that he had voicemail. Picking the paper up, he saw that the Farmington game received front page coverage of the sports section. Opening up to the rest of the high school baseball standings, he noticed that Farmington-North did indeed defeat Quallin Regional, fourteen to eight.

Placing the paper on his desk, Connor picked up the phone and dialed for his messages. There was a voicemail from the league commissioner indicating that the game would be played at Farmington against Farmington-North, under the lights on Friday night at 7:00. It was a bit unusual of a start time, but with the new stadium, the league must have thought it would be a good draw.

Making a few calls, Connor contacted each of his coaches to come down to the school to begin preparing for the game. He did not know very much about Farmington-North, but between now and Friday, he would learn as much as he could.

No one could make it until 2:00 in the afternoon. Joe had to leave work early and promise to make the time up the following morning to even make it that early. Dom picked Rickey up on his way to the school.

"Farmington-North, eh?" Dom asked. "Good team."

"What do we know about them?" Connor asked.

"They have three power hitters in the middle of their lineup," Dom said. "I've seen these guys playing ball since they were kids at Pure Hitters. They're good."

"As good as Lamont?" Rickey asked.

"One is definitely better," Dom sighed, as if admitting that was difficult. "The other two are probably comparable."

"That's going to give Dane trouble all game," Corey said.

Connor had to agree. Dane was so touchy of a pitcher. He could be the most confident player in the world, but if he gave up a couple of home runs, he would likely have a complete breakdown.

"Should we go with someone else?" Joe asked. "Let Osamu pitch again, or go with Troy?"

"It's the playoffs," agreed Dom. "No need to stick to normal rotations."

Connor did not like the idea of bumping Dane without even giving him a chance to pitch. He and Troy were the only two pitchers not to get into the Timberlin game. One of them would start this one.

"Osamu will have had four days between games," Rickey added. "That's more than enough time off."

"This is a team," Connor said. "Not a one-man pitching show. We beat Blackfield twice when they insisted on pitching only Roger Collins. You can't win with just one player. Osamu pitched Game One. Maybe, if we make it, I'll let him pitch again in Game Three. For now though, Dane or Troy are the pitchers we're looking at for this one."

"If that's the case, might as well stick with the rotation," shrugged Joe.

"I'll keep a close eye on him," Corey said. "If I see his confidence wavering, I'll step in and have Dane relieved."

"Okay," Connor agreed. "Dane gets the start as scheduled. Let Troy be a reliever in this one just in case. Anything else?"

The coaches broke down whatever they knew about Farmington-North. In addition to the three power hitters, the team was mostly seniors, and mostly big. Two players—both pitchers—had received full scholarships to pitch in college. Neither of them had pitched the first game in the playoffs, meaning one was undoubtedly being held in reserve for Farmington. That had been a pretty brave and risky decision to bypass one of their best pitchers for the first game of the playoffs.

The keys to winning this game were fairly easy: they had to find a way to challenge the pitching staff, score runs, while maintaining solid defense behind Dane Olney. Unless Dane had a great game, odds are this would be a high-scoring one. It was a game Connor expected to have to really be on his toes for, making the little adjustments and tweaks all game long. He had confidence in his players, but the second round of the playoffs would be a considerable challenge.

CHAPTER 46

If there wasn't rivalry and hatred between the two teams before the game, there certainly was by Friday night. That week, Farmington had been vandalized, with lockers, walls, and doors all spray-painted with profanities and insults geared at the baseball team. The William Edward Blake Memorial Field was also broken into and had been toilet-papered—how they got that much toilet paper into the stadium to cover almost every seat remained an unsolved mystery.

Everyone had been outraged, nobody more so than the Governor, who petitioned the league to hand out stiff penalties to any player caught while attempting a vile act of vandalism. He then ordered the Farmington Police to keep an eye on both schools to make sure that there was not either a repeat performance or any kind of retaliation.

Principal Daniels made an announcement that volunteers were needed to help clean the school and stadium in time for the game. Almost every student who chose to attend Farmington answered the plea, scrubbing the lockers and walls until evidence that they had been victims of a crime was washed away. The memory, however, would not fade nearly so quickly.

Even as the game was about to begin, Connor had to personally go to the other team's bench along with Dom to get their lineup. He had sent Chrissie, but they refused to even acknowledge that she had been there as an official team staff member. That is, the coaches did, but the players teased her and were quite vulgar in their exclamations of profanity. If there was one team that Connor wanted his players to absolutely slaughter without letting up even an ounce, it was Farmington-North.

Dane Olney began the game with two strikeouts before the third batter sent a ball over the left field wall. The cleanup batter almost did the same in center, but Alejandro Izquierdo made a phenomenal catch by scaling the wall and robbing them of the home run. They were down by a run, but it was certainly a decent first inning.

Pat Dillingham stepped up to the plate to lead things off for Farmington, and the very first pitch struck him in the helmet, knocking Pat out. An uproar of shock and disgust filled the stadium as Connor called for paramedics to come check on him.

Pat lay on his chest where he had collapsed, unconscious. The paramedic checked his neck, then turned him over and removed his helmet. They worked on him a little longer, forcing Pat awake and examining him to see if he was coherent. Pat's words were slurred, his eyesight blurred, and he could not manage to stand up on his own.

A stretcher was brought out and they carefully moved Pat onto it, who raised his hand and waved, as if he was trying to tell the crowd that he would be all right. The crowd, which had been deathly quiet since the impact, erupted into cheers at the sight of the wave.

Connor walked back to the dugout, looking at Dom. "What do you think?"

"Either move Tyrell to left and have Gary go in to right, or just let Jacque Jennings play the game in left."

Connor agreed with his assessment. Letting Gary play meant going with the guy who had been with them longer. But, Jacque Jennings was the future starting left fielder, and he had the better stats on the year in JV. He also was much swifter, and he was replacing the leadoff batter.

"Mr. Jennings, grab your helmet, you're in," Connor said.

Chrissie walked over to the other bench to announce the switch, calling it into the dugout and then walking away without worrying about whether they acknowledged her or not.

With Tyrell at bat, and Jacque at first, Connor decided to try and get a quick run back. Tyrell could bunt, and with his speed, it may not even be a sacrifice. Connor sent the sign to Rickey at third, who relayed it to the batter. As Tyrell squared the bunt, he found himself leaping back as the second pitch of the game also came close to striking him on the head.

The crowd began booing and shouting at the pitcher. He was one of the scholarship recipients, and everyone knew that he was throwing at the batters intentionally. Missed by the crowd, Jacque Jennings made his way down to second on the pitch.

On the next pitch, Jennings was off for third. Tyrell, who was signaled not to bunt and put his head even closer into the pitch, swung and missed. The throw was made to third, but Jennings slid under the tag and was safe. On the next pitch, Tyrell bunted on his own, scoring Jennings and reaching first safely.

"Okay, okay," Connor clapped. "That's the way to do it."

Alejandro Izquierdo stepped up to the plate, looking to add another run onto the board. Like Tyrell, Alejandro spun out of the way to avoid the pitch.

"Come on, blue, do something!" Connor shouted to the umpire, but to no avail.

Alejandro stepped back and further from the plate. The pitcher took advantage by throwing to the outside of the plate and getting a strike on the batter. When Alejandro stepped closer again, another pitch soared close to his chin.

With each pitch thrown at his batters, Connor was growing more and more angry. Farmington-North had had a good season: they went eighteen and two on the year, and beat Quallin Regional in the first round of the playoffs. The school had a reputation as being full of trouble-makers and bullies, but he never believed that until he saw what was happening, both in the days leading up to the game and here in the first inning.

Alejandro swung at the next pitch, but it was inside and his swing was more defensive than a true attempt at swinging at the ball. The pitch struck his fingers on the base of the bat, and he jogged toward his bench, waving his hand and cringing in pain.

Connor and Dom both rushed out to see Alejandro, who insisted that he was fine. Shaking it off, he jogged down to first base.

Connor stopped Lamont as he was going to the plate.

"Yeah, Coach?"

"Be careful—but if you can, bury him," Connor said.

Lamont nodded.

Connor walked away, hating that he felt this way, but feeling justified. Once, in a Frostbite league, there was a game when he went to help one of his players who ran a team and was going to forfeit without a couple of replacements, there had been a pitcher who was overly obnoxious and rude. The guy insulted everyone at the plate, made fun of the team, and overall created a considerable distraction to the team. Since it had not been the WildCard, Connor was not as concerned about the overall success of the team, but he still had the undying urge to make the opposing pitcher shut up and help the team he was playing for win. Instead of hitting like he normally would, Connor had focused on the pitcher, and sent a shot right back at him. If the pitcher had not reacted quickly enough, the ball would have struck him in his genitals. Connor did not mind so much that he was out, but regretted that the pitcher had reacted so quickly as to deflect the ball. All he accomplished was a pair of batters getting to the plate without insults, and then the verbal barrage began again.

This, however, was worse. This was not playing with people's heads and trying to create an advantage. It was actively attempting to hurt his opponents. Pat was really shaken up, but hopefully he would be all right. What would happen to the next player who was hit in the head, though?

Lamont had the most power on the team. If he got a good pitch, he could send one over the fence. With a good pitch, and some focused concentration, he could send a ball back at the pitcher at twice the velocity that the pitcher had thrown the ball. This was exactly what he had done.

The pitcher barely managed to get out of the way, with the hit drilled into the outfield. As Lamont rounded first, he shouted something to the pitcher. Connor did not hear the words over the cheer of the crowd, but by how angry Lamont looked, he imagined that it was some kind of threat if the pitcher did not begin pitching without trying to hurt his players.

They scored another run on Lamont's hit, putting Farmington in the lead over Farmington-North. Robert Griffin stepped up to the plate, and receiving a pitch right down the middle of the plate, he hit it over the head of the second baseman, scoring another run.

Farmington scored another three in the inning before being retired, making the score six to one. The team had already gone into the game angry about the vandalism, and the way Farmington-North began playing made it even worse. This was going to be a battle more than a game, and nobody on the team expected it to be pretty.

It wasn't only the pitcher who was acting up, either. In the third inning, one batter hit a shot between Alejandro and Tyrell, and easily had a triple. The batter rounded first, headed to go around second, but instead of rounding and going to third, he overran second and slid into Robert, who was standing several feet from the bag and waiting for the cutoff throw.

On one hand, he was not in his regular position since he should have been on the grass, but he was also far from being near the bag. No matter how much the base runner protested by saying that Robert had been in his way, the crowd and players all knew that they had purposefully taken him out of the game for getting two hits in two at bats already.

Robert hurt his ankle on the play, and with assistance, limped off of the field. Karlic Kulin replaced him at second for the remainder of the game.

After Robert was taken out, Dane began his breakdown. He gave up five consecutive hits, and the score was tied at eight. Troy Kane was warming up, but he still needed time since Dane fell apart so quickly.

Connor glanced imploringly at Corey. "Can you calm him down?"

"I'll see what I can do," she said, heading out to the mound for a conference with the pitcher. Then—in the most amazingly unexpected moment in baseball history—rather than talking to Dane, Corey began dancing with him on the mound. They were actually waltzing, as if dancing to their own personal tune.

The home plate umpire looked at Connor questioningly, and then made his way to the mound to break it up, but even then, Corey and Dane ignored him as they continued to dance. The Farmington-North team began laughing and taunting them, but the crowd drowned them out with cheers. The digital scoreboard showed the pair dancing on the big screen in the outfield.

Finally, the umpire broke in, and Corey headed back to the dugout. Dane was grinning from ear to ear, looking more happy than Connor ever remembered seeing him.

"That was different," Connor said.

"I figured it was what he needed to loosen up," shrugged Corey.

"Hey, can I have a dance?" Dom asked.

"In your dreams," Corey replied with a wink.

With the bases loaded, the score tied, and a dance with the pitching coach, Dane Olney faced the Farmington-North batters with renewed vigor. He struck out two and then got the third batter to ground out to Marty Dillingham at shortstop, who threw the ball to first to finish the play.

By the fifth, Troy Kane was on the mound, and Farmington-North was maintaining a strong three-run lead. Pitching had been consistent since Coach Corey danced with Dane Olney on the mound—although, where Dane did not throw at opposing batters in retaliation, Troy Kane beamed two of the three power hitters in the lineup before both benches were warned—but the fielders were making mistakes: costly mistakes.

Rickey was pacing the dugout, clapping his hands, and shouting words of encouragement. One could never tell what to expect from the mouth of Rickey Urban. He came up with quick little quips and launched them in quick succession. Things like, "We may not be the Backstreet Boys, but we can still get 'N Sync."

Troy Kane was ejected from the game in the seventh for throwing too close to a batter. Connor ran out and argued with the umpire claiming that it was not intentional, and that unlike his opponents, his pitcher would not do that, especially after being warned. The argument was in vain, and Troy was sent to the showers early.

Connor wasn't sure how to go after that. Troy had been pitching a good game, keeping it from getting out of hand. They were still behind by three though. Ramon Diaz was the logical choice in the seventh, but Jimmy Kerrigan or even Osamu Ishikawa were the better options with the game on the line and the chance for elimination.

"What about Ryan?" Corey asked.

It was a simple question, and Connor liked it. Ryan Wolf could switch from third to pitcher, which shafted Ramon Diaz, but Connor just wasn't sure he wanted him in this situation. Ryan was also a hard thrower and could potentially help keep them in the game.

The only thing left to determine was who went into the field for Ryan. Brian Dickson was the obvious choice with a good bat and being a natural third baseman, but his defense also was not nearly what Connor would hope for in the field. Julio Diaz did not have as good of a bat, but he would be phenomenal in the field.

After a quick chat with Rickey and Dom, Connor decided to put Julio in at second, have Karlic switch to short, and Marty take over at third. Again, Chrissie went to the other dugout to make the announcement, but did not wait for acknowledgement.

Ryan Wolf finished the seventh, only giving up a single hit, and pitched a perfect eighth. Farmington came up with six potential outs to go and the game on the line. In hopes that they took the lead, Jimmy began to warm up to pitch the ninth.

Julio Diaz was leading off, followed by Ryan Wolf, then Marty Dillingham, and—if he got up—Jacque Jennings at the top of the order. Julio drew a walk, and stole second and third as two balls were thrown in the dirt to Ryan Wolf. The Farmington-North coach made his way to the mound, taking the ball from the starter. As he walked off of the field, he was booed again for his performance and demeanor through-out the game.

Another pitcher came in, but Farmington-North did not have player names on jerseys and nobody came to announce the substitution. Chrissie went to their bench to try and figure out who was in the game, but as they had all evening long, she was ignored. Returning to the bench in frustration, she threw the clipboard onto the bench and shrieked in frustration.

"Pick it up," Connor said.

"They won't even acknowledge me," she shouted.

"Pick it up," Connor said again. "We play this game the way it's supposed to be played, no matter how they treat us or try to tear us down. Just put number twenty-nine on the scorecard instead of a name for the new pitcher."

When the pitcher was ready, Ryan Wolf stepped back up to the plate. He had two balls and no strikes as the count. He watched the first pitch with his bat in front of him and his hands on the barrel, making it obvious he was not going to swing. It was still a habit that Connor hated—he liked the patience at the plate, but he did not agree with what basically amounted to taunting of the other team's pitcher. Though he did find that in this particular situation, against this team, he did not care quite as much about taunting them in return.

Ryan got into his normal stance, and swung at the second pitch in a violent swing that twisted him completely around. If he had connected, there was no doubt that it would have been out of the stadium.

The catcher said something to Ryan, who glared at the player and looked as if he wanted to tear the catcher's head off of his body. When the next pitch came in, he took his frustration out on the ball, and sent it soaring over the left field wall for a two-run homer.

Down by a run with no outs in the eighth, Marty Dillingham bunted himself on with a drag bunt for a base hit. Jacque Jennings then came up, the starting JV left fielder, and sent a rocket to right center, bouncing the ball off of the wall. Marty rounded third and scored from first, tying the game, with Jennings sliding in safely at third base.

With the game tied, there was another pitching change. The new pitcher—also in the game without the courtesy of announcing the substitution to the Eagles—struck out Tyrell Witham and Alejandro Izquierdo on six straight pitches. With two strikes on Lamont Aronson, Aronson got a piece of the pitch, enough to bloop it over the heads of the infielders and in for a base hit. Jennings scored, giving Farmington the lead again.

Karlic Kulin got a hit, and then with two on, Roger Nauth grounded out to first base to end the inning.

Before the ninth, Connor walked out to talk to the home plate umpire. The conversation was brief, and then Connor made a double switch. Ryan Wolf returned to third base, and Jimmy Kerrigan came in to pitch with Julio Diaz coming out of the game. The infield shifted back to their original positions before Ryan pitched as well.

They had the lead—only a run, but the lead. Jimmy Kerrigan was the closer, and with the game on the line, Connor had all the faith in the world in his nephew. He watched Jimmy with pride, almost as if he knew the outcome before it even happened. It took four batters to record the three final outs of the game, but Connor's vision came true: the team charged out of the dugout and in from their positions, grabbing Jimmy and lifting him onto their shoulders, cheering in victory.

CHAPTER 47

That weekend after the Farmington-North game, Connor combined two traditions. The first was the annual Blake Barbeque, which was generally on the Fourth of July, but had switched dates in past years because of vacations and availabilities. Regardless, every year, the entire family got together at the Blake's house in Holliston for one giant barbeque celebration.

The second tradition was one he did every year while coaching softball. It was also a barbeque, this time for the team, but began with a home run derby, followed by a co-ed softball game, and then ended up at the Blake's for the barbeque.

After such a trying game against Farmington-North, and while they waited for news about the final playoff game—who they were playing, when, and where—Connor figured that the old softball ritual was exactly the way to go. The home run derby, for those who were interested in participating, began at 9:00 AM at the William Edward Blake Memorial Field. Coaches were also participating in this one, and as the winner in two out of the four years they had the derby, Connor was determined to give Lamont Aronson and Ryan Wolf a run for the title.

The derby would probably last about an hour or two, followed by the softball game. Anyone was welcome at the game, including players, coaches, wives, girlfriends, cheerleaders, and any other person involved in some way with the team. If they had too many people, then perhaps they would play a pair of games, but softball was next.

When the game was over, everyone would return to the Blake's house where Connor would host both the team and family barbeque. To prepare for the volume of people coming, Connor brought his own grill to add to his father's, and also called both of his brother-in-laws to ask them to bring their grills as well. Between the four, they should have enough to keep people fed throughout the day.

The first event of the morning though was the home run derby. In softball, if time was running out, everyone seemed more interested in the derby than they were the co-ed game. Connor enjoyed the co-ed game because it was just for fun. Rather than playing first base like usual, he went out to centerfield and just enjoyed himself. He had thrown-out his elbow in college, and playing the outfield in a competitive game was no longer really an option; but for fun, that was where he wanted to be.

When he and Marina reached the field, Connor was pleasantly surprised to see that the parking lot was practically full already. Every player was there, including Domingo Milas, Pat Dillingham, and Robert Griffin, his three injuries. Pat was still a little shaken up and on medicine, so he came to watch, not participate. Robert had a bit of a limp, but was bandaged up and said that he could still do something for fun. The desire to play, through injuries, is something that Connor knew all too well.

Not only the players came though, but also their families. Connor saw as many children as he did adults. The cheerleaders were also there, as well as some girls Connor assumed were girlfriends of his players.

"Well, let's get this party started!" he said as he unlocked the doors. Everyone made their way into the stadium, and Connor went directly to the home dugout where his coaches joined him to discuss how to go about the day. Dom had brought a dry-erase board with him to keep track of how batters do in the contest.

Once they were ready, Connor shouted out for everyone to gather around. "Okay, this is a day for fun, and that's what we're going to have. No concerns about the playoffs, stats, or anything. Here, we're having a home run hitting contest, followed by a co-ed softball game. First up is the home run portion of the day.

"As many batters can participate as they want, whether it's three or thirty," Connor said.

"That's one way to be here all day," Marina teased.

"There will be three rounds," Connor continued as if his wife hadn't made the comment. "The four best batters will advance into round two. The best two will advance into the final round. The first round will have ten outs, the second round will have five outs, and the final round will have only three outs."

As he finished his explanation, he glanced at Marina with a look that told her the format would not keep them there all day. "Coach Corey will be the pitcher for all batters. If there are any ties in the first round, it will be decided by a pitch to each batter until one batter does not hit a home run. Ties in the second or third round will take combined home runs on the day into account.

"Any questions?" Connor looked around, waiting. Other than a few remarks about beginning, nobody asked anything about the format. "Anyone not batting, we would appreciate having people scattered around the field or in the bleachers to shag balls. Remember, if it's not a home run, it's an out."

Dom placed his board on a tripod easel. "Who wants to go first?"

"You know it, baby!" Ryan Wolf said. "Everybody else should just quit right now. You know I'm going to win this thing."

Dom wrote Ryan's name down, and grinned. "You think you'll win over Lamont?"

"Heh—easily," Wolf added.

"I guess that means I'm in too," Lamont said.

"I'd like a shot at that," Brian Dickson said.

"Can we do it? Being JV until the playoffs and all?" Jeremy Oulevay asked.

"You're on this team, or affiliated with it—you want in, you're in," Connor said.

"Then sign me up," he said excitedly.

"Just to show that anyone can do it, I'm in too," Rickey Urban said.

"A coach?" groaned Wolf. "No way."

"Afraid of the competition?" Dom asked, writing his name after Rickey's.

"Might as well add me, too," Connor said. He had not brought his batting gloves and favorite bat for nothing.

"You can count me in," Alejandro Izquierdo added.

"Anyone else?" Connor asked. "Nobody?"

"I'll still beat you all," Wolf snarled.

Looking angered, Robert raised his hand. "I'm in."

"You sure?" Connor asked.

"I can bat," he said confidently, glaring at Wolf.

"Anyone else?" Connor asked again. "No? Then nine it is. Good luck to us all."

Since Wolf volunteered first, he was the first to bat. He didn't use batting gloves, just took his bat and walked up to the plate, grinning triumphantly without even taking a practice swing. "Time to show this group how a winner hits," he boasted.

Corey was on the mound, John Turner catching behind the plate. Younger siblings and some players were scattered throughout the field to catch the balls that did not make it out of the park. Corey checked with Wolf to see if he was ready, and then began pitching. He swung at the first pitch, sending it foul down the third-base line for an out. His second and third pitches landed in the same place for three outs and no points.

Wolf stepped out of the batters box, finally taking a warm-up practice swing. He then stepped back in, glaring at Corey with hatred seething from his eyes. Her fourth pitch was launched into the left field bleachers. "That's it! Now we're playing baseball."

His next pitch he rocketed as well, but it drifted just foul. Rather than accepting the out, he began shouting at Chrissie as she erased the three outs and put it as four. "That was a point!"

"An out," Connor sternly replied.

Wolf's next two were both home runs, followed by three balls that struck the wall but didn't get over it. He hit one more home run before fouling out, hitting a grounder, and then launching one to the warning track that didn't make it out. As he walked out of the batters box, with only four home runs, he looked pale as a ghost.

"Lamont, you're up," Connor said.

"Go show them how it's done, kid," Dom said.

Lamont took his practice swings, stretched, and then stepped up to the plate. The first pitch he sent over the right field fence. The next three landed in the same place, tying Ryan Wolf without recording a single out. He hit a foul and an out, and then sent one soaring into the center field bleachers for his fifth home run. By the time he hit his tenth out, Lamont had sixteen home runs, scattered to all sides of the field.

"I *told* you he could hit—yes!" Dom shouted as he clapped profusely. "Way to go, Lamont!"

Brian Dickson was next up. He was a good hitter, with tremendous potential at the plate. He hit five home runs, sending Wolf into a litany of profanities and slapping his head with both fists.

Jeremy Oulevay was all smiles as he took his swings. Every hit was a good one, probably landing, if this was a game. But by the time he hit his tenth out, he only had one home run. Rather than being upset, he knew the true spirit of the contest, still smiling, thanking Coach Corey for pitching to him.

"Come on, Coach Urban—let's see a little hitting display," Connor shouted as Rickey went up to bat. Rickey had won the softball home run derby once, with eighteen home runs before they ran out of balls because too many were hit and lost in the trees and creak beyond the fence of the field.

"A little lesson to everyone," Rickey said as he tapped his bat on the plate. "You can wait for your pitch. If you get tired, don't swing. If you swing when you're not ready, it's an out." He then got into his stance, which was one he adopted from Ken Griffey Jr. Standing there, his eyes blinking quickly, the bat and his upper body shifting, he could pass for a younger Griffey.

He hit six home runs before getting an out, and then another seven before he was done. It was good for second place, and, probably to advance a round.

Ryan Wolf was quiet now, watching each batter. At the moment, he was still alive. If the last four batters hit four or less, then he still had a chance. The first round was a warm-up round for him. All he needed was to advance, and then he would give Coach Urban and Lamont a run for their money.

Dom Petrioli was up next, but he struggled to get into a rhythm. He acted nonchalantly as he finished with only three home runs, but Connor knew him well enough to know that just under the surface, Dom was a raging volcano waiting to erupt. Three home runs to him would be akin to a sin.

Connor put on his batting gloves, black and white ones, and took his lucky bat. Rather than wearing the Farmington colors, he had on his old pinstripe pants, black button-down WildCard shirt and hat. It was not that he did not want to play in his Farmington uniform, but he always felt more like a ballplayer in his black and whites of the Wild-Card.

Though he would never admit it to anyone—perhaps other than Marina—his only goal at the moment was to hit at least five home runs to effectively bump Ryan Wolf from round two. Wolf had settled down somewhat since his suspension, but his arrogance, respect issues, and superiority complex were always brimming at the surface.

When the fifth home run went trailing over the left field wall, he had a tingly feeling deep inside. Even if he was eliminated now and did not hit another home run, he would be content with the way things had gone. However, he still had three outs, and in those three outs, he hit an additional four home runs to end with nine on the first round.

Alejandro Izquierdo came up to the plate; already a freshman batting champion and Most Valuable Player winner. Connor had no doubt that by the time he was a senior, he would be a power hitter too. For now though, he hit line drives, gap shots, and could placement hit. He could even beat out quite a few infield hits with his speed. For the derby though, none of that mattered. Like Ryan Wolf, he hit four home runs on the morning.

Robert Griffin stood by Chrissie and the scoreboard, studying it. "I need six to advance?" he asked.

"Six," she confirmed.

"Six it is," he nodded.

Robert went up to bat, facing it much like Rickey had, watching several pitches and then swinging. He was in no rush and focused on his timing. Even though he was playing, his ankle was still sore from the prior night, and his balance was a little off. With a few adjustments, he found his swing by the time he had four outs, and hit his six home runs. Rather than continue, he just check-swung at the last two pitches for outs, accepting the six he needed to advance.

Since Joe Lane was not participating in the derby, he took over as the announcer for Connor. After Robert got his final out, he thanked Chrissie for keeping the score, and then walked forward to address the batters. "Our four players who have advanced to Round Two are Lamont Aronson with sixteen home runs, Coach Urban with thirteen, Coach Blake with nine, and Robert Griffin with six. Congratulations to you all.

"In Round Two, batters shall bat in the same order as they did for Round One. That means Lamont is up. Good luck," Joe finished.

Lamont stepped up to the plate again. In this round, the pitches were cut in half from ten to five. After hitting sixteen home runs, fairly well dispersed, it should not be that big of a problem. However, Rickey hit most of his home runs early on, and then slowed down. Lamont kept that in the back of his mind.

Whether he was over-thinking it, or was perhaps tired after having the most home runs in the first round, Lamont only hit three in the second round.

"Good try, good try," Dom said, clapping his hands.

Rickey stepped up to bat and took five pitches before swinging. His first swing sent the ball soaring over the left field wall. He took three more pitches before swinging again, hitting his second home run to left. He hit two more before recording an out, putting him on top of Lamont Aronson. He then got three more before getting his final out for a total of seven.

Connor stepped up to the plate. All he needed was eight to advance. Regardless of what Robert did, eight would get him into the final round. Since he hit nine with ten outs, getting eight with five might be tricky, but he also picked up the pace near the end, getting into a good groove. Hopefully, he would keep it going.

The first pitch Corey threw, Connor groaned as he watched it soar foul. The next pitch he got a hold of, but it didn't have the distance. Taking a deep breath, he took a pair of pitches to calm himself, and then refocused. He hit six home runs before getting his third out, and then hit three more before the round was over for a total of nine, matching his first round total.

Lamont Aronson was the first to congratulate Connor, shaking his hand and wishing him luck in the final round. Connor accepted it, and briefly wondered if it had been a bad idea to let the coaching staff participate. This day was for fun, but maybe Lamont deserved to win the derby after all of his hard work and production all season.

The final batter was Connor's nephew, Robert. Like his last at bat, he paced himself, making sure he could adjust his stance to accommodate his ankle. Then, pitch-by-pitch, he put on a hitting display, driving eight home runs before he made his check-swings for the final three outs like he had in the first round.

"Maybe we found you a new stance," Dom said as Robert walked over to the board. "This injury may be the best thing that ever happened to you."

"I could always hit home runs," Robert said. "But Uncle preaches speed and consistency, so I hit for average and moving batters along. The power is there if I need it."

"Well I'll be," Dom chuckled. "He's been holding out on us all season."

"The final round is between Coach Blake and Robert Griffin," Joe announced. "Coach Blake—you're up first."

This round only had three outs. It didn't leave much room for error, or for trying to get into a groove. Connor had needed two to three outs in each round before getting the ball out of the field. This would be his biggest challenge.

Like the last two rounds, his first two pitches were outs. Connor then got three home runs before getting the final out. As he walked to the dugout, he patted Robert on the back, saying, "Go get it." It was good to be playing again, and certainly good to be in the final round, but deep down, Connor wanted one of his players to win the trophy for this little event. Who better than his nephew?

Robert went out and did exactly that. He had four home runs with an out to spare, and stopped with the win assured. Joe and Corey met Robert at the mound and gave him a little trophy that they had pooled their money to buy for the winner. It did not have Robert's name, but it said, "2007 Home Run Derby Champion" on it.

After the derby they played the co-ed softball game. Connor played center field for his team like he wanted to. His nieces both played on his team, with Kimberly behind the plate and Chrissie at shortstop. Coach Corey was on the mound, Lauren was at first, and Marina was in right field, completing the lineup with the girls. In softball there are always four outfielders. The second center fielder was Alejandro, and the left fielder was Jimmy. Marty was playing third, and Robert was at second to complete the roster for Connor's team.

There had been enough people to make four teams in all. Rather than remaining in the stadium, they went to the fields where they had spring training and played a pair of games at once. The winners then played afterwards, and the losing teams also played each other. Connor's team won both games, the second one in the ninth inning when Chrissie hit a shot through the infield to score Marina.

With a full day's activities of baseball and softball—laughs and enjoyment all around—most of the players and families made their way to the Blake house for the barbeque. It was one long progression of cars following each other, almost like an army invading Holliston.

Some people went swimming. Some sat and chatted. Connor also caught a couple of people—Dane Olney and one of the cheerleaders, who he later learned was Dane's cousin—making-out in the front yard behind one of the bushes. At night, he set off some fireworks—nothing major, only roman candles and things like that. People then gradually began making their way back home. It was a fun day. Everyone seemed to have enjoyed themselves. Even—Connor was glad to see—his mother, who had been gracious enough to host the barbeque in her yard. Days like this, Connor thought, were just what people needed sometimes.

CHAPTER 48

The following Wednesday, the final game was upon them, and it was none other than Corinth. Connor should have known that this magical season would not end without having to go through his father's old team one last time. Principal Murphy had told him when he went to try and get a job there that they had a great team and thought that they would compete for the state championships. Now they were there, but so were Connor and Farmington.

It should have been a game that Troy Kane would start, but he had to come in and pitch in the game against Farmington-North. Instead, Connor was going with Osamu Ishikawa, making it a rematch of their late-April game where they had won fifteen to three, giving Corinth their only loss of the season.

Of course, Connor believed then that they had caught Corinth by surprise. After the pre-season scrimmage, being defeated so handedly, the Corinth team and coaches thought that Farmington would be an easy win. They quickly learned that that wasn't the case, and could not catch back up after they fell behind. Now, in the final game of the State Tournament, there would be no underestimating the other team.

Farmington's lineup would look a little differently for this game as well. Pat Dillingham was able to pinch run, but he was still having a little trouble judging balls hit to him in the outfield. Connor would rather him not play at all as a result, but Pat was adamant that he could play if needed. Instead, Connor and his coaches decided to stick with Jacque Jennings in left field.

Fortunately, Robert was able to play at second. He still had his ankle wrapped, but he was no longer limping or showing any sign of visual discomfort. If he did during the game, Connor would quickly pull him for Karlic Kulin, but for now, the infield was better with Robert leading it, and that was where he would be.

Just like with the last two playoff games, the band came out to play the national anthem. When they were off the field, the final game of the year between Corinth and Farmington for the state championships was on.

Connor sat on the bench, trying to not be overly anxious. He was sure that at some point he would begin pacing and shouting out instructions to his players, but for now, with Osamu Ishikawa finishing up his pre-game warm-up pitches, the mood Connor wanted to be in was one of calmness. They had fought hard to get here for this game, and here they were.

"Play ball!"

"Okay, okay," Connor said, clapping and resisting the urge to stand up and walk to the edge of the dugout.

"Good luck, Uncle," Chrissie said, once again beside him on the bench.

"To us all," Connor said.

"Grandpa is with us, you know," she added.

Connor thought about it for a moment. He had seen things since his father had died—like the cloud formations looking like a helicopter—but he had never really been a spiritual man. Believing in some kind of afterlife had always escaped him. Yet, that didn't stop him from having the undying urge to go to the cemetery and wish his father a Happy Thanksgiving when he was driving near, or promising his father that he would take care of his mother. Perhaps he believed more than he thought he did.

"I hope so," Connor said. "I hope so."

For someone who professed not to believe, Connor had gone to the cemetery and read the rest of the book he had written and his father hadn't gotten through before he died. He also listened to his mother talking all the time about how she speaks to him every morning before she gets out of bed while looking at his picture. Whether there was something beyond the years one had in their lifetime or not, the belief and hope that your loved ones hear and understand you could keep someone going. If not that, then why was he truly coaching this year?

Lost in thought, Connor did not even register the top half of the first inning until he saw the players coming in and Rickey and Joe heading to their bases to coach. "What happened?"

"Three strikeouts," Chrissie said, looking at him curiously. "Where did you go?"

"Just lost in thought," Connor said. "It won't happen again."

The pitcher for Corinth wasn't one of the players Farmington had seen before. Connor had read a lot about him in the newspaper coverage leading up to this game. Like Osamu, he was only a sophomore, but he had the best ERA, the most strikeouts, and the most wins from the Corinth pitchers. He wasn't their ace—at least the season did not start that way—but he became the go-to guy by the end of the season.

Connor watched his warm-up pitches. He was nowhere near as fast as Osamu with his fastball, but his movement was phenomenal, even better than that of Dane Olney. He was a kid who seemed to know how to put it all together, and that meant a very likely pitcher's duel between the two teams.

Jacque Jennings led off in place of Pat Dillingham, and chased strike three in the dirt for the first out. Tyrell Witham fared little better, striking a ball with a full swing that wound up dribbling back to the mound for an easy out at first. Alejandro Izquierdo got the first hit of the game, but as the pitcher got ready to face Lamont Aronson, he spun quickly and nailed Alejandro while taking his lead from first.

Joe, who had been the first-base coach, crouched down in front of Connor, whistling. "That's an impressive pick-off move."

"Deceptive," Rickey agreed as he joined them.

"Keep an eye on it," Connor said. "Our running game is one of our strengths. With this pitching matchup, a few stolen bases getting players into scoring position may make all the difference."

Projected by both media and coaches as a pitching duel, neither pitcher disappointed. In the fifth inning, the score remained zero to zero with only a few scattered hits here or there for either team. Lamont Aronson came close to a home run once, but a stellar play in left field made it a really long out instead. Between the two pitchers, through the first five, there were twenty-one strikeouts out of a possible thirty outs.

Connor's desire to remain calm and seated had also been lost in the fourth when Lamont had his near-home run. He had been on the front step of the dugout and pacing ever since.

In the seventh, the score still the same, Marty Dillingham got a rare walk against the pitcher. After two unsuccessful pick-off attempts, he ran for second on the pitch. Every player in the dugout was praying that someone would make it to second in this game, and like his brother Pat, Marty was fast. Sliding into second, the steal just inches away, Marty found the second baseman lowering his glove just in time to apply the tag to end the inning.

A collective sigh of disappointment escaped the lips of the coaches, players, and fans in the stadium.

In the bottom of the ninth, Alejandro got a double with two outs. Corinth then intentionally walked Lamont to face Robert. Connor pulled Robert aside before he went up to bat, thinking of the home run derby and how Robert could end this with one swing of the bat.

"We only need one to win, so with Alejandro's speed, a base hit will do it," Connor said.

"I've got it," Robert replied.

"But, if you get a pitch you want, feel free to go deep."

"Really?"

"Who am I to argue with the home run derby champ?" Connor grinned, winking at his nephew.

Robert swung for the fences on the first pitch, sending one deep to left field, trailing foul at the last moment. Once again, a sigh filled the stands, along with a collective groan. After swinging for the fences,

Robert decided to go for the hit. If he tried again and missed it, he would be down to one strike and at a disadvantage, especially the way this pitcher was throwing. Instead, if he could hit the ball to right, Alejandro should be able to score.

The second pitch came in, Robert swung, and· it sailed as a line drive down the first-base line, again, slicing foul.

With two strikes on him, the Corinth pitcher decided to throw around the plate to make Robert chase one. Each pitch was close enough that it could be called a strike. Robert did lay off of the first one, but then swung at the second one, popping it up in the air for the final out of the inning.

"Extra innings," Connor said, exhaling slowly. "What a game."

"At least there will be a new pitcher next inning," Dom said. "Hopefully we'll get to him."

"Hopefully," Connor agreed.

With Osamu Ishikawa pitching nine complete innings, giving up four hits, no runs, and striking out nineteen batters on the game, he was replaced in the tenth by Troy Kane.

Troy Kane pitched with his normal flair and passion for the game. A ball was hit to shortstop, and Troy pointed at the ball, shouting the entire time, "There, there!" Once Marty fielded it, Troy was shouting and pointing at, "First, first!" When Marty threw the ball to first for the out, Troy pumped his fist and shouted, "That's it! You know it! That's the way it's done!"

Each batter was like a theatrical performance for Troy Kane, who was even more pumped up because of the playoffs. In the end, three batters faced in the tenth, three outs.

To everyone's surprise, the Corinth starter came back out in the tenth to continue pitching. With two strikeouts and one line drive that was caught, he looked just as dominant as he had all night long.

Two innings later, Corinth finally pulled their pitcher after giving a leadoff hit to Robert, and then walking Roger Nauth. With a new pitcher coming in, Connor had a big decision to make. Troy Kane was pitching great and could easily for two or three more innings. But, he was also at bat. With two on and no outs, they may be able to win this game right here and now, and Troy wouldn't be needed on the mound again. However, if he pulled Troy and they did not score, then it might be asking Jimmy a bit much to pitch deep into an extra inning game.

As the pitcher threw his last warm-up pitch, Connor made the decision. "Brian Dickson—go bat for Troy." Even the pinch hitter was a bit controversial to Connor. Karlic probably had a better chance of getting a hit, but with Robert's ankle possibly flaring up the longer the game goes on, he wanted Karlic available to play the field. He also knew that if he needed another pitcher, and Ryan Wolf went to the mound, he would need Karlic in the field as well.

"Tricky," Dom said.

"Brian's a good hitter," Connor replied.

"Karlic's better," Dom added.

"But we may need him," Connor said.

"You're playing defensively," Dom pointed out. "This is the playoffs. There is no tomorrow. We should be going for the win."

"If we use our best bat off the bench and don't get that run across the plate, it weakens us later in the game," Connor countered.

"You're the head coach," Dom shrugged.

He was, and that meant, in the end, it would be him who had to answer to the reporters and angry parents. Brian hit into a double play, and Wolf struck out to end the inning.

With the score still zero to zero, Connor called on Jimmy to go in and keep the score the same. It was a non-save situation, but he had faith in his nephew. Jimmy would not let him down, and he came through: Jimmy pitched four innings, bringing the game to the bottom of the sixteenth, and still a score of zero-zero. With the bullpen on the mound, both teams looked close to scoring, but each time, a spectacular defensive play, or a strikeout ended the threat.

In the sixteenth, Connor had Alejandro leading off, followed by Lamont, and then Robert. It was the heart of his order. He did not want to fall into the trap of thinking that if they were going to win, it would be right now, because—truth be told—he had thought that several times already that night. But the pitcher's shoulder was drooping just a bit, and he had his best players coming to the plate.

Alejandro drove the ball to deep center field on the first pitch. The fans jumped to their feet cheering, thinking that the game was finally over. Even with such a long extra-inning game, not a single spectator had left the field. But the center fielder made a diving catch to come up with the ball.

Lamont Aronson got into the batters box, but the Corinth coach sent the signal for him to be walked. With Lamont jogging down the first-base line, Connor had another big decision to make. Pat Dillingham could go in and steal a base or two, making it easier to get that one run across the plate to end this game. But, if they did not, he would lose both Lamont's bat in the lineup, and his glove at first base. The bat may not be so bad since Corinth had intentionally walked him in each of his last five plate appearances, but that was still a base runner every time he got up to the plate.

Glancing at Dom, he recalled what he had said about taking chances. This was a big one. "Pat, go run for Lamont."

Dom's eyes widened. "Are you serious?"

"What happened to taking chances?" Connor replied.

"That's pulling a pitcher for a pinch hitter. This is taking our best bat out of the lineup," argued Dom.

"A risk is a risk," Connor said.

As Lamont reached the dugout, Connor got up and patted him on the back. "Great game tonight, Lamont."

"Thanks, Coach."

Connor then signaled Rickey at third base. Robert was to be patient at the plate, giving Pat a chance to get into scoring position. Rickey then signaled Joe to let Pat know he had the green light, and Robert to know not to be too aggressive at the plate.

The Corinth pitcher, expecting Pat to try and steal, threw the ball to first four times before throwing to the plate. On the first pitch, Pat was off, sliding head first into second. Connor held his breath, especially with the head-first slide and Pat's injury from the last game, but the umpire shouted, "Safe!" and after the dust settled, Pat asked for time out to get up and dust himself off.

Connor gave the new sign. Robert could swing if the pitch was right, but Pat was to try and get to third regardless. The pitcher watched Pat as he took his lead, faking a throw to second, but not actually sending the ball. He threw the ball home, a ball in the dirt, and Pat made it easily into third without having to slide this time.

"Okay, okay," Connor said, clapping his hands and feeling a sense of exhilaration on his chest. He then gave the signal for Robert to swing away.

The pitcher set, threw the ball home, and instead of swinging, Robert lowered his bat into a bunt. Nobody was expecting it. Pat began running from third. The pitcher ran from the mound to try and get the ball. The third baseman, who had been covering Pat at third, swore as he began sprinting as fast as he could toward the ball. The catcher began to go for it, but backstepped when he saw Pat bearing down on him. Robert was running to first as fast as he could go, a limp beginning to make him hobble about halfway there as his injured ankle flared up.

The pitcher got to the ball first, throwing home to try and beat Pat. The catcher blocked the plate, making it difficult for Pat to score. The throw was made, the catcher had the ball and brought it swinging down. Pat stepped closer to the umpire and slid feet first, dragging his left hand across the plate and his body away from the tag.

"Safe!" the umpire shouted.

Robert rounded first and leaped into the air, cheering. The bench cleared with every player running onto the field, some toward Robert to congratulate him on the hit, others to Pat for the slide away from the catcher that scored the winning run.

The dream-season ended in a dreamlike way: an extra-inning game with the final score of one to nothing between the two best teams—the team Connor coached, and the team his father used to coach.

The celebration for the win did not end with the players alone. The stadium itself was erupting with cheers. Connor sought out his mother behind the home bench, locking eyes with her and seeing the pride she had both for her grandson's game-winning hit, and for everything that Connor had accomplished with this team. By her side were Marina, Cindy, and Lauren, all clapping and cheering right along with the fans.

The coach of Corinth sought Connor out, shaking his hand. "Great game, Coach. Your father would have been proud."

"Thank you," Connor said. "You guys had a great season, too. I wish it wasn't you we had to beat."

"This is the way it should have been," the Coach said. "Enjoy your victory. We'll see you again next year."

"You can count on it," Connor replied, the excitement of the moment beginning to sweep him up.

A bucket of Gatorade was spilled over his back. Connor cringed, then turned around to see Ryan Wolf and Lamont Aronson as the culprits. That was one tradition his softball players had never maintained, but he should have expected it after this game.

The league commissioner came out to the pitcher's mound with a microphone and a trophy. After a short presentation and congratulatory wish to Farmington for their unbelievable season, he presented it to Connor.

Connor held the trophy—the State Championship Cup—over his head to a standing ovation from the fans. His eyes met his mother's again, and he smiled, as if reminding her that this was all for his father.

"Thank you," Connor said after the crowd settled down a bit. "This is more than I ever could have dreamed about when I first decided to honor the memory of my father and coach this season. But, I promise to keep this brief. I just wanted to thank Governor Shilalie, Superintendent McGovern, and Principal Daniels for giving me the opportunity to coach such a fine group of young men.

"I would also like to thank Coaches Corey Forester, Dominic Petrioli, Rickey Urban, and Joseph Lane for all of their hard work and dedication throughout the season. We would not be here today without all of their efforts and insights into this game.

"I would also like to thank Satoshi Ishikawa, who has gone well-above and beyond by building this beautiful stadium and helping to insure that Farmington will have not just baseball, but a competitive academic program for years to come.

"And, I would like to thank every player who donned a Farmington Eagles uniform this year. You guys fought all season long—when the whole world seemed to be against you, you kept fighting to prove that we belonged where we are; and your hard work, dedication, determination, and undying passion is what turned this high school team into an exceptional team, an elite team of champions. Thank you all."

With the trophy in his hand, Connor held it tight, knowing that there was one other person who was not here that deserved to be thanked: his father, the man who taught him everything that he knew about baseball, the man who turned Connor into a coach and champion.

Looking to the sky, Connor thought, *This is for you, Sir. This is all for you.* With his eyes still on the sky, thinking of his father, Connor saw a most inexplicable sight: the clouds actually resembled his father's face, and he was smiling down upon his son. As Connor watched the clouds, feeling more warm and content than he had since he first received his mother's frantic call, he accepted, in that moment, that his father knew what he had done, and that as always, he loved him and had pride in him. Within moments, the clouds shifted, and the image of his father was gone, but Connor knew that his father had been there, looking down and smiling at him, and that was all that mattered.

Also available from Silver Leaf Books:

CLIFFORD B. BOWYER

The Imperium Saga

Fall of the Imperium Trilogy

An evil tyrant weaves a tapestry of deception as he plots to conquer the Imperium. Only a few heroes are brave enough to uncover the mystery and face Zoldex directly. Follow the adventures of the heroes of the realm as they try to preserve the Imperium and confront Zoldex's forces. Their hearts are true and their intentions noble, but will that be enough to overcome such overwhelming odds? Find out in the *Fall of the Imperium Trilogy.*

The Impending Storm, 0974435449, $27.95
The Changing Tides, 0974435457, $27.95
The Siege of Zoldex, 0974435465, $29.95

The Adventures of Kyria

In a time of great darkness, when evil sweeps the land, a prophecy fore-tells the coming of a savior, a child that will defeat the forces of evil and save the world. She is Kyria, the Chosen One.

From the pages of the Imperium Saga, *The Adventures of Kyria* follows the child destined to save the world as she tries to live up to her destiny.

The Child of Prophecy, 0974435406, $5.99
The Awakening, 0974435414, $5.99
The Mage's Council, 0974435422, $5.99
The Shard of Time, 0974435430, $5.99
Trapped in Time, 0974435473, $5.99
Quest for the Shard, 0974435481, $5.99
The Spread of Darkness, 0978778219, $5.99
The Apprentice of Zoldex, 0978778227, $5.99
The Darkness Within, 0978778243, $5.99
The Rescue of Nezbith, 0978778251, $5.99
and more to come!

ILFANTI

Known as an adventurer, the dwarven Council of Elders member Ilfanti is one of the most famous Mages in the realm. Everyone knows his name, and others flock around his charisma. But even Ilfanti is at a loss for why the Mage's Council is ignoring the fact that Zoldex has returned and none are safe as his plans go unchallenged.

The Empress has been kidnapped while in the midst of trying to unite the races. Her true whereabouts are unknown, but her return is vital to the survival of the Seven Kingdoms. The Mages are doing nothing, and Ilfanti can no longer condone avoiding the obvious signs that are plaguing the realm.

Follow Ilfanti as he returns to a life of an adventurer and battles against time to save the Imperium. Experience the adventure and learn if the charismatic adventurer can complete one last mission in time to save the realm.

Ilfanti and the Orb of Prophecy, 0978778278, $18.95
and more to come!

CLIFFORD B. BOWYER
CONTINUING THE PASSION

Continuing the Passion follows the story of Connor Edmond Blake, a best-selling novelist who, after suffering the tragic and unexpected loss of his father decides that the best way to honor the memory of his father is by carrying on the legacy that his father left behind.

Connor's father, William Edward Blake, a Hall of Fame High School Baseball Coach had led his team to numerous state championships. Most of Connor's memories and moments he shared with his father have something to do with and revolve around the sport of baseball. As a former coach himself, of a men's softball team, Connor decides to at least make the attempt to coach a High School team in attempt to honor his father.

Continuing the Passion is seen through the eyes of Connor Blake as he experiences the tragedy of the loss of his father, and his pursuit to help his family find a way to overcome the loss.

Continuing the Passion, 097877826X, $18.95

STUART CLARK
PROJECT U·L·F

Imprisoned for a crime of passion, Wyatt Dorren is given a second chance at life on the Criminal Rehabilitation Program. Dorren becomes the rarest of breeds: an ex-convict who has become a productive member of society, trapping U.L.F.'s—Unidentified Life Forms—from newly discovered planets and returning with them for exhibition at the Interplanetary Zoo. Dorren inspires loyalty and courage in his team members, but nothing from his dark past, or his years trapping dangerous aliens, can prepare him for what's in store now.

Project U.L.F., 0978778200, $27.95
and more to come!

MIKE LYNCH & BRANDON BARR
SKY CHRONICLES

Since the dawn of time, an ancient evil has sought complete and unquestioned dominion over the galaxy, and they have found...us.

The year is 2217 and a fleet of stellar cruisers led by Commander Frank Yamane are about to come face to face with humanity's greatest threat—the Deravan armada. Outnumbered, outclassed, and outgunned, Yamane's plan for stopping them fails; leaving all of humanity at the mercy of an enemy that has shown them none.

Follow the adventures of Commander Frank Yamane and his crew as they struggle to determine whether this will be Earth's finest hour, or the destruction of us all.

Sky Chronicles: When the Sky Fell, 0978778235, $18.95

Try these other novels by author Clifford B. Bowyer.

ABOUT THE AUTHOR

Clifford B. Bowyer is the creator and author of The Imperium Saga universe. His novels include the Fall of the Imperium Trilogy, and the young adult spin-off series, The Adventures of Kyria. Bowyer graduated from Bryant College with a degree in both Management and Marketing, and received his MBA from Babson College. Currently a Project Manager in the Finance Industry, Bowyer continues working on developing future installments of The Imperium Saga novels, an RPG game based upon his world, and other book projects such as Continuing the Passion and Gen-Ops. He resides in Massachusetts, where he also coached and played softball for the better part of a decade. He also has a pet bunny named Fribble.

www.CliffordBBowyer.com